Bernadette:

Princess Under Protest

By Cate McDermott

Dedicated to my brother and sister,
Without whom this book would never have been written

Table of Contents

Book One: In Which It All Began

Book Two: The Chronicles of Their Adventures

Book Three: And What Came of It

Book One

In Which It All Began

Chapter One
Morning in the Palace

"Will it please Your Royal Highness to rise now? 'Tis well-nigh past nine o' clock."

Princess Bernadette yawned and stretched, allowing herself to enjoy the smooth, cool feel of the silken sheets for one more blissful moment before she opened her eyes. She blinked at the rush of sunlight that met her vision, flowing in through an unusual gap in her damask bedcurtains. Once her eyes became accustomed to the light, Bernadette recognized the figure of her lady-in-waiting, Camille, standing beside the bed, holding back the curtains to let the sun shine through.

"Close the curtains! It's too bright! And I don't want to get up yet!" Bernadette laughed in a merrily complaining tone; and, giving another impressive yawn and sinking back into her goosedown pillows with exaggerated drowsiness, she reached out and tugged to close the curtains back again.

But Camille drew them away, and gently re-insisted: "You really must get up now, Your Highness. It is an entire hour past your accustomed time for rising, and . . ."

"Well, is it my fault I had to dance at that silly ball last night 'til two in the morning, Camille?" Bernadette demanded, sitting up in bed. "I could hardly help being tired after that."

"Indeed, yes, Princess, I understand; and so do your most royal parents, who gave me orders to let you sleep late this morning. But if I allow you any later, you will not make it to breakfast on time. And it was not a silly ball, my dear Princess Bernadette; it was a most glorious

7

affair. You looked so lovely, especially with that handsome officer who was so often your partner, Sir Timothy. And the young baron of Uscared—with the elegant red cloak, you must recall him?—praised your singing so highly, though indeed no more highly than you deserved. You were simply magnificent, I do declare, and quite delighted all the guests. And the entire occasion—the lights, the banquet, the flowers, the music—was perhaps the most opulent and engaging of the year—in any kingdom from Scartazin to Eglebreth, I heard one of the Ambassadors from Hegaltrith say; and he must know, for he has been to—was it over a hundred?—royal events in just the past six months. You are becoming such a charming hostess, Your Highness, just like your esteemed mother, the Queen. Why, I heard one of the elderly Dukes of Marschedulechlin tell his wife that . . ."

"Yes, yes, of course, it was all that," Bernadette at last managed to interrupt. "And I do love to dance—but six hours gets to be a little much, you know. And although Sir Timothy was, certainly, a most entertaining and sensible conversationalist—I greatly enjoyed talking with him about his travels—most of the men are not. I get so bored and frustrated making elegant and civil replies to the most errant nonsense all evening long! And what is even more annoying than trying to make conversation with those coxcombs who can't for the life of them talk sense at all—which includes Mr. Red-Cloak Baron Hubert, I am sorry to say—what really frustrates me is when a group of men are talking rationally amongst each other or with the elder guests; but then as soon as I attempt to join the conversation, they automatically switch the subject to something fashionably unintelligent—as though they think that young ladies of title have neither the ability nor the inclination for reasonable discussion! Humph!"

Bernadette flung the bedclothes over the foot of the bed onto the floor, and swung around so that she was sitting on the edge of her feather mattress, with her bare feet dangling out over the side. She sat there for a moment in silence, swinging her legs and frowning thoughtfully out of the nearby window at the sunny landscape beyond, while Camille stood by, quietly watching her mistress. Presently Bernadette sighed and added, regretfully: "Although I must confess, that as far as most girls are concerned, they are quite justified in their belief; I rarely meet a girl whom I can have a sensible, pleasant conversation with, either. That's excepting you, of course, my darling Camille!" Bernadette, who was inherently good-humored and never stayed somber for very long, sprang out of bed and ecstatically hugged her maid and close friend.

Camille permitted but did not return the exuberant caress, smiling in the tolerant, slightly puzzled manner with which she usually responded to Bernadette's frequent complaints about court society and almost-as-frequent philosophical observations on life in general. Camille was a kind-hearted maiden with a great deal of common sense and a gift of simple tactfulness; but she had no inclination towards abstract discussion concerning *why* things were what they were. To Camille's way of thinking, everything was simply what it was. Court society was court society, and in court society you behaved in a certain manner, and that was all there was to it.

Furthermore, Camille did not have time to ask questions about how to live: she was far too busy solving the dilemmas generated by actually living. And she was presently completely occupied with the one significant problem of getting the princess to breakfast on time.

So, quietly freeing herself from Bernadette's arms, she stepped over to a brocade-covered chair and picked up the ornately embroidered dressing-gown lying across it. "Come, Your Highness, you must come now," she repeated, draping the garment over her mistress's shoulders and herding her gently but persistently towards the door leading from the bedroom to the dressing room.

Bernadette, resigning herself to her fate, sighed with mingled frustration and amusement. There was no use in trying to start a conversation with Camille until after one had already fulfilled all the demands of royal schedules and procedures. Therefore, Bernadette trotted briskly ahead of her maid into the next chamber, throwing the ribbons of her dressing-gown over her shoulders and freeing her long, flowing blonde hair from her collar with a swift, careless motion, saying brightly, "Well, I guess I'm about ready to get up and about, anyway, Camille darling. What would I ever do without you? Mercy, how bright and fresh it looks outside this morning! I do hope Father will be able to come riding with me today—Ah, good morning, my little one!" Bernadette broke off in her stream of merry chatter to greet her sister, Princess Roxanne, who was already in the dressing room, having her hair brushed out by *her* maid.

"Good morning, my dearest sister," the younger, more delicate princess replied, lifting her eyes (she did not dare to turn her head, for fear of ruining the maid's painstaking efforts for her adornment) to Bernadette's face with a look of intense affection.

Bernadette paused beside the dressing-table, bending to drop a light kiss on her little sister's cheek, but likewise taking great care not to disrupt the maid's proceedings. "Up and dressed already! I'm really quite ashamed to be such a lie-abed this morning. Did you enjoy yourself last night, Roxanne? I didn't see you after the third quadrille, had you gone up to bed already? Soon you'll be able to stay up the entire time, and then what larks we'll have!—Yes, yes, Camille, I'm coming!" And with a last pat on her sister's shoulder, Bernadette turned to survey the assortment of gowns that Camille had spread out for her inspection. "Oh, I think I'll wear my gray satin today," she said, selecting one of the remarkable creations of sumptuous fabric and ribbons, and skipping behind the embroidered screen in the corner of the room to put it on.

"Cloth of *silver* satin, Your Highness!" Camille called after her, half reproachfully, as she organized the combs and brushes on the other dressing table.

"Whatever," Bernadette giggled from behind the screen. A moment later she came out again, her dressing-gown and nightdress carelessly bundled up together in her arms. "Will you lace me up, Camille? No, I just want my hair done the usual way; I don't like to have to bother with fancy puffs and coils when I don't have to. By the way, Roxanne, did you see that headdress that Princess Margarethe of the Northern Virkweld Province was wearing last night? I can't imagine how she kept it on, wiring I suppose. I mean to ask her about it, if I see her before she leaves this morning . . ."

So, chatting away as only blithe young girls can, the princesses and their attendants soon completed their breakfast preparations, and then the rest of the lovely young ladies-in-waiting entered to accompany the royal highnesses to the dining room. Bernadette, being the elder of the two princesses, had twelve ladies-in-waiting besides Camille; Princess Roxanne had ten in all.

"Good morning, Your Most Royal Highnesses," the ladies-in-waiting chorused as they swarmed into the dressing-chamber and gathered about the princesses, each one surreptitiously striving to be one of the privileged few who would carry the princesses' trains, help to arrange the enormous armfuls of flowers that palace protocol dictated that the royal ladies bring to breakfast, or walk at their left hand (the right-hand position was reserved for the chief lady-in-waiting).

"Good morning, ladies," Bernadette replied, with a certain dignified coolness which we have not hitherto observed creeping into her manner.

"Good morning," echoed Princess Roxanne, with no diminution of her sweet cheeriness of tone.

"Oh, Your Highnesses, *have* you heard the news?" breathlessly cried one of the ladies-in-waiting, who had just rushed into the room, a couple of seconds behind the others. She hastily elbowed her way through the crowd of girls towards the princesses' flower-covered dressing tables, wearing a hopeful expression. But Bernadette swiftly gathered up her bouquet with both hands before she or any of the other ladies-in-waiting could offer to assist her.

"What news, Letitia?" she inquired coolly, making her way as well as she could towards the door leading into the upstairs hall. Bernadette didn't put much stock in the "absolutely thrilling" reports that the rest of the maidens in the castle gossiped about endlessly. The topics of such rumors rarely interested her; and furthermore, half the time they weren't more than half accurate.

Camille caught Bernadette's eye as she took her place beside her and shook her head slightly, with a look of mild remonstrance. Bernadette merely frowned and tossed her head in reply, but her bored expression instantly vanished as Letitia eagerly replied.

"Oh, Princess Bernadette, a messenger arrived this morning—I just heard while I was passing through the hall—and informed the King—I beg your pardon, His Royal Majesty your father—that a division of

Royal Guard soldiers, led by Sir Peter, is on its way to visit the castle, and should be here tonight!"

"Cousin Pete!" Bernadette cried out in delight, stopping so abruptly on the threshold of the door that her sister's chief lady-in-waiting accidentally bumped into her. "Oh, no, it was entirely my fault, Hannah," she assured the excessively apologetic maiden, before turning back to Letitia, now with an eagerness that matched that young damsel's own. "Are you quite certain, Letitia? Who did you hear it from?"

"Positive," the girl responded confidently, delighted to have impressed her princess. "I had it from the maid of the Duchess Rosamond of Callifwis, who had it from her brother the Duke, who had it from his valet John, who had it from the ironing-maid that brought him his master's pressed collar-frills this morning, who had it from the butler's assistant Egbert, who actually overheard the messenger telling the King while he was on his way through to the pantry."

"In that case, I guess it must be certain, if so many people are already aware of it," Bernadette said, trying to stifle a chuckle and carefully avoiding Camille's eye. "That's marvelous!" But she privately resolved to check with her father before rejoicing with too much assurance over this confirmation of the report.

Upon rounding the curve of the grand crimson-carpeted staircase, Bernadette craned her neck to see over the polished balustrade, hoping to obtain a view of whoever was on duty as door-porter in the castle's Great Hall below. She easily accomplished this (Bernadette was rather tall), and her face immediately broke into an even wider smile. The porter standing below, who was looking up to catch a view of the ladies-in-waiting and princesses quite as eagerly as Bernadette was looking down, was not her favorite, the grandfatherly old Cecil; but what was next best, the handsome and chivalrous young porter Stephen, one of her greatest friends in the palace. However, it was not at Bernadette that he was looking as the flock of silken-attired maidens descended the last few steps into the three-story-high foyer, but at the quiet, modest, dark-haired figure beside her.

"Good morning, friend Stephen!" Bernadette called, bestowing a slight, cheery nod upon him in greeting, rather than the more informal, friendly wave she would have preferred to give, if only her hands had not been filled with that burdensome mass of flora, as she privately considered her mandatory bouquet.

"And an equally fine one to you, my most highly esteemed Princess," replied the young servingman with a low bow, but he still had his eyes on Camille as he straightened himself again.

Suppressing a smile, Bernadette detached herself from the crowd of maidens and took a few steps toward her friend, adroitly managing to keep Camille, and only Camille, by her side as she did so.

"Another beautiful day, isn't it?" Bernadette said casually, as she came up to Stephen. "Marvelous weather we've been having lately." She gazed out of the nearest window with a look of apparent abstraction as she spoke. "You'd almost think it was summer already, instead of just the beginning of spring."

"Yes, indeed," Stephen agreed amiably. "Very good weather for traveling, it is—oh, have you heard the news of your cousin Peter's coming, Princess?"

"I have indeed," Bernadette replied, smiling. If Stephen was also helping to circulate this report, it testified far more strongly in favor of its truthfulness, in her opinion. "He'll be here in time for the Blossom Festival, isn't that splendid?"

The Blossom Festival was the merriest and most anticipated event of the season in the Kingdom of Berklesgilands. A celebration of the arrival of spring, the Festival was a favorite with both the lower class, as they laid aside all their labors and closed down the usual operations of the entire village for the day, and also with the nobility and royal family, who delighted in the opportunity for some slightly less ceremonial entertainment.

"I do hope that the weather will continue to stay this fine for the celebration; that would make the festivities all the more enjoyable, do you not agree with me?" Bernadette looked from Stephen to Camille as she posed the question.

"Oh, yes, most assuredly!" Stephen responded, taking his eyes from Camille long enough to exchange meaningful glances with his princess; and then, returning his gaze to the face of the maiden, he asked softly, "And what think you, fair Maiden Camille?"

Camille had not raised her head since Bernadette and Stephen had begun to talk to one another; her cheeks had deepened in color, but not with pleasure. In fact, she appeared mildly irritated, and seemed to be entirely occupied with attempting to refasten the shoulder clasps of her young mistress's mantle. Upon Stephen's addressing her, she replied quickly and civilly, but still without looking up: "Indeed, I am certainly looking forward to the Festival, and I would by no means stand in the way of any prospect of pleasure for my mistress; however, as delightful as this unseasonably warm and clear weather may seem to us, such a consistent lack of rain can have a devastating effect upon the crops and the peasantry. And I am sure that you would not wish that, would you, my dearest princess?" Camille at last raised her eyes upon completing her moral pronouncements, but directed her gaze only towards Bernadette, as if the conversation had only involved the two of them.

"Ah, no, indeed, I would not!" Bernadette exclaimed in reply, struck by her maid's insight. "How could I be so thoughtless! Well, in that case, I hope that it rains every day between now and the Festival, but is just as clear and warm as today on the day of! That would work out nicely, don't you think?" she concluded merrily, glancing over at Stephen again, and then returning her gaze to her maid.

"Well, perhaps," Camille replied, somewhat indifferently. "But now, Princess Bernadette, I believe it is time we were going into breakfast. Come." She turned as if to walk away.

"Good morning, then, Stephen; I'll see you later," Bernadette was forced to give a rather hurried farewell to her friend, accompanied by a sympathetic shrug and half-smile, as she hastened after her lady-in-waiting, leaving the young man standing in the hall, an expression of decided disappointment upon his countenance.

As Bernadette once again reached the side of her principal waiting-maid, just as they approached the entrance to the breakfast-hall, Camille immediately raised a pair of accusing eyes—a fitting accompaniment to her flushed cheeks—to her mistress's face.

"Well, really, Camille," Bernadette whispered hastily, responding to her friend's unspoken reproach, "I don't see that there is any reason why you shouldn't be courted, just as much as myself—more reason for you, if anything." Her face hardened into an abstracted little frown as she spoke, as though her words held more meaning than was immediately apparent.

Camille's own face softened proportionately in response, while she replied in an equally soft, reassuring voice: "But, my dear Princess Bernadette, I cannot allow myself to be distracted from what is presently my first and foremost duty in life—my services to you and, by extension, the rest of your esteemed royal family. Therefore I cannot now spare the time and effort for encouraging suitors and pursuing my own secure establishment in this world, until you are taken care of . . ."

"Oh, as if I couldn't take perfectly good care of myself, really, Camille!" Bernadette retorted flippantly, with a good-naturedly impatient toss of her head, briskly moving a couple of steps forward. Camille only smiled quietly as she followed; this was clearly a common topic of discussion between them.

Having thus pleasantly dismissed the subject, the two maidens now entered the breakfast hall together; Princess Roxanne and the rest of the ladies-in-waiting following behind.

Chapter Two
Pete Arrives

Bernadette, accompanied by her sister, Camille, and Princess Roxanne's chief lady-in-waiting, headed directly for the King's Table in the center of the room, where the royal couple sat ready to greet their daughters. It was a pleasant prospect, indeed! The handsome, ruddy-cheeked, portly King Friedrich was already beaming radiantly upon them from where he sat at the end, and the dark-haired, elegant Queen Anna Marie had turned in her chair at his right hand to bestow her gracious smile upon them as they approached.

"Good morning, Father!" sang out Bernadette as she reached him, stooping down to kiss the king's cheek with unceremonious daughterly affection. "Isn't it such a lovely day?"

"It is that, indeed!" responded King Friedrich enthusiastically, returning the kiss and then leaning over to bestow a similar caress on his younger daughter. "Good morning, good morning, everyone! Do sit down. Everything's hot and ready!"

Bernadette, having already kissed her mother as well, quickly slipped around to the other side of the table to sit in her chair across from the Queen. Camille sat down beside her, across from Princess Roxanne. As soon as grace was said, before she had even picked up her spoon, Bernadette turned eagerly back to her father, fixing her eyes on him in obvious anticipation. He took a moment to notice.

"Did you want something, my dear?" he asked teasingly, working away busily with his knife and fork.

"Oh, I was just wondering whether what I heard—didn't you get a message this morning, that you might want to tell me about, Father?" Bernadette responded in the same tone, dipping unconcernedly into her bowl of wheaten porridge.

"About your cousin Pete's arrival, you mean?" the King said knowingly, raising an eyebrow. As his daughter nodded, he continued: "Yes, you heard right—for once! He should be here before dinner-time today."

"Oh, hooray!" Bernadette shouted, leaping up and dropping her silverware to her plate with a noisy clang that attracted the attention of several of the other diners in the room. She hastily sat back down again.

"Gracious, Bernadette, do not raise your voice in such an unladylike manner!" admonished her mother, elevating her eyebrows in astonished censure. "You may better demonstrate your delight over your cousin's approaching visit by giving due assistance to our preparations for his arrival."

"Yes, Mother," Bernadette responded meekly, trying to curb her rising excitement, now that she was sure her cousin was really coming. Sir Peter had not visited the castle in over a year; he had been away with his regiment.

"Do you know how long Pete will be able to stay with us this time?" she asked eagerly, picking up her silverware once again.

"Well, as it so happens that your royal father has decided to assign him to a different, higher-ranking division in another area of the kingdom, I suppose that he will remain here until all the necessary arrangements can be made for his transfer—in other words, for as long as we can keep him," Queen Anna Marie replied, with a significant smile at her daughter. King Friedrich confirmed his wife's statement with a conspiratorial wink around the table.

"Hoo—" Bernadette stopped herself in the middle of another display of unladylike exuberance, halting her hands in mid-clap. She cast a sheepish glance at her mother, who returned it with one of indulgent serenity, before resuming her conversation with her husband, in regard to the luncheon arrangements for him and the company of ambassadors from Hegaltrith.

"Oh, I don't think that there will be any need of particularly elaborate preparations for today's luncheon, my dear," said the King, carelessly. "We still have a good deal to cover in our negotiations today, and so we will all eat more or less irregularly during the conference in the Council Chamber."

"But such a manner of dining will require certain arrangements of its own; I will speak with the cook immediately after breakfast," Queen Anna Marie replied with quiet decision.

Bernadette looked up alertly. "But, Father, will you still have time to go riding with me today?"

"I'm afraid not, daughter. I will be in council with the ambassadors all day. Perhaps tomorrow."

"You said that yesterday, and the day before that, too," Bernadette grumbled slightly, stabbing at a piece of fruit dumpling.

"Sorry, that's the way it happens sometimes. We'll just have to make the best of it," her father responded philosophically.

"Besides, daughter, I will need your help today to prepare for the guests arriving with your cousin, as I already mentioned," the Queen interjected. "While there will not be time to organize as grand a welcoming celebration as we perhaps should like, we shall at least prepare for a fine banquet dinner with dancing afterward; and I shall require your assistance, particularly in decorating the ballroom. So make haste with your meal. We have a great deal to do today."

"Yes, and after you have finished helping your mother, I will need to see you in the study later this afternoon, once the council is over, to go over the proceedings with me," the King added.

Bernadette brightened considerably at this remark. "All right, Father! And I'll be ready as soon as may be, Mother," she promised, hastily consuming the remainder of her breakfast. "Come on, Camille, Roxanne; let's go!"

The preparations for the coming guests seemed to take forever. Bernadette tended to think that the arrangements for royal celebrations were always extremely overdone. Pete certainly wasn't going to notice any of the particularities of the flower arrangements! But by four o'clock that afternoon, everything was at last in order, and Bernadette ran gladly away from her completed duties before her mother could think of anything else.

As she headed up the stairs towards her room, she heard her father calling to her. "Ah, there you are, daughter; I was just looking for you!" King Friedrich leaned over the upstairs railing, smiling affably down at her. "The negotiations are just over; come right on up to the study."

"All right, Father!" Bernadette bounded up the few remaining stairs with alacrity, and cheerfully tripped alongside her father down the hall to the King's private office. He pushed the door open and stood back to let Bernadette enter first.

The room was quite dark and cluttered inside. But Bernadette was used to that; she knew where everything in the study was, so she easily threaded her way around the bulky leather-covered armchairs and toppling piles of manuscripts, and pushed aside the curtains. The late afternoon sunshine poured in, the warm golden light illuminating every corner of the chamber.

"There, that's better," Bernadette said with satisfaction. King Friedrich looked up from where he had already seated himself in his elaborately carved throne-chair before his ponderous oaken desk, and laughed robustly.

"You like to have a little light on the subject, don't you, my dear?" he said lightly, drawing up another chair beside his own for her. "Well, I must say that I agree with you, although just having you in here already brightens up the place considerably for your old father! Now, let's go over these minutes from the meeting," he concluded in a more businesslike tone, reaching for a nearby bundle of parchment manuscripts. Bernadette immediately seated herself beside him and took up an enormous goose-feather pen, preparing to take notes on the proceedings of the diplomatic meetings.

Here in the Kingdom of Berklesgilands, when the eldest daughter was also the heir to the throne, the Princess Royal was expected not only to fulfill her primary duties in the management of the royal housekeeping, hostessing, and elegant leisure activities (such as spinning and embroidery and flower-gathering), but also to thoroughly learn about and assist in the actual governance of the realm. Therefore, ever since Bernadette had turned fifteen, over a year before, she had divided her time between studying how to run a proper royal household at her mother's side, and sitting with her father at his ledger-cluttered desk, buried deep in calculations of internal economics and foreign affairs and common law and obscure precedents. (And after all this, of course, she was expected to dance into the wee hours nearly every night, and be exceptionally charming to all her attendant swains the while.)

After half an hour of studiously attending to matters of state, Bernadette dropped her pen to take a brief rest, stretching her cramped fingers and straightening her back against the cushions of the massive armchair. It would be nice, she thought, once Roxanne turned fifteen. As soon as her sister was old enough to begin assisting more with the social duties in the palace, Bernadette would be free to involve herself more deeply in public affairs, without being overly encumbered by her other ceremonial obligations.

It must be confessed, that Queen Anna Marie did not quite share her daughter's views on this subject. It was by no means standard policy in that day for succeeding princesses to know anything about how to actually *govern* their kingdoms. The fact that such was the case in Berklesgilands was due solely to the somewhat unorthodox, but generally sound, judgment of King Friedrich, who delighted in having his daughter's interest and aid in his political undertakings, despite his wife's implicit disapproval. Bernadette gladly backed herself with her father's sanction, for she would not have willingly given up one iota of her share in the governance of the kingdom for, well, a kingdom.

So when the Queen entered the chamber now, with a slight furrow between her fine brows, and announced uncompromisingly to her husband that she required Bernadette's presence downstairs as soon as possible, Bernadette instinctively gripped her pen tighter and inwardly groaned with dismay.

"What's left to do, Mother? I thought we had finished all of the preparations," she said plaintively, trying desperately to think of a plausible excuse for avoiding any further involvement in excessive and irrelevant ballroom-decorating projects. Nothing came to her mind.

"All of them that could be done in advance. But there are always some things that must be done immediately prior to the visitors' arrival; and furthermore, I have changed my mind about certain details of taste, and wish to consult with you as to how they should be redone. Come now." She beckoned imperiously for her daughter to rise and follow her.

"Bernadette will be down in a minute, my dear," interposed King Friedrich good-humoredly. "We can set aside the rest of these affairs for a later date—we are nearly done now, anyway—but we must just finish our overview of today's agreement on trade quotas and tariffs. Very important details for a future sovereign to understand thoroughly." He smiled proudly and winked at Bernadette.

"Indeed, and I know not why you esteem it so necessary for our daughter to comprehend all of these official matters!" the Queen exclaimed impatiently. "Her husband can attend to all that. Bernadette will have more than enough to do with the management of the royal household, once it falls to her care."

"But the kingdom as a whole will fall to her care, my dear; she is the rightful heiress," replied the King, firmly, raising his eyes and regarding his wife with a serious expression.

"Besides, my husband will have lands of his own to care for," Bernadette muttered rebelliously, recklessly twirling her goose-quill between her fingers and frowning fiercely out the window.

"Granted; but not an entire realm, so he shall be well able to attend to the administration of the kingdom here as well, where he will reign with you as joint sovereign," Queen Anna Marie rejoined decisively.

Bernadette sighed, but made no further response. The line between her own brows deepened considerably as she reflected on her mother's words. This matter under discussion was perhaps the bitterest drop in Bernadette's royal cup; namely, the issue of her impending union to Prince Gerald Reginald of Saxe-Habsburg, third son of the reigning sovereign of that nation, King Vincentius. Her father had been the bosom friend of the aforesaid King Vincentius during their youth, and the betrothal of two of their offspring to one another, from the time of their birth, had naturally followed. Their marriage was set to take place in little over a year, but as yet Bernadette had never so much as seen her intended spouse. She did not like to think about the prospect.

Therefore, she was quite relieved to turn her mind to other matters, on her mother's saying, "Well, if you must finish these documents, I suppose you must. But please come directly to the Grand Dining Hall once you have finished."

"Yes, Mother, I'll be there," Bernadette promised obediently, bending back over the sheaf of parchment minutes spread out before her and King Friedrich. The Queen paused in the doorway to smile back at them, engrossed in their work. They made a fine, noble picture, the father and daughter, so alike with their golden heads bent close together, and their broad faces equally serious as they attended to the matters before them.

When the heralds at last called from the tower to announce the visitors' approach, all was in readiness, and the Royal Family was drawn up in state in the Throne Room to receive them. Bernadette could hardly contain her excitement. She didn't dare bounce up and down, under her mother's watchful eye; but she alternately rose and fell upon the toes and heels of her satin slippers, her eager gaze fixed upon the door opposite, in readiness for the entrance of Pete.

She had not long to wait. Barely five minutes later, the tramp of militarily-bred feet was heard outside in the hall; and in another moment a dozen or so handsome young soldiers entered the room, led by a young knight who could be none other than cousin Pete.

It required only one glance to tell from which side of the family he was. His slightly tousled blond locks, clear blue eyes, powerful physique, and strongly-marked features proclaimed his relationship to King Friedrich almost as obviously as Bernadette's own did.

Sir Peter was, indeed, the nephew of King Friedrich, the only son of his younger sister, the late Princess Margaret, who had, in her maiden days, fallen in love with and married one of the most honorable knights in the Royal Guard. Pete was their only child; and he had never known his father, for he had died in battle almost immediately after his son's birth. Everyone had expected that Princess Margaret would have followed him but shortly after, for she was heartbroken by her loss. However, she was a woman of nobility and steadfastness, and she had rallied from her grief in order to devote her entire life to the care and upbringing of her son. She cared nothing for herself now that her husband was gone, but only for Pete; and as soon as he was firmly established at the Royal Military Academy of the Kingdom of Berklesgilands, she had quietly passed away, her work accomplished.

As his closest remaining relatives, the Royal Family was strongly attached to Pete; and the King had offered him one of the foremost positions in the ranks upon his graduation. However, Pete possessed a strong streak of independence and sense of duty, and had insisted upon proving himself in the regular forces before he would consider accepting any superior position. And King Friedrich, who would have been the less pleased with his nephew had he accepted his initial offer, had allowed him to go his own way. But he had been sincerely delighted by the opportunity provided, through the recently received report of Sir Peter's unexampled acts of valor on the field, to present him with a justly earned promotion and an extended furlough. And, truth be told, Pete himself was nothing loath to accept this prospect, now that he might do so with integrity; he delighted in nothing more than a chance to visit his beloved royal relations.

"Bernie!" With this hearty exclamation, the youth hastened forward, catching his cousin around the waist and spinning her around in a merry dance, lifting her feet quite off the floor. This was his usual manner of greeting Bernadette, and had been since they were four years old.

"Pete!" Bernadette laughed in response, hugging him tightly around the neck. "Oh, I *am* glad to see you! It's been so long!"

"Really?" Pete said, with an incredulous grin, as he set her back down. "An if I mistake not, your final words to me, when I left the last time, were that you never wanted to see me again! Isn't that so, Camille?" He appealed to the maiden, who was standing near them, a soft blush mantling her cheeks.

"Oh, for goodness sakes', Pete," Bernadette half-scolded, not giving Camille a chance to answer. "Are you really so dense as to not know what I meant by that? Aren't you like a brother to me?"

"*To* be sure," was the careless response. "And it's the fate of brothers all over the world to have to deal with incessant displays of base under-appreciation from their sisters."

"Does it hurt you so very much, poor fellows?" Bernadette inquired pityingly, her eyes dancing with mocking merriment.

Pete deigned no reply, but immediately turned to his uncle and aunt. He bowed very low to them, saying in tones of great respect mingled with deep affection, "I hope I see you well, my dear uncle and aunt and royal sovereigns? Thank you for your readiness to receive me and my comrades with so much attention and at such short notice. I can never tell you how much you mean to me," he concluded, embracing them each in turn.

"Tush, my boy! As if you didn't mean just as much to us?" retorted King Friedrich, slapping his nephew heartily on the back. "I'm sure we are more than repaid for what little arrangements we may have made for you and your friends' comfort. It's a positive delight to have you all here! Is not that so, my dear?"

"Indeed it is," was all that Queen Anna Marie said, but her eyes shone with a tenderness almost as great as that she demonstrated towards her own daughters, as she took the young knight's hand and pressed it between both her own.

Pete bent to kiss the tips of her slender white fingers. "And a joy to me to be with you all again, aunt," he said simply.

"And how are you, my little one?" Pete added merrily, turning to whirl Princess Roxanne about in her turn, albeit somewhat more gently than he had her sister. "My, how you've grown! Quite the fine young lady now, aren't you, gracing the banquet-table and dance floor at all times with your fair presence, I suppose, eh? May I crave the honor of Your Highness' hand in the first set at tonight's ball?"

"Hey!" Bernadette protested indignantly, pushing in between them. "That's always been *my* dance with you, Pete, and you know it. Why would you want to change it now?"

"Well, life would grow rather boring if there were never any changes, now wouldn't it?" Pete inquired, with a lazy yawn. "Besides, we might as well start preparing ourselves for the inevitable, Bernie; once you're married, we won't be able to dance the first dance with each other any more." Now it was time for *his* eyes to twinkle wickedly at his cousin.

Bernadette flushed and tossed her head back, the shaft having hit home. "Well, I prefer to put off that fateful day for as long as I can," she retorted in a half-whisper, to prevent her mother hearing. "And don't call Roxanne 'my little one'; that's my name for her," she added adamantly, putting her arms possessively around her sister.

Pete rolled his eyes. "Well, then, my not-so-large one," he said, with exaggerated emphasis on the corrupted title, "may I claim the honor of your hand for the third dance, then? I would ask for the second, but since around here we are apparently not allowed to deviate in the slightest from our accustomed practices, I must perforce offer myself as partner for that one to Maiden Camille, as is our usual custom."

"But not a mandatory custom," Camille protested hastily. "And I would not wish to stand in the way of any arrangement that you and Her Highness may desire, Sir Peter . . ."

"No, no, I was only in jest," Pete assured her hastily, his eyes taking on a far more gentle expression as he looked at her. "I would not trade my dance with you for anything," he added earnestly, whereupon Camille blushed very deeply indeed and cast her eyes upon the ground.

Bernadette eyed them suspiciously. Camille had been her constant attendant since her childhood, when she and her cousin had been inseparable companions; and therefore a natural intimacy had sprung up between these two closest friends of the princess. Of late, however, Bernadette had begun to discern signs of a deeper connection blossoming between them. She wasn't sure yet how she felt about this prospect, and determined, as she now observed them together, to watch them very closely during Pete's stay with them.

"Well, shall we now adjourn to the banquet hall?" inquired the Queen, taking her husband's arm. "I am sure we are all very eager to hear a full account of all that has passed since the time you were last with us, dear Peter."

He bowed in response, replying, "It will be a great pleasure to tell you all that you may desire to hear, over the grand dinner I am sure you have provided, Aunt Queen Anna Marie." His eyes danced with boyish delight over the prospect of a magnificent meal. Then, turning lightly away from Camille, he offered his arm to Bernadette, saying in a high-and-mighty tone: "I suppose you will desire me to escort you, Your Most Esteemed Royal Highness, since such has been our accustomed practice? I would not wish to cause you undue distress by creating upheaval in your settled routine. Seriously though," he dropped his voice back into an easy, familiar tone, "I want to make the most of our time together during this visit, Bernie." And with a smile of affectionate good-humor at his cousin, who, despite her attempts to appear offended, couldn't help laughing as she accepted his arm, they left the room together quite companionably. Camille and Princess Roxanne followed behind them, each escorted by one of Pete's soldier companions.

Chapter Three
The Village Festival

Bernadette turned slowly around in a circle, unsure of where to look first, as the various sights and sounds of the Blossom Festival swirled around her.

"Fresh-pressed elderflower wine! O come to my booth and drink my sweet elderflower wine!"

"Flowers and garlands and magnificent wreaths! O come and buy a garland for your lady, come and buy!"

"Ring toss here! Everybody's a winner at the ring toss!"

"O come and try my just-baked strawberry pastries—the taste of spring!"

"Oh, what shall we do first!" Bernadette hugged herself and tapped her toes up and down in happy anticipation, eagerly glancing first one way and then the other as the village merry-makers hurried past her.

"We can't do anything until Uncle and Aunt get here; we promised to wait for them," Pete observed with lazy moralism, his arms crossed in provoking indolence as he leaned nonchalantly against the wall of a shuttered corner shop. He winked down at Princess Roxanne and Camille, who were primly seated on a stone bench next to him. Bernadette was standing on the curb, as near to the action as she could get.

Rocking back and forth precariously on her toes, impatiently poised to be off, Bernadette glanced over her shoulder at her needling cousin and wrinkled her nose at him in frustration. Was there *anything* he enjoyed more than to irritate her?

"Well, where are they?" she demanded, whirling around and sweeping her gaze out over the distant plaza, where a crowd of nobility was still gathered about their parked coaches, straining hopefully to see her parents emerge and come towards her. "I don't know how it is," she continued impatiently, turning back to Pete, "but whenever this family goes anywhere, we never manage to get there until at least half an hour later than we were supposed to!"

"Then you ought to prepare yourself and plan your time accordingly," her cousin responded coolly, taking out his handkerchief and brushing off the sleeve of his mail shirt as if that were the only matter of consequence at the moment.

Bernadette made a horrible face at him, which he didn't see, and returned to her occupation of watching the street crowd surging past her, bouncing slightly as she attempted to contain her eagerness to join in the celebration. Bernadette had been rushing the Royal Family to hurry up and get to the Festival since the crack of dawn that morning, and had been absurdly pleased with herself since she had managed to get them to depart from the palace an entire three minutes ahead of schedule. But then, of course, just as soon as they arrived at the village, the Lord High Chancellor *would* choose that very moment to come up to them with a most pressing matter, that absolutely *had* to be resolved by their Majesties prior to their joining the festival entertainments. They had been discussing it at the carriage door for ten minutes already (by Bernadette's timing; it was only fifty seconds according to Pete's calculations, and two minutes by Camille's watch), and Bernadette was beginning to think that they would never come to join the rest of them at all!

But at last the King and Queen did arrive, arm in arm and all gracious waves and smiles to the passing crowd. Bernadette immediately hopped off the curb onto the cobblestone pavement below, ready to rush off and take part in as many of the festivities as she possibly could. "Come on, Pete; you can polish your sword later! Let's get going; we're already missing out on all the fun!"

"Here, hold on a minute, can't you, daughter mine?" protested the King, laughing, as he breathlessly followed his speeding daughter down the street with the rest of his family in tow. "What's the great rush? We've got all day to spend here at the Festival, haven't we?"

"Not the part of it we've already missed," Bernadette retorted, casting her eyes hungrily over the line of booths and stalls arranged along the path to the village's Central Plaza. "Oh, look, there's Johanna!" she cried, pointing to a booth staffed by a pretty, dark-haired young woman, who waved and called out a pleasant greeting to her. "Her cakes are always the best; do let's go and get some right away, before they're all gone, please?" She turned a childishly pleading look, like a toddler begging for candy, upon her father.

"Well, I don't know . . ." King Friedrich began, half-hesitatingly, but he was already reaching into the leather money-bag tied at his side, as he turned towards the bakery stall.

"No, daughter," Queen Anna Marie interposed in her gentle but decisive manner, "there is no time just now; we are already expected at the Royal Pavilion."

"Oh, Mother, must we go there first?" Bernadette cried in dismay. "Once we get there, we'll never be allowed to leave. So we simply *must* have some fun first."

" 'Must' is a word I do not particularly like to hear from you under such circumstances, my daughter," replied the Queen, with quiet severity. "And duty comes before pleasure; I have taught you better than that. Now come along; we have lingered long enough." She moved

33

on towards the enormous raised pavilion overlooking the Central Plaza, from which the Royal Family traditionally observed the festivities of the Blossom Festival.

"But we *could* get something to eat on the way, my dear," hopefully suggested the portly, food-loving King, with a sympathetic glance at his elder daughter's disappointed face, and a surreptitious one back towards the tantalizing attractions of the bakery stall.

"No; there will be plenty of dainties available at the Pavilion, and we can come back here later," the Queen spoke firmly, and having thus decided the issue, she gathered up the flowing train of her skirt with one hand and led the way down the avenue towards the plaza. King Friedrich hastened along behind her; and Bernadette, who knew from years of experience that "later" on Festival days meant "never," heaved a great sigh and dropped back to the end of the procession.

But after a few moments, a new thought apparently occurred to Bernadette, and she hurried to catch up to her parents. "Oh, Mother," she asked, carefully offhand, in hopes of catching the Queen off guard, "may I join in the dances today?"

"Which ones do you mean?"

"The circle dances of course, round the Blossom Pole in the plaza," Bernadette endeavored to reply quite lightly and naturally, but the look she directed at her mother, out of the corner of her eye, was rather timid and uneasy, as though she already knew what the answer would be.

"Positively not." There was absolutely no trace of any willingness to compromise in the Queen's voice. "Those dances are strictly for the pleasure and entertainment of the peasantry and townsfolk; they are most unsuitable for a lady of royal station. You will take part in the formal dances at the Royal Pavilion, as usual, and that should be more than satisfactory to you."

"But Mother, you let me join in the village dances that one year, with Father," Bernadette persisted resolutely, hopeless as she knew her efforts would be.

"You were younger then. Now it is high time that you began to behave more in accordance with your position in life," Queen Anna Marie replied without concession.

"You always used to tell me I couldn't join in the dances because I was too young to do so without a chaperon; and now that I am old enough, you say that I am too old to join in at all!" Bernadette complained. "And those dances are so much more fun than ours! Oh, please, Mother; I'll be extra good and ladylike in other ways if you'll just allow me this one exception today! Please!" She clasped her hands together and leaned forward in appeal, her eyes fixed imploringly on the Queen's inflexible countenance.

"You cannot take part today; so let me hear no more about it." Queen Anna Marie waved her hand slightly, indicating that she considered the conversation to be at an end, and moved on in her most stately fashion. Bernadette cast an entreating look at her father, but he remained silent, and his expression indicated his tacit agreement with his wife upon this subject.

"Come on, you can dance with me, isn't that good enough?" Pete interposed teasingly, tugging on the end of his cousin's hair.

"No, it isn't!" Bernadette jerked her head away and placed herself on the other side of her father, where she remained for the rest of the walk to the Royal Pavilion, occasionally casting suspicious sidelong glances at her cousin, as if she expected him to make another assault upon her tresses. Pete, for his part, did not seem to notice her at all as he strode along with his easy martial stride, in between Camille and Roxanne, all three of them chatting merrily away together.

Just as they reached the steps leading up into the pavilion, Pete uttered a delighted cry.

"Why, Thomas! Richard! What brings you two here!" He hastened to shake hands with two knights of about his own age, both wearing grins so broad they threatened to split their faces. "The three of us were at the Military Academy together," he informed his royal relatives, as the two soldiers bowed to their sovereigns respectfully.

"Our regiment is on its way to its springtime quarters by the southern border, Pete," explained the one whom Pete had addressed as Sir Thomas.

"And our commanding officer gave us leave to stop over here for the weekend, to enjoy the Festival," added the other, Sir Richard, directing a bright, inquisitive smile at Bernadette, who blushed and tossed her head back self-consciously.

"A pleasure to make your acquaintance," said Queen Anna Marie graciously. "Will you not do us the favor of joining us in the Royal Pavilion for the day, to observe the Festival?"

"We would be most glad of your company, indeed," boomed the King heartily, seconding his wife's invitation.

The two knights exchanged glances with each other. "We are most honored, to be sure, Your Majesties," replied Sir Richard, slowly. "But we have already committed ourselves to joining the dances in the plaza; I trust that you understand?"

"Oh, of course!" laughed King Friedrich. "What were we thinking? Never fear, my fine young gentlemen; we would not wish to deprive you of your expected pleasures for the day—nor those of the young ladies to whom you have committed yourselves," he added, significantly, while the two young men blushed.

"Why don't you join us, Pete?" asked Sir Thomas, hastily.

"And your cousin, the Princess?" added Sir Richard, with another admiring look at Bernadette, who drew a quick breath and glanced towards her parents, hopefully.

But Pete gave his aunt and uncle no chance to reply. Shaking his head, he responded: "I thank you, my comrades. But I am duty bound to give my company to my relations this day, as is her Royal Highness, Princess Bernadette. But I hope to see you later at the feast. Good day to you!" he bade farewell, beginning to mount the stairs.

"Good day!" echoed the two young soldiermen, as they were quickly swallowed up in the milling crowd around the Royal Pavilion.

Bernadette watched them go, regretfully, as she followed her cousin up the steps. "And since when couldn't I answer for myself, Pete?" she hissed, in an undertone that only he could hear.

"You know Aunt and Uncle would never have let you go, anyway," Pete answered in the same low key. "You should be glad that I spared you the embarrassment of having them refuse you in front of my friends," he added, helping her up the final step into the Pavilion, and then turning to give his hand to Camille, who was just behind her mistress.

Bernadette scowled at him, but she couldn't think of any compelling argument to make in reply (perhaps because there *wasn't* any; Pete was right, and Bernadette knew it). Without another word, she turned on her heel and strode across the Pavilion to where her parents were greeting the nobles and courtiers. It was a tiresome business; Bernadette didn't even know half of the people, but it was necessary to ensure that no one felt neglected by their sovereigns and the heiress to the throne.

The dances had not started yet, but more and more villagers were pouring into the Central Plaza, putting the final touches on the gorgeously garlanded Blossom Pole, securing their partners for that all-important first dance, and making sure that all was in readiness for the grand opening moment, while the village orchestra tuned for all it was worth. Oh, how Bernadette wanted to join them. She decided to make one last effort. Bidding a polite farewell to the noblewoman she had just greeted, she turned and walked over to her parents, who were talking with the Duke and Duchess of South Perewerdland, old friends of the Royal Family.

The Queen looked up and smiled at her daughter as she approached. "Yes, dear, what is it?" she asked, encouragingly.

Emboldened by this sign of ready indulgence, Bernadette ventured to ask once more: "Mother, may I *please*"—the Queen's smile had already disappeared at the wheedling note in her daughter's voice— "take part in just this one dance today? It's my very favorite, and I'll never have another chance . . ." her words trailed off hopelessly.

"I told you to let me hear no more about it, and I meant what I said," her mother replied sternly. "Be grateful for what you have, and don't demand more. You need not come along at all, if your position here does not satisfy you." The Queen turned back to her conversation.

Vastly disappointed, and feeling quite ill-used, Bernadette marched off to the other end of the pavilion, where there was no one that she knew well, and sat and watched the mounting excitement below with a corresponding increase of frustration inside. She was beginning to feel lonely, too; Pete and Camille were off on the other side of the pavilion, engrossed in their own conversation; and Princess Roxanne was likewise standing at a distance, gracefully discoursing with an elderly ambassador and his wife.

Doesn't she ever get bored, with all these demands of royal protocol? Bernadette wondered, eyeing her sister with mingled amazement and irritation. She sighed and slumped back in her seat,

38

dismally anticipating an entirely unproductive and dreary day all alone in a stuffy royal enclosure. Well, there was nothing she could do about it.

Chapter Four
At Old Saphronia's Cottage

"Cecil! Oh, Cecil! Cecil, can you hear me?" Bernadette crouched down low behind the banisters, peering around the curve of the Grand Staircase to catch a glimpse of the elderly porter below, who was looking about him perplexedly. "Cecil!"

"Is that you, Princess Bernadette?" inquired the honorable old servant, looking up towards where her voice was coming from. "I can't see you."

"Good; I don't want you to see me," came Bernadette's quick reply. "I'm around the curve in the stairs, and I want you to turn around and look the other way until after I've come down; so that if anyone asks you, you can honestly say that you haven't seen me."

"Eh, now, what new mischief are you up to, Your Highness?" Cecil asked drily, raising an eyebrow in apparent censure.

"I'm not up to anything, truly, Cecil," Bernadette responded half-plaintively, half-irritably. "I just want to go for a walk alone on the grounds—nowhere far off or where I'm not supposed to go, I promise." Bernadette frowned; she was still frustrated over her failure to get to join in the fun at the Festival the day before, and determined to find it in some other way. She had decided, therefore, to head down to the peasants' cottages, where she knew they would be involved in the yearly jam-making, a pastime Bernadette loved. However, she rarely had the time to spare from her palace duties to join them; and when she did go, she had to keep it profoundly secret. Court society looked down its nose at any royal association with the peasants that was not strictly charitable or official business transactions, such as collecting rents. The King and Queen themselves did not object to their daughter's interactions with their tenants; but Bernadette did not want anyone else in the castle to know what she was doing: her ladies-in-waiting would gossip about her forever if they found out!

Therefore, as soon as she had finished helping her mother overview the linen closets and prepare the menus for the week, Bernadette slipped away to her room and put on her darkest full-length cloak, pulling up the hood to cover her blonde head. If any superfluous decorating tasks came up that afternoon; well, they would just have to be done without her! She went to the door, and after a cautious glance up and down the hall, headed for the top of the stairs, hoping that Cecil would be on duty and would fall in with her plan.

As has been seen, as least the first part of her hopes had been quickly answered. Bernadette remained crouching and half-hidden behind the banisters, watching the kind old porter with bated breath, hoping that he would comply with her request. He bit his lower lip and considered for several seconds before responding, his sympathy for his young princess struggling to overcome his notions of strict adherence to the unwritten code of conduct for palace society. "Very well," he said at last. "I won't have seen you. That's about the right idea of what you want of me, is it not, my fine young Princess Bernadette, eh?" his eyes were beginning to twinkle.

"Yes, yes indeed," Bernadette returned promptly, immensely relieved. "Just turn around, please, until I've passed you and shut the outer door."

"All right then," replied the porter, suiting the action to the word. Once his back was safely towards her, Bernadette crept down the stairs and tiptoed across the marble floor of the Great Hall foyer to the door.

"I'll be back by dinner-time, Cecil," she whispered, poking her head back around the edge of the portal as she slipped outside. "So I'll see you then. You can turn around now," she added humorously, pulling the door shut behind her and stepping down into the sunny courtyard, heaving a great sigh of freedom. Picking up the edges of her gold-embroidered skirts, she ran lightly out of the palace yard, into the wide, sweeping meadow slopes behind the castle.

Bernadette knew exactly where she was headed: the cottage of Old Saphronia, an elderly widow who lived alone in one of the peasants' cottages nestled away in the hollows of the hills behind the castle. Old Saphronia was well advanced in years, at least something past eighty-five; and although she was remarkably spry and capable, she still gladly welcomed any visitors who might be willing to assist her with the heavier duties of peasant life, while listening to her long spun-out tales of the old days. Bernadette loved to visit her cottage and have a chance to participate in such absorbing tasks as butter-churning, egg-hunting, and candle-making, which made her feel useful as well as being entertaining. And furthermore, Old Saphronia was an understanding, grandmotherly woman, who was always ready to lend a sympathetic ear to a younger person's troubles.

She was not alone in her cottage today, however. Bernadette found an entire company of Old Saphronia's daughters, grand-and-great-granddaughters, grandnieces, and distant cousins assembled there, busily preparing a fresh store of jam from springtime berries picked the day before. They all knew Bernadette well, and greeted her enthusiastically, as she got right into the midst of the action.

"But tie this apron around yourself first, Your Highness; it would *not* do for you to get berry stains on your fine attire," instructed Old Saphronia, handing the worn-out, voluminous garment to Bernadette, who obediently slipped it on. One of the younger children, who had only met Bernadette a few times and was still in thrall over being so close to a princess, tied the apron-strings for her—into triple knots that would have to be cut later.

Jam-making was messy but fun, and all the women and older girls talked and laughed continuously as they worked, only ever ceasing in their chatter to call out a warning reprimand to a child who was wandering too far away from the open cottage door or venturing too near the fire. Of course, they all wanted to hear about the Festival; and so Bernadette told them what had occurred, and they all sympathized with her heartily. After all, they would have liked to have been at those dances themselves! Only the most well-off of the cottagers ever had the time to take off from work or the means of conveyance to the village that would enable them to take part in the festivals there.

"But, anyway, I think all of you probably had a nicer day yesterday than I did, out berry-picking. My, but these are delicious," Bernadette popped a "second-rate," rather squashed berry into her mouth. "Did you eat anywhere near as many as you brought back for us?" Bernadette giggled slightly, and munched another berry.

"What kind of a question is that, Your Highness?" demanded Estrella, Old Saphronia's eldest great-granddaughter. "Of course we did; that's what they're there for. But we brought plenty home for the jam-making—and extras in case of inexplicable reductions in our store while we work today"—here she gave Bernadette a meaningful look, and ate one of the berries herself. "And there's still some left on the bushes, if you want them," she added, once she had swallowed the luscious morsel.

"I probably wouldn't be allowed to go there to pick any, even if I did want more," Bernadette grumbled, swiftly hulling a pile of the small crimson berries. "I suppose you got these out on the Western Range; I can't go that far away from the palace unaccompanied."

"Well, I wasn't unaccompanied either, Princess Bernadette; there was a whole party of us, my brothers and sisters and cousins," Estrella responded, moving over to pick through another pile of berries.

"And cheer up, child; you're not the only one barred from these berry-gathering jaunts." Old Saphronia looked up from her boiling kettle. "I didn't get to go yesterday either; it's too far and high a climb for my old legs, and I also wasn't at the Festival, dancing or not dancing. Couldn't do that either, even if I had the opportunity, so count your blessings, both of you."

"Yes, ma'am," Bernadette and Estrella echoed in unison.

After all the jam was boiled down thick, strained, and jarred, and all the old stories and recent news had been told and retold, and the kitchen-area swept and scrubbed clean of berry-stains, the other women and girls at the cottage packed up the children and their share of the jam-jars, bade farewell to Bernadette, and departed, leaving Bernadette and Old Saphronia alone together in the cottage. The latter sighed and sat down in one of the only two rickety chairs in her dwelling.

Bernadette looked at her. Why, she hadn't realized until now that Old Saphronia really *did* look rather old today. And lonely. It must be hard upon her, to have all her flock settled, if not far away, still not in her own house with her. And as she slowly grew more feeble, it would be nice for her to have someone else with her all the time.

"Would you like me to fix you a cup of tea, Old Saphronia?" Bernadette asked rather shyly, not knowing how to put into words what she was feeling. "And maybe slice up some bread and cheese for us? I'd like to sit and talk with you a while longer."

"Ah, that would be nice, my dearie," responded the elderly woman, gazing at Bernadette fondly. " 'Tis indeed about my supper-time, and I'm rather worn to be making it myself. Not that I wouldn't do it, though," she added more strongly, straightening her bent shoulders. "But it is nice to see a lady be handy about the fireplace and foodstuffs, like yourself, Princess; and to have someone else tend to the victuals on occasion."

"Oh, I'm only too happy to!" Bernadette exclaimed, quickly putting the kettle on, and then setting out the rough cloth and chipped pottery and ironware upon the table, before she took down the loaf of black bread and sheep's-milk cheese that composed the peasant woman's simple supper fare.

"But will you be able to eat with me, Princess Bernadette? Won't they be expecting you to dinner at the palace?" Old Saphronia raised one eyebrow inquiringly. "I don't suppose you thought to get permission to spend the entire evening down here with me."

"Well, no, I didn't," Bernadette responded, rather slowly, as she poured the tea from the kettle into an old handleless cup. She didn't bother to explain that she hadn't asked permission to come at all. "But I would love to stay," she added wistfully, looking at the homey meal and cozy, well-kept, although humble surroundings.

"And I'd be glad to have you. I wish you could be with me all the time, Your Highness; you're such a grand help to me," Old Saphronia picked up her steaming cup and began to slowly sip from it.

Bernadette gazed over at her, a warm feeling springing up in her heart. How nice to be wanted by someone, to be a true benefit to them! A glimmer of longing, for something that she could not quite define, came into her mind.

"But I'm afraid I must go," she said regretfully. "You're right; they will be expecting me back at the castle."

"Well, then, run along, Princess Bernadette; I shall see you again soon."

"Oh, yes! Goodbye, and thank you for having me, Old Saphronia," Bernadette made her respectful farewell, and then ran out of the cottage and back over the hills towards the castle, hoping that she would make it back in time for dinner. For the shadows were already stretching out long beneath the trees, and the sky glowed with the mellow tones of early sunset.

Chapter Five
The Bargain

Halfway up the hill, she ran into Pete. "Well, and where have you been all day?" he asked, dropping into step beside her. Bernadette gave him an angry look and did not answer. She had still not forgiven her cousin for interfering with her attempts to join the dancing the day before. "I've been looking for you."

"Yes, I'm sure you have!" Bernadette snapped back. "Just so you could prevent me from having any fun, like you did yesterday."

"Bernie!" Pete stopped on the hillside and stared at her in astonishment. "That's not fair for you to say. What, do you think that I deliberately interfered with your chances of getting to dance in the plaza? I told you, I knew you wouldn't be allowed to go and was just trying to keep you from being humiliated in front of everyone, that's all. And I came looking for you now because you've been gone all afternoon and no one knew where you were, so I thought I had better look out for you. I should think you would appreciate it."

"It isn't my fault if you were silly enough to be anxious about me; you should know that I can take care of myself," Bernadette retorted with a scornful toss of her head, swinging her skirts back impatiently as she continued on up the hill.

"And how could I possibly know that, when you can't?" Pete rejoined mockingly, leaning around to peer into his cousin's face. "You don't have any experience in looking after yourself; you've always had other people to take care of you, and you wouldn't last one day out on your own."

"How dare you, Pete!" Bernadette exclaimed indignantly, swinging around to face him. "I guess I know just as much about it as you do! It's not my fault that I've never had the opportunity to prove it."

Before Pete could respond, King Friedrich came riding up over the crest of the hill.

"Ah, there you are, daughter!" he exclaimed in evident relief. "I've been wondering where you were. It's nearly dinner-time."

"I went to visit Old Saphronia; I told Cecil I'd be back for dinner," Bernadette replied, a little defensively. "I was just on my way back now, when *Pete* had to come after me, like an officer after an escaped convict!" She darted another wrathful glance at her cousin, who rolled his eyes disparagingly.

King Friedrich only laughed. "Well, well, no harm done by that now, is there? We're all still on our way back to dinner; and I can eat, too! Riding certainly gives one a magnificent appetite!" Rubbing his stomach anticipatively, he glanced keenly over at Bernadette. "But why didn't you tell the rest of us what you were up to this afternoon, my daughter?"

"I didn't want to, Father," Bernadette sighed, suddenly feeling only weary and depressed instead of angry. "I didn't want to be . . ." she stopped abruptly, not wanting to give Pete another opportunity to mock her by disclosing her real reasons for not informing anyone of her whereabouts that day. "I just wanted to be alone," she said tiredly, gazing out over the valleys of the castle grounds.

Her father looked over at her in concern. "What's troubling you, my child?" he asked gently. "I think it's something a little more serious than brooding over not getting to dance yesterday, isn't it?"

"I guess . . ." Bernadette hesitated, not sure exactly what she felt. And then, suddenly, the hint of an idea that had half-formed itself in her brain while at Old Saphronia's cottage broke out into a full-fledged plan. "Father, I don't want to be a princess any more," she said decisively, looking up at him with her most resolute and mature expression. "I want to go live with Old Saphronia and help her. She's all alone, and really getting on in years, and she said just today that she wished I could be with her all the time. And after yesterday—knowing how much I would have preferred to dance in the plaza instead of up in the Pavilion, but couldn't—I've realized now that I would much rather spend my life doing what peasants do rather than what royals do. I know it's a more strenuous life; but it's simpler, and not as restrictive. In other words, I want to abdicate; Roxanne can have the throne."

King Friedrich regarded Bernadette solemnly; he did not appear to be questioning the sincerity behind his daughter's proposal, although he did seem a little—but only a little—surprised. "I see, daughter," he replied slowly. "But have you thought well of the ramifications of such a course of action? About any negative impact that it might have on your life or that of others?"

"It couldn't have any negative impact on my life, Father; I'd love it," Bernadette responded, inwardly picturing the amount of freedom such a life would give her. "And how could it possibly have any effect on anyone else, other than giving Roxanne a kingdom?"

"Would you not miss us, daughter?" The King's voice was very sad, though still calm and accommodating.

"Why, Father, I wouldn't be going away!" Bernadette was shocked at the idea. "What difference does it make whether I sleep in my own room in the palace, or just a stone's throw away at the cottages? I'd be scarcely further away from you than when I am on one side of the palace and you are on the other."

"But your duties and life would be centered on Old Saphronia and the cottages," the King replied, as they continued on over the hill; "you would not have time to spend with us: helping your mother, riding with me, embroidering in your boudoir with your sister, or taking your meals with us. And can you so lightly give up your royal role and privileges? I thought you enjoyed giving me your aid in the governance of the kingdom, and were justly proud of your abilities in doing so. Also, I would miss you," and now there was finally a slight tremble in the King's voice as he continued. "It would be impossible for us to continue to have the same depth of relationship; for though you would always be my dearly beloved daughter—nothing could ever change that!—a peasant girl and the king of the realm cannot spend the same amount of time together as a princess and her kingly father. Think well on it, my daughter; it is kind of you to think of Old Saphronia, but still, she is not your true relation, and the first claim on your loyalty belongs to them. I am sure you love us best."

"Of course I do!" Bernadette was now a trifle concerned herself. "But you all don't really *need* me; I want to be needed, to do something that no one else would do if I wasn't there," she tried to explain.

"Someone else can nearly always be found to do someone else's duty," her father responded gravely. "But the question is: is it *right* to take up other duties than one's own, and leave those for another? Can you, in good conscience, cast away all that you have been brought up for, and devote yourself entirely to a new life? And are you certain you would not be disappointed, and find that your new life really had no more benefits or fewer aggravations than the old?"

"I'm pretty sure I wouldn't be disappointed, Father; though of course I couldn't know for certain until I had tried it," Bernadette replied, growing more troubled by the minute. This was all getting to be a little more complicated than she had thought at first. "But as far as giving up my royal station goes—I'm sure Roxanne would love to have it; to be the sole heiress and future ruler, instead of just an extra princess with really no specific royal role to fulfill. It's not like I would be taking her away from her own duties to attend to mine."

"And what about your betrothed? Is this fair to him, that he would have to give you up now without any reason or consideration?" Bernadette had hoped her father would not mention this.

"What does it matter to him?" she challenged, frowning fiercely over the subject. "He won't care as long as he can marry the heiress of Berklesgilands; Roxanne can have him."

"Well, I still think you need to be very sure, more sure than one day at the Festival and another of visiting the cottages can make you, that you really would prefer and could better fulfill the purpose for which you were put on this earth in a peasant's situation rather than in a royal one." As he spoke, the King swung his leg over his horse's back and dismounted in the front courtyard of the palace.

"But Father, how can I decide that?" Bernadette sighed in frustration. "And really, how do I even know that either of those two paths is the right one to take for my life? It could be something entirely different; something that I haven't even thought of yet." All kinds of hazy notions about different ways and means of living darted through her head, and she became aware that she wasn't very clear on what *any* of them might actually entail or how well they might suit her. "How can anyone ever decide what kind of role in this world is best for them?"

King Friedrich stood regarding his daughter gravely for a moment, and then his face abruptly broke into a smile. "Would you like to try an experiment, my daughter?" he asked, a mischievous expression crossing his face.

"What do you mean?" Bernadette asked, suddenly alert. She liked it when her father looked like that; it usually portended *something* in the realm of fun or excitement.

"I'll make a bargain with you. You can take a year—this next year, before your scheduled wedding-date at age seventeen—to travel around the Kingdom of Berklesgilands and the neighboring realms, to try out all of the different ways of living that you think you might enjoy, so that you can find out which you like the best. If you like one of them so much better than your royal station that it can reconcile you to parting from all of us and giving up your birthright of both duty and privilege, then when the year is up, you can continue living that way and Roxanne will become the heir to the throne and marry your betrothed. Otherwise, you will remain the heiress and go through with your wedding as planned. But you will first have had a year of freedom, adventure, and new learning experiences, which would doubtless make you a better queen in the end, anyway. Now, what do you say to all this?"

"Oh, do you mean it, Father?" Bernadette gasped in amazement. "I should love to! It would be so exciting, like a treasure hunt, like going off to seek one's fortune, or like—like . . ." she couldn't think of words to properly express how she felt about it: exhilarated and confident, but a little scared, too, somehow. "Oh, thank you, Father!" She rushed to throw her arms around his substantial waist and hugged him tight. "You won't be disappointed in me; I won't abuse this precious opportunity you're giving me. Oh Father, you're so understanding and—and always right; you knew this is just what I need to sort everything out in my own head, and I can't thank you enough."

Bernadette drew back a little and dabbed at her eyes with her handkerchief; she was surprised to find them moist.

"However, there is one catch to all of this," King Friedrich continued, the look of mischief on his face deepening. "Pete has to go with you."

"Wha-at!" Bernadette gasped in horror as she turned to look at her cousin, who had said nothing throughout the course of her and her father's conversation, but had remained at her side all the way back to the castle. "Oh, Father, why? I don't want *him*," she protested, glaring at Pete as irritably as she could, while he grinned cheerfully back at her, having quite recovered his accustomed good-humor.

"Afraid I'll cramp your style, cousin, is that it?" he inquired teasingly.

"Yes," returned Bernadette, too much ruffled to say anything other than the absolute truth. "Must I, Father?"

"I'm afraid so," replied the King, much amused by her reaction. "It isn't safe for a young maiden to travel alone these days—or any days, really—and it isn't proper for her to travel with a man she is not related to. Besides, I don't suppose we really want to get outsiders involved in this. And there isn't time to send for another one of your male relations to accompany you: if you want to get a whole year of travel and adventure in, that is."

"As if any of them could be better than Pete, anyway!" Bernadette exclaimed, with an abrupt change of tune. Nothing reconciled her to her cousin faster than someone else saying something that could possibly be turned into a slight against him. "All right then, let's go!"

Both Pete and King Friedrich chuckled at her obvious enthusiasm. "Don't you think we might want to pack a little first?" Pete suggested, taking her elbow and guiding her towards the castle. "And make something of a plan?"

"Spoken like an officer," Bernadette sighed, pretending to be disconcerted by the proposed delay. Suddenly, a new thought caused her to stand still in dismay. "Oh, no!"

"What is it?" Pete asked, alarmed. He hoped she hadn't thought of anything that might prevent their trip: in spite of his affected nonchalance about the whole thing, he was really just as keen on the prospect as Bernadette was.

"What about Mother?" Bernadette returned, despairingly. "Do you think she'll agree to this?"

"Um—no," Pete answered honestly, looking rather disheartened.

"Leave that to me," said King Friedrich, in a tone of authority, giving his horse's reins to the groom. "But I can tell you one thing: the Queen *certainly* won't agree to it if you're late to dinner, so go on, you two." He shooed them through the front door of the castle, past a broadly grinning Cecil.

Chapter Six
Hasty Preparations

Well, Queen Anna Marie was hardly enthusiastic about the idea when it was first presented to her, and at first refused to even consider it. But after a private conference with her husband that night, while Bernadette tossed and turned between hope and dread in her own room, the Queen finally gave her consent to the journey.

Over the next few days, all was bustle and preparation for Bernadette and Pete's impending departure, at least within the castle: the proceedings were kept secret from outsiders. As King Friedrich pointed out, there was no way that Bernadette could get away from her royal status to try out other livelihoods, if everyone in the country already knew about their princess's proposed adventure. She'd have to travel in disguise, and Pete too. Bernadette rather liked that part of the plan; it lent quite an air of mystery and romance to the undertaking.

Speaking of which, Bernadette did manage to find time, in between all the packing and planning, to finally approach Camille about her feelings for Pete.

"Camille, you rather like Pete, don't you?" she asked in a carefully offhand tone, one time when the two of them were alone in her room, packing.

"Why, yes, to be sure; he is a remarkable gentleman and worthy of the highest honor from any maiden," Camille replied without hesitation, and apparently without any embarrassment. Bernadette twisted around to look up at her, but Camille was bending over a trunk, and she couldn't see her face.

"But I didn't mean that, Camille!" Bernadette protested, not at all satisfied. "Don't you feel a stronger sense of admiration for Pete than you do for just any gentleman of honorable reputation?"

"Well, of course, naturally; we have been close companions from childhood, and I do believe that I have, as a result, a deeper relationship with and greater understanding of him than I do of anyone else, other than your own Most Gracious Highness, my dearest princess," Camille answered, in the same tone as before.

Eventually, having failed to glean any more explanatory remarks from Camille, Bernadette gave up, despairing of obtaining any satisfactorily revealing information from that quarter. But a few days later, on the very morning of their scheduled departure, she managed to corner Pete in the front hall.

"Pete, what are your intentions towards my maid?" she demanded, unequivocally, fixing him with the most severe gaze of which she was capable.

"Well, we *are* getting vigilant, now, aren't we?" Pete retorted, grinning, apparently not in the least impressed. "And who died and made you Camille's official guardian, Bernie?"

"Camille has no guardian, and well you know it, Pete!" Bernadette shot back immediately. "She's entirely dependent upon her position in our family for her support and guidance for her future—but that's not really the point here," she brought herself up short, determined to not allow Pete to sidetrack her into squabbling over entirely irrelevant details about Camille's situation. "I just want to know," she ended, lamely.

Pete shrugged in response, unconcerned. "I don't know what you'd want to know that you don't already know, Bernie. I've nothing to tell you, really. Camille and I have always been friends; we understand each other, and now that we're getting to an age where our relationship can accomplish its natural and desirable conclusion, well . . ." he shrugged again.

"So you do intend to marry Camille, then?" Bernadette had to come directly to the point at last, utterly exasperated by her inability to achieve the answer she wanted by delicately beating about the bush.

"Someday, I suppose; though not until after we get back, of course," Pete replied with nonchalant humor.

"But, Pete!" Bernadette exclaimed, astonished by his matter-of-fact coolness towards the situation. "Don't you realize—don't you know that Camille has no intentions of marrying anyone, at least not for right now, as she's made quite clear with Stephen . . ."

"Oh, so he's still in love with her, is he?" Pete inquired with sudden alertness. "I noticed that the last time I was here. She hasn't managed to discourage him yet?"

"Only to keep him at a distance, using me as the excuse. But I'm not going to stand for that any longer, if that's not her real reason for avoiding courtship. I don't think it's at all fair that she'll allow such attentions from you but not from Stephen, when there is no difference in how either of you interfere with what she perceives as her duty towards me . . ."

"Ah, but that's where you're wrong, Bernie!" Pete interrupted her, quickly. "In the first place, I'm your cousin, and we're very close, so I can understand how Camille feels about leaving you before you're settled yourself."

"Stephen's my friend; so he can understand, too!" Bernadette insisted, quick to resent the slight towards the young door-porter.

"Not like a member of the family, Bernie; you know you don't really think so. Besides, Stephen is around all the time, while I only visit occasionally. See, I'm already leaving again today, and I've scarcely been here two weeks. If Camille allows my attentions whenever I'm here, but keeps Stephen from doing the same until some time in the future, we'll both end up having the same total amount of time to court her, and then she can make a fair decision. But we all already know—or at least, Camille and I do—what that decision will be."

"I still don't think it's fair, though, not to me and certainly not to Stephen," Bernadette reiterated, puzzled but unconvinced by Pete's line of argument. "And what do you mean, that you already know that she'll pick you over Stephen, when you haven't yet given Stephen any chance as a fair rival? And he really does love her, while I can't see that there's anything that special between the two of you."

"Oh, what do you know about love and such, Bernadette?" Pete responded, impatiently. "The only dealings you've ever had in the marriage market thus far have been those of prearranged policy and convenience."

"You needn't rub it in!" Bernadette exclaimed, indignant. "You're right; I don't know anything about love for myself, and I never will. I'm either going to have to marry that Prince Gerald-Reginald; or else I'll never marry *anyone*, of that I can assure you. This whole betrothal situation has left a really bad taste in my mouth. But I do know what Stephen's love is like for him, for he's told me about it; and I support him in it wholeheartedly!" she ended heatedly, feeling more incensed than ever by her failure to provoke Pete to any demonstrations of jealousy. He only shrugged yet again as she concluded.

"Support whom you please, it won't make any difference in the end to the only two who are really concerned in the matter; and may the best man win, say I," and Pete walked away, whistling quite unconcernedly.

Bernadette shook her head, frustrated. But she didn't have time to dwell on the question any longer at the moment: there was so much to do with last-minute packing and innumerable other departure preparations. She didn't even see Pete again until just before they were ready to leave, when King Friedrich called both of them into a private antechamber just off of the Great Hall.

"Yes, Father?" Bernadette skipped inside the room, half-closing the door behind her for privacy. Pete was already sitting down, and King Friedrich was standing before the desk in the center of the room, his hands clasped thoughtfully behind his back.

"There's just one more, rather important, matter that I wish to clarify to the two of you before you go," said the King, somewhat gravely, although with a mischievous little twinkle in the depths of his eyes: "that is, the question of who is really to be in charge on this mission. It is your experiment, Bernadette; and therefore you are to have the final word on all disputed decisions. Pete is going along as your bodyguard and companion, not as your leader. Do I make myself quite clear to both of you?"

He evidently had. Pete looked extremely dissatisfied, and Bernadette was smirking triumphantly.

"But—"and the King made a tantalizing pause, while the mischief-loving expression in his eyes deepened as he looked from his daughter to his nephew and back again—"what I wish to make explicit to you, my dear, is that your being the one in charge doesn't necessarily mean you can do whatever you please. Pete knows some things and has had some experiences in the world that you have not; and so, while he is not to initially tell you what to do, you need to listen to Pete if he warns you rationally against your own plan. I want your assurance that you will not stubbornly insist on doing things your own way when Pete knows that it won't work out and tells you so. Will you give me that assurance, daughter?"

"Yes, Father," Bernadette replied obediently, with a disillusioned little sigh. She did wish that people would trust her to be capable of making her own decisions!

It was Pete's turn to smirk at his cousin now; and to his credit let it be said, that he really didn't do it at all—well, hardly. The corners of his lips did curl up a trifle complacently, but he merely said to King Friedrich: "Yes, Uncle, my liege; I fully understand my role in this adventure, and you need not fear that I will take advantage of it."

"Oh, I don't fear that you will; no, not at all!" the King threw back quickly, his eyes twinkling more than ever. "I *know* that you will, both of you! Neither one of you could ever stand taking orders from the other; and whenever a disagreement comes up, as it inevitably will, each one of you will be absolutely certain that this particular instance is one in which you have the ultimate authority over the decision. But I hope—it's a very slight hope, to be sure, but better than nothing—I hope that the remembrance of what I have so clearly outlined as your respective duties towards each other will prevent you from getting to the point where you'll never speak to each other again. I know you won't do as I've told you; but I figure, that if I hadn't told you, you might do a great deal worse!"

"Oh Father!" Bernadette cried out in protest—and then suddenly looked over at Pete, whose face was as bright red as a cherry, and put a hand over her mouth to keep back a sudden storm of irrepressible giggles. The laughter that Pete himself was trying to smother broke out then, and King Friedrich's booming guffaws rang out louder than either of theirs.

"We're a fine pair, I know," Pete spluttered, once he got his breath. "And I dare say we're a hopeless case of irreconcilable self-confidences, Uncle Friedrich. But we'll manage all right; and whatever goes wrong between us will probably turn out to be nothing more than a great joke in the end. Even if we do stop speaking to each other."

There was no time for them to discuss the matter further: the entire palace household was assembling out in the Great Hall to say goodbye. All was such confusion and hugging and affectionate farewells, that Bernadette had no time to think or fully realize what was happening until she found herself seated in the carriage, Pete at her side and the coachman on the box, waving frantically to her family members, ladies-in-waiting, and the palace servants, who had all gathered in the front courtyard to see her off.

"Good-bye, my princess and best friend!" Camille cried, waving her handkerchief and otherwise behaving in an unusually demonstrative manner, tears running down her cheeks as the coach carried her beloved mistress out of the courtyard.

"Good-bye, Camille darling! I'll be back before you know it!" Bernadette called in return, past the lump quickly forming in her own throat. "Oh, goodbye, goodbye, dearest Father and Mother and Roxanne; I love you all so much. And—" catching sight of another familiar figure standing and waving over on the edge of the assembled crowd—"goodbye to you too, Stephen! Take good care of Camille till I get back!" Bernadette leaned as far out of the window as she could, waving to her friend as significantly as possible, a look of droll triumph chasing away the one of regret over leaving all her dear ones.

"I will!" Stephen shouted back, his own face flushed with delighted confidence and renewed hope, as he waved madly after the departing carriage, while making his way to Camille's side. Bernadette just barely had time to catch a glimpse of her maid's crimson cheeks and appealing eyes, before they turned the corner and all the assembled company in the courtyard was lost to view. She pulled her head back in the window, settled back against the seat cushion, crossed her arms in satisfaction, and grinned exultantly at Pete.

He had also turned a little red by now, but all he said was: "Well, he's certainly got a more enviable job than I have; that is, taking care of *you* for the next year, Bernie."

Chapter Seven
The Adventure Begins

Some five or six days later, anyone journeying along the mountain passes of the King's Highway in the middle of the morning might have chanced to notice two travelers riding briskly along the edge of the road. Two blond-haired young fellows they were, in simple but striking attire and mail coats, obviously knights of some degree. One of them was very tall and strongly built, and he rode his horse, a glossy brown stallion, with the purposeful air of a man of the world who knows what he is about. The other, slighter and nearly a head shorter, sat astride a fine black horse, and looked around curiously at the passing scenery, in a somewhat more uncertain manner.

Of course, you have already guessed who these two knights are. After a great deal of discussion—and, it must be confessed, some argument—held in the carriage after their departure from the castle, Bernadette and Pete had ultimately determined that their first disguise would be that of common soldiers—"I should think, Pete, that you'd like to start off on our adventures in a capacity with which you're already familiar," Bernadette had said, clinching the matter without allowing Pete to further protest the impracticality of the endeavor.

And therefore, after a brief visit with Bernadette's Aunt Helen, Duchess of the nearby city of Girenthia—during which Pete had instructed Bernadette in the rudiments of broad-sword fighting and secretly purchased two fine war-chargers for them in the town market, and Bernadette had had two sets of squire's clothing made to fit her and cut her knee-length golden hair into a cropped page-boy style—the two cousins had set out together to enact their first disguised role. And hence their appearance on this particular road on this fine bright morning.

"So, Pete, and just where, exactly, does this pass lead to?" gaily asked Bernadette—who was, of course, the slighter knight on the black horse.

"Well, it doesn't exactly lead *to* anywhere," Pete responded, pulling up his mount for a moment and mopping his forehead beneath the pushed-up visor of his mail helmet. This spring was well on its way towards being one of the hottest on record in the Kingdom of Berklesgilands. "It just leads *through* this range of the Highring Mountains, to the crossroads where all the other thoroughfares converge."

"And where do they go?" Bernadette persisted, finding the topic extremely interesting.

"Oh, there's three or more different ways you might go," Pete explained carelessly. "The King's Highway picks up there—widening out to its usual broadness—and leads clear across to the other end of the kingdom. Then there's a twisty little road that leads back into the mountains and the villages up there. And then there's the short road that leads straight out into the Kingdom of Lurkenwild next door, through the lowlands."

"And is that it?" Bernadette asked. "What about the towns in the upper end of Berklesgilands, below the High Ranges? The King's Highway doesn't lead to them, does it?"

"No; if you want to get there, you have to follow the path—it couldn't even be called a road—into the Burlon Forest, and travel through to the other side. But that side of the country's mostly wilderness, and there's hardly any roads. Even the path that leads into the Burlon Forest fades out after a few miles." Pete evidently knew this area quite well; he spoke very knowledgably about it.

"But there are ways to get through the forest, even without a road?" Bernadette leaned forward in eager inquiry.

"Oh, certainly; if a person is skilled in traversing the woodlands, he could get through easily enough," Pete replied carelessly.

"Then could we go that way?" Bernadette's voice was tense with excitement. "It would be so much more of an adventure than just going along the road; and I'd like to learn how to live in the woods. You know how, don't you?"

"I should think so!" Pete might be pardoned the touch of scorn in his voice: the very idea that he, a knight of the Royal Military Academy, might even be suspected of not knowing how to survive in the wilds! "We'd be less likely to be noticed along that route, too. Well, I'm fine with the idea; but you know, Bernie, the Burlon Forest is not the safest area of the country. There's wild beasts and outlaws a-plenty that roam in there, not to mention the difficult and dangerous terrain."

"You don't think I'm *afraid*, Pete, do you?" Bernadette flung him the question like a challenge. "You don't think that I could brave the dangers just as well as you?"

"Well, maybe not quite as well as I, but well enough," Pete added on the last clause imperturbably, checking Bernadette's indignant exclamation. "Shall we head in that direction, then?"

"Yes, we shall head for the Burlon Forest," Bernadette returned with prompt decision, deftly handling her reins to guide her mount in behind Pete's charger, as he led the way down the winding mountainside.

When they reached the bottom, they drew rein next to each other; and Pete pointed across the valley, past the cross-roads and a brief bit of meadow beyond them, to where the black, ominous fringe of the

Burlon Forest loomed. Thick and tangled, it looked like a solid, twisted mass of overgrown branches and thorns. Other people might have thought it looked threatening. Bernadette thought it looked amazingly exciting, although—how in the world did you get in there?

"Ready to go?" Pete was surveying his cousin appraisingly, wondering what her reaction to this uninviting prospect might be. He really—although he would hardly have admitted it—had quite a high opinion of Bernadette's courage and ability to handle tough circumstances, but then these qualities in her had never been deeply tested. And she *was* only a girl, after all. Maybe she wouldn't like the prospect of trekking through this dense, gloomy forestland, now that she had seen it.

But any doubts Pete had about the matter were quickly cleared away. "Ready to go?" Bernadette breathed, her eyes sparkling like stars. "Oh, yes, I'm ready. Now this will be an adventure!"

Pete smiled, half admiringly and half self-reproachfully, his faith in his cousin's strength of character triumphantly restored. "Well, let's go then!" he cried merrily, and setting their spurs to their horses, the two thundered across the green and entered the Burlon Forest.

The tangle wasn't really as thick as it had appeared from a distance. There was plenty of room between the thick old tree-trunks for Pete and Bernadette to ride side by side. Pete had not minded taking the lead while they were on the road; but in this treacherous woodland, he was not taking any chances of Bernadette falling behind him and possibly getting lost or into danger.

Bernadette, for her part, was looking in all directions at once, drinking in the wild loveliness of the forest. She had never imagined anything so splendid, so overwhelmingly majestic. Everything in the forest looked more intense, more gorgeous, more enchanting than anything else ever seen in reality—so much so that it almost didn't look real at all. Bernadette was loving everything she saw. Dangerous? How could a place this lovely be dangerous?

And it was so nice to be out of the sun's direct heat. Bernadette's mail armor was not particularly heavy, but she was still not entirely used to it, and had found it somewhat oppressive and hot while riding out in the open earlier that day. She removed her helmet now and hung it from a strap on her saddle, enjoying the cool freshness of the breeze on her bare head, ruffling the edges of her short hair.

The two cousins scarcely spoke as they rode along: Pete, although not as mesmerized as Bernadette by the wondrous glory of the forest, nonetheless had a high appreciation for its beauty and did not care to be distracted from it by useless chatter; and besides, he was fully occupied with keeping them headed in the right direction. And so they traveled on in silence; the immense, imposing hush of the forest enveloping them in its age-old mantle.

Presently, though, a new sound broke the stillness: a stealthy, disturbing kind of rustle, as if something—or someone—did not wish to be openly observed, but nonetheless meant that its unseen, insidious presence should be felt. This noise first came from somewhere off to Bernadette's left, the side of her on which Pete was *not* riding.

"What was that?" she asked abruptly, but rather indifferently; she was not particularly alarmed. She knew that Pete was a magnificent swordsman and archer; and besides, Bernadette had often gone hunting herself in the woods around her castle. Her hand went almost instinctively to her bow, hung at the front of her saddle, with the calm, quick responsiveness of one well prepared to deal with unforeseen situations at a moment's notice.

Pete was still less affected by the sound than his cousin: he probably would not even have noticed it had she not mentioned it. "A deer, perhaps; or a fox or wolf seeking food or shelter," he responded unconcernedly, with a brief shrug of his shoulders. "The animals around these parts are not accustomed to human intruders; they may, on occasion, come nearer to us than is usual, because they won't have expected us to have so brazenly invaded these sacred grounds. But upon realizing their mistake, they will doubtless go away and leave us in peace. They don't want us any more than we want them—less, if anything, for there will be times when we will have no objection to fresh meat for dinner."

Bernadette laughed, now quite undisturbed, for his bantering tone had fully assured her that there was no cause for alarm. "Still, it is always better to be cautious," she replied, with a great show of prudent wisdom. "And don't bandits often endeavor to imitate these sounds, in order to avert any suspicion of their approach?"

"They do, but not that well," Pete replied, still entirely unperturbed. "I've had enough experience so that I can tell the difference between the two: this one is definitely a real wild animal, not a vagabond masquerading as one," he stated confidently, as the rustling sounded again, this time considerably in advance of them. "We've got nothing to worry about by day, provided that we keep on the alert. It's only at night that there is true need for vigilance: but a good fire and taking turns at watch will doubtless prove a more than sufficient safeguard for us."

"When and where are we going to stop for the night, anyway?" Bernadette queried, turning her head to observe the flight of a wood-bird, who, disturbed by the hoof-beats of the travelers' mounts, had just made a hasty retreat from her roost on a nearby tree.

"Well, as to when: as soon as it gets too dark to see our way any longer; and as to where: how should I know?" Pete retorted bluntly. "Wherever there is sufficient open ground for our camp, low branches to tie our mounts, and, hopefully, running water nearby. But that won't be for a while, Bernie; we want to make our way as far as possible beforehand. Let's go!"

Chapter Eight
Night in the Woods

"Pete, don't you think we ought to stop and set up camp now? We'll want there to be enough light left to see to gather wood for our fire. There's a stream not far off from us; I can hear it." Bernadette cocked her head in the direction of the faintly musical, rippling sound. "It's somewhere off to the left; shall we head that way?"

"The ground should be more level there," Pete agreed, turning his horse's head towards the sound. Bernadette followed after him.

"The underbrush seems to be getting thicker, Pete," she noted.

"Naturally; the proximity to running water is good for vegetation," Pete returned, drily.

Bernadette bit her lip before replying. "But don't we want a clear spot?" she asked finally.

"Yes, of course, we won't camp right next to the stream where it's all overgrown; but I just want to see where it is, so we can get to it easily when we want water." Pete ducked under a low-hanging limb and uttered an exclamation of satisfaction. "Ah, there it is! And Bernie, there's actually a bit of meadow on the other side that's comparatively open; why don't we ford the stream and spend the night over there?"

"All right." Bernadette managed to prevent her nervousness from showing in her voice; she had never forded a stream so wide and swift as this one before. But she followed Pete gamely through, suppressing a gasp as the rushing water buffeted against her legs and her horse's sides, threatening to sweep them away at the slightest misstep. But her mount's footing was sure, as was Pete's; and they both reached the other side in safety.

Bernadette drew a long breath of relief and glanced behind her, re-measuring the stream with her eyes. Actually, it hadn't been that hard. Few things are once you've actually done them. It's only getting up enough nerve and determination to make a start that takes a real effort.

Pete had already dismounted and tied his horse's reins to a nearby branch. He now turned to offer a hand to Bernadette, but she shook her head and slid quickly down to the ground without his assistance. "You mustn't help me, Pete; you'll give us away! We're both knights now, remember, and we have to act like it," she half-scolded.

"Okay, Bernie, I know, I know," Pete returned quickly. "But it'll take some getting used to, getting out of the habit."

"Oh, all right." Bernadette dismissed the subject. "Now, shall we start gathering the wood?" Pete was already kneeling down, pulling up the grass to make a bare circular spot where they could safely build their fire. "There's a lot of that brushy growth like what we just came through, downriver."

"Well, you can get some of that if you like, to start the fire with," Pete replied. "But we'll mostly need heavier wood—fallen limbs and such—that will burn more slowly. We want this to keep going all night, or else we'll be at a decided risk from wild beasts. Probably the best place to look would be further away from the stream; I'll come and join you in a minute, once I get this clear. Until then, I think you should stay close by and just get the shrubs," he added, as Bernadette slowly began to walk away towards the deeper part of the forest, where the dusk was swiftly deepening into nightfall.

"Don't tell me what to do, Pete," Bernadette retorted, almost haughtily. "I'm not such a fool that I'd go out of sight of the campsite

71

and get lost. I know I'm not as experienced in forest travel as you, but I'll learn!"

"Yes, you will," Pete responded cryptically, speeding up his work and then deciding that he could wait to clear the rest of the space until after they got back with the wood. Better to not let Bernadette go running off by herself just now, not until she was more experienced and less concerned with *proving* her capability.

Together the two cousins collected a substantial pile of wood and returned to their camp, where Pete finished clearing the circle while Bernadette gathered a few sticks and shrubs to start the fire.

Once they had the fire going nicely, Pete piled the rest of the wood into a convenient stack, and Bernadette went over to get the food for supper and their blankets out of the saddlebags. She decided that they had better have the jam tarts that night, before they got completely smeared over everything else in the bags.

Before long, the two cousins were seated on opposite sides of the fire, toasting their bread and cheese over the flames, while they munched on apples and cast occasional longing, sideways glances at the sticky-smashed jam tarts that were waiting for dessert.

"We don't have to sleep in our armor, do we, Pete?" Bernadette inquired presently, shifting her position to lessen the pressure of the mail coat on her shoulders. "Oh!" she made a frantic grab at her bubbling cheese-covered toast as it fell off her stick into the blaze.

Pete, fortunately, had seen mishaps like this before. Laying his own bread aside, he sprang nimbly around to Bernadette's side of the fire and raked her bread out of the coals before it had a chance to burn up. As it was, it was deeply browned and sizzling, and Pete had to blow out some flames still clinging to it.

"You can have mine, if you'd rather, Bernie," he offered. "I like them this way."

"Oh, no, thanks; I'd like to try it coal-roasted myself," Bernadette giggled, accepting her toast from him. "Thanks for rescuing it for me. I guess I'm not much of a hand at this."

"Nonsense," Pete scoffed, walking back to his side of the fire. "I've seen dozens of seasoned camp-travelers drop their food in the fire—and most of them don't know how to get it out, either. It's quite a joke; and we laugh about it—in some cases it's not so funny, though, when that's the only ration you have for the night and you can't get another. Somebody else is nearly always willing to share, however, even if they will jibe you about it," he added, swallowing the last crumb of his toast and reaching for his tart.

"Well, I suppose you can learn great lessons about self-denial in such situations," Bernadette observed quietly, her eyes fixed musingly on the dark branches opposite, just barely illumined by the leaping flames. This trip was certainly going to be very enlightening, and character building, she thought to herself, as she began on her own jam tart.

"So, anyway, what was it you had been asking me, Bernie?" Pete inquired lazily, stretching out his long arms and flopping back in a relaxed attitude next to the fire, his hands behind his head.

"Just whether we are expected to sleep in our mail, as thoroughly-equipped knights always ready for action," Bernadette responded, swallowing the final bite of her tart.

"Oh, no, of course not!" Pete chuckled at the bare idea. "Unless you're expecting to be ambushed any second. And most of us have become very practiced in the art of girding our mail coats and helmets back on in double-quick time, so we don't have to sleep in them even

73

during emergency situations. We race, you see. The leaders only allow you to remove your armor during nights on the battlefield if you can demonstrate that you can put it back on in less than twenty seconds. Perhaps you ought to learn how too, just for the fun of the thing, for I don't suppose we're going to be in any real battles . . ."

"And why not?" Bernadette interrupted, looking rather irritated at the insinuation, as she supposed, that she was not capable of enduring the conditions of an actual battle.

"Because there are no wars going on in the vicinity at present," drily returned Pete, who had meant nothing of the sort, "and as we are not a pair of hired mercenaries, I presume that we are not going to go looking for one, just to have the battle experience?" He raised an eyebrow and regarded his cousin steadily.

Bernadette flushed at the rebuke, and said nothing in reply. After a few moments of silence, Pete continued on with the same subject:

"So, no, Bernie, we won't sleep in our armor tonight. You may as well lay yours aside now; I'm sure you're good and tired of wearing it, and I should have mentioned it before; there was no need for you to keep it on during dinner. But I forgot, you see, since I wasn't taking mine off. Selfish enough of an excuse, but it's the best I've got."

Bernadette laughed, and willingly divested herself of the chain-link overgarments that had encumbered her all day. Looking a very attractive, if disheveled and boyish, picture in her squire's tunic and leggings, she sat down again, cross-legged, and asked, pertly:

"But why don't you also take off your armor, Pete? It's a good deal more comfortable, I assure you, for sitting cozily round the fire." She leaned back with affected laziness to better demonstrate her point.

"Because whoever is on watch should keep his armor on, in case of any surprise attack; so no use taking it off just to put it on again," Pete replied, getting up to toss another log on the fire.

"And who said that you were going to take the first watch?" demanded Bernadette, sitting up abruptly.

"I did," Pete returned calmly, sitting down again.

"Oh, and without so much as a 'by-your-leave' or even thinking it worth discussing with me?" Bernadette rushed on, hotly. "Don't I get any say in these matters? I believe that Father said that this was *my* adventure, did he not?"

"He did." Pete showed no inclination to deny the fact.

"Well, then?" Bernadette challenged.

"Well, then, I have experience in keeping watch, and you don't, so it makes sense for me to take the first one and demonstrate," Pete retorted. "Not to mention the fact that you aren't as accustomed as I am to long days of hard travel, so I feel it's only fair to let you get some sleep first; I'm sure you're more tired than I am. And finally, no matter what you may be wearing or what role you've currently chosen to play at being, you are still a lady; and my honor as a gentleman and a knight forbids me to allow you to serve and protect me in any way before I do you."

"Oh, that's all rubbish, Pete! Who needs to be shown how to sit by a fire and just keep a look-out for invaders, really! And I'm *not* tired; I'm just as capable and tough as you are, even if I am a girl! I get so tired of hearing that girls aren't as good as boys, and . . ."

"If you can get that interpretation out of what I just said, then I give you up as a hopeless case," Pete interjected, still lounging indifferently beside the fire. "Be that as it may, I am still going to take the first watch tonight; this is one of the areas where I believe I am entitled to

command the benefit of my expertise in deciding the situation."
Bernadette made a face at him, but didn't bother to respond.

"So, Bernie, why don't you get a couple of hours' sleep, now that dinner's over?" Pete suggested more pleasantly. "We have to get up early tomorrow, you know. And then I'll wake you and you can take your turn for an hour."

"But you just said that you were going to keep watch for a couple hours," Bernadette noted suspiciously.

"I am; I think it's only fair that I should take longer watches than you until you get used to it," Pete replied, still in the same conciliatory manner; he didn't want to frustrate his temperamental cousin any more than he could help, especially considering that this was only the first day of their journey.

"Well, I don't!" Bernadette retorted angrily. "Turn and turn about, fair play; that's what I think."

It was on the tip of Pete's tongue to say that Bernadette didn't think at all, but he suppressed the inclination. Inwardly resolving to actually wait longer before waking her than she had stipulated, he stuck a stick into the ground to measure the time by its shadow cast by the moonlight, which filtered down abundantly through the few branches that criss-crossed over the glen. Bernadette composed herself to sleep on the other side of the fire, watching Pete through half-closed eyes as she reclined on her blankets, drawing their edges up around her shoulders. She saw through his intentions rather better than he supposed, and a slow smile curved her lips in response. But she was soon asleep.

Chapter Nine
The Surprise Attack

"Bernie, wake up; it's your turn now." Bernadette squirmed away as Pete prodded her awake with his foot, and sat up, rubbing her eyes and blinking sleepily in the light of the fire as she tried to get her bearings.

"All right, all right, Pete," she half-grumbled, half-laughed, shifting her position so that her back was towards the fire, and placing her bow in readiness to her hand. "I'm ready to stand guard, so you can turn in now! Thanks for letting me sleep so long," she added drily, glancing over at the time-stick.

Pete did not answer; perhaps he had not heard, as he was busy arranging his bedroll on his side of the fire. "Be sure you wake me up in *exactly* two hours, Bernie," he instructed peremptorily, as he lay down. "And earlier if anything happens. The point of having someone on watch is so that he can rouse the rest of the camp to take action when required, not so that he can defend everyone entirely on his own."

"I know what I'm doing," Bernadette replied coolly, piling up her arrows next to her and girding her mail coat back on. "There's no need to disturb you if nothing more than one wolf comes along, which I could easily take down on my own. By the way, did anything come by while I was sleeping?"

"No." Pete's eyes were already shut; his experience as a soldier had taught him how to both fall asleep and fully awaken in the blinking of an eye. "I mean, there were some rustlings and wild beasts passing by at a distance, but none of them cared to come near the fire. It's rare that there is any *evident* reason for keeping watch; it can be a boring job."

"But the one night you decide not to do it, is the one day you should!" Bernadette laughed, understanding him perfectly. Pete again did not reply, being already well on his way into the depths of slumber. Bernadette glanced over at him with twinkling eyes, admiring how very handsome her cousin was—which is always easier to do with semi-irritating people when they are asleep. Then, with a happy little sigh, she settled down and prepared to keep good watch, gazing about on her surroundings with a delighted eye. The moon was high above the horizon by now, touching the edges of every leaf and blade of grass with silver. Bernadette thought herself in a veritable fairyland, as she gazed about her, eagerly drinking in every detail of the scene and attempting to impress it indelibly upon her memory.

However, she did not allow her occupation with the beauties that surrounded her to entirely distract her; upon hearing an unaccountable rustle behind her, she turned ready for action, her hand on her bow.

With a sudden snarl of outrage at the intruders of his domain, a sinewy panther crouched to spring from a low-hanging branch at the edge of the circle of light, his eyes glowing their reflection of the flames that terrorized him, but could no longer hold him back. Bernadette stared into those viciously haunting and unblinking orbs, mesmerized; but mechanically raised her bow and fitted an arrow into it, feeling herself nearly hypnotized and powerless to look away in the face of the savage, unconquerable ferocity of her opponent.

As the great cat gathered himself for the final leap of attack, Bernadette gave one quick gasp of alarm and drew the string back, letting her arrow fly. Her aim was true: with a wild scream of agony, the beast fell to the ground and rolled over, pawing at its chest, before expiring not three yards from where Bernadette had sprung to her feet, prepared for further fight had it been necessary.

"What happened?" Pete had woken at the sound of the panther's cry, and was already on his feet as well.

"Nothing; I took care of it," Bernadette responded, still gazing at her fallen foe. "Apparently one of the residents of this area decided that his dislike of trespassers surpassed his fear of their incomprehensible weapons. A foolish preference, as he has found to his detriment," she concluded wryly, pointing out the body of the powerful animal to her cousin.

"You killed it with one shot?" Pete exclaimed, half incredulous, half impressed. "That's well done, Bernadette; there's not many who can do that."

"I was afraid that if I didn't get him the first time, I'd be too rattled to do it right the next," Bernadette replied. "But I was ready to shoot again if I had to," she added, showing Pete her bow, with another arrow ready on the string.

"That's right; that's the way you have to do things in the forest," Pete approved. "You really *are* a natural, Bernie." The cousins smiled warmly at each other, their earlier disagreements forgotten in their mutual feeling of victory.

"Although I must say, I really should have been the one to face the beast; you were supposed to wake me up half an hour ago," Pete rather spoiled the moment by this observation, as he glanced down at the "moon-dial." "I'll take over now."

"Fine," Bernadette replied shortly, putting her bow aside and settling herself down to sleep again. She was well enough satisfied; at least she had proved her ability to single-handedly meet and counter an attack on an unfortified camp. Not a bad night's work, on the whole.

The next two days passed in relatively the same manner: constant travel through difficult terrain by day, with only a brief rest at lunch

and an occasional stop for Pete to show Bernadette some of the
essentials of forest life, such as how to distinguish between a nutritious
mushroom and its similar-looking poisonous cousin, or learning how to
use fallen sticks and bent bushes to discreetly mark one's trail so that
only friends and not enemies could find you, and so forth; and then
camping on the hard ground by night, cooking a meagre supper over
their defensive fire, and taking turns at watch while the other slept.
After the one incident with the panther, they had had no further trouble.

"How much longer does the Burlon Forest continue on?" Bernadette
inquired, towards sunset on the third day. She tried not to allow her
weariness to show in her voice; she was truly glad of this opportunity
to learn how to survive in the wilds, but still—a night in a real bed
under a friendly, sheltering roof was beginning to look like a more
inviting prospect than it ever had before!

"We should be close to the edge by now; but we probably won't
make it out tonight," Pete replied, a trifle regretfully. "We could have
made it in three days, but we've stopped in order to acquire important
new skills and experiences. But once we're out, it's not far to the next
village. We can get there by midday tomorrow, easily. It's a nice-sized
town; I've passed through it a couple of times, though I've never stayed
overnight. But I've had lunch there, and I know there are good inns and
shops to buy food—"

"Which is a good thing, since we're starting to run low, and what we
do have is going stale very quickly," Bernadette interjected, with a
significant pat to the almost-empty saddlebag that hung on the right
side of her saddle (the other, which contained most of the jewels and
gold they had brought along to pay their expenses, was still quite full).

"We can get new mounts there, too, if we wish," Pete continued.
"Ours are pretty worn out by now," sympathetically slowing the pace

of his steed. Pete and Bernadette weren't looking quite their best and brightest selves, either. Bernadette had long since given up on trying to remove the thorns and twigs that accumulated in her hair during every day's journeying. "Or we could just stay for a couple of days in the village, and then travel on once our horses are rested."

"Well, we can decide all that once we get there," Bernadette determined. "Since we aren't going to make it out of the forest this evening anyway, why don't we stop for the night now? I can hear water, can't you?"

"What kind of water is it?" Pete had been teaching Bernadette how to note the subtle differences in forest sounds.

Bernadette cocked her head and listened closely for a moment. "A pool with a bit of a waterfall at the side; I can hear the plash of the falls over the stones at the edge," she decided.

"I think you're right," Pete agreed, guiding his horse in the direction of the sound.

And so she proved to be; it was a charming little woodland glen, that seemed better suited for a fairies' tea party than for two knights' campfire meal. However, Pete and Bernadette had too keen of appetites to care, and enjoyed their supper with a relish.

Pete still insisted on taking the first watch every night, and Bernadette had decided not to argue the matter any more for the time being. Besides, she was very tired, and only too happy to get a little rest.

Truth be told, Bernadette actually had a great deal of difficulty staying awake for *any* of her watches that night, even after she had gotten some sleep. She kept catching herself on the verge of nodding off, and would start up suddenly in alarm, glancing about to see if she had missed anything. And when Pete woke her for her third turn on guard, he had such difficulty in arousing her, that he asked whether she was sure she wanted to take any more watches that night; he was quite willing to do the rest if she didn't.

"Certainly not," Bernadette snapped, extremely frustrated—with herself, really, not with Pete. Her tired body was pleading for more rest; and Pete, she knew, was not as weary as she was; he was used to this. But her pride would not allow her to admit her sleepiness or take on one jot less of the work than Pete.

It was not a good idea. Pete knew it wasn't; but remembering his uncle's instructions, he reluctantly let his cousin have her way and fell asleep with his accustomed promptness. Bernadette, sitting bolt upright across from him, tried to refrain from even blinking in the dazzling moonlight, knowing that if she closed her eyes for even the fraction of a second, her chances of opening them again were quite slim. She was not as alert as she generally was on guard; and all at once she was abruptly startled from her daze by some stealthy, unusual sounds on the darker side of the glen, where their horses were tied.

As she rose slowly to her feet, grasping her weapons a trifle nervously, one of the horses gave an anxious whinny, as though it sensed her movements and was calling for help. Peering into the darkness, Bernadette could just barely distinguish the forms of the animals beneath the trees, and surrounding them, several figures of vaguely human size and shape. Bandits!

Well, they weren't going to steal their horses, not if Bernadette had anything to say about it! She moved steadily across the glen in the direction of the unwanted visitors, keeping in the shadows and treading as silently as possible.

She was within a stone's throw of the thieves—there were three of them; one was untying the horses and the other two were preparing to mount them—when she stopped, half-obscured from view by some overgrown shrubbery, and called loudly, her hand on her sword-hilt: "Who goes there?"

There were a few alarmed ejaculations; and then, jerking the horses' reins entirely free, the bandits turned to gallop away with their spoil. Bernadette dashed forward in an attempt to stop their getaway; only to be immediately knocked down by her own horse as it thundered past her. The bandit astride her former mount slashed at her with his sword, but could not reach her as she fell to the ground.

"What's going on?" Pete had awakened immediately at the sound of Bernadette's cry, and now came running up to his cousin and pulled her to her feet, his sword already drawn and ready for action.

"Bandits; they got our horses before I noticed them; I wasn't soon enough," Bernadette gasped out, leaning against Pete for a moment to recover her equilibrium and then straightening up again, swiping her hair out of her eyes and taking a firmer grasp of her own sword. "Come on, we've got to go after them!"

"No use; they'll be too far ahead of us already for us to catch up on foot," Pete shook his head in dismay. "Why didn't you wake me immediately; we might have had a chance to fight them then!" he exclaimed impatiently, annoyed at the inconvenience of their predicament.

"There wasn't time, Pete! And there won't be time to stop them now, either, unless you hurry up. Come on!" Bernadette started to run in the direction the bandits had taken; she could hear their hoofbeats rapidly receding away ahead of her.

"I'm telling you it's too late; we can't waste our time or our strength in useless pursuit," Pete insisted, catching her arm as she began to dash off. "At least we still have our armor and our weapons; thank goodness, they weren't able to sneak up all the way and get those!" The implied rebuke of her negligence stung considerably.

"Who cares!" Bernadette cried, indignant. "They've got our horses and everything we own is in the saddlebags—all our money and our jewels! How can we go on without them? We've simply got to get them back, or else—*what*? Let me go!" and jerking her arm free with a desperate movement, she dashed frantically forward, following the distant thuds.

"Bernie, stop! Oh, don't be a fool, come back, you positive little piece of imprudence!" Pete shouted, racing after her. But Bernadette had already left him far behind; she was covering the ground between herself and her quarry as rapidly as if she had been given wings for her pursuit, taking shortcuts through the underbrush to cut off some of the distance between them.

At last, panting for breath, Bernadette broke through a row of trees and found herself in a small clearing. And at that instant, the moon broke free from a momentary cloud-cover, revealing the figures of the three riders just vanishing into the trees on the other side of the glen.

"Stop!" Bernadette shouted, waving her sword and crossing the clearing almost at one bound to come up alongside the lattermost of the bandits, who was astride her own horse. He shouted to his companions ahead, and endeavored to get to his sword to fend off Bernadette's attack. She was hanging on to the reins now, and deftly using her own sword to hinder the thief's efforts to get to his. Terrified by the commotion, the black horse reared up, almost unseating his rider, who dropped his just-drawn sword, inches from Bernadette's shoulder.

By now, the other two bandits had come back alongside them. Bernadette felt herself surrounded; and so, taking one second to ascertain which of the saddle-bags on Pete's brown horse was the fullest—and therefore the one that held gold—Bernadette quickly slashed the thongs that held it to the saddle, grabbing it before it could drop to the ground. The robber seated upon that stallion growled a threat, and thrust out his sword; Bernadette swiftly turned the blow away, giving the ruffian's wrist a painful twist as she did so. Dodging the approach of the other two bandits, Bernadette slashed off her own valuable saddlebag. The third robber was roaring and clutching his useless injured hand, while his horse, feeling the slackening of the reins, turned and galloped frantically away. His companions rushed after him, dismissing their lost booty for the moment.

Bernadette seized the jewel-bag, which had fallen to the ground, and then turned and hastened out of the clearing. As she ducked back into the protective darkness of the overhanging vines and branches, she could hear the outlaws returning.

"He got the bags! Should we go after him?"

"We'll not find him in this wretched blackness; let him go," growled a surly, authoritative voice, obviously that of the leader. "We've got their horses anyway; much good the rest of their stuff will do them, stranded here in this wilderness! And we have the other bags; doubtless there's just as much of good in them. Come on; let's be off before others come to his aid." In a few moments, the sounds of the horses and riders died away in the distance.

Bernadette, crouched under cover of a bush and scarcely daring to breathe, while they were so close to her, could still hardly refrain from laughing aloud when she heard their conclusion. "They think I'm a fool, do they? Not clear-headed enough to know which bags were worth saving and which weren't? They'll get nothing more out of the others than moldy cheese and stale bread, and much good may it do them!" Satisfied that they were far enough away from her by now, she straightened up and looked alertly about her, trying to discern the signs that would guide her back in the direction from which she had come.

She had taken no more than ten steps back toward the little glen, when she suddenly froze, her ear having caught the sound of approaching footsteps. As silently as possible, she shrank back into the shadows.

"Bernie? You there?" Slight as the rustling of her movements had been, Pete's trained ear had caught them, and recognized them as being too light to belong to heavily-laden beasts and hefty bandits.

"Yes." Bernadette emerged from her hiding-place, limp from the exertions of her adventure, but mightily proud of her accomplishment nonetheless. "I got back the jewels and gold, but they've still got our horses and food."

"Humph!" Pete grunted, as he took one of the saddle-bags from her and swung it onto his shoulder. "Well, you'll just have to put your newly-acquired woodland skills into practice sooner than we had expected; we won't make it to the village for more than three days now, traveling on foot, and we'll have to live off of what roots and berries we can find." He didn't seem overly impressed by her success in having retrieved *anything* from the thieves.

"But at least we'll have money to buy more provisions when we do make it to the village!" Bernadette offered, looking at the brighter side of the picture. "Shall we head back to our camp now? Do you know the way?"

"Yes; but I don't see any reason to go back," Pete responded. "I put out the fire before following you, and I picked up our bedrolls while I was about it. Here, you can carry yours." He tossed it indifferently over to her. "We might as well start on our way now; it's dawn any minute."

"Okay," said Bernadette agreeably, shifting her bedroll and saddlebag into the most comfortable positions for carrying. "I'm ready to start on again, if you are. I guess I had enough sleep for tonight."

"I'm sure you did," Pete returned wryly, leaving the rest of his thoughts on the situation unspoken. Bernadette gave him a "well, I made up for it as best as I could, didn't I" look in response, and then the subject was forever dropped between them as they headed deeper into the Burlon Forest together, now truly at the start of their adventures.

Book Two

The Chronicles of Their Adventures

Chapter Ten
The Village Inn

The sun was low in the sky when the two weary travelers finally trudged up the main street of the bustling village, situated in a welcoming, cozy valley between the labyrinths of the Burlon Forest and the sparser woodlands on the other side. Pete and Bernadette, tired and disheveled after four days' traveling on foot, were trying to decide what their next move should be.

"We need to buy horses and food for continuing our journey, of course; but in order to do that, we'll have to trade in some of our jewels. We should save the gold for emergencies, when we don't have time for bartering beforehand. And then, of course, I take it you'll want to stop at the inn for the night?" Pete cocked an inquiring, slightly mocking glance over his shoulder at his cousin, who was trudging along a little behind him, clearly much more worn out from their recent trekking experiences than he was.

"Well, naturally, what else?" Bernadette demanded, plucking up a little spirit in the face of his obvious indifference to her sufferings. She'd show him that she was just as tough as he was! "I don't suppose you particularly want to sleep out in this road, either. But if you do, that's your look-out; *I'm* going to the inn. Do you suppose they'll be serving meals yet? I'm *so* hungry, Pete," Bernadette concluded somewhat pathetically, her weariness and longing for sympathy getting the better of her pride.

"I know; I am too," Pete admitted. "But the inn won't be serving anything at this hour; it's still too early—Hey fellow-well-met!" he startled Bernadette exceedingly by breaking off in the middle of his sentence to call out to one of the passerby, a brisk-looking young man who was obviously out on an errand for his master or his father, for he was walking purposefully and rapidly along, evidently bent on getting somewhere in particular. But, as is generally the case with young apprentices who have gotten an unexpected break from shop-work, he was not in *too* great of a hurry, and turned obligingly to speak with Pete and Bernadette.

"And a good day to you, sir knights! Newcomers to town, aren't you?" he greeted them, raising one eyebrow curiously as he took in their soiled attire, but simultaneously their sturdy mail that garnered his respect.

"We are indeed," Pete responded; "just come through the Burlon Forest. My companion and I are looking to spend the night at the inn and travel on in a day or so. Can you inform us of which inn is the best here in town? Oh, and where we might be able to purchase new horses for ourselves? Ours were stolen by robbers back in the forest."

"That's too bad," sympathized the young man. "They're getting really bad these days; far too bold, those outlaws! I wish His Majesty King Friedrich would send out a dispatch of his guard to round them up; but then, there's only so much he and the army can take care of at one time! And who's going to inform the King of our problems out here, anyway? But I can answer both of your questions at one shot, young sir: the finest inn in town, bar none, as everyone acknowledges—except perhaps the proprietors of the other inns—is "The Gander and Cheese" just halfway down the side road there; you can't miss it," pointing as he spoke. "And the owner, worthy Grand, as his name is, has horses for sale. He owns some of the finest animals around here; you can certainly get mounts that will suit your needs, of that I can assure you."

"That is grand news," Pete rejoined heartily, as Bernadette heaved a sigh of mingled delight and longing, casting an eager glance down the street wherein lay the ready solution to all their problems. "And would you also happen to know, my good fellow, where we might be able to obtain some victuals at this hour. For I can assure *you*," he added, with a half-smile, "that we are well-nigh famished after our journey."

"Of that I am quite certain, sirs," assented the young man, earnestly. "And it is my good fortune to be able to likewise tell you where you may find nourishment—and good nourishment it is, too! Grandma Myrtle makes the best gingerbread in the village; and, I should say, in the world! Her shop is down that way: around the first corner, and then three doors down. It's the low gray-stone building with the burgundy shutters and green curtains; you can't miss it! If I didn't have to get these tools sharpened for my master, I'd join you; it makes my mouth water just to think of her good baking!" he smacked his lips appreciatively. Bernadette ran the tip of her tongue over hers, her own mouth watering at the thought of the luscious treats the young man's glowing recommendation had conjured up before her. "Anything else I can help you with?" he inquired, preparing to stride off.

"No, thank you—but indeed we do thank you!" it was Bernadette who replied to him this time, with a warm, glowing smile. The youth returned it, giving the second of the two knights a rather puzzled look; he was not accustomed to seeing such gentleness and gratitude in the face of a hardened warrior. It really was almost as if—but of course, that couldn't be, and so with a bow and a pleasant farewell, the young man continued on his errand, quite dismissing the incident from his mind. He never so much as thought of the two knights again, even though the one of them had showed evidence of possessing quite an interesting character for his profession!

Bernadette and Pete, quite unaware of the impression they had made, were eagerly winding their way down the crooked narrow streets of the village, to where an equally crooked wrought-iron sign, sticking out at the queerest, most picturesque angle, bore the half-legible legend of "Grandma Myrtle's Bakery Shoppe—Best Breads and Confectionery."

Now, whether that gingerbread really was the best in the world, as the young apprentice had claimed, or whether it just seemed so to Bernadette because she was so hungry, is a question that will never be satisfactorily answered. Be that as it may, it certainly was the case that she and Pete easily devoured the nearly full pan that the one gold piece they had been willing to spare had purchased; and, greatly pleased by their obvious appreciation for her baking talents, a beaming Grandma Myrtle gave them each another piece for free!

Greatly refreshed by the wholesome treat—and wholesome it was, I assure you; gingerbread in those days was far more worthy of the "bread" part of its name—Pete and Bernadette then found their way to a nearby second-hand jewelry store, where Pete took care of trading in a couple of their jewels for regular coins (after a half-hour of haggling over the appropriate price).

"It's enough to spend three nights at the inn, and buy horses and provisions to last us to the next town, anyway, Bernie," Pete told her, as they left the shop and headed back toward the main street of town, following the directions their earlier acquaintance had given them to "The Gander and Cheese."

"Splendid!" Bernadette approved heartily, as they rounded the bend in the road and approached the inn. It was a pleasant, low-eaved building set somewhat back from the road, with a good bit of land around it and a large garden and thatched stable behind.

Pete swung open the yard-gate and strode across the courtyard, with his cousin hurrying close behind him. "Come on, Bernie, let's go in! It must be supper-time by now." And he and Bernadette ducked under the low doorway into the smoky front hall of the village inn.

It was the supper-hour, most decidedly! A busy hum of conversation and bustling service came clearly through the open dining-room door on the right. People were talking and laughing and thumping mugs on the table; and a loud, cheerful voice, apparently that of the proprietor, could be heard above all the rest, urging everyone to "Eat hearty, eat hearty! There's plenty more in the kitchen . . . Hey, Sally, my girl, where did you disappear to? There's mugs to be filled—Good evening sirs, walk in, walk in!"

As Pete and Bernadette responded to his invitation and followed him inside, Bernadette couldn't help wondering how she and Pete were going to find seats in the crowded dining room, that already seemed to be bursting at the seams. There was only one long oak table, the benches along its sides packed full of patrons; and yet, as Bernadette and Pete headed for the table, the rest of the guests somehow managed to squeeze even closer together, leaving just enough space for two more. Pete, stepping nimbly over the rough boards and seating himself, was already giving his order to the innkeeper: "Two bowls of soup— what kind do you have? Either onion or cabbage?—well, two bowls of onion soup, then, with black bread and a *big* assorted dish, please, of whatever pickles you've got. And—hey, Bernie," he turned around to look at her, since she was still occupied with climbing awkwardly over the bench, devoutly hoping that no one would notice her.

Bernadette gave Pete a black look; couldn't he tell that she wouldn't want any attention drawn to her at this point, and respect that? And besides, they had already agreed that their names were now to be "Sir George" and "Sir William." So why was Pete still calling her Bernie? Thank goodness, at least the nickname did not sound obviously feminine! But even so—"What?" Bernadette demanded, snappishly, as she finally fell, decidedly ungracefully, into her place on the bench.

"Do you want ale or cider, eh, friend George?" Pete was using the same free-and-easy bantering tone, accompanied by friendly elbowing, that he would have used towards any other "genuine" knight. But Bernadette knew him well enough to see that he was just putting it on; and she was torn between being irritated that he thought her knighthood such a joke, and frightened lest his flippancy should give them away. So she merely replied shortly, "Cider, please," and hunkered down in her seat, trying to make herself as inconspicuous as possible. Pete didn't appear to notice her discomfort; he merely finished giving the innkeeper his order, and then immediately plunged into a lively conversation with several of the diners around him.

It didn't make Bernadette feel any more comfortable when she realized that, other than the innkeeper's four daughters who were acting as servers, she was the only woman in the room. And she had not expected so large of a crowd—didn't anyone in this village stay at home for dinner?

This question was shortly cleared up, however, by a remark Bernadette overheard from one of Pete's conversation partners: "Yes, we all arrived just this evening; our camp is three days' march from here: we came as soon as we had word of the invasion. Had you not heard of it?"

"No," Pete replied. "It happened last week, you said?" Upon a nod from the first speaker, Pete continued, "My comrade and I were traveling through the Burlon Forest at that time, and met no one who could have informed us about the attack."

"We've been recruiting more forces along our way," the knight across the table went on. "Would you and your companion be able to lend us your aid, or are you committed to another mission just now?"

"Nothing that could stand in the way of an opportunity to serve our king and country, particularly in the company of such a noble band as yours, sir," Pete replied promptly, without looking at Bernadette. She was not looking at him, either; tense and burning with excitement and nervousness at the thought of joining a real military campaign, she leaned forward involuntarily, gazing intently at the knight who had raised the proposal. However, he had resumed his meal, and did not appear to notice Bernadette's fixed attention upon him. After a moment, Bernadette realized that such obvious staring might arouse the curiosity of her table companions, and quickly turned away. Fortunately, the innkeeper had just brought out her and Pete's bowls of soup, so she had something else to claim her attention. But after the first few bites, Bernadette sneaked another look at the knight across the table. He caught her glance and smiled affably.

"Had you ought to request of me—Sir George, I believe I heard your companion call you?" he inquired, pleasantly.

"Yes, that is right," Bernadette said, a little confusedly. It was rather difficult for her to conceive of herself as a "Sir George." She snuck a glance over at Pete, but he was talking with someone else now, so she plucked up her courage for a solo interview with someone who sincerely believed that she was an official knight, just like all the rest of them, and plunged blindly into it. "I wondered if you had any more information about the invasion?"

"Well, it seems that they attacked the border city of Strolenburg—you know it?" Bernadette nodded, and the other continued, easily, "but fortunately the forces within the city were strong enough to withstand the raid, and the enemy troops apparently decided to adjust their plans and pursue a course directly into the heart of the kingdom. It is up to us to stop them before they can reach and attack another, less well-fortified city."

Bernadette racked her brains for an appropriately military-sounding response. Eventually, a little tentatively, she inquired: "And what are our plans for doing so?"

"That will be arranged tomorrow: we will hold a council of war once we arrive at our final camp, where we will prepare to approach our enemy," the knight replied, with a confidence that marked him as a born leader. Bernadette studied his handsome, strongly characterized face closely. Something about his manner seemed familiar: where had she seen him before? "Anything else you wish to ask me just now, Sir George?"

Well, she wasn't going to ask him who he was, of that much Bernadette was certain. "No; I thank you, Sir . . ." Bernadette hesitated.

"Timothy," the other supplied, with a comradely smile.

Sir Timothy! Of course! This was the very same knight that Bernadette had danced with, and actually enjoyed talking with, at that long-ago ball. Bernadette distinctly remembered talking about him with Camille the morning after. How strange, how very strange that they should meet here, where he could not, must not, be allowed to find out who she was! With renewed anxiety, Bernadette abruptly cut their conversation short and returned to her meal.

Around the rest of the table, however, talk flowed as freely as the refills poured from the innkeeper's daughters' jugs into the mugs of the patrons. The innkeeper himself had brought out an enormous roast of venison, which he was carving expertly, and passing the juicy slices around the table in plenty. His wife had also emerged from the kitchen, carrying an enormous tray of savory pies, which she served to whoever requested them. Bernadette had no objection to speaking to her, and did request a pie. She immediately regretted having done so, however; for the cheery woman teased her about how "young growing lads" need so much to eat, and asked what her mother was thinking to let her lad out into the world while he was yet so skinny! Several of the other knights at the table overheard this, and roared with laughter and chaffed Bernadette pleasantly on the score of her supposed youth. Naturally, with her high voice and slender frame, Bernadette had been assumed to be a younger knight, just barely above a squire in rank. Blushing deeply—"as deeply as a girl!" one of the knights remarked jocularly— Bernadette stammered as she tried to think of how to repudiate this half-serious, good-natured mockery of her inexperience. Pete was no help: he laughed as loudly and bantered as much with his "young friend George, who needed to get used to the rougher side of knighthood," as did the rest. It was ultimately Sir Timothy who managed to subtly but firmly interfere, and turn the tide of the conversation into less personal matters.

Relieved, Bernadette kept her head down and devoted herself to devouring the pie that had caused all the trouble, as well as two muffins that the kindhearted innkeeper's wife had slipped onto the "poor young lad's" plate upon seeing the distress she had inadvertently caused him. But as she ate, Bernadette kept her ears open, determined to learn all she could about how knights talked and acted, so that she might not embarrass herself again on the morrow.

There was plenty to listen to: the banter and shouted conversations down the full length of the table and endless thumping of mugs set Bernadette's ears to buzzing. However, the innkeeper was used to such pandemonium, and so he was able to distinguish an unrelated clattering noise over the stones outside, and quickly excused himself from the room to show in his late-arriving guest.

A few moments later, the clamor in the dining-room died down slightly, as several of the knights turned to look upon the newcomer, as he entered and stood momentarily in the doorway, hanging his cloak on a peg in the wall. He was well worth looking at, too; a tall, sturdy figure clothed entirely in black mail, even to his helmet. From beneath the visor of the dusky hood, a pair of piercing, far-seeing eyes swept the crowd in the room, with the expression of one accustomed to take charge evident in their bold gaze. He was young, but that obviously had no diminishing effect upon his utter self-possession and marked confidence.

Bernadette, who had turned to see what everyone else was looking at, instinctively felt the weight of this commanding presence as he met her gaze evenly, before turning away to send an inquiring look about the rest of the table. Feeling strangely resentful and oppressed by the dominant character of this black-garbed new arrival, Bernadette quickly turned away again and continued eating. But after another moment of surveying the assembled company, the knight strode purposefully up to the table and took his seat directly in between Pete and Bernadette, without so much as a by-your-leave. Bernadette stifled a gasp and cast an appealing look at her cousin, but he did not appear to be distressed by the behavior of this audacious newcomer; in fact, he must have moved aside for him quite readily, otherwise there would have been no space for him on the bench, as Bernadette most certainly had not moved!

Bernadette was now more distressed than ever; even though Pete had not been helping her out at all, it had still been a comfort to feel him sitting right next to her. Now Bernadette was in between two strangers, both of whom she greatly feared to give herself away to, especially this new black knight now sitting on her left.

So determined was Bernadette *not* to talk with this stranger, who had dared to come between her and her cousin, that she actually did begin to talk with the knight on her right. He, fortunately, was a rather shy and inexperienced young fellow himself, so he and Bernadette had plenty in common, and the rest of the meal continued on quite pleasantly.

Pete, who for some reason seemed to have determined to make himself as unaccommodating as possible to his cousin that night, soon found an excuse to involve the new arrival beside him in his conversation. Bernadette tried not to listen to what they were talking about; she was too profoundly irritated to betray any interest in what they had to say, but anon a dangerously familiar subject struck upon her ear, and forced her to pay closer attention.

"Have you heard the rumor about the princess?" inquired one of the knights sitting next to Sir Timothy, a tousle-headed, bright-eyed chap who exuded an air of profound interest in things which did not concern him.

"Which one?" inquired the newcomer in the black armor, drily, with one eyebrow pointedly upraised. "There are two of them, you know."

"Well, then I guess you haven't heard, or you would know which of them I meant!" the other retorted. "It's about the elder one, Princess

Bernadette. They say that she has left the palace, for no one knows where."

"Oh, yes, I'd heard about that," Bernadette's right-hand partner eagerly joined in the conversation. "They say that she left to explore and experience other lifestyles within the kingdom, that she was tired of the palace, and that she may never return at all."

"Indeed!" the knight in black appeared interested. "It must have been a sudden decision on her part; I wonder what prompted it?"

"I don't know: perhaps the King and Queen always intended for their daughter to travel incognito and learn firsthand about the day-to-day life of her subjects, once she was old enough," Sir Timothy remarked, with grave consideration. "The experience would certainly be an aid to her when she becomes the ruler. And now that I recollect, when I met her last month during an official visit to the palace, she seemed extremely interested in all I had to say about my own travels. It is quite conceivable that she was already planning this then."

"Perhaps," the youth who had brought up the subject responded with a shrug. "But, Timothy, I have only one objection to your otherwise thoroughly profound explanation of the Princess Royal's behavior, and that is: how does it account for the rumor that she does not intend to ever return to the palace?"

"My response is that the said rumor is exactly that, a rumor," Sir Timothy rejoined somewhat sternly. "And I do not choose to account for unfounded rumors and make judgments on others' behavior based upon them."

"You are right, sir," agreed Bernadette's young right-hand neighbor. "It would indeed be strange, and hardly creditable, to automatically assume that the Princess has so little regard for her privileged life in the palace that she would be ready to leave it forever."

"Yes, and she certainly does have everything she could possibly want there!" exclaimed Sir Timothy's tousle-headed companion. "I didn't get to meet her at the ball they held while Timothy and I were there, and why was that? Because she was so constantly in demand. I never knew a girl to be danced attendance on so constantly and be so thoroughly reverenced and esteemed, as was the case with Princess Bernadette."

"Well, she is the princess; and, what is more important, a very intelligent and upright young lady." Sir Timothy's voice was quiet but very decided in tone. "And thus it is as it should be, that she should receive the admiration and honor that is her due."

"I wish I could have met her!" groaned the tousle-headed knight. "You're so lucky, Timothy; you got to dance with both the princesses, and I didn't so much as meet either one!"

"Surely Princess Bernadette greeted you; that is a requirement of her royal station." Bernadette spoke up impulsively, in her own defense. She had no great liking for this young knight, but she did not want him to think that she had purposefully neglected him.

"Oh, of course, she did! And she was so sweet and down-to-earth, and yet so dignified and sophisticated at the same time, that I would have given anything to have a chance with her! But all I could do was bow, and then she went on to some more fortunate chaps," he concluded dolefully.

"You should have asked her to dance; I'm sure she would have said yes," Bernadette said, somewhat loftily. "And what do you mean by 'having a chance with her,' anyway?" She wrinkled her forehead in confusion over the other's terminology.

"Oh, my, aren't *we* the young innocent!" Sir Tousle-head returned, mockingly. "As if you didn't know that every young knight dreams of an opportunity to court Princess Bernadette! But no, we all get cut out on behalf of those higher-ranking, stuffed-shirt nobles."

"But she's already betrothed to Prince Gerald Reginald of Saxe-Habsburg!" Bernadette protested, astonished. "Surely you knew that?"

"Oh, of course she's betrothed; but what does that matter? Nothing's certain with that until she's actually married to the fellow, what's-his-name. There's no objection to courting her, anyway; and a fellow can dream, can't he?"

"You surely don't mean . . ." Bernadette almost gasped in her shock ". . . that no one regards this betrothal as official or binding on anyone in any way?"

"Oh, don't be so dramatic," Sir Tousle-head said, contemptuously. "It's not as if no royal betrothals had ever been broken before. If Princess Bernadette falls in love with someone else, why shouldn't she break the betrothal for him?"

"Well, I've always been under the impression that a betrothal does not allow people the opportunity of backing out so easily," Bernadette retorted, becoming somewhat incensed. She could feel Pete looking at her warningly over the black-armored knight's shoulder, but she refused to meet his eye and continued to glare across the table at her opponent.

"Ah, that's all *you* know," the patronizing superiority in the other's tone was polished to a nicety. "Rumor has it, so I hear, that the Princess Royal may—just may, mind you—be intending to break her betrothal regardless; that she is abdicating and leaving her betrothed to her sister."

"Yes; but not because she is planning to marry someone else!" Bernadette exclaimed. "The whole idea of betrothal is that no one else can court either of the parties concerned, at least not until after the betrothal is broken, if indeed it ever is."

"So, it is not true that the princess has considered breaking—or shall we say, abandoning, her betrothal if she decides not to take up her throne?" Now it was the knight in the black armor who raised the question.

"I'd not venture to speak definitely on such a delicate matter concerning the princess's own personal decision," Bernadette responded, cautiously. Raising her eyes to her interlocutor's face for a moment, she continued firmly: "But if she does not remain at the palace as ruler, that would certainly void the betrothal: the arrangement is dependent upon her position as heiress to the throne of Berklesgilands, of course."

"I don't see what's so 'of course' about that; how do you know that it is not the princess herself, as a person and not simply a political figure, that is the object of Prince Gerald Reginald's betrothal?" Bernadette could not meet the other's steady, frankly questioning gaze any longer, and hastily averted her own. She accidently caught Pete's eye, twinkling merrily at the ludicrity of her present position, as she did so; but not wishing to look at him just now, either, she fastened her own eyes back down on her bowl of soup as she replied, brusquely:

"Of course such is not the case; how could it be, when he has never even met her? And I can assure you, if he had, he would be well aware of the fact that the Princess Roxanne would be much more suitable as a wife; she is so sweet and gracious and agreeable in every way!" Bernadette looked up again now, carried away by her enthusiastic praise of her sister, and encountered Sir Timothy's sympathetic gaze across from her.

"I have to say I agree with you," he said. "Princess Bernadette is undoubtedly a most admirable woman, and I believe she is eminently suited to be our next ruler; however, her sister was decidedly the most charming young woman I ever met in my life, of the highest level of the gentle and compassionate nature a man desires in a wife, to be a complement to his own, which too often is sadly lacking in those necessary qualities."

"Well, that may be what you and Sir George find most attractive in a wife, but who's to say that the prince of Saxe-Habsburg would not prefer a more strong-minded woman for his bride, such as is Princess Bernadette?" the sable-clad knight on Bernadette's left challenged both of them.

"Exactly; who's to say?" Pete had apparently decided that it was time he took matters into his own hands. "And while we are on the subject of what's preferred; I've met Princess Bernadette before myself, and I can assure you, she would definitely prefer that we not continue to canvass her private concerns in this casual manner, when we might be far better occupied in discussing the campaign and the rest of the current military state of the nation." He set his mug firmly down upon the table to emphasize his point.

"You are undoubtedly in the right, Sir William!" the black knight exclaimed, grandly, turning his attention away from Bernadette and Sir Timothy to Pete, raising his own tankard in salute to him. "I drink to your very good health and in acknowledgement of your prudent wisdom," he added, clinking his stein against Pete's before taking a satisfactory draft from it. Bernadette, for her own part, was relieved to have the dangerous subject closed and attention diverted from herself, and accordingly remained silent and withdrawn for the rest of the meal.

Chapter Eleven
Midnight in the Stable

As the evening drew to a close, the noise around the supper-table gradually began to die away as the tired knights straggled out one by one to find a suitable place to bed down for the night. Pete and Bernadette were among the last to leave the dining room; Pete had been occupied in conversation with the knight in black and Sir Timothy until the latter retired, with a gracious good-night, to the chamber he was sharing with several of the other knights in his regiment, including Sir Tousle-head, who followed Sir Timothy willingly out of the room, yawning sleepily.

Sir Timothy and Sir Tousle-head were among the lucky ones; there were not rooms enough in the inn to accommodate all the knights, far from it! A number of them were already stretched out on the benches around the dining room, or out in the hall where Bernadette and Pete now headed, with Pete still talking over his shoulder to the black knight, who was leisurely following them, eating a final piece of meat pie. Bernadette wondered irritably why he couldn't find some other party to attach himself to, and she was furious at Pete for encouraging him.

"Here's a couple spare benches; suppose we bed down for the night?" the stranger knight proposed, swallowing the last of his meal and preparing to recline on one of the benches he had indicated.

Bernadette panicked; she had no intention of sleeping out here in this public space. But where could she safely sleep in this knight-infested inn? Fortunately, Pete, as usual, already had the situation well in hand.

"Aye, I think you have a fairly good idea there, comrade, so far as bedding down for the night is concerned!" he said with an easy laugh, at the same time surreptitiously taking hold of Bernadette's elbow and edging her towards the door. "But not here; Sir George and I are going to join the rest of the division in the stable."

"More room there, I suppose," the knight in black said agreeably. "But I'd rather not move; I'm quite comfortable here." He leaned his head back on the flat bench cushion.

Without another look behind her, Bernadette followed Pete out across the yard to the stable. Just inside the door, they paused. Bernadette looked around her, a trifle uncertainly, as Pete, his back turned to her, struggled to fasten the latch.

It was much quieter in the stable; only the low nickering and shifting sounds of the animals settling down for the night could be heard clearly. The air was still and peaceful, heavy with the warm scent of sleepy horses and cattle.

"Well, I guess I'll go up and get some blankets," Pete broke the silence, having finally got the door shut.

Bernadette looked over at him alertly. "So, where are we going to sleep, Pete?" she asked.

"There's no 'we' about it, Bernie," Pete responded, heading down the narrow passageway between the stalls. "*I* am going to sleep in the hayloft with the rest of the fellows. But I don't suppose you'd feel comfortable doing that, being a girl and all, even if no one knows it, so I suppose you can sleep somewhere down here. There should be a tack room somewhere about—ah, here we are!" He kicked open the door of a small room at the end of the hall, full of saddles and harness and oiling tools. "There's a bench here that you can sleep on, Bernie; so I'll go up and get you a couple blankets and you'll be quite comfortable for the night."

Bernadette didn't know that she agreed with him. The bench looked very narrow and hard. For a moment she wished that they had stayed in the inn to sleep on the wider, cushioned benches, Black Knight or no Black Knight. But in a moment she rallied. She had asked for this, and she wasn't going to shrink from the discomforts of these crude accommodations any more than the most hardened knight!

So she nodded to Pete, quite brightly. "That sounds reasonable," she said briskly. "Thanks for offering to get the blankets; I'll wait here." She sat down on the bench and began removing her armor.

"Right." Pete vanished, and Bernadette could hear him scrambling up the ladder to the hayloft and crunching through the hay. A moment later he was back with two coarsely-woven, woolen blankets. "Here you are, cousin," he said cheerily. "And no one even saw me bring them down. Anything else I can do for you?" Upon a reply in the negative, he turned to go, saying over his shoulder, "Good night, Bernie; and if you need anything else in the night, just sing out; I'll sleep in a corner where I can hear you but no one else will. The fellows up there who aren't sound sleepers will be deafened by the snores of those that are."

"I don't think I'll be needing you, though, anyway, Pete," Bernadette responded, lying down upon the hard bench and drawing the rough blankets up around her shoulders. "Good night."

"Good night."

Pete's footsteps died away once again, and Bernadette was left alone in the darkness and her discomfort. She was also very cold; the spring nights were still quite chilly and the wind poked bitingly into the drafty tack-room. Bernadette shivered and clasped the blankets more tightly about her shoulders; she wished Pete had thought to bring her a couple more, but then there were probably only a limited number that had to be evenly divided.

The whooshing sound of one of the sleeping animals in the stable letting out its breath gave Bernadette an idea. She got up stiffly from the hard bench, dragging her blankets with her. She would go and sleep in one of the stalls; it would be warmer near the animals, and the hay in the stalls would be softer to sleep on.

At the far end of the stable passageway, Bernadette ran across a double stall. There was plenty of room for a young girl to curl up on the pile of hay at one side of it. As Bernadette gently pushed open the door and entered, the horse inside lifted its head and turned intelligent eyes on Bernadette, almost as if inquiring about the reason for the intrusion.

Bernadette loved horses. She simply could not help going over and stroking the forehead of the noble animal, which was marked with a beautiful white star. Otherwise, the horse was completely black.

"Oh, my beauty!" Bernadette murmured, stroking the horse's firm neck and burying her chilly hands in the warm mane. "Aren't you the loveliest horse ever! Oh, black horses are always the prettiest! Although I've always had to ride a white one; princesses are expected to, you know. I wish I had a treat to give you, my beauty!" The mare nuzzled Bernadette's hand in response. "Is Beauty your name, I wonder?—no, that's too obvious. I think I'll call you Midnight; yes, that will do." Bernadette squirmed around and laid her head comfortably against the horse's side, covering herself up with her blankets. Midnight turned her head to regard her new companion for a moment, and then sensibly went back to sleep. Bernadette too fell asleep right away; it was so nice and warm in the stall, deep in the soft hay. Soon she was far away in the land of dreams, riding as fast as the wind under a star-studded midnight sky, on a horse as black as the midnight itself, with a star matching those in the heavens on its forehead.

Chapter Twelve
The Unaccepted Offer

Bernadette was awakened very abruptly the next morning, as Midnight coolly got up and walked over to munch some hay, sending Bernadette's head to the floor with a sudden thump that sent all her dreams flying away.

Laughing, Bernadette sat up and rubbed the back of her head. "What a perfectly self-possessed, impudent creature you are, Midnight!" she exclaimed, leaping up and going over to pat the animal's neck. "And such a splendid horse! I'll tell you what, I'm going to buy you! Yes, I am! We have to have new horses, Pete and I, so I am going to buy you! How would you like that, ho, my beauty?" Midnight gave her a benevolent look, and then bent her head to take another bite of hay.

Bernadette laughed again. It was a beautiful, bright morning; just the kind of day when it is easy for a young girl to laugh at everything. "Once I've bought you, I'll come back and bring you a treat! Then maybe you'll pay some attention to me!" she tossed the last words back gaily over her shoulder, as she ran out of the stall and down the hall to the ladder leading to the hayloft. Flinging her blankets over her shoulders, she scrambled up to the shelf-like room in the rafters, crammed full of sweet-smelling prickly hay.

All the knights were already out in the courtyard, preparing to set out on their day's march. Bernadette could see through the window under the eaves that the sun was already well up; she had slept longer than she had meant. So Bernadette folded up her blankets rather hastily and tossed them onto the pile where the other knights had left theirs—

she would have liked to refold some of those, too, but there wasn't time. As she scrambled back down the ladder, she fortunately happened to look down at her knees, and realized that she was still only wearing her leggings and tunic; she had left her armor in the tack room.

"Thank goodness I remembered in time," Bernadette giggled to herself, catching sight of her reflection in a sharp-bladed harness tool. Her shorn hair, tousled from sleep, looked far more girlish than she desired, tumbling in loose, curling tendrils about her flushed cheeks. With the help of the reflection in the blade, she managed to smooth it down into appropriately indifferent-looking, stringy flat locks. Then she ran into the tack room, sat down on the same hard bench—which somehow seemed less uncomfortable on this bright and shining morning than it had the night before—and hastily girded on her armor once again.

Still fumbling with the buckles of her sword-belt, Bernadette ran gladly out of the stable into the yard, where all the young knights of the regiment were eating their breakfast standing up, as they prepared to continue on their campaign march—checking the status of weapons, packing provisions into saddlebags, harnessing up their horses. The innkeeper was out in the yard as well, beaming benevolently upon his erstwhile customers, and generously pressing "yet one more" helping on them before their departure. His booming voice could be easily heard above the rest of the bustle.

Pete emerged from the midst of the throng and elbowed his way through to Bernadette, with a none-too-angelic expression on his face. "Where were you, Bernie?" he asked in an irritated half-whisper, upon reaching her side. "I went to the tack room first thing this morning, and you weren't there. What happened?" Despite his clear annoyance, he seemed relieved to see her.

"Sorry if I worried you," Bernadette smiled reassuringly. "I meant to get up before you, but I slept in instead! I went to sleep in one of the stalls, because I couldn't fall asleep in the tack room; it was too cold and uncomfortable."

"Better get used to it," was Pete's curt advice. "Had any breakfast yet?"

"You know I haven't; I just got here," Bernadette responded, somewhat nettled by his attitude. She followed him through the press, capably imitating his example in pleasantly but unyieldingly elbowing other people out of the way, exchanging greetings as they went. Bernadette caught sight of Sir Timothy, leaning against the wall and munching black bread with Sir Tousle-head, nodding a friendly good-morning to her; and she waved back, her spirits soaring once again. "Oh, Pete—er, I mean, William," she began eagerly, "the horse in the stall last night was the most beautiful creature ever; can she be one of the ones we buy?"

"If the innkeeper is selling her, I suppose so," Pete returned, taking some bread off a tray set up on a stump in the center of the yard, and offering a piece to his cousin.

"Oh, I'm sure he will," Bernadette returned confidently, accepting the meager fare with alacrity. "Weren't we told that he was selling horses?"

"Yes, but . . ." Pete was interrupted by the innkeeper himself, as he came bustling up to them, easily balancing yet another well-filled tray upon his substantially broad shoulder. "Ah, sirs, you have been undoubtedly overlooked this morning! Here, you must have some of this cheese before you depart; no one can rightly leave "The Gander and Cheese" without trying, well, the cheese, now can they?" He filled Pete and Bernadette's hands full of the semihard yellow curds as he spoke. "Taste it, good young sirs, and then tell me, if you dare, whether my Dorothy's cheese is not the best in the country, or no?" He stepped back and placed his hands confidently on his hips, beaming with the assurance of an affirmative answer.

"I have to say," Bernadette remarked, savoring the morsels of creamy deliciousness with great relish, "that it seems that everything in this village is the best in the country!—including your horses! I say, good Grand—" swallowing the last luscious mouthful—"Sir William and I are in need of new horses for this campaign, and we were told that you had some for sale."

"Indeed I do, sirs," responded the worthy innkeeper, swelling with delight over the reaction his wife's cheese had produced. "I raise horses simply for trade with the regiments who pass through here; I have no need of them for myself, other than that good horse-raising is one of my favorite pursuits. There is such satisfaction to be found in the knowledge that one has the care of such well-bred and appreciative animals," he wound up with the romantic sigh of the true enthusiast.

"Ah, yes; especially that beautiful black animal of yours in the far-end double stall!" Bernadette rejoined eagerly, now sure of her purchase.

"The mare Sultana, you mean, my lad Sir George?" inquired the innkeeper familiarly.

"I called her Midnight," Bernadette responded, laughing a little. "And I suppose whoever buys her can call her whatever he wants, right?"

"Oh, I suppose so, although he seemed to be just fine with the name I gave her when he made the purchase," the innkeeper spoke so jocularly that Bernadette did not immediately realize what he was saying. "I sold her this morning to the knight who came in late last night; but any of our other horses are available for sale, if that is still what you desire?"

"Undoubtedly, we do," Pete replied hastily, seeing that Bernadette had not yet completely grasped the situation.

"Sold her this morning? But how could you—it *is* morning," Bernadette said stupidly, unable to comprehend this sudden and unexpected loss of what she had already claimed as her own. "When— and how?—and who?"

"To that strapping young fellow who sat with the two of you last night; the one in that unconventional black outfit," the innkeeper replied. "He was up at dawn asking to purchase her; said he'd seen her before he came into dinner and determined then and there to buy her. I wish I'd known you wanted her too, Sir George: perhaps I'd have held out and had the two of you bid for her; I might have gotten a better price!" he concluded jestingly.

"You still can; I'll give you twice what he paid for her," Bernadette offered, forgetting all else in her earnest desire to possess Midnight.

"Bernie . . ." Pete said warningly. Bernadette scowled at him, daring him to interfere further. "How can you offer that, George, when you don't know how much the fellow paid for her and whether we have twice that amount on hand? And even if we do, it's foolish to pay more than the horse is worth when we could get two other perfectly good ones for a better price."

"But I want Midnight!" Bernadette exclaimed, unreasonably determined. "All right, so maybe not twice as much; but I'll give you more for her than he did, worthy Grand."

"Well, that's fine by me, but you'll have to take it up with him; here he comes now," the innkeeper responded, gesturing across the yard towards the stable door, from whence the black-garbed character had

116

just emerged, leading Midnight. The elegant creature stepped daintily, sniffing the air and apparently quite at home following her new master.

The sight made Bernadette's blood boil. Ignoring Pete's efforts to restrain her, she headed determinedly for her competitor and *her* horse. The Black Knight noticed her approach as he made his way across the yard, and he paused and waited for her to come up.

"A very fine morning to you, Sir George!" he greeted pleasantly, if in a somewhat boisterous tone. "Splendid weather for our campaign today, don't you agree?"

"I suppose," Bernadette returned ungraciously. "The innkeeper Grand just told me that you purchased the very horse I wanted."

"*This* is the horse I just purchased," the Black Knight replied, a trifle deprecatingly, rubbing Midnight's nose as he spoke. The mare rubbed her head lovingly against his arm. There was gratitude for you!

"Yes, I know; she's the one I wanted to buy, and I told the innkeeper I'd buy her for more than you did," Bernadette continued insistently.

"So you know how much I paid?" the other raised one dark eyebrow in critical inquiry.

"No, but I don't care," Bernadette retorted. "If you'll return her to her previous owner, I'll buy her from him for more; or I'll buy her directly from you now and give you a profit."

"Well, I must say that you have a strange take on common business sense, Sir George!" the Black Knight threw back his head and laughed heartily. He did not loosen his hold on Midnight's halter.

"Nothing of the sort!" Bernadette exclaimed hotly. "I just want to buy Midnight, and I'm willing to do whatever it takes to fairly acquire her."

"Oh? Then it's all a mistake here," the young man returned, quickly, and evidently glad that the matter could be settled so easily. "This horse isn't your Midnight; she's called Sultana."

"That may be what you call her, but her real name's Midnight; I decided that last night, which is also when I decided to buy her!"

"Well, if we are going to make timing an issue, I decided to buy her as soon as I rode in yesterday, which was before nightfall and therefore before you made your decision." The Black Knight shrugged good-humoredly.

"Enough of this parley, sir," Bernadette put on her stateliest manner, which generally had worked very well for her at court. Whether it would work equally well in this barnyard setting remained to be seen. "I wish to purchase this horse from you, so name your price and that will be all we need to consider further."

"Indeed? And what if I don't wish to sell?" the Black Knight's eyes twinkled mischievously.

Bernadette was not amused. When you are accustomed to having completely unrestricted access to all the horses in the Royal Stables, and when you know that everyone else in the country would be only too delighted to loan, sell, or even give you their mounts, just so that they could say that their animal had been ridden by the Princess Royal, then it is rather difficult to immediately come to terms with the fact that you cannot always have whatever you want simply because you want it. So Bernadette ignored his last remark, and continued to press the issue. "What did you pay for her?"

"I don't see why that matters, since I don't intend to sell her; and furthermore, I don't wish to divulge details of my private transactions." The Black Knight flicked a bit of lint off the saddle.

"And why won't you sell her? Just to disoblige me?" Bernadette demanded, her face flushed with ill-suppressed anger.

"No; because I don't see that it would be a practical bargain for either of us. Why should I trouble myself to sell, and then buy another horse when I already have a perfectly good one? And certainly you should not waste your hard-earned wages on paying extra for one horse rather than another, when each horse is pretty much just like the next. You might thank me for preventing you from such rashness." He met her indignant gaze steadily, with a rather odd expression in his eyes. A mixture of amusement, mild contempt, inexplicable admiration, and almost pity—Bernadette could not guess what he was thinking.

"Well, if you don't think it matters what horse you have, why should you care if I do?" Bernadette asked heatedly. "I want to buy this horse, and not a different one."

"You've made that quite clear, Sir George."

"You already have a horse; you said you rode in last night; and I don't!" Bernadette was growing desperate. "And how fair is it that you should have two horses, and I none?" Bernadette posed the childish question as though there were no possible response to it.

"Life's not fair, Sir George," the Black Knight sighed heavily, as though he could have wished it otherwise. "And my other horse is too worn to travel further, which is why I had to purchase another for this campaign."

"Why can't you just rent one, and let me have Midnight?" Bernadette was running out of arguments.

"Her name is Sultana, and I have already bought her, and I don't wish to sell. And that, Sir George, is all there is to it. Therefore, unless you have another topic of greater worth to discuss with me, I will bid you good morning." Raising his helmet in farewell, the Black Knight made his way to the mounting block and climbed astride Midnight's sleek dark back.

"Just a minute! What do you think you're doing!" Now completely beyond herself, Bernadette rushed forward to prevent him from riding off, but a strong grip on her arm stopped her in her tracks.

"Are you mad, Bernie?" Pete whispered furiously in her ear. "Why will you persist in making a spectacle of yourself? Come on; we will barely have time to purchase and tack up the horses we *can* get before the campaign starts off." Still grasping her wrist, he turned to head back to where the innkeeper was waiting.

"I don't want any horse but Midnight!" Bernadette insisted.

"Fine! You can march the whole way then; I don't care." Out of patience, Pete let go of her arm and headed back to talk with the innkeeper.

Chapter Thirteen
The Military Campaign

Pete did manage at last to provide himself and Bernadette with two suitable mounts; and then, taking leave of the worthy innkeeper, they departed with the rest of the regiment, whom Sir Timothy had already organized into official ranks for proceeding.

Bernadette, it must be confessed, did not make much use of this opportunity to evaluate whether or not a career as a knight was a good choice for her. When she thought back on it later, she could remember very little about the technical details of the day-long march, and practically nothing at all of the conversations that went on among the "genuine knights" around her. She spent most of her time grumbling beneath her breath over the slowness and ungainliness of her mount, a chestnut stallion a little past the prime of life with a scraggly mane. The only good thing about the day was that Pete was not nearby to aggravate her; he had been assigned to a position in the rear guard, keeping watch for any unsuspected enemy attacks.

By mid-afternoon, everyone was tired and dusty and bored from the unremitting jolting of the ride, and few people were in any better humor than Bernadette herself. The Black Knight was an exception; he whistled and sang the whole way, as well he might, being blessed with so splendid and comfortable a mount!

Just at sundown, the campaign halted to camp for the night. Bernadette was the first off her horse, only too ready to stretch out her cramped limbs, and willingly offered to be part of the detachment deployed to bring back firewood and water. Anything was better than being assigned to the care of the horses. Besides, the Black Knight was one of those who had elected to remain and pitch camp. Bernadette didn't want to have anything more to do with *him*, either.

Bernadette found her young right-hand companion of the night before, and the two of them stuck together like silent, uncertain shadows as they gathered up two heavy leather buckets apiece and headed for the stream, somewhat behind the rest of the group, who all seemed to know each other and were laughing and talking loudly—too loudly. Bernadette's head ached, and she was hungry. Once the buckets were filled, she and her companion trudged slowly back to the camp, hoping they would not have to make another trip before dinner.

Pete was standing by the newly-kindled fire, carefully endeavoring to balance a heavy iron cauldron of soup bones and wilted vegetables on a decidedly tippy makeshift tripod. "I'm on KP, as you can see, Sir George," he greeted Bernadette with a wry smile. "Just pour the water in here, will you?"

"Sure." Bernadette stood on tiptoe and carefully emptied her buckets into the cauldron. "We'll still need some more." She sighed; her hands were already blistered from the buckets' rough handles.

"I'll get it, Bernie; you stay and stir the soup. 'Women's work,' anyway," Pete teased in an undertone, as he grasped the buckets capably and prepared to dash off.

"Pete, be quiet!" Bernadette hissed, darting a nervous glance about to see whether anyone had overheard her cousin's unguarded remark. No one was within earshot except the Black Knight; however, he was occupied in counting over the stockpile of extra weapons stacked by the fire, and had not looked up.

"Soldiers and comrades! Now that we are all gathered together, it is time to plan our strategy for the morrow." Sir Timothy was standing before the blazing bonfire and the ranks of weary knights, who had sprawled themselves comfortably upon the ground and nearby stumps. Hands clasped behind his back, head erect, gaze meeting every eye frankly and pleasantly, he was every inch the ideal knight; and everyone sat up a little more at attention as he addressed them. "And the first thing to do in this circumstance, therefore, is to choose a leader."

"No one better suited for that position than yourself, sir," Pete said easily. He very much admired Sir Timothy—as did most of the other soldiers, judging by the chorus of approval that greeted Pete's suggestion.

Sir Timothy himself, however, raised a deprecatory hand to check the demonstrations of support. "I am deeply gratified by your confidence in me, but there are many other men in our ranks who are more qualified than I in preparing military strategy, including Sir Rombart"—indicating one of the older knights who had assisted in organizing the march that day—"and our friend here," he laid his hand upon the shoulder of the Black Knight, who was standing next to him.

"Why *him*?" Bernadette grumbled beneath her breath. Her opinion was supported by a general murmur of dissatisfaction among many of Sir Timothy's division, who did not take kindly to the idea of being under the command of a comparative stranger. Others, though, influenced by the very human tendency to assume that anything new and untried must be better than that which is already known and tested, cheered their support of Sir Timothy's modest deferral.

"I propose we put the matter to a vote; the man who gathers the most adherents will doubtless have the greater success in leading the entire division," Sir Timothy went on. "First let us determine who else will be under consideration for the position."

123

After some discussion, four other knights were proposed as candidates alongside Sir Timothy, Sir Rombart, and the Black Knight, and then the voting began. As there was no paper in the camp, the votes were cast by making a specified number of notches in a stick, and then placing them in separate piles according to their number. Sir Timothy's number was three, the Black Knight's was one, and so forth. Whoever ended up with the greatest number of sticks in their pile would become the leader.

Bernadette, Pete, and Sir Tousle-head all cut three notches in their sticks and put them in Sir Timothy's pile. It was already evident, Bernadette observed as she looked round at the other piles, that the only serious competitor Sir Timothy had was that same old mysterious Black Knight. Oh, dear! If it hadn't been dishonest, Bernadette would have gone over and cut extra notches in half of the sticks in his pile, and transferred them to Sir Timothy's.

But of course she couldn't do that, and therefore sat on pins and needles, ignoring her supper of watery soup and black bread, while a couple of squires counted over the voting sticks. Only Sir Timothy's and the Black Knight's piles were significant enough to be counted.

". . . thirty-seven, thirty-eight . . ." the young lad droned, handing each of the Black Knight's sticks to his companion as he counted them. There were fifty-six in all.

Then Sir Timothy's were counted. The squire's voice must have been more tired by now, for although Bernadette strained to hear, she soon lost track of the exact numbering. But the final total was clear.

"Sixty-one!" the lad proclaimed, as he laid aside the last stick, as proudly as though the procedure had gained *him* the leadership role.

"Sir Timothy is our leader! Hooray!" Bernadette led the three cheers for their new commander.

"Thank you so much." Sir Timothy inclined his head in acknowledgement. "You were a worthy competitor, sir, and I congratulate you on the support you received," he politely commended the Black Knight, shaking hands with him.

"And you well deserved to win, sir," the Black Knight returned quickly.

"All right, then, Timothy: now that you're the leader, what's our strategy?" demanded Sir Tousle-head, who had been awaiting his friend's victory with visible signs of impatience.

"Well, that is the next step in our planning," Sir Timothy laughed, sitting down cross-legged and accepting the final bowl of soup from Pete, who was still on KP. "The enemy army is still, I pray, unaware of our approach. However, it would be wise to send scouts out tonight and also a small scouting party ahead of our campaign tomorrow, to ensure that they are not on the watch for us. If they are, then we will have to change our strategy.

"But supposing that to not be the case, a divided attack would doubtless be the most effective. We will divide into two parties: I will lead one; and as the second most endorsed as our leader, I believe that you should take command of the second, sir," Sir Timothy addressed the Black Knight.

"I am honored," the other replied, with a gallant bow. Bernadette drew a quick, annoyed breath, hoping that she wouldn't end up in his division! As he accepted the command from Sir Timothy, the Black Knight turned his gaze out over his potential subordinates, as though selecting those he would wish to enlist; and his eye met hers and he smiled confidently. Bernadette tossed her head back and frowned at him, indignant at the liberty he was taking.

". . . and so you will take your troops and circle around behind their camp, early tomorrow morning," Sir Timothy was still outlining the plan of attack to his co-leader, who turned back to listen to him attentively. "And just at dawn, I and my division will fall upon them in a surprise attack. You will wait for my signal—a special wave of the flag, known only to our soldiers—which will be delivered by my aide at the very height of confusion in the battle, just when the enemy has come to think that they are prepared to counter our strategy. Then you and your soldiers will quickly fall upon them from behind, and thus caught between two armies, 'twill be short work to overcome them fully."

How simple, and yet how profoundly ingenious! Bernadette swelled with pride at these clear signs of her chosen leader's strategic genius. She glanced quickly around to see whether Sir Timothy's clearly-outlined plan had made the same impact on the rest of the knights. Most of them were beaming their admiration, approval, and loyalty to their new commander. Well satisfied, they all returned to their dinner and soon began singing, gathered around the fire in cheerful concert. Presently, however, Sir Timothy cautioned them to remain quiet.

"We do not wish to alert any chance enemy spies to our presence," he reminded them, and the knights murmured acquiescence to the wisdom of his words. "And furthermore, we now must turn our attention to appointing our lower officers and dividing our ranks for the morrow. You may choose first, sir." The selection of their subordinates took up the entire rest of the evening.

"I select you, Sir George, as my aide. Pray stand to my right for the remainder of the selection, sir," Sir Timothy gestured to Bernadette. She cast an alarmed glance at Pete, who had already been assigned to a position in the Black Knight's command, hoping that he could somehow signal to her what the correct manner of accepting her new role ought to be. But he wouldn't even look at her, but continued standing straight at attention with his gaze fixed unswervingly before him. Thus left to herself, Bernadette could only do what she was quite sure was the wrong thing, but that no one could possibly argue with: she just did what Sir Timothy had told her to. This unique strategy worked quite well, and then she had nothing more to worry about until the morning.

In spite of their having been assigned to separate divisions, Bernadette managed to slip around the edge of the camp to unroll her bedroll next to Pete's. The two of them were at the very outskirts of the camp, just barely within the circle of firelight, and not too close to any other knights.

Nonetheless, Bernadette waited for more than a quarter of an hour, until a steady chorus of snores assured her that any doings on her part would be largely unobserved, and then cautiously raised herself on one elbow. "Pete, are you still awake?"

"No," came the unequivocal answer, Pete still keeping his eyes tightly shut. "And you shouldn't be, either. We've a big day ahead tomorrow."

"As if I didn't know it! Pete, what exactly does an aide do?" Bernadette whispered. She had been immensely flattered by Sir Timothy's choosing her, but she was still deeply concerned that she would not know how to properly fulfill the duties of her position.

"Simple." Pete hadn't opened his eyes yet. "Just follow orders, like everyone else. And stick close to Sir Timothy—you'd want to do that anyway, I'm sure. Always remain on guard to defend our commander if he is in any danger; that's your main job. He may send you around with his messages to other officers or have you support him in leading charges; just pay attention and you'll do fine. Oh, and you have to carry the flag and give that signal, too, when Sir Timothy calls for it."

"But I don't know the signal! What am I to do?" Bernadette sat all the way up in her anxiety.

"I forgot about that; we all learned it at the Military Academy, and of course, you weren't there." Pete's eyes were still comfortably closed. "I can't tell you what it is; it's a dead secret that no one is ever allowed to utter; but here, give me your hand and I'll show you the moves you'll have to make." He guided Bernadette's hand to the edge of the blanket, and proceeded to demonstrate the secret signal and patiently guide her hand through the correct pattern over and over until she had it down. I can't describe how the signal worked, of course, that would betray the all-important confidentiality of the sign, which guaranteed its continued usefulness to the King and Country of Berklesgilands.

"All right, I've got it now, Pete. Thanks so much," Bernadette whispered, drawing her hand away and lying back down to sleep.

"You're welcome." And without having once opened his eyes throughout the entire process, Pete went composedly off to sleep as well.

Chapter Fourteen
The Battle

"Halt!"

Bernadette lurched forward in the saddle as she hurriedly pulled her horse up short at Sir Timothy's command.

"Now is the time to send forward our scout party," Sir Timothy continued, in low tones. "Sir Leopold, Sir Hugh, and Sir Randolph, you will be our scouts: you will circle the enemy camp and bring back any indications of their movements or their awareness of ours. Watch out for any scouts of theirs as well. We will wait for you here, barring any developments. Speed and dispatch are your watchwords; onward!" With smart salutes of acknowledgment, the selected knights immediately galloped off upon their mission.

Bernadette wondered where Pete was. He, along with the rest of the Black Knight's command, had set off two hours earlier to take a roundabout route to the back of the enemy camp. Had they arrived yet? What was happening there? She shifted restlessly on her horse's back as the minutes passed, waiting for the scouts' return. Dawn was just beginning to break when Sir Randolph and Sir Hugh at last came galloping back to the rest of their comrades-at-arms.

"Well?" Sir Timothy asked crisply.

"They are yet unaware of our approach, sir," Sir Randolph replied with bold certainty. "There were no signs of readiness to meet any attack. The army is enjoying a rest before continuing its march of invasion; many of the men were still sleeping, no one seemed to be on watch, the weapons were piled carelessly at the edge of the camp, and the war-horses were picketed out to graze."

"Hum! We will have to call them out, then; 'twould be most dishonorable to fall upon them while so helplessly unprepared. Taking unawares is one thing; taking defenseless is quite another," Sir Timothy observed, whilst a murmur of approval for their leader's ethics ran through the ranks. "Where is Sir Leopold?"

"He went to inform the other division that there was no change in the enemy's condition, and therefore likely no change in plan. He will be waiting for us at the edge of the camp," Sir Hugh responded. "I trust we did not overstep our duties in delivering said message?"

"Nay; 'twas most judicious on your part; what I would have bidden you do myself," Sir Timothy responded. "Anything further to report?"

"No, sir," the two scouts returned promptly.

"Fall in just behind me and Sir George, then. Forward march!"

The regiment surged forward with an eager but subdued tramp. Bernadette, astride her mount beside the leader, felt a rush of excitement. There was a certain solidarity in being part of such a strong group, bent on a valorous mission.

It was not long before they came across Sir Leopold, who was waiting for them with his finger on his lips. "Any news?" Sir Timothy asked, low.

"No, sir; but the enemy is just beyond this line of trees. Look there, and you may see their camp," the knight replied, pointing.

Sir Timothy rode forward and gazed steadily through the gap in the underbrush for several minutes, carefully marking and evaluating the position of the enemy, and then returned to his former position. "Have the archers ready to shoot in case of any treachery. We will give them just time to take their weapons and mount, and then you all know what to do," he concluded significantly, and then turned to Bernadette. "Stay close behind me; do not speak unless I request your corroboration of some point, and carry the standard raised high that they may see it and know that we are fighting for our own noble King Friedrich and in defense of his and our glorious country," his eyes glowed with his patriotic sentiments. Bernadette smiled back proudly.

Sir Timothy, with Bernadette at his side, then proceeded boldly out into the open. "Hail there! Who commands this regiment?" Sir Timothy demanded, drawing up his horse at the edge of the green, and sending a sweeping gaze out over the untidy rows of tents and bumbling, just-arisen soldiery. Bernadette followed his look without attempting to conceal her contempt.

From the largest of the tents, a rather alarmed-looking, ill-featured knight emerged. The crown on his helmet proclaimed his royal status as commander of his own realm's army. "Are you the invading king?" Sir Timothy inquired, just to be sure.

"Well, I am the king, all right," growled this unprepossessing personage, gesturing uneasily to his men, who began surreptitiously to arm themselves and head for their horses.

"And we," Sir Timothy continued, "as you may see by our standard"—Bernadette held the flag yet a little higher, to ensure that the enemy king could see it clearly—"are the true and loyal knights of the sovereign ruler of the Kingdom of Berklesgilands, His Royal Majesty King Friedrich the Twelfth, sole and rightful monarch over all these lands, and long may he reign!" Sir Timothy's ringing voice stirred the leafy branches of the tree limbs above. "And we hereby denounce you as unlawful invaders, and call upon you to meet with us in armed battle, unless you will give a guarantee of peace and return immediately to your own country by the way you came."

"Just the two of you?" sneered the enemy king. "Or is King Friedrich here himself, hiding in the underbrush?"

"No is my answer to both questions," came Sir Timothy's unruffled reply. He was not here to bandy words, but swords. "I am the leader of this regiment, fighting on His Royal Majesty's behalf today. My troops await behind me for your response to our challenge."

The enemy gave no verbal response, but a sudden volley of arrows and a rush from the knights who had managed to get to their horses, waving their swords and yelling as they advanced, seemed to indicate their acceptance of the challenge. The archers from Sir Timothy's brigade sent an answering volley into this charge of cavalry, felling several men and horses to the ground. "Forward, my noble knights, and quit yourselves like men!" Sir Timothy shouted, and the regiment rode into the field.

And so the battle began. Encouraged by the much fewer numbers of Sir Timothy's regiment, the enemy knights were careless and confident as they rode in for the first encounter, expecting that a few crossed swords would result in a rout that would leave them in undisputed possession of the field. But the sure aim of the archers and skillful swordsmanship of both the mounted knights and the foot soldiers in Sir Timothy's forces, soon proved them wrong, and the battle waxed fast and furious.

Bernadette, at her commander's side, was ever in the thickest of the battle. Her position required her to guard Sir Timothy constantly from any unexpected attack; and well schooled as she had been by Pete, and confident after her experience with the robbers, she easily turned aside the most tricky and subtle of sword-thrusts, and got in a few notable ones of her own.

"Keep the banner high, Sir George," panted Sir Timothy, pausing to wipe his sword at the end of a fiercely close struggle, "and tell me, can you see where the enemy leader is?" He would not call him "king."

"Aye, sir, just under that linden tree, surrounded by a score or more of his strongest knights," Bernadette replied, gesturing in their direction. "But Sir Anthony's men are hard on their left rear flank; soon there may be a breakthrough, and then is your opportunity, sir."

"Then now is the time!" Sir Timothy cried. "Follow me, Sir George, and give the signal!" He set spurs to his horse and galloped towards the indicated position, with Bernadette right behind, presenting the secret flag signal. There was no immediate response; perhaps they could not see it through the trees and the battle commotion, so she continued to repeat the signal.

Then, with a rousing shout that astonished the enemy army, the reserve forces rushed upon the field. The enemy troops gathered around their king turned to meet this new and unexpected attack; and so Sir Timothy and Bernadette easily pressed through their ranks, and Sir Timothy at last crossed swords with the enemy king himself. Despite his pretentious and indolent appearance, the king was skillful enough with his rapier when circumstances demanded, and he had a decided advantage on Sir Timothy with regard to size. Furthermore, his outrage at being challenged by a mere common soldier lent a furious intensity to his thrusts. Sir Timothy had all he could do to keep him at bay; but when Bernadette, anxious, came to his aid, her commander waved her off. "Nay, Sir George; two against one is never fair fight! Keep the others off!" In response to his orders, Bernadette withdrew to a respectful distance, loyally providing a barricade from the rushes attempted by the enemy knights against her commander.

Meanwhile, the battle raged hot around her. The Black Knight had just successfully felled two of the enemy army's chief officers, who had both attacked him at once but found him more than a match for them. An infantryman slashed at Midnight's front legs; Bernadette inadvertently cried out in alarm, but that clever mare had the sense to rear up and neatly avoid the blow. The Black Knight kept his seat with amazing dexterity, and upon Midnight's coming down on all four feet again, horse and rider galloped as one through the remaining ranks of the enemy, skillfully avoiding their blows and scattering them on all sides into helpless confusion.

Completely demoralized by now, the enemy knights were fighting "every man for himself" against whomever of Sir Timothy's soldiers they could find; and no one was attempting to come to the aid of their king, who was now facing Sir Timothy on foot. Bernadette was holding Sir Timothy's mount by the halter; the king's was nowhere to be seen.

Just at this moment, Pete came careening furiously by Bernadette, his horse running madly alongside one of the enemy knight's, with whom he was exchanging blow for blow in rapid succession. Bernadette backed her horse to let them pass, and swept an appraising look over the rest of the battlefield. A group of foot-soldiers from her side were battling to overcome a last cluster of those belonging to the enemy at the far side of the field; their ultimate success seemed a foregone conclusion. Sir Timothy beckoned to her to restore his horse to him; a wounded enemy cavalryman had offered his horse to the king, who was already astride it. Bernadette hastened over and assisted her commander to mount, keeping the king off the while with a bit of nimble sword-play, before deferring the honor of concluding the fight to her leader.

"Order Sir Anthony to gather his forces and drive off or take prisoner as many as possible of the remaining stragglers, and then return immediately to me," Sir Timothy commanded in a nearly inaudible aside, crossing swords once again with the enemy king.

Bernadette galloped off, calling to all of her fellow knights she met on the way to come with her, and so presented Sir Anthony with a ready-made force along with her message. As she rode back at a furious rate, avoiding the thrusts and challenges of the remaining enemy soldiers, intent on returning to her post, she vaguely observed the Black Knight, who had completely vanquished the last three knights he had encountered and was now unemployed for the moment, standing at his ease in the center of the field, regarding the melee around him with some measure of detached satisfaction.

And then Bernadette caught sight of Pete. Whether his horse had thrown him, or his opponent had violently unseated him, was unclear; but he was lying prone on his back, apparently stunned, in front of his adversary, who had dismounted and was standing over him, sword in hand. Pete made a dazed effort to rise, feebly striking out with his own sword; but the other fellow knocked his weapon out of his hand, and had Pete at his mercy.

Bernadette was horror-struck. No one else was near who could come to Pete's aid; the enemy knight would run him through in a moment. And she—her soldier duty as aide required her to give first service to her commander before lending any assistance to her other fellow knights, even her cousin. Sir Timothy had commanded her to return immediately, and given her no license to turn aside on any other purpose.

But no. Bernadette didn't hesitate for one moment. There are laws that supersede even those of military strategy. Bending low over her horse's neck, her sword outstretched, she bore down upon the enemy with all the force that blinding speed could gather. He fell to the ground beneath her horse's heels; Bernadette swerved to one side, not wishing to trample upon the fellow unnecessarily, and swiftly dismounting, helped her still-unsteady cousin to his feet and assisted him onto her horse. "Hang on, Pete; go and join Sir Anthony's routing force yonder. Here's your sword." Without waiting for any response, she set off at a run, back to Sir Timothy.

She met with no resistance in her path. The battle was as good as over: Sir Anthony and his men had rounded up a goodly score of prisoners, the foot-soldier skirmish at the edge of the field had ended in victory for Sir Timothy's infantry, and Sir Timothy himself, Bernadette could see as she hastened towards him, had at last overcome the enemy king and was currently occupied in binding him securely. What few of the remaining enemy knights were not lying scattered about the field in various conditions of indisposition, had fled the scene and were making all judicious haste back to the border of their own country, never to cross it henceforth again.

Sir Timothy did not immediately look up when Bernadette arrived breathless at his side, still holding the flag high. But as he finished securing the enemy king and rose to his feet, victorious, he met his aide's eyes with an even gaze.

"A man who knows his duty to a friend, is one that a commander may safely trust to know his duty to his superior officers and the military cause as well. Well done, Sir George," was all that he said, but Bernadette felt herself well rewarded for her efforts as a knight that day.

Chapter Fifteen
Captured!

"Oh, Pete, do let's stop and have lunch here; look how pretty this place is!"

"You certainly got being a manly knight out of your system quickly; already taking the *attractiveness* of the situation into account," Pete retorted with lofty condescension, nonetheless dismounting from his horse and turning to help his cousin down from hers.

After the successful conclusion of the campaign, Bernadette and Pete had parted company with Sir Timothy's regiment, who were to bring the enemy prisoners into state custody. They had been urged to remain; nay more, to enlist permanently in the regiment's ranks, but they had refused on the plea of pressing business that could no longer be delayed. Most of the other volunteers, including the Black Knight, had immediately left the division as well, bent on pursuing new adventures.

Pete and Bernadette, however, had headed in a different direction from any of their former fellow soldiers. Once well distant from any chance observers, they had stopped to confer as to what their next occupation should be. After considering the nature of the countryside in which they were currently situated, they had decided that the role of peasants would be the most practicable. At this time of year, young men—and sometimes women too—might leave their winter homes and go seeking temporary work on larger farms to earn a few extra coins. And this area of the country was nearly all farmland, where they could easily find such employment.

For this stage of the journey, Bernadette had decided to dress as a girl again—she wasn't interested in spending her whole life masquerading as a boy unless it was for the sake of a career, such as that of a knight, that a girl typically could not follow at all.

So, as they sat beside the sparkling brook that had caught Bernadette's admiring attention, she smoothed the coarse brown skirt of her rustic gown with positive satisfaction. It was nice to be wearing a dress again, especially when it was a simple one that you could ride and work and lounge on the grass in without worrying about stains. Pete was dressed in rougher garments as well, although he still wore some of his mail.

"It's quite normal for peasant lads to volunteer for campaigns like the one we were just in, Bernie, and girls sometimes go along too, as cooks or washerwomen; no one will think it unusual for us to have been camp-followers for the past couple of weeks," Pete explained, lolling comfortably on the mossy roots of a tree and enjoying to the fullest the frugal repast they had purchased at the last village.

"And no one will ask where we came from before then?" Bernadette inquired, leaning back on her elbows and crunching satisfactorily into a juicy apple.

"They may—but they'll be satisfied to be told that we are from a distant part of the country and seeking work. Peasant folk usually have more important things to do than probe too deeply into other people's affairs," Pete responded, flicking a stray beetle off his sleeve. "Pass the cheese, will you? We mustn't waste our provisions, of course, but I'm still hungry." Bernadette laughed carelessly and tossed a lump of yellow cheese at her cousin. It hit him on the shoulder and then rolled triumphantly into his lap, as if to say, full of its own importance: "Here

I am, as requested!" Pete looked his exasperation over Bernadette's playfulness, but picked up the cheese and sank his teeth into it anyway.

"Ho, what goes on here?" suddenly demanded a strange voice, as the bushes behind them parted and a young man, a little older than either Pete or Bernadette, emerged, wearing a slightly hostile expression. At the sight of him, Bernadette started and dropped her apple into the brook; mindful of Pete's earlier caution, she dove hastily to get it before it sank.

"What do ye, strangers, here on my father's grounds?" the newcomer repeated, looking somewhat less surly as he watched Bernadette's rescue of her apple.

"We did not know that they were anyone's grounds," Pete replied, rising from the tree-roots and drawing Bernadette protectively towards him. "I beg your pardon; we will be on our way now. But stay, is your father in need of field laborers by any chance? We are travelers looking for such work."

"I'm sorry to say that we have no need of more hands at this time; my father is fairly well off and keeps his hired men year-round," responded the young man, who grew increasingly friendly as he took in their rustic appearance, realizing (or assuming) from this that Pete and Bernadette were simply harmless peasants like himself. He was quite satisfied by Pete's assurance that they had not *meant* to trespass. "But I can tell you where you might find work; Farmer Geoffrey on the other side of the Green Woods usually hires extra help for sowing his wheat-fields around now, and I don't think he's found anyone as yet; at least he hadn't when he stopped by last week. I don't know that he'd usually ask a maiden," nodding to Bernadette, "to help with such a strenuous part of the planting, but if he couldn't get anyone else . . . and his daughter just got married last month, so his wife probably wouldn't object to some extra help in the kitchen, either."

"All right then, we'll head for his place, and thank you very much for the recommendation. Sorry again for trespassing. Can you direct us towards this Farmer Geoffrey's?" Pete inquired.

"I can indeed, my good fellow and fair maiden; but first won't you stop and rest a bit at our place up over the hill"—pointing as he spoke—"and sup with us tonight? Perhaps you carry news from the farther country?"

"Yes; had you heard of the invasion?" Pete inquired, falling into step beside their new acquaintance as he headed back towards his dwelling. Pete was leading his horse, and the other young man insisted, with country politeness, on taking Bernadette's. She was more than willing to let him, as she still felt a strong repugnance towards the unwanted animal, and then she dropped back to walk behind the two youths, who were already deep in conversation—the farm lad was greatly impressed by Pete's having actually volunteered and fought in a real battle, "with real knights, really?"—and paid but scant attention to her.

"I guess we are going to 'stop a bit' at his house, even though no one ever actually accepted the invitation!" Bernadette chuckled to herself as she trailed along, enjoying the meadow views and the climb over an enchanting twisty fence around the farmyard—the young man helped her over even though she didn't really need it; his agreeableness had really increased amazingly during their short acquaintance, especially since he had noted that Bernadette had no wedding-ring on her finger and was therefore undoubtedly Pete's sister and not his wife.

The young man's pretty sister was quite as much impressed with Pete, who didn't even notice her, there being six or so other strapping young fellows of his age about the place, who were much better company when it came to discussing the news of the late invasion and the crops and prospect of a good harvest that year. Bernadette liked the jolly farmer—he reminded her a little of her father—and his bustling wife, who made almost as much of Bernadette for having traveled so far, as their sons and hired men made of Pete due to his having been in battle! Pete managed to catch his cousin's eye unobserved at one point during the conversation, and winked at her knowingly. Imagine what these good people would have thought if they had known their female guest had handled herself quite as ably on the field of arms as her male companion!

They had a marvelous supper— mainly fresh-laid eggs and home-baked bread, plus so much cold roast meat that Bernadette wondered how there could be anything left on the farm for the next day's meal, and foamy milk and mugs of home-brewed ale. After supper, Bernadette insisted on helping the farmer's wife and daughter with the dishes; she was not at all tired from her journey, really, thank you. Glancing back over her shoulder into the main room as she dried the heavy earthenware plates and bowls, Bernadette could just barely discern the contented smiles on the men's faces through the thick cloud of the smoke from their pipes, as they sat together by the enormous fire and re-talked over all the same old news most comfortably. The farmer's wife and her daughter gossiped quite as cheerfully through the soap-suds and splashing water in the kitchen, and made Bernadette feel quite at home with them. If this was a peasant's life, she could get used to it very easily!

It was well into the evening when Pete finally rose and requested the first fellow they had met to show them the way to Farmer Geoffrey's, for they wished to make their way there before dark if possible. The young man went to the window, inspected the sky critically for a moment, and then returned to the hearth, shaking his head. It was already dusk; Farmer Geoffrey's was at least a two-hour ride away; much better to spend the night here and ride on tomorrow. The rest of the farmer's family added their persuasions to try and convince Pete and Bernadette to stay. Bernadette would have had no problem with that, until Pete mentioned that if they waited, they might lose their chance of employment at Farmer Geoffrey's. Under such considerations, the family reluctantly withdrew their protests, and their son went out with Pete and Bernadette to show them the way.

"I'll take you as far as the Green Woods, and show you your path through it," their new friend said, springing lightly onto his own sturdy plow-horse and following Pete and Bernadette through the gate, pausing to latch it behind him securely. "It'll be a full moon tonight; that's one good thing, although it won't show much through the trees. Sure you wouldn't rather spend the night with us?" he inquired solicitously, with one eyebrow raised.

"Well, that's up to Bernie. Do you want to stay?" Pete looked thoughtfully at his cousin.

Bernadette did want to stay, but it seemed more polite to spend the night in a place where you were going to start working the next day, rather than imposing on others' hospitality too far. So she said, brightly, "Oh, I think we'd best be on our way, as you said earlier, Pete; but thank you so much for the offer, we do appreciate it," she added, smiling at the young man, who by this point considered her to be one of the fairest and most delightfully engaging young maidens he had ever seen.

Approximately half an hour later, they reached the edge of the Green Woods—Black Woods would really have been a more appropriate name for it, at least at this time of day, when its gnarled old trunks towered gloomy and menacing against the reddened sunset sky. But Pete and Bernadette, after their recent adventures in the Burlon Forest and the battlefield, were not at all daunted; it was just a bunch of stunted trees, that was all.

"Thanks awfully for showing us the way, old chap," Pete said familiarly, turning in his saddle to shake hands with their companion. "Great to meet you; regards to all your family, and hope we meet again before we have to leave the area and move on. So it's about an hour and a half from here? Not bad, and you'll be home before dark, at any rate," he concluded gaily.

"I'll head just into the beginning of the woods with you, to show you which markers to look for, and then head back," returned the other lad. "Here, fair maid, you had best ride in between us."

These were issues that Bernadette argued only with Pete. She coolly took her place in between the two young men, and rode on silently into the tangled mass of woodland. There really was no path at all, but certain trees had had their branches bent in a certain pattern that marked the trail, though only for those who knew and were looking for them.

Before the blackness of the forest had even entirely shut out the view of the sunset sky, their companion took his departure, bidding them be careful and make their way to Farmer Geoffrey's property as speedily as possible. "You will see it as soon as you emerge from the woods." Pete and Bernadette bade him a cheery farewell; and he rode back and they rode on, soon swallowed up entirely by the surrounding trees.

Bernadette could see the stars overhead through the twining boughs as they rode along, and called Pete's attention to them. "We certainly won't lose our way, Pete, even if we miss a marker-bough or two. Isn't there a way to tell direction by the stars?"

"Yes," Pete replied, casting a hasty glance up at the spangled sky above, and then returning his attention to their more immediate surroundings, his hand touching his sword involuntarily as rustlings sounded in the nearby underbrush. The animals in these woods seemed louder and more restless than usual tonight.

"Can you teach me how?" Bernadette pursued, still more interested in the stars. She took out her bow, however, and hung it on the saddle before her.

Pete obliged, after peering very hard into the tangled foliage beside them for some minutes. The rustlings died away, and then began again. Bernadette rather liked it; the animals showed no disposition to attack, and the soft padding sounds were quite lulling. She might have fallen asleep on her horse if she hadn't kept talking to Pete about the stars and their directions, boring of a topic as he evidently thought it was.

Suddenly, with a malignant whoop that filled the night, shadowy figures came rushing at them from all sides, wrapped in capes and kerchiefs that hid their faces from observation. Pete shouted, and pulled his horse nearer to Bernadette's. "Stay close and fight our way through!" he cried, drawing his sword.

As she reached for her own sword, Bernadette felt rough hands grasp her and attempt to drag her off her horse, while another of the figures rode up alongside her and seized her bridle, diverting her mount's course away from Pete. Bernadette screamed and struck out wildly at her captors, evading their efforts to subdue her as well as she could. She managed to slip to the ground and turned to run, but she stumbled and felt herself swooped up again by one of the dark riders. Before she could utter another scream, a heavy piece of cloth was wound around her face and mouth, effectively silencing her. Successful, the riders turned to gallop off with their prize.

At a distance, Bernadette heard Pete cry out, a dreadful groan of mingled pain and despair. Terrified at the thought of what might be happening to him, she renewed her struggles with increased vigor. Her captor wrapped the bandage tighter about her face with a cruel twist; Bernadette could scarcely draw her breath through it, and ultimately lost consciousness.

Chapter Sixteen
At the Gypsy Camp

"Well, and where am I *now*?" Bernadette muttered crossly to herself, awkwardly raising her head to take stock of her surroundings.

There wasn't much to see, only the dingy, once-white walls of the tent where she lay, securely bound hand and foot, on the dirt floor, across from a pile of rags in one corner. Her captors had thrown her carelessly down here, after a wild ride through the night deep into the forest to this isolated settlement. They had taken away the handkerchief around her mouth once they had put her in the tent, and left without heeding either her futile shrieks for help, reproaches for their unlawful behavior, or demands to be informed as to the fate of her cousin. Still stunned by what had happened, Bernadette had lain there in a daze until past daybreak, when the sunlight filtering in through the tent walls at last roused her entirely.

"They might at least have left me in a less uncomfortable position," she grumbled, trying to shift her weight off of her elbow, which was already numb. It was broad daylight by now, and Bernadette was glad of that, for throughout the night, she had been very cold under the insufficient shelter. "And just how long, pray, do those ruffians plan to leave me here, and what are they going to do to me?

"And where is Pete?" Bernadette might have added, but she did not, even in her thoughts, although this question was truly her greatest concern. She did not dare to think of what might have caused him to so cry out, or what might have occurred afterwards. But even without thinking of it, her alarm grew greater with every passing minute, as the sunlight grew stronger, and no one came.

Bernadette did not cry, she was too deeply alarmed even for tears; and besides, if Pete needed her help, she would have to remain calm and brave and strong. Between conquering her weaker feelings and watching the sunlight creep excruciatingly slowly across the ground and tent walls, Bernadette whiled away another dismal hour.

She was gazing distractedly at the dust specks flying around in one sunbeam, when the steady tramp of nearing feet suddenly caught her attention. She tried, again ineffectually, to raise herself on her elbow and dropped back again, waiting breathlessly.

Two swarthy, dark-haired men entered the tent, bearing a limp bundle in between them. They were dressed very carelessly, in ill-fitting blouses and loose trousers and no shoes, but their clothes were very brightly colored, especially the handkerchiefs around their necks and foreheads. Without even glancing in Bernadette's direction, they deposited their burden on the pile of rags in the corner and left the tent, dropping the flap shut behind them and tramping away the same way they had come.

The bundle was Pete, his clothes torn and coated with dried blood. Bernadette called his name, in a terrified whisper; but he lay with his back to her, so still and for so long that she was beginning to fear the worst, when he suddenly uttered a deep groan and rolled over, revealing a deep gash in his upper right arm.

"Oh, Pete, you're hurt!" was all Bernadette could think of to say.

"You're here, then, Bernie?" Pete languidly opened his eyes, peered vacantly at his cousin for a moment, and then shut them again. "I wondered why they brought me here; I was tied up in one of the wagons all night, to keep me secure after the fight I put up, I guess. But this morning I was so weak from loss of blood that I suppose they figured I couldn't do any harm out here, so they brought me to be with you. Very considerate of them, I'm sure," he concluded with biting sarcasm.

"Who are they, Pete, and what do they want with us?" Bernadette demanded anxiously, more nervous now than before.

"I'm sure they want ransom, if indeed they want anything besides to work their mischief on unguarded travelers," Pete responded, with scarcely repressed fury, although his eyes remained closed. "They're gypsy bandits, that's what they are, and this is one of their camps."

"Oh." Bernadette had never met any gypsies before, and she knew very little about them, other than that there were a moderate number of them living in the woods, far away from the palace and capital city of Berklesgilands; and she had always had a mild curiosity to know what they were like and how they lived in the woods. Sometimes they were involved in border riots along with disgruntled peasants, and she remembered now that Pete had been involved in at least one campaign to put down such disturbances, so doubtless he knew more about them than she did. But she didn't dare ask Pete anything further; he had shown a strong disinclination to pursue the subject, and besides, just breathing was giving him enough difficulty at this time. He was very pale, and his face worked with pain in spite of his best attempts to shrug it off. Bernadette's gaze wandered piteously back to his wound, which was really a very nasty one and had clearly not been treated or bound up at all. If only she could do something! She started to tug quietly at her bonds, but they were much too tight and well secured.

Footsteps approached again, and the same two men entered, accompanied by three or four others. Pete opened his eyes again and, by dint of furious concentrated effort, pushed himself up into a sitting position, and stared defiance into the eyes of their captors. Bernadette still couldn't move, but she glared at them too.

"Get up. You will be attended to outside, in the center of the camp," ordered the tallest of them, evidently unimpressed by his prisoners' hostility. The others cut their bonds and jerked them both to a standing position. Bernadette's limbs were cramped, and she was forced to lean momentarily against the arm of the man who had raised her in order to regain her balance. Pete reeled, and would have fallen but for the timely intervention of another one of the gypsies, younger and more sympathetic-looking than the others; he caught hold of Pete, and insisted that they carry him out.

Bernadette blinked as they headed into the sunshine, and looked around curiously. The camp was situated in a small clearing, surrounded on all sides by tall, thick trees that appeared to serve as grim sentinels, shutting out the rest of the world. The camp itself consisted of thirty or so brightly colored wagons, some finer and larger than others, circling the area, and then a dozen or so more tents such as the one in which she and Pete had been held. The center of the camp was mostly bare earth, with here and there a fire-pit, anvil, or rude table. There was a crowd of people waiting right in the very middle, evidently expecting the prisoners' arrival. Most of them, Bernadette noted with relief, seemed to be as innocently curious as herself, and more friendly-looking than otherwise. A few appeared sullen and disgruntled, but no one was exhibiting any signs of violence.

The gypsies set Pete down as they reached the crowd, and stood guard around him and Bernadette. One of the crowd, a muscular, fierce-looking young man of gigantic proportions, whom Bernadette thought she recollected as being at the head of the raid last night, stepped forward, surveying them critically. "Who are you?" he demanded at last, in a voice as rough as his looks.

Pete, who was swaying on his feet, despite the support of his guard, raised his head and looked directly into the other's eyes. "What is that to you? What do you want with us, brigand?" His voice rattled hoarsely, but carried clearly through the crowd, who murmured and drew closer together.

"Your money, stranger," the other laughed in an ugly manner.

"You have it. Now let us go; we have no more to give you."

"I'm not so sure about that, stranger. Peasant folk, as your dress would seem to identify you, don't carry jewels and gold and fine armor in their saddlebags. I would guess you are people of better quality than you let on, aren't you?"

Pete managed to shrug indifferently. "We've nothing to hide," he responded distinctly. "Yes, we are not poor peasants; but every traveler dresses and acts as though he were less wealthy than he truly is, to have a better gamble at getting past you fellows. But the chances were obviously still against us, so you may take your triumph along with our resources, and let us go again, as poor now as we appear."

"But who are you?" repeated this unpleasant individual.

"That we don't intend to tell you," Pete said firmly, although he coughed and bent nearly double with the effort to speak. There was a ripple of sympathy throughout much of the crowd, but no one moved to assist the prisoners; they cast uneasy looks at the man who was questioning them instead.

"Don't try to talk, Pete; let me handle this fellow," Bernadette cried, overcome with distress at his predicament. "Since you've got all our goods and money, sir, how could our names possibly do you any good? Answer me that, sir," she folded her arms together contemptuously.

"You might have relations who would pay us more," the man replied. "We won't let you go until you've given us the information we want, and we'll get it out of you, too!" he added with a menacing gesture. Some of the surly-looking young men around him surged forward, as though intending to try the effect of force. The nice young fellow supporting Pete moved forward a little, to shield Bernadette from their approach as well. Obviously, not all of the gypsies were in agreement as to how to treat their prisoners. But they all seemed to be too afraid of this giant ruffian to oppose him.

Before he or his men could reach them, however, an elderly man at the edge of the throng called the ringleader to his side, and whispered to him earnestly for a moment. The other did not seem to be either impressed or pleased by what he said; but it apparently was not entirely without effect, for when the fellow returned to his place at the front, he merely said, gruffly: "We will give the prisoners a little time to consider their situation before we deal with them further. But if you don't give your names and tell us where to send for ransom, rest assured it will go hard with you!" he threatened. "Tie them up at the edge of the camp, and don't anyone go near them until I call the assembly together again." He stalked off without another word, following the elderly figure to the largest and best wagon, with the roughest of the men accompanying him. The rest of the gypsy band dispersed, quite readily it seemed, and the guards dragged Bernadette and Pete over to a stout short pole stuck in the ground at one corner of the camp. The two cousins were pushed down into a sitting position on either side of it, back to back, and their guards bound them together with several loops of rope around their upper bodies, and tied their feet together. The kind-hearted young gypsy (he was barely more than a lad) brought them both some water, and then he left with the others.

For a while, neither Pete nor Bernadette said anything. Bernadette leaned her head back against the pole and stared vacantly up at the fluffy clouds passing each other in the blue sky above. Her mind was a blank; she had no idea what they should do or what might happen to them.

After several minutes, she felt Pete shift behind her, and heard him stifle a groan, his breath coming now in panting gasps. "Pete, are you all right?" she cried, twisting her head around to look at him.

"No . . . don't move, Bernie; you shift the ropes and they're cutting into my arm enough as it is," Pete gritted between clenched teeth, beads of perspiration rolling down his face. "The cowardly wretch! Won't meet a man in fair fight, but slashes at him in the dark and then still trusses him up like a fowl for roasting! Ugh!" he writhed again against his bonds, trying to shift the already blood-soaked ropes down so that they wouldn't press directly on the wound. Bernadette judged from his words that it had been the rough gypsy leader himself who had wounded him. "Don't think I'll give in, though, Bernadette; I don't care for the pain. We'll show him, the ruffian, that he has tougher customers to deal with than he supposes! Oh, what I wouldn't give to meet him in a fair fight, now!"

"You're in no condition for any kind of fighting, Pete; I think diplomacy is our better strategy," Bernadette replied quickly and compassionately. "Most of these people seemed willing to hear us and treat us more kindly: if we can but stir them to support our cause, we might make it out of here all right yet. But I'm just worried about your wound," she craned her head carefully to look down at it. "It already looks infected."

"I don't care; all I want is to gain the victory over that fellow, and get us safely away from here!" her cousin exclaimed, his face flushed with a feverish glow.

Bernadette could see that Pete might become really ill if his injuries were not speedily attended to. She looked around, hoping that their friend from earlier might be within sight and willing to bring them aid, but he had vanished with the rest of the camp. It seemed that everyone was in their tents or wagons; no one was out in the open. If she wanted anything done, she could depend on no one but herself.

"Pete," she said calmly, speaking as decisively and encouragingly as she knew how, "I've got to get help. There's got to be a way we can loosen these ropes."

"There's no way, and I'd probably faint if we tried it," Pete returned, hopelessly.

"I thought you just said you weren't going to give in. Now, come on, make one effort and I'll do the rest. Are your feet tied really tightly?"

"Not too tight, but what's that matter if my hands aren't free?" Pete sounded puzzled.

"I mean, do you think you could stand up, leaning against the pole and me, without your ropes tripping you up? This pole scarcely reaches above our heads even while we're sitting down; if we could just stand up, the ropes would be so much looser, without the pole between them, that I could probably slip them off and go get help. I think it will work."

"I don't know . . . but I can make one try at it, I suppose. You're right, Bernie; we mustn't give up," and clenching his teeth together once again, Pete leaned back hard against Bernadette, who reached back to clasp his hands in hers, to help him push up. Both of them bent their knees and planted their bound feet flat on the ground, and at Bernadette's "One, two, three . . . now!" they made a terrific effort and pushed back and up against the pole to try to stand.

At first they were unsuccessful. Every time they pushed halfway up, one or the other would lose their balance and slide back down to the ground again, dragging the other along. Pete cried out once or twice in agony, but he set his jaw and kept trying valiantly. Bernadette was perspiring heavily by now, too, which made the pole just that much more slippery to get up, but she was still determined. Another try, and yet another . . . it takes so little time to tell, and yet to them these ineffective efforts seemed to take forever.

At last, with a grunt and a shove that threatened to break the pole in two, the cousins strained their utmost and gained their footing for one second. Before they could slip down again, Bernadette got her elbow on the top of the pole and, using that to support them both, untangled the ropes around them and pulled them up over her head. Now free, she toppled back to a sitting position and began untying the ropes around her feet. Pete had fallen down on the other side of the pole, the ropes still wound around him, faint from pain and exhaustion.

Bernadette cast an anxious glance at him as she threw aside her former bonds and got to her feet again. Hurrying to his side, she bent over him and, ripping off her sash, wrapped it securely around the wound in several folds. It would staunch the flow of blood at least until she got back.

But where was she to go for help? Whom could she trust in this camp? Bernadette suddenly felt more overwhelmingly lonely and helpless than she ever had before in her life. And yet . . . throwing her head back determinedly and plucking up all her courage, she headed off. If she failed in her mission, it should not be from lack of will or effort on her part.

Pausing on the very edge of the camp, Bernadette took a careful survey of the wagons. Oh, if only she had noticed which one belonged to that nice young gypsy lad! But as it was, she would just have to take her chances and see what came of it.

As she stepped hesitantly towards the nearest wagon, her attention was suddenly drawn to a nearby stream running past the camp, which she had not noticed before. And what was more, an elderly gypsy woman was kneeling down by the creekside, filling a bucket. As Bernadette watched her, she straightened up and turned back towards the camp.

Alarmed, and not wishing to be seen yet, Bernadette shrank back to hide behind the wagon wheel. The woman passed quite close to her, entered the wagon, and came back out again after a moment with another bucket. She walked bent nearly double; the bucket was clearly very heavy for her, and she was aged and infirm. In fact, she reminded Bernadette a little of Old Saphronia.

That gave her an idea. As the gypsy woman stooped at the water's brink again, Bernadette emerged boldly from the shadow of the wagon and approached her. Tapping her lightly on the shoulder, she said, with a false brightness of tone (her anxiety was nearly choking her): "Please, ma'am, shall I help you with that?"

The woman looked up, startled. She looked ten times more startled still once she realized that this young girl was one of their prisoners, but she gave her the bucket. She watched as Bernadette filled it and turned to take it to the wagon, and got up to follow her there. As they reached the steps, she put her wrinkled hand on Bernadette's shoulder.

"Why have you not run away, my daughter?" she asked, in strongly compassionate tones, mingled with curiosity.

"My cousin is badly wounded; and oh, if only you would help us!" Bernadette put down the bucket and clasped her hands beseechingly. Now the tears began to flow.

"We shall bring him here, then, daughter," the woman replied, quietly. "I have no liking for these unlawful raids, and would not see one of their unfortunate victims suffer for lack of any help that I can give. 'Tis well you approached me; I am the best healer and nurse in the band. Come, we shall have young Ivan help to bring him in." She turned to lead the way; Bernadette followed after her, still scarcely believing that it was really going to be all right.

Young Ivan, of course, was their kind-hearted guard, who was only too happy to help Bernadette carry Pete over to Mother Veronica's wagon. In less time than it takes to tell of it, Pete was comfortably established on a cot bed inside, his arm bound up carefully with healing herbs, and with Mother Veronica trotting back and forth from his side to her little stove, where another medicinal mixture was brewing. She had prepared some strong broth that she was feeding to Pete (who was already feeling so much better that he wished she wouldn't), and had given Bernadette a lunch of bread and cheese. Ivan had gone back to his own wagon, promising to return if needed.

"Run down to the brook and get me some more water, my daughter," Mother Veronica told Bernadette. "Your cousin will do very well."

Now as blithe as a bird, and feeling herself quite the happiest girl on earth, Bernadette seized the bucket by its leather handle, and swinging it gaily, sprang lightly out the wagon door—and found herself face to face with the scowling visage of the dreadful fellow who had captured and threatened her and Pete. Trembling, she shrank back inside the wagon; he came up the steps and followed her in.

"What is all this, Mother Veronica?" he demanded roughly. "These are my prisoners; what right have you to interfere with my treatment of them?"

"They are my adopted son and daughter; I need someone to help me with my work now that I am old, and I am a poor widow with no living children of my own," Mother Veronica replied calmly and without looking up, apparently completely absorbed in pressing a damp cloth to Pete's forehead. "You would not demand ransom for two hard-working young members of our band, now would you? My daughter, it is time to set the table for our midday meal. You will find the dishes in the cupboard over the other bed."

Bernadette, amazed at the old woman's cleverness, moved to obey as though she were walking in her sleep. The hulking ruffian, who was really too large for the inside of the wagon, stood staring at Mother Veronica for a minute, and then, muttering something about her being responsible if they were to get away, turned and left. He hit his head on one of the tin pots dangling from the doorway, and with an enraged howl, he leapt off the wagon steps and hastily made his way back the way he had come.

Pete and Bernadette and Mother Veronica all looked at each other, and burst out laughing. Beaming triumphantly, Mother Veronica put down her damp rag; and, forgetful of the dishes, Bernadette ran over and gave her a tremendous, grateful hug.

Chapter Seventeen
The Guest-Dance

"Here, Bernadette, move over! Some of the rest of us need to fetch water, too!" a merry young voice cried, at the brink of the stream.

Bernadette sat back on her heels and looked up, frowning slightly, as she brushed the damp hair back from her forehead. "Oh, hello, Esmeralda," she replied, dipping up a bucketful. "I thought you had already gotten your water for the day."

"I got the water earlier and I'm back again already!" the other responded with mocking gaiety, as she moved past Bernadette and knelt down by the stream. She was an extraordinarily pretty girl, about Bernadette's age, with thick black hair curling around her symmetrical oval face and a vivacious pair of dark eyes. Her figure was as perfect as her features, and well set off by the gypsy attire she wore: a brilliantly colored striped skirt, an embroidered vest girded with a gold-link sash, a white blouse with full, flowing gauze sleeves, a bright beribboned kerchief in her hair, and an abundance of hammered-metal bangles.

Bernadette was dressed similarly; she and Pete were recognized members of the gypsy camp now. It had been nearly two months since their capture, and they had been with the band ever since. They had already moved camp several times, but every place they dwelt was as secluded as the first. Pete and Bernadette had never yet had a chance to run away. Mother Veronica had advised them against it.

"You'd be captured again and brought back long before you were out of the forest. Be patient. Eventually we will arrive at a camp near enough to a village that you can reach safely before you are pursued.

And, speaking purely selfishly, I am in no hurry for that time to come; it is a blessing for me to have you and your help. I love you like my own children."

"We love you, too," Bernadette said earnestly. "But we have to think of our own families as well. Don't you think they'll be terribly worried?"

"You told me that you and Peter were traveling for a year, and that no one will be expecting to hear from you before then. Time enough to worry about it after that time arrives," Mother Veronica responded. She still did not know exactly who Pete and Bernadette were; she thought it would be wiser for her not to know the details. The gypsy band was satisfied to know that they had gained a decent supply of goods from their new members, and that they were quite one with them now, at least to all appearances. Bernadette really did enjoy living in the gypsy camp; the hard-working, open-air lifestyle appealed to her sense of adventure. And she was learning many new things, particularly various kinds of beautiful gypsy craftwork, and medicinal arts from Mother Veronica. By now, Bernadette was friends with nearly everyone in the camp, especially Ivan and the girls of her own age. Once their chores were done, the younger gypsies spent hours roaming the woods gathering berries and flowers, swimming in the stream, playing lively games and music, and telling stories round the evening fires together.

Pete was not as fond of his new lifestyle and companions as Bernadette was; his previous experiences with gypsy peoples had tended to prejudice him against them, and the circumstances leading to their current position among them had only intensified these feelings: but complaining was not part of his nature. He worked with a will, chopping logs and repairing the wagon and caring for Mother

Veronica's horse. And whenever strong lads were needed to help work the anvils for the gypsy metalsmiths, Pete would be first in line.

All this flashed through Bernadette's memory by the time the other girl had arisen from the stream, her buckets overflowing, and turned to walk by her side back to the camp. "But why are you getting more water now, Esmeralda, if you already fetched it earlier?" Bernadette queried, puzzled.

"Three guesses!" the other challenged promptly.

"You needed more for something you were doing at home?"

"Oh, what a boring explanation! You think I'd have you guess for something as mundane as that? No, try again."

"You're getting it for someone else in the camp who couldn't come to fetch it themselves today."

"Getting warmer; but still not quite. It's not for anyone from the camp."

"Then you've captured more prisoners who need water for wounds and fever. Is that it?" Bernadette raised an eyebrow with a wry, meaningful grimace.

"Oh, mercy me, no!" Esmeralda stopped short and doubled up with merriment. "We haven't *captured* anyone—oh, how sour you look about it, to be sure! But a group of traveling knights has stopped at our camp to be our guests for the night, and we are going to give them a grand feast. This water is for their horses. We gypsies are very hospitable people, for all our faults, you know," she glanced over at Bernadette, her luminous eyes twinkling with indescribable mischief.

The news of these arrivals was exceptionally pleasant to Bernadette. "I'll help bring the water, as soon as I bring Mother Veronica hers," she offered readily. "Which side of the camp are they on?"

"Over there." Esmeralda nodded in the direction. "I'll meet you back at the stream." She skipped off, the water sloshing over the sides of her buckets.

Bernadette walked more slowly back to Mother Veronica's wagon. Balancing her buckets carefully, she climbed up the steps, ducked under the low doorway, and poured the water into the cauldron on the stove. Mother Veronica was chopping vegetables at the table, and Pete was standing on one of the cot beds, repairing a broken window sash high up on the wall.

"There, it should keep the wind out now, Mother Veronica," he said, stepping down. "Not that it really matters, while it's so hot out! What's the news, cousin?" he glanced over at Bernadette's animated expression.

"We've got visitors," she announced importantly, grasping the handles of the buckets once again, and preparing to depart. "Esmeralda told me. Unless you need me, Mother Veronica, I'm going to go help her water their horses. And there's going to be a feast tonight; I'll be back once I find out more details to help you prepare. Why don't you come with me, Pete?" She was already halfway back down the wagon steps.

"Certainly; I'd like to see these new arrivals for myself," Pete rejoined, ducking out after her and bidding farewell over his shoulder to Mother Veronica, who looked up from her vegetables to nod goodbye to them as well. "Who are they, Bernie," he asked in a lower tone, as they left the wagon behind.

"Traveling knights, Esmeralda said," Bernadette replied with suppressed excitement. "Are you thinking what I'm thinking? Perhaps they could help us to . . ."

"Hush!" Pete cautioned, looking around warily for chance eavesdroppers. "We'd better not talk about it. But the sooner we make their acquaintance the better. Here, give me one of the buckets."

They filled their buckets at the stream, where Esmeralda was waiting impatiently, her own already refilled. "Come on, or you'll be too late. Seems everyone got word all at once and is rushing to be the ones to wait on these highly respected guests of ours. It's not as though we get any very often, you know," she said flippantly, walking ahead of Pete and Bernadette to the wooden water-troughs, beside which a crowd had eagerly clustered about the newcomers.

There were six of the young knights, each with his own horse, and several pack-horses in their train besides. Their armor and harness proclaimed them to be well-off knights of noble station, as did the good breeding with which they responded to the barrage of questions and curious gazes darted at them from the pressing crowd.

Esmeralda pushed easily through the gathered assembly, creating a path for Pete and Bernadette to follow behind her. They poured their buckets into the trough, filling it up to the brim. Pete then offered to show the knights where they could rest a bit before the festival evening, hoping to gain an opportunity to start a conversation with one of them unsuspected. Esmeralda fell back into the admiring throng, watching every move of these new, and therefore extremely interesting, arrivals.

Bernadette, of course, was looking at the knights' horses. They were fine, lithe animals of magnificent proportions.

"Well, aren't you a beauty, now," she whispered to one of them, running her hand under the black mane of the sleekest mount. The dark, handsome animal raised her head from the trough, water dripping from under her jawline, and turned to regard Bernadette with gentle eyes, revealing a white star on her forehead.

"Midnight!" Bernadette gasped in shock, and then hastily repressed her astonishment and moved on to inspect the other horses with pretended interest, hoping no one had noticed her outburst. Fortunately, most of the gypsies had followed after the knights, farther into the camp. Bernadette sneaked a look over at them, and yes, there he was—the Black Knight, striding purposefully along next to Pete, and chatting with him quite amicably. He caught Bernadette's eye and nodded to her carelessly, apparently thinking she was just one of the gypsy maidens furtively admiring him.

"Of all the people who *could* have turned up, it would have to be *him*, wouldn't it?" Bernadette grumbled into a palomino's sympathetic ear.

"Come, my daughter, you can pet the horses more later. We must join the other women at the fire-pits to prepare the meal." Mother Veronica had come up unobserved behind her.

"Oh—all right." Bernadette darted another look over at the Black Knight, and a wistful one towards Midnight, as she slowly followed Mother Veronica to the center of the camp, adjusting her kerchief to hide as much of her blonde hair as possible. The knights had all disappeared into a wagon by the time they reached the chattering throng gathered to cook up the feast, and Bernadette was able to relax a little.

And it was a grand feast, indeed, that they prepared! The guests, well rested and refreshed, were loud in their praise as they sat in the places of honor about the long rough-hewn wooden tables, and feasted on fare that would have put many a palace banquet to shame. Everyone enjoyed themselves very much, even Bernadette, since she was seated well away from the Black Knight and his companions, and was quite sure that he had not recognized her. Pete was sitting across from her;

and she had been able to discuss the situation with him privately earlier, by the fire while they were cooking. Pete had not brought up the subject of their escaping to the knights yet; there had been too many people around, but he had made friends with them all and was quite confident that they would be willing to help them.

Once dinner was over, it was time for the dancing to begin! The fiddlers and other musicians climbed up onto the just-cleared tables, to serve as a performing-platform, and tuned their instruments until everyone was worked up to the highest pitch (forgive the pun) of anticipation. Then they struck up the first tune of the night, and one and all entered into the dance.

There were no stately strictures to the gypsy dances; you could keep to the simplest moves possible, or the most complicated ones you knew. Some danced in couples, others by themselves in the center, and still others joined hands and circled the rest of the merry-makers in a swirling ring.

The best dancer of all was Esmeralda. Graceful and lively as a flower twirling in the breeze, she danced alone, spinning and executing the most complicated steps of anyone. Every gypsy fellow and all the visiting knights wanted to dance with her; so she swung lightly from one partner to the next, never staying with any one for very long, and then returning to her own place in the middle to continue dancing by herself until she received the next invitation.

Not long after the dance began, the Black Knight offered himself to Esmeralda as a partner. She took his hand indifferently, evidently expecting that he would be just like all the others. However, the Black Knight soon proved himself her match when it came to graceful maneuvers and intricate footwork (as even Bernadette was forced to admit), and they continued to dance together long into the night. The rest of the crowd soon fell back into the ring, where they could continue dancing while still watching Esmeralda and her partner in the center.

The moon sank low below the stars, but still the dancing went on. Bernadette clasped Pete's hand on one side, and Ivan's on the other, and whirled and sang along to the glorious tune, feeling that this night of feast and festival would prove a fitting end to her experiences as a gypsy maiden.

Chapter Eighteen
Betrayal!

Keeping in the shadows, Bernadette skirted the edge of the camp, intending to wait until the guests had retired before returning to her wagon. The knights would be sleeping in some of the extra tents on the edge of the clearing. They intended to rise earlier than the rest of the camp to depart the next morning, and wished to be closer to their horses so as to leave without creating any disturbance. And therefore, they were expressing their thanks and farewells to the gypsies tonight before going to bed.

Bernadette waited impatiently, tapping one foot on the ground as she watched the crowd in the firelight, taking their time as they gathered up their sleepy children and gradually drifted away in groups of two or three to the wagons. Pete and Ivan were helping the knights set up their tents. Bernadette supposed she should join them; after all, the more the knights saw of them, the more likely they would be to remember who they were when they approached them early the next morning to ask to go along with them. But Bernadette really did not want to meet with the Black Knight again any sooner than was absolutely necessary; it would be good enough for Pete to cultivate an acquaintance with him.

Everyone else had turned in for the night by this time. The tents were up and the knights were inside; Pete and Ivan were checking the ropes outside to make sure they were secure. Bernadette supposed she should head for the wagons now; she'd rather walk with Pete and Ivan across the camp. It was best not to be the only person out after dark, even in this secure clearing.

But as Bernadette got up from the stump where she was sitting, brushing bits of bark and grass off her skirt, she abruptly realized that she was *not* the only person out here. Someone had just passed behind her, crunching twigs beneath his feet. His enormous shadow identified him as the rough gypsy who had led the capture of Pete and Bernadette two months before.

What was he doing out again at this hour? Bernadette had seen him go into his wagon; why had he left it? Suspicious, she crept after him. He had not observed her, and strode carelessly along until he reached the wagon belonging to the elderly gypsy chief. Bernadette knew by now, after living here for so long, that this ruffian was actually the chief's grandnephew, and that he mostly made the older and weaker man do as he pleased, especially since he had the backing of all the most aggressive and insubordinate fellows in the band. What was he up to now?

He was not alone, either. As he reached the wagon, he gave a low whistle, and all his followers emerged from where they had been waiting for him, concealed in nearby shrubs and thickets. There were nearly a score of them altogether. Bernadette halted at a slight distance, crouching down by a bush to hide herself from view, and waited until they had all entered the chief's wagon. The grandnephew went in last of all, latching the door securely shut behind him.

Bernadette, trembling with mingled apprehension and curiosity, stole cautiously over to the wagon and went up the steps herself. She bent down and peeked through the keyhole.

All the young ruffians were sprawled carelessly about in various attitudes on the chief's good furniture, putting their boots up on the fine

167

woodwork, and quaffing mugfuls of strong liquor. Only their leader, the chief's grandnephew, was standing, in the center of the room. The chief was sitting in the best chair before him, his head hung low.

"You have nothing to do with it, uncle," the grandnephew was saying in a loud voice, "I am the leader in this undertaking, and I can take the responsibility myself."

"But you are not the chief yet; it is my position to be held accountable," the elderly man replied wearily. "And it would be a disgrace to our name to fall upon these men, our guests; a rank betrayal of our reputation and duty of hospitality."

"You took care of the presentation of hospitality to them earlier today, and quite enough there was of it, too," responded the other with a coarse laugh. "And so now it is my turn to take care of our own people: these men are nobles, with gold and connections that will serve us well. We must look to ourselves and our own purposes, uncle!"

The aged chief shook his head, but it was only too clear that he was completely powerless in the hands of his forceful grandnephew. Besides, the other young men in the wagon, fired with zeal, expressed their intentions of carrying out their leader's plans with cheers and vigorous stamping, clanking their mugs together and taking deep draughts from them again. "Down with the landed gentry!" they cried with enthusiasm.

"You fools!" cried the chief, his voice quavering with hopeless rage and anxiety. "Do you not realize that you jeopardize our safety and our hard-won freedoms by your unlawful and rebellious activity? Will King Friedrich overlook this forever, and not take a just retribution, which will affect not only our own band, but doubtless all of our people in the kingdom?"

"Let him try; we'll take care of him and his army, too," growled his grandnephew. "Can they follow us into the mountains, and navigate the wilderness as we do? And the more of his knights we get out of the way now, the fewer we shall have to deal with when it comes to that. No more words, uncle; we are determined, and you cannot stop us now." He moved away, placing his hand on the handle of the door. Bernadette shrank away, alarmed lest he should come out and see her. Suddenly, the sound of light footsteps approaching the wagon caught her ear. Bernadette was forced to leap off the steps to avoid discovery; she fell her length in the dirt by the wagon, fortunately concealed from view by the shadow of the wheel, watching as the slender figure of a young woman climbed up the steps and entered the wagon, silhouetted for a moment against the light from within. Esmeralda! What was *she* doing here?

"Well, what news?" the chief's grandnephew demanded curtly, shutting the door behind her again. Bernadette could hear still them talking, and also see their shadows on the shade pulled down over the window.

"All quiet, master," Esmeralda replied respectfully, but with a trace of reluctant sullenness in her voice. "Our guests—the intruding gentry I mean—are yet unsuspicious; the captive Peter and Ivan have retired for the night. I hobbled the knights' horses so that they cannot slip away unawares, as you bade me. And I noted which saddlebags and pouches about their tents contained valuables worth pursuing, and marked them with our secret sign so you could tell which they were."

"And no one saw you?" the leader spoke quickly and harshly. His great-uncle groaned and sank his head into his hands.

"No one notices a girl," Esmeralda replied with a shrug. "Well, master, what do I get for my pains?"

"Your tasks are not over yet," the chief's grandnephew retorted. "But here, take this piece of gold to hold you for now, and go back out and keep an eye on our victims while you lay the usual traps that will trip up their mounts and prevent them from escaping, even if they do get their horses loose before we observe them. If anything rouses them, inform me immediately. Well, get you gone, girl!" Esmeralda silently withdrew, putting the gold coin in her pocket as she descended the steps and headed back into the darkness. "The rest of you wait at your posts until my signal to fall upon them, which will be at approximately an hour before dawn, unless one of us discovers some development that will change our plans before that," the outlaw leader ordered, turning to leave the wagon himself.

The old gypsy chief essayed to speak once more, but his voice was drowned by the shouts and cheers of the other ruffians, as they rose in a body to follow their captain and swarmed out the wagon door and down the steps. Bernadette drew back underneath the wagon as the brigands tramped past her, carefully watching where they went. To Bernadette's relief, no one headed for the side that she would have to pass in order to reach her own wagon. As soon as the leader had returned to his wagon, she crawled out towards the open center of the camp. Holding her breath, Bernadette darted swiftly across the bare spots, staying in the shadows of the tables and anvils as much as possible, until she reached her side of the camp, where she crept along behind the wagons until she came to her own. Finally daring to breathe, she stole noiselessly up the steps.

"Bernie, where have you been?" Pete rose to meet her from where he had been waiting outside the door, speaking in a whisper. "Mother Veronica is asleep; but come away, she might oppose our plans as rash if she overheard them. I still couldn't tell the fellows about our plight with Ivan there; but I know what time they're rising, and I said we'd be there to help with their departure, which hopefully will be ours as well, at daybreak tomorrow, and so . . ."

". . . it won't be *anyone's* departure, unless we leave long before that, and you listen to what I have to tell you now!" Bernadette hissed. She quickly informed Pete of what she had heard.

"The wretch!" Pete muttered between his teeth. This atrocious betrayal of common hospitality was nearly incomprehensible to him. It went against all the accepted principles of both gypsy and settled society. "Well, we'll have to warn them and get away as soon as possible, then, Bernie. Let's get the few things the ruffian left to us, and act now!"

"But what about Esmeralda? I didn't see exactly where she went to lay those traps, and she's watching the knights' tents. We can't get out without falling into her snares or having her alert the ruffians and their leader," Bernadette objected anxiously.

"Leave her to me; I'll find her and manage it so that she won't be able to give us away," Pete replied briefly, as the cousins headed back to their wagon to pack hastily. "All you have to do is go and warn the knights now," he directed, as they left it again, Mother Veronica still slumbering in peaceful unconsciousness inside.

"Maybe I should track Esmeralda, and you should warn the knights?" Bernadette suggested, shifting her burden.

"No; in situations like these, men would be more likely to heed a warning from a guileless maiden than from another man; and a girl is more easily cowed by the commands of a robust fellow than those of another damsel," Pete returned.

"You won't take this out on her, though, will you, Pete? I believe that she is involved in all this somewhat against her will," Bernadette appealed to him beseechingly.

"What kind of an honorable knight do you take me for, to think that I would harm a defenseless maiden?" Pete inquired with justifiable scorn. "All I intend to do is prevent her from hindering our escape. Give me your sash, Bernadette; I may need it."

Bernadette complied a little hesitantly, wondering what he was planning to do; but Pete's face was stern and resolute, so she decided not to ask him. The sash having been accordingly handed over, the cousins parted company, and Bernadette hastened over to the knights' tents. She cast a nervous glance over her shoulder before entering; but all was still and there were no signs of anyone observing her movements. Drawing a deep breath, she ducked inside the tent.

It would be just Bernadette's luck that the tent she chose to enter was the very one in which the Black Knight was sleeping. And the two others in the tent appeared to be very sound sleepers, the kind who would wake up very noisily when they finally *were* aroused, so Bernadette had to go over and shake the Black Knight's shoulder.

He sat up immediately, and looked very surprised to see who it was. "What is it, maiden?" he inquired softly, reaching for his mail and weapons.

"You and your companions are in danger here," Bernadette said shortly. "The chief of this band is a good man, but he is old and helpless, and his lawless grandnephew is determined to go against him in taking you prisoner and seizing your goods. I know whereof I speak; my cousin and I are also his captives here. We must get away from this place before daybreak, for they intend to fall upon you then. My cousin is now engaged in deterring their main spy, and we are ready to help you escape. Will you let us come with you?"

"Of course!" the Black Knight was now on his feet. "Johnson! Wilhelm! Up, and let us be going!" he roused his companions.

"It's too dark to leave yet," groaned one of them, rolling over.

"We are betrayed by lawless brigands, and must get away now if we value our lives, freedom, and property," the Black Knight said with decision, buckling on his sword. "Silence and dispatch are our watchwords. One of you must go to each tent to rouse the others, and then we will all meet in the thicket where our horses are tied—stay," he turned back to Bernadette, "where are their spies watching for us?"

"There's really only one, the one my cousin is trailing; the rest are all on the other side of the camp lying in wait," Bernadette replied, still curt and to the point. "If we are careful to make no noise, we can slip out into the thicket unobserved. Your horses are still there, but they are tied up to hinder our progress."

"We must only go once, then. Collect everything in the tents and bring it all along," the Black Knight directed his comrades, who nodded and left the tent as silently as shadows to alert their fellows. "Will you help me to gather what we have in this tent?" he went on to Bernadette, stooping down himself to roll up the bedding and collect the coins and weapons in the corners. Bernadette nodded and began to bundle together the articles in the tent as swiftly as possible. The sooner they packed everything up, the sooner they could join the others at the horses, so that she wouldn't have to be alone with this Black Knight any longer!

Pete, meanwhile, had strolled away to the outskirts of the camp. He had watched as Bernadette's shadowed form slipped almost unnoticeably into the guests' tent, and smiled with satisfaction, certain that no chance spies could have observed so slight a motion.

But here he was wrong. Directly in front of him, a figure rose up and turned, regarding the tents fixedly for a moment. She did not observe Pete, back in the shadows, and began to run lightly across the camp towards the grandnephew's wagon to give the alarm.

Pete was upon her in a moment. With one swift motion, he grasped her by the shoulder, bringing her to a full stop, twisted Bernadette's sash securely around her mouth before she could cry out, and forced her to the ground, holding her tightly by the wrists. Esmeralda was not easily subdued; she fought and twisted against Pete's grip, and he had a few difficult moments handling her before he could bind her securely with his own bandana and neckerchief. Then he stepped back and stood regarding her sternly, as she stared up at him with a frankly terrified gaze.

"I'm not going to hurt you," Pete said loftily. "You have nothing to worry about, provided that you will behave yourself like a respectable woman and lend me your aid. For shame, really! What can have possessed an innocent young girl like yourself to offer your services to these lawless ruffians? But we haven't time to go into all that now; if you will give me your maiden word of honor that you will not cry out or alert anyone, and will assist me and these worthy guests of your people to escape unharmed, I will free you. Will you?"

Esmeralda nodded, so Pete stooped to unbind her and removed the sash from around her mouth. "What would you have me do?" she whispered, regarding him earnestly.

"First of all, take up the traps that you have laid for these unsuspecting gentlemen," Pete commanded briefly. "Every one of them, mind."

"I had barely begun," Esmeralda responded haltingly, heading into the bushes and stooping to undo the nooses she had hung so craftily there. "But some of them cannot be reversed, tar and such. But I can show you how to avoid them at least. You are fleeing, too?"

"Yes," Pete said shortly. "What, do you think we would consent to remain prisoners when chance was offered us to escape? And that reminds me, do you know where the goods which were taken from us are?"

"No, I do not . . . exactly," faltered the girl, darting another frightened glance up at his severe countenance.

"That means, I take it, that you can easily find them," Pete retorted grimly, his arms crossed uncompromisingly across his chest as he looked down upon her.

"But sir! You cannot . . . you do not know what I risk by aiding you even so far. That man—the leader of these brigands—he is my master, and oh, what he will do to me if he finds out that I helped you escape! Not to mention if I helped you to retrieve the goods he hoards for his own. Oh sir, have pity on me, and do not ask it!" Esmeralda pleaded despairingly, raising beseeching eyes to Pete's stern face. Unnerved and knowing herself to be powerless to oppose anything Pete might require of her, she buried her face in her hands and began to sob hopelessly.

Pete's gaze softened slightly. Despite his hardened soldier exterior, Pete had a very tender heart, which he usually only demonstrated towards his beloved relations and closest friends. But the sight of this helpless, misguided girl weeping worked on his susceptibilities, and he could not help speaking more gently to her.

"You don't have to be afraid: if you will help us get away, I will protect you from your savage leader; I give you my word of honor as a gentleman," he assured her, quietly.

"But how can you do that?" Esmeralda raised her tear-stained face to stare up at him again.

"We'll take you safely away with us, of course. Now, finish untying those snares and go get our money and jewels; we need to get over to the horses as quickly as we can, so you can direct us in unhobbling them and we can get away without any more delay."

"I'll try." Esmeralda got up from her completed task in the bushes, and walked a little ahead of Pete across the camp, keeping to the shadows. "But he keeps the finest articles hidden in his own wagon, and I couldn't sneak them out under his very nose. And some of your things have been traded away to other bands already. The rest are hidden with the rest of their hoard, in some hollow trees outside the camp; I could probably find them readily enough. However, all the other men are in hiding on that side of the camp, and I am not supposed to be there, so . . ."

"I know all your plans, so spare your breath in recounting them to me," Pete cut her off. "If anyone stops you, you can easily enough represent yourself as carrying out some new orders from your master. It appears to me that you are his main right hand in these stratagems."

"I'm no better than his slave," Esmeralda muttered. "Well, then, I'll get you the jewels, sir, and the gold as well, come what may of it." She straightened herself and set her face determinedly. Pete glanced over at her with a slight feeling of admiration.

They had reached the other side of the camp by this time, passing by the chief's wagon. Esmeralda paused. "You had better not come into the woods with me; I will go and bring back the goods if you will wait here."

"Very well; but you know what the consequence will be if you betray us," Pete warned her significantly, sitting down to conceal himself in the shadow of the wagon wheel while he waited for her to return.

Esmeralda flitted into the grove without another word; only the faint rustling of the branches betrayed her movements. Pete heard no sound of anyone discovering or confronting Esmeralda for her activities. He strained to hear what might be going on at the other side of the camp, but nothing carried to his ear. Inside the chief's wagon, the elderly man was still sitting up; Pete could see his silhouette shadowed against the window shade. Pete shifted his weight impatiently and glanced at the sky, which was already fading from its earlier velvety blackness to a more grayish hue. An hour before dawn was not far off. Where was Esmeralda, and how long was she going to take?

At last she returned, breathless and weighed down with heavy bundles over her shoulders. Pete got up and took one of them from her, swinging it capably over his own shoulder. "Come on, let's go."

"Sorry it took so long," Esmeralda managed between gasps, as they hastened towards the other side of the camp, where the knights awaited their coming in the thicket. "I couldn't find the place at first. I think I got everything of yours that was there, and I brought another bag of gold and some extra trinkets as well. It can't very well be returned now, so we might as well take it along. Better that we have it than *him*," she stressed the final word with unwonted venom.

Pete glanced over at her, but he had no time to say anything in reply before a low voice hailed them from within the thicket. "Who goes there? Stand; are you friend or foe?"

"Friend; Sir Peter and a companion now on our side," Pete responded, low, as he and Esmeralda ducked into the thicket. The Black Knight, who had spoken to them, took their loads and packed them into the saddlebags, along with his own and his companions' belongings. Bernadette was kneeling beside one of the horses with the knight named Johnson, endeavoring to loosen the hobbles about its front legs.

"You do that, Esmeralda; you tied them in the first place," Pete ordered, pushing her forward. Bernadette looked up, surprised to see her there, and moved aside. Esmeralda knelt down and began working at the knots. "Hurry up; we've got to get going."

"I know, I know," Esmeralda answered between her teeth, straining at the tight leather bands. "I'm in as much danger as any of you—or more. He'll only take you prisoner again, unless you put up a fight. But if he catches me helping you . . . the tortures he would devise. . ." she shook her head and shuddered.

"I gave you my word of honor for your safety, didn't I? As soon as you get those undone, we'll be off and you with us," Pete rejoined impatiently, working with his knife to get the last set of hobbles off of Midnight, who stood patiently and perfectly composed despite the unusual proceedings of this night.

Bernadette moved over to stand guard at the edge of the thicket with one of the other knights. The Black Knight was busy checking the girths of all the horses, and making certain that everyone had a suitable weapon handily girded to their side, including Bernadette and Esmeralda.

Bernadette silently took the sword he held out to her without looking towards him; she kept her gaze fixed on the wagons and center of the camp. Suddenly, she caught sight of some motion on the far side.

She leaned forward to get a better view; yes, there were several people standing by one of the wagons, talking and gesticulating, apparently trying to attract someone inside. The door of the wagon opened and someone came out—it was the chief's grandnephew! Even from this distance, and in the dim starlight of early morning, Bernadette could see his face redden with rage.

Bernadette slipped further back into the thicket. Everyone could hear the shouts now. "They are alerted! Where have they gone! Summon the rest of the men; cut off their retreat, you fools!"

Esmeralda looked up and blanched with horror, the hobbles she had just managed to unfasten falling unheeded from her hands. Then she suddenly sprang to her feet and, throwing her hair back from her face and cupping both hands around her mouth to enable the sound to carry, she shouted: "By way of the south ford, men; be quick if you wish to catch up to them!

"We can take the other way, and hopefully that will put them off the track long enough for us to get a fair start," she explained hastily. "I just hope they couldn't tell where my voice was coming from."

"In all this commotion, I doubt it," the Black Knight replied, sounding amused. The entire camp was roused by now. The old chief, torn between relief and renewed anxiety, had come out of his wagon and was adjuring his people to stand by the right, to not go against the sacred values of hospitality and permit these outrages against their erstwhile guests. Although most of the other gypsies were afraid to directly oppose the grandnephew, they still managed to hinder the leader and his band, running to and fro and creating a general disturbance.

"You and I had better take the first horse; you must not be discovered by them above all, and besides, you have to guide us around the traps and away from their pursuit," Pete commanded, grasping Esmeralda around the waist and swinging her up onto one of the horses, immediately springing on behind her.

"I know the shortest way out of this forest, too," Esmeralda replied, gathering up the reins and heading out of the thicket at breakneck speed. They were forced to cross a small open space by the camp before re-entering the main body of the forest, and shouts from the chief's grandnephew's band, who had just begun to cross the stream at the south ford in response to Esmeralda's clever diversion, told them that their movements were discovered. Esmeralda took one look in their direction, cried out in terror, and then she and Pete galloped madly away, into the forest. The other knights leapt upon their own mounts and prepared to follow.

Bernadette found herself standing beside Midnight, with the Black Knight next to her. Their eyes met and he gave her his hand, and then, springing into the saddle and drawing her after him, they were both astride and riding off after their companions.

Bernadette, slipping around on the smooth back ridge of the saddle, gripped the Black Knight's shoulder-sash tightly to keep her balance. Her fellow rider guided his mount with an unerring hand, speeding across the turf without seeming to touch the ground. They were nearly caught up to the others by now.

Then suddenly, out of nowhere it seemed, the ugly, swarthy face of the chief's grandnephew materialized beside them, one enormous scowl as he bore down upon them. Bernadette gasped, and reached for her sword. But the Black Knight was ahead of her; his blade sliced through the air, a silver flash, and neatly unhorsed the outlaw, who fell sprawling into a thorn-bush below, howling with rage.

His band was all around now, but the fall of their leader covered them with confusion. The knights easily beat them back and galloped on. A ways ahead, Pete and Esmeralda called to them to follow.

Bernadette and the Black Knight galloped on, at the rear of the company. But Midnight soon gathered speed and began to overtake the other horses, leaving the sounds of their former pursuers far, far behind. The wind blew through Bernadette's hair; she put up one hand to smooth it back and shifted into a more secure position, thoroughly enjoying the adventure and their triumphant escape, and the pleasure of riding as fast as the wind itself on the loveliest horse to be found anywhere. On and on they galloped into the remnant of the night; those perfectly smooth and swift motions carrying them away to safety.

Chapter Nineteen
Their Own Place

Upon reaching the edge of the forest, the fugitives from the gypsy camp had gone their separate ways. The knights had headed for the nearest village, inviting their deliverers to come along with them; but they had been politely declined. Bernadette had already had her full experience with knights, and she had other vocational plans to pursue. Esmeralda, for her part, was terrified to even remain in the country, where the chief's grandnephew could easily track her down. Therefore, Pete (who didn't care what they did), Bernadette, and Esmeralda purchased their own horses in the next nearest village, crossed the nearby border out of Berklesgilands, and traveled deep into the heart of the neighboring kingdom.

It was here in this new country that the three of them discovered the Midway Inn, a picturesque stopping-place in a pleasant little wayside glen, situated halfway between two villages. The day that they first arrived there, at lunchtime, they were at a crucial point in their travels.

"We can't go much further without cashing in more of our jewels; our gold is practically gone," Pete said, feeling in his half-empty saddlebags. "We need to figure out what our next trade will be, so that we can earn back some of the funds we've spent—or lost," he added significantly.

"I got back all I could; I wish you would stop bringing it up," Esmeralda retorted, tossing her dark hair back indignantly. "Well, then, mastermind, and what is your marvelous proposition for rectifying this sensitive situation? *I* can turn my hand to almost anything; just let me know what it is. We gypsies are generally very handy people, you know." Her eyes sparked with pride not unmixed with scorn, as she turned to fix her gaze on Pete's indifferent countenance.

"Don't ask me; this is Bernie's adventure, as you are well aware," he responded with a shrug. Esmeralda knew all about Pete and Bernadette's identity and mission now; Bernadette had told her, feeling that now that she had joined with them, Esmeralda had a right to know all about what they were doing. Pete had been rather against a full disclosure, but Bernadette had convinced him that there was no feasible way to keep Esmeralda in the dark for long, so it was better to tell her all about it up front. Pete had reluctantly agreed, but had been none too gracious about it to Esmeralda in consequence. But he was never very gracious to her anyway, so it didn't really matter.

So now Esmeralda turned to Bernadette, her brilliant smile flashing in the sunlight. "So, Princess, what do *you* suggest we do? I await your royal commands; what do you desire, Your Highness?" she inquired mischievously. Esmeralda was exceptionally delighted to be traveling with "a real princess," having never encountered one before meeting Bernadette.

Bernadette wrinkled her nose at her. "Maybe we can find employment at the next village; we'll look and see which businesses are hiring. Perhaps we could become bakers or perfumers or even candy-makers; wouldn't that be fun! But for now, why don't we stop for lunch?" she suggested, dismounting before the Midway.

As it turned out, the owners of the Midway, an elderly couple, were tired of running their inn and wanted to sell it and retire to a small farm nearby. Bernadette and Pete, presenting themselves as a young couple out to make their own way in the world, with a small portion of jewels to set them up, offered to purchase the inn for its full worth. The elderly owners were only too happy to accept; and so the bargain was struck then and there, and they still had plenty of their jewels left over.

And therefore, on a bright early autumn morning some time later, Pete was standing on the front step, cheerfully surveying his property and the fine day, with his hands buried satisfactorily in the capacious pockets of his rough breeches underneath his full belted tunic. Even those who knew Pete well would have hardly recognized him in this garb of a prosperous innkeeper, with his hair tousled and broad face sunburnt, observing with great affability and satisfaction the approach of a party of travelers. "Hey, girls," he called, heading back inside to the enormous brick-walled kitchen. "Looks like we may have some new customers! Can you get something hot ready fast?"

Bernadette looked up from where she was sifting flour for biscuits. With her sleeves tucked up above her elbows, wisps of hair just escaping from her tightly wound bun, and a voluminous apron swathing her practical, full-skirted brown dress trimmed in bronze ribbons, she presented the perfect picture of a capable, pleasantly bustling housewife. Few would have made any connection between this competent young woman skillfully working at her dough, and the easily bored, inexperienced Princess Royal of Berklesgilands.

"Certainly, Pete," she replied now, brushing the back of her hand across her hot forehead—the entire kitchen felt like the inside of one of the ovens that lined its walls! "I'll get these biscuits baking, and throw some chops over the fire right away. Essie . . ." she peered inside a bubbling iron cauldron hanging over the fire, "I think it's about time we added the vegetables to the stew; will you run out to the garden and get some, please?"

Esmeralda, as she flitted about the kitchen, storing away the shiny tin cups and utensils she had just dried, in her bright green dress with crimson ribbons, and with her hair flowing loose over her shoulders in spite of her best attempts to keep it tied back, "still looked every inch the gypsy that she was," as Pete never failed to point out, and did so now.

"Well, and why shouldn't I?" she retorted, pausing in the doorway leading out to the garden to look back at him. "I'm not ashamed of it; *I've* got no reason to conceal my identity." With this parting thrust, she departed.

"You really shouldn't tease her so, Pete," Bernadette remonstrated, taking down a crock of pickles and beginning to arrange a plate of nibbles to put out ready for the guests as soon as they came in. "Why do you always have to go out of your way to provoke her? That's not like you." She raised a concerned eyebrow, and when Pete did not respond, added testily, "And you'd be better employed out front, ensuring that our coming guests don't pass us by due to our lack of welcome." She then bustled out into the front hall, with her snack platter in one hand and a freshly sliced loaf of bread and its accompanying crock of butter in the other.

Pete headed out under her reproof, and could soon be heard adjuring the travelers to come in and rest themselves over a hearty lunch. A couple of guests who were already there, in the back parlor, called to Bernadette to please refill their drinks. Bernadette scurried back into the kitchen to fill the mugs, and then hurried back to the parlor with three in each hand, and stayed there for a while, chatting affably with her customers.

Esmeralda, meanwhile, had returned to the kitchen, her apron full of fresh produce. With a flushed face and downcast eyes, her chest heaving with strong emotion, she took down a great butcher knife and began to chop the vegetables with a great deal of energy, as though it were a relief to her feelings.

Outside, Pete had easily convinced the travelers to stop there, and so they all tramped cheerfully in, standing around the front hall, munching pickles and rye bread and putting in extensive orders for a "real luncheon," which sent Bernadette flying back to the kitchen to prepare, while Pete put up the horses.

It was hard work, but worth it! This newest party of arrivals had intended to leave after lunch, but finding their surroundings and the service so pleasant, decided to stay the night. Along with the guests who were already there, and with Pete and Bernadette and Esmeralda mingling pleasantly with their customers, they all spent a cozy evening, with plenty of hot stew and fresh baked pies, singing and joking round the fireplace. And the fun didn't stop after the guests went up to bed; then the three landlords went back to their kitchen, where Pete was playfully forced into service to dry the enormous pile of dishes and mugs that Bernadette washed up in a vast trough of soapsuds, and Esmeralda put away. They chatted merrily while they worked, in subdued tones so as not to disturb their customers, and then went wearily but contentedly off to bed, to be up and working again at dawn the next day.

Innkeeping, Bernadette had soon found, was a hard life, but a very fulfilling one. You always had something to do, and it was in your power to make so many people happy! And you *owned* something. The inn was yours, and the business was yours, and you could keep it up and run it any way you wanted to. The only limit on what you could do was the exceptionally comfortable and sensible limit of having to make people happy with your services, and it was no end of fun to figure out new ways of showing your customers that, so long as they are under your roof, they are the most special people in the world.

It was the exact opposite from palace life. At the palace, while you could technically do whatever you wanted and not concern yourself with whether it made people happy or not, no royal was actually in control of how life was arranged there. There were no end of maddening restrictions and procedures that had to be fulfilled whether they made any sense or made anybody happy or not. The monarch is never really the true ruler of his or her country; the monarchy is, and a monarchy is not something you own, it owns you!

Bernadette was thinking of this one day, as she pulled weeds in the front yard. It was a matter of pride with her that the Midway always looked at its best and most inviting whenever anybody rode up, that people would feel rested and invigorated by the pleasant sight as they passed even if they didn't stop to come in.

It seemed to Bernadette now, as she thought it over, that she had always lived this way. Her time with the gypsies and her adventures as a knight were long ago, madcap escapades that had been fun while they lasted, but could never sustain a full life. And still further back, her former life as a princess was a distant memory, classed with the fairy-tale, impractical dreams of childhood. It would never have worked, her becoming a queen someday! Nonsense! Bernadette was well aware that there were still other professions that she might look into, but why do that when you have already found the one that suits you perfectly? That would be akin to meeting your true love, and then leaving him dangling until you had courted everyone else in town!

So, taking one thing with another, Bernadette had just about made up her mind that at the end of the year, she was going to return just long enough to resign the throne to Roxanne, and then immediately return to her chosen life's work, insisting that the entire Royal Family come along and stay at her inn for a long, well-deserved vacation. She was blissfully planning how she would arrange the flowers in her mother's room, and how proud her father would be to see what a splendid set-up she could provide, when a voice near at hand called her back from her happy day-dreams to reality.

"Good day to you, maiden, and are there any rooms available at this inn for tonight?" It was an exceptionally cultured voice that spoke: a voice that signified a valuable and worthy customer.

"Yes, indeed," Bernadette exclaimed, leaping to her feet and brushing grass-stems off her skirt, and turning businesslike all at once. "Our best room was vacated just this morning, after being held for a week. Nearly all the other rooms are taken, but if you do not object to company in the dining-room and about the fire of an evening, it is in our power to make you comfortable for as long as you might wish to stay . . ." her voice suddenly trailed off and she forgot all the other pleasant and inviting words she had intended to say to this prospective guest, upon raising her eyes to his face. The young man who stood before her, with the halter of his horse, a fine black mare, wrapped carelessly about his arm, his dark eyes fixed intently upon her and a slight smile of amusement at her warmly professional reception just touching his lips, was a young man she knew only too well—it was, in a word, the Black Knight himself!

"Well, in that case, I suppose I will take the room, then," he said graciously, after waiting for Bernadette to make any further remarks, which at the moment she was quite unable to do. "Have you a groom who will take my horse and see that she is well rubbed down and fed? We have had a long ride out here, and I am sure that she is more weary than I am," he said, rubbing Midnight's nose with the affection of a good master. Midnight whinnied appreciatively.

Bernadette clenched her teeth, a hot flash of jealousy getting the better of her momentary paralysis. "I can take your horse; if you will go through the front door here and call for the landlord Hugh, my brother, he will see you comfortably established in your room." For their disguises here at the inn, the three of them had taken other names: Pete, as just now mentioned, went by Hugh; Bernadette was Gertrude, or Gertie for short; and Esmeralda was known to their customers as Bertha. As for the matter of relationship, it required much fewer explanations for Pete and Bernadette to just call themselves brother and sister, which they had always practically considered themselves anyway.

"I thank you, maiden," and the Black Knight bowed and withdrew. Bernadette did not look after him as she led Midnight away to the stable behind the inn, but she could hear his boots clumping up the front steps and heading into the front hall, and then his energetic, hearty voice calling good-humoredly for "Hugh! Hugh, my worthy landlord, if I might have speech with you?"

"How did this happen?" Bernadette stopped short in the stable doorway and stared bewilderedly at Midnight, who tossed her graceful head, as much as to say, "Don't ask me; *I* had nothing to do with it, indeed no!"

Bernadette patted her neck and led her into the best stall, pouring fresh water into her trough and kneeling down next to her to rub her sweaty legs clean with a towel. "I'm glad to see *you*, at any rate, my beauty. But still, what an unfortunate coincidence this is, you must agree with me?" She lifted her head and peered anxiously out the stable window towards the inn. "I don't believe he recognized me—why would he, in this outfit and these surroundings, where you'd never expect to find a runaway gypsy girl or a disguised knight. I just hope he doesn't recognize Pete, and that Pete will have the sense to keep him thoroughly in the dark. Somehow, Midnight, I just don't trust that man." She patted her beloved equine friend one last time before hurrying back towards the inn kitchen, wiping her hands on her apron and walking far more slowly as she neared the building.

"Where's Bernie?" she could hear Pete haranguing Esmeralda about the million and one things that needed to be done today, what with new distinguished customers coming in and all, and how they couldn't possibly be done unless she told him where Bernadette was. Esmeralda, with characteristic impudence, was informing him that if he would kindly lower himself so far as to inform *her* of what it was that needed to be done, he might find to his astonishment that she was perfectly capable of doing it!

"You might need to sit down first, though; I don't fancy having you faint dead away from shock on my just-polished floor," she added mockingly, rubbing her cloth over the last of the tiles and rising to face Pete, when they were both diverted from their wranglings by Bernadette's entrance.

"Hullo, Gertie!" Esmeralda greeted her exuberantly. "Guess who's here! That handsome fellow who stayed that night at our camp and ran off with us in that daring midnight escape of ours, remember him?"

"Of course I do; I let him in, worse luck!" Bernadette responded, scowling. "The question that's more to the point right now is: did *he* remember *you*, or any of us?"

"I don't think so," Esmeralda replied, puzzled. She was not aware of Bernadette's antagonism towards the Black Knight. "He didn't seem to know you, did he, Pete? And of course he would be even less likely to recognize me, as I only met him once. But there's nothing stopping us from telling him, of course . . ."

"We'll do nothing of the kind!" Bernadette snapped. "And we're getting out of here the first minute we can. Until then, any services he may demand will be your responsibility, Essie, since as you say, he has had the least contact with you and so there's less danger of his realizing who we are if you wait on him instead of me. If he recognizes me and Pete as the same two he met, first in the guise of knights, and then as captive peasants at the gypsy camp, and now as innkeepers, he's bound to get suspicious. And I can't have him learning who I really am."

"Don't see why you should care if he knows; you didn't mind telling Essie," Pete remarked sagely, from where he was lounging carelessly against the wall by the oven, his wide sleeve in imminent danger of being caught by the occasional spurting flames.

"That was a different matter entirely! Even you should be able to see that!" Bernadette shot back indignantly, putting her arm defensively around Esmeralda's shoulders. "Essie is one of us, our *friend*! That outrageous Black Knight is a total stranger, and a most disobliging stranger at that! He stole my horse, remember?"

"You still haven't gotten over that?" Pete asked, laughing. "Now, really, Bernie, do be reasonable. We can't just pack up and go because we've gotten one customer that you happen to feel a personal resentment towards. If he bothers you all that much, Bertha here and your humble servant Hugh will attend to all his needs with pleasure. You needn't worry about it."

"But I am worried! I don't want him to discover who we are; we need to get out of here before he figures anything out!" Bernadette reiterated frantically.

"And how do you suggest we do that? Just leave the inn to run itself, with all our customers still in it, and take their money and go? Hardly what I'd call ethical," Pete observed.

"Will you be quiet, for a change?" Esmeralda hissed at him. "Or is that too much to ask of you? I'm sure we can think of something, Bernadette, dear."

"Maybe the couple we bought the inn from are bored with having nothing to do in retirement, and would want to buy their old place back," Bernadette suggested hopefully, but was immediately disheartened by Pete's cynical snort. "But surely someone would be willing to buy the Midway; it's such a fine inn! And requires hardly any work; we've kept it up so well. What about that couple who were thinking of buying property in the next village, since they couldn't find any around here? Or that current guest of ours, the traveling merchant's son? He might think it a good investment; I'll go talk to him about it right now." Bernadette prepared to decamp from the kitchen.

"Beggin' yer pardon, but is anyone in?" inquired a nasally voice from the kitchen-garden door. The three friends turned swiftly around to see a wizened little man peering in at them, a sizeable pack on his back. "Is dish-yer a public-house, or some such sort?" he pursued earnestly, fixing his beady eyes on first Bernadette, then Pete, and finally Esmeralda.

"Why, yes, it is," Bernadette replied hospitably, pushing quickly past the others to take charge of this new situation. "I am sorry that you had to come around to this door to find anyone to give you service! Can we accommodate you with a meal or a room for the night, perhaps?" She smiled in her most welcoming fashion, although at this moment it cost her a great effort and felt decidedly fake.

"That might be right nice, missus," the little man replied, shifting his pack. "But I come to dish-yer door because I'm no fine high-riding payin' guest; I'm a common peddler, and me family with me. If you'd care to look at my wares and see what you might wish to buy, I'd be right happy to accept pay in the form of room and board for me and me family for the night, if that's how you'd like to arrange it. Or you can pay in coin or barter other goods; it's all one to me," he finished with a deep breath and mopped his face with a handkerchief almost as large as he was. He obviously wasn't accustomed to making long speeches. "*Would* you care to inspect me goods?" he reiterated earnestly. "Wanting to buy anything pertickular today?"

"Yes; we'd be more than happy to buy *all* your goods," Bernadette responded promptly, a full-fledged plan presenting itself immediately to her active brain, "and we'll sell our inn to you in trade. How would you like to settle down and own your own place instead of having to tramp all over creation for the rest of your life?" she proposed enthusiastically.

"Well, I'd have to ask the missus and me girl," replied the peddler, shifting his pack once again. He seemed disposed to consider the suggestion favorably, however, and turned to speak with a withered little middle-aged woman, with a kindly but tired face, who stood behind him on the step. After a brief conference, it was positively concluded that the peddler's wife would be only too happy to settle down permanently, and thought it would be quite a good thing for their girl, a well-built lass of about twenty, who was standing a little ways down the garden path, waiting for her parents to make arrangements.

And so the peddler and his family became the new landlords of the Midway, and after a quick briefing on how to run an inn, with specific instructions concerning their present guests, Pete, Bernadette, and

Esmeralda left the owners to the management of their property and slipped up to their rooms to pack and change into clothes more suitable for traveling, heavy broadcloth attire and full-length cloaks. Then, repairing once again to the ground floor, they bade farewell to the former peddler and his family, gathered up their new wares, and departed. What the guests at the Midway thought when they found out at dinner-time that their current lodging-place had just been entirely turned over to new management, was never discovered.

"I know nobody else here wants to hear my opinion . . ." Pete began, as the three of them began to trudge away down the road leading to the next village.

"You're right, we don't!" Bernadette effectively silenced her cousin, who could only, after that, muster up the bravado to mutter to himself that he still thought it was a foolish and far too hasty maneuver.

Bernadette turned her head and looked back at the Midway as it sat proudly beside the road, looking so homey and delightful in the warm glow of the sunshine. It was hard to leave behind the one place that she had been able to call and enjoy as completely her own, and she kept looking back at it until a turn in the path hid it entirely, although unshed tears had already obscured her view.

Chapter Twenty
Turning Homeward

Winter had passed and spring had come again. Bernadette and Pete and Esmeralda were still journeying onward, now heading for the seacoast, where Bernadette's uncle, her mother's brother Theodore, governed a small independent principality. Bernadette was very fond of "Uncle Ted," as she called him, and so the three of them naturally stopped to pay him a visit.

Uncle Ted's domain may have been little, but it was extremely wealthy. Uncle Ted's palace by the sea was one of the most opulent and tastefully decorated on the continent—all his serving plates were rimmed with gold and each window was draped in silk and every master-painted ceiling of the many spacious rooms was held up by solid marble pillars. Uncle Ted was a cheery old bachelor, but he had more than half-a-dozen wards living with him, jolly boys and girls, who were always ready to give and take part in a splendid time for their "cousin" and other guests.

Esmeralda was in a state of constant shock and rapture at Uncle Ted's. She had never before seen luxury such as the fairy-tale elegance and sweet comforts of his palace. Esmeralda could hardly believe that she was really allowed to wear the silken gowns provided for her and Bernadette, play with ivory chess sets, and dine on poached eggs and salads that were arranged like works of art on the plate. She was so hesitantly curious and awe-struck about everything, that it was really almost laughable. No one did laugh at her though—except for Pete, who seemed to take a certain provoking delight in exposing her ignorance of the behaviors of polite society. Fortunately, Uncle Ted and his wards were the type who cared more about people than perfect etiquette, and Bernadette protected and taught Esmeralda as much about upper-class protocol as she knew. Watching her fascination with it made it much more enjoyable for Bernadette herself, to be wearing fancy gowns and crooking her little finger over her teacup again.

And so the time wore pleasantly away, until it was time for them to return home to the Kingdom of Berklesgilands, if they were to arrive within the allotted time for Bernadette to make her decision. She, Esmeralda, and Pete bade farewell to Uncle Ted and his crowd of cheerful charges, and set out once again.

Now they were traveling as a middle-class merchant's children— that is, Pete and Bernadette were. Esmeralda was going along as Bernadette's supposed lady's maid (the middle-class version of a lady-in-waiting).

But as they drew nearer to the border of Berklesgilands, they began to hear some disturbing rumors, which increased in frequency and certainty, the closer they got to the border. Apparently, while Pete and Bernadette had been out of the country, the Kingdom of Berklesgilands had been attacked and had gone to war with the largest neighboring realm.

"Well, we just need to get back all the faster then, so we can help in the war, now that I know how to fight." That was Bernadette's view on the situation.

"What you don't seem to understand, Bernie," Pete argued, "is how we are to get back at all, let alone fast. If they are fighting along the border, as the rumors we've heard would indicate, we won't be able to get through. Civilians are not allowed to travel through war zones."

"There's got to be some place where we can get through; I don't believe half these rumors, anyway," Bernadette returned doggedly.

"I'm not going to risk it; not now that I have *two* girls to look after," Pete retorted, with just that hint of scorn in his voice that always jarred considerably on both Bernadette and Esmeralda.

"We'll look after ourselves, then!" Esmeralda entered the conversation, an indignant tone in her voice. "Besides, even if the armies are fighting along the border, they are certainly not fighting up in the High Ranges of the Border Mountains. Why shouldn't we cross back into the country that way?"

"Good grief, Esmeralda! Talk about risk! You're right; the armies won't be fighting there, and why? Because it's such dangerous and precipitous terrain, no one travels there," Pete responded, turning his mount in through the open yard-gate of the village inn that they had just reached.

"Have you actually forgotten, Sir Peter, that yours truly is a *gypsy*?" Esmeralda demanded with more than a little sarcasm, as she dismounted, disdaining his offer of assistance. "I'm more at home in the tops of the mountains than anywhere else except the forest, and the rockier the better. I can travel through there, and guide the two of you with perfect ease as well."

"Thank you; I don't fancy committing myself to your care," Pete responded curtly, turning to go into the inn. "I'm going to ask around, Bernie, and find out the exact truth about these rumors. Maybe there will be a place we can get through, after all," he said over his shoulder as he went.

"Just a minute! What did you mean by that? So you don't think that I could . . ." Esmeralda followed Pete into the building, from whence the sound of their voices raised in heated argument soon issued.

Bernadette did not go in. She gave their horses into the care of one of the stable-boys, and then wandered about the inn-yard, where there were a few people lounging around on barrels and chatting comfortably together. Bernadette half-listened to their conversations, to see if she could pick up any news about the war, but she didn't feel inclined to join in the talk herself.

To tell the truth, Bernadette was a little upset about the situation. She had enjoyed the adventures along her journey more than she could have ever expressed, but by now she was tired of the constant excitement and upheaval. And she was lonely. Bernadette loved Pete and Esmeralda dearly, but she missed the rest of her family and friends terribly. She couldn't bear to think that this war might keep her away from them for still longer. Afraid that she might give way to tears, and not wishing anyone to observe her, Bernadette leaned against a corner of the inn wall, at a distance from any of the idlers and stable-boys, and closed her eyes to better concentrate on her thoughts.

She was day-dreaming about the welcome they would get once they reached home, and wondering who would come to meet them first, when a voice at her elbow said, "Excuse me, miss, but my master asked me to tie this horse out here to graze in the sun."

Bernadette turned to see one of the stable-boys looking anxiously up at her, holding a black horse by the bridle and gesturing at an iron ring set into the corner where Bernadette was leaning.

"Oh, of course!" Bernadette moved over so that the boy could tie the horse to the ring, settling herself against the wall a little further down. As the boy walked off, the horse turned its head and looked inquiringly at Bernadette for a moment, before daintily stretching its neck down to munch on the nearby grass.

Bernadette gasped. "Midnight, is it you?" She ran around to the front of the animal and bent down to look at the noble forehead, marked with that unmistakable star.

"Oh, Midnight, how wonderful to see you!" Bernadette rushed to hug the mare about the neck. "How are you, my beauty? I guess you must live here now; the stable boy said he was putting you out here for his master, who would be the innkeeper. I wonder—we have to trade in our horses now if we are going any further; maybe I can trade for you! Oh, I will! Won't it be a wonderful end to my adventures, to ride home on you." She leaned her head against Midnight's warm side, patting her neck with one hand, while she held out a bunch of grass with the other, which Midnight took appreciatively.

"I see you are admiring my horse, maiden!" a nearby voice exclaimed heartily, all of a sudden. "And she is well worth it indeed, isn't she?" The Black Knight stepped up beside her and began stroking Midnight's neck as well. "I have owned many fine animals in my life, but none that ever compared to this mare. I would not trade her for a king's ransom in gold." He then turned and looked over at Bernadette, who was still standing there, stunned, with her hand frozen on Midnight's neck. He took in her fine clothes at a glance. "Traveling with that large party inside, maiden?" he queried conversationally.

"No, I'm just with my brother and my maid," Bernadette replied, shortly. The other looked at her somewhat quizzically, but then smiled and turned away to continue stroking Midnight. Bernadette felt uncomfortable; maybe she should have kept on with being Pete's cousin. But then they had acted as brother and sister at the inn, and the Black Knight had seen them there, too—oh, it was far too confusing, having to keep track of all your various disguises just for the sake of one annoying, constantly recurring intruder! It was on the tip of her tongue to inquire whether "he made it his life's business to follow her around," when his next remark fortunately stopped that in its tracks.

"Ah, but you are still strangers in town? So am I; just stopping over on my way to my next assignment. And who are you, and where are you from, and whither are you bound for?" he asked, raising a dark eyebrow in friendly inquiry. "Too many questions at once?" he went on, smiling affably down at her when she made no immediate reply. "Well, I'll start with one, then. What is your name, fair maiden?"

Bernadette's mind was still in a whirl. She didn't want to give him her real name. But what should she call herself? This may not seem like it should have been so difficult for her; after all, Bernadette was well accustomed to disguising herself by now. But it is quite one thing to disguise yourself from people who wouldn't know you in any case, and entirely another to meet someone you knew under one identity, and pretend immediately to be someone else. It almost seemed dishonest. But she had to tell him something before she could civilly withdraw.

"My name is Cecilia," she said hastily. Bernadette had just been hoping that her favorite door-porter Cecil would be on duty when she arrived home; it seemed rather a tribute to him to take his name on this occasion.

"And mine is Sir Colin," the Black Knight replied pleasantly, even though Bernadette had not remembered her manners so far as to ask his name.

"Pleased to meet you," Bernadette said reluctantly, seeing that some kind of response was expected of her, and feeling more deceitful than ever. She *wasn't* pleased, and this wasn't the first time they had met, either.

"Likewise." Sir Colin bowed, and returned his focus to Midnight, stroking her nose. Midnight didn't seem too happy about his attention, as it interfered with her dinner, and she whinnied impatiently. Her owner laughed. "I guess she wants us to leave her alone, eh, you unsociable animal?" he remarked lightly, patting her one last time. "Shall I see you inside, Maiden Cecilia?"

"That won't be necessary; I'm not going in," Bernadette returned bluntly, turning her back on him. It didn't occur to her to even thank him for the offer. He didn't appear to mind that, however, and immediately bowed and withdrew. He headed inside the inn, calling greetings to several of those around as he went.

Bernadette wandered about the yard again in a daze. Now what? Well, they'd just have to move on again, making sure to take a different path than the Black Knight, or Sir Colin, or whatever he called himself. But what if the war prevented them from moving on at all? Would they be stuck here at this inn along with the Black Knight until it was all over? And who knew how long that would be. Bernadette was seriously depressed by the time Pete and Esmeralda came out of the inn and rejoined her, back petting Midnight again. That beautiful horse was her only comfort at the moment.

"Hey, Bernie!" Pete was now far more cheerful than his cousin. "What've you been doing all this time? I thought you'd be coming in."

"Well, I didn't," Bernadette returned, scowling. "And please don't call me Bernie here, Pete; I'm Cecilia now."

"Yes, so I've heard!" Pete laughed. "The Black Knight's here."

"I saw him." Bernadette looked up, alarmed. Had he recognized her after all? Or Pete?

"He came up to me in the bar, and asked whether I were the brother of Maiden Cecilia, whom he had met in the front yard. Said we looked alike." Pete's eyes were brimful of merriment. "I caught on to the act quick enough, and said, yes, I was; and I gave him the whole rundown on our being the son and daughter of a wealthy merchant, traveling back together from a trading trip I had been on for our father. So everything's settled so far as he's concerned, and now we all know what we're playing at right now."

"I gave my name as Violetta," Esmeralda jumped in, giving Pete a black look, "since I remembered you didn't want him to know our real names. Pete still said he was Peter, though, but that's a common enough name so that we don't have to worry about it. What's wrong, Ber—Cecilia; did we overlook something important?"

"No, no," Bernadette replied crossly, tracing lines in the dirt with her foot. "I just—I don't want to be around him, whether he figures out who we are or not. Can we leave tonight?"

"Where for?" Pete leaned back comfortably against the wall. "That's the bad news I have for you, Bernie. The entire traversable border is a warfront now; we can't get through, nor expect to for at least another couple months or more."

"But that's too late! We have to get back into Berklesgilands before then if we are to make it home in the allotted time," Bernadette protested, desperately.

"Sorry, Bernie; we're just going to have to wait. Uncle will understand why we're getting back late; and believe me, he'd rather have us return after the intended date than never return at all because we were killed or captured going through the battle lines."

"Which leaves us with three options; or actually, only two," Esmeralda picked up the thread of the conversation. "One was to stay here until the war's over, but obviously that's not going to work, unless the Black Knight leaves for somewhere else. Or we could go back to your Uncle Ted's for a while; I'd like that—don't you say anything, Pete!" she frowned indignantly at his mocking expression. "Or else, of course, since Pete has such an aversion to traveling over the mountains, you and I could go alone together over the High Ranges; *I* know we could make it, and Pete can do what he pleases, go join the war effort or whatever." She shot another scathing glance in his direction, and moved over to stand next to Bernadette, linking her arm through hers.

"Oh, what a pair you two make, to be sure!" Pete laughed, but there was a ring of irritation to the sound. "A couple of Babes in the Woods! I'd just like to see you, trying to make it alone over the mountains!"

"So you think I've learned absolutely nothing from all my experiences?" Bernadette demanded indignantly. "I beg leave to differ from you. I can take care of myself now, thank you, as you may one day discover to your discomfiture. Now, go back inside and find out whether or not that Black Knight fellow is staying on here or not, and Esmeralda and I will make plans." She waved her hand in dismissal, and she and Esmeralda turned to walk up and down the yard together. Pete turned to go inside, and then glanced back at them, absorbed in earnest discussion, and smiled at the pretty picture they made.

Bernadette and Esmeralda sent inside to have their meal brought out to them, and then perched precariously on top of the inn stable fence while they ate, balancing their plates on their laps and discussing their options. Bernadette did not want to backtrack to Uncle Ted's; but at the same time, she wasn't sure that she and Esmeralda could convince Pete to remain behind while they went over the mountains by themselves. And Esmeralda was certain that if Pete came with them, he would spoil the entire venture just to show them that they were incapable of it and that he had been right all along. Bernadette had a slightly better opinion of her cousin's priorities than that; but the question was, would he ever agree to go through the High Ranges? They still had reached no conclusion when Pete came out of the inn again and headed towards them, accompanied by and chatting harmoniously with the Black Knight.

Bernadette looked up, sighed impatiently, and slipped down off the fence. She wanted to be prepared to face this fellow standing up, at least! Esmeralda got down after her and took her plate, preparing to carry them both inside as her position as a maid dictated.

"No, don't go in yet, Essie," Bernadette whispered, grabbing her by the arm as she turned to go. "I want you here for moral support. Oh, *why* did Pete have to bring him out!"

"He would; what did you expect?" Esmeralda said vindictively, standing staunchly by Bernadette's side, and facing the two newcomers with anything but an inviting countenance.

Pete did not appear to notice. "Hello, girls!" he said breezily. "I've got good news now! We can travel over the mountains after all!"

"What made you change your mind?" Bernadette asked uncertainly, glancing from her cousin to the other young man standing before her, and then back again.

The two young men exchanged glances, and then faced the suspicious girls sturdily. "Because Sir Colin here—" Pete indicated him with his hand, as that gentleman bowed in acknowledgment—"has kindly agreed to travel with us. So I won't be one fellow with two girls to look after; you'll both have a protector in case of emergency."

"We don't need protection!" Bernadette exclaimed hotly. "And besides, Essie and I haven't decided yet that that is the best plan."

"Well, if you don't want to get back in time, that's no concern of mine," Pete rejoined indifferently, turning as if to go back into the inn. "Come on, Colin; we'll let them think it over for a while. You know what girls are like."

"No, wait." This was a very bitter pill to swallow, but Bernadette knew that Pete was right. She hesitated, glanced at Esmeralda, who nodded reluctantly, and finally turned back to the two young men, who stood waiting patiently for what she would say. "So there is no other way that we can convince you to travel through the mountain passes, Pete?" she made one last effort, imploringly.

"What, do you object to my company, Maiden Cecilia?" Sir Colin inquired in a booming, jovial voice, grinning at her so infectiously that no one could have found the heart to say they did.

"No, of course not," Bernadette replied miserably. Yet another forced falsehood!

"It's settled then! We'll stay here tonight, and tomorrow we'll be merrily on our way! Come on inside, girls," Pete turned to lead the way back in, with Sir Colin still at his side.

"Merrily indeed," Bernadette muttered, trading despairing glances with Esmeralda as they followed. A life of constant deception, like this, definitely was not one that appealed to her.

Chapter Twenty-one
On Top of the High Ranges

"Whew, it's cold as December up here!" Pete took off his helmet, wrapped his scarf around his head, and pulled his helmet back down firmly over it, tucking in the ends.

"Of course, at this high of an altitude; what else did you expect?" Esmeralda inquired acidly, steering her mount capably around a pile of loose stones. She was unquestionably the most skilled at this form of travel. The cold wind and occasional showers of snow on the tops of the Border Mountains did not deter her at all.

Bernadette, riding behind her with bowed head, shrunken within her wraps, was not finding the trek so easy. But not for worlds would she have complained; Pete and Colin lorded it over them enough without their showing any demonstrations of weakness! Neither one of them had yet admitted that Esmeralda was the best mountaineer of them all, or let her take the lead. Right now, Pete was leading and Colin was bringing up the rear, just behind Bernadette. She glanced back at him now, sitting up straight and tall astride Midnight, and he caught her glance and smiled amiably at her. She quickly turned her head back into the biting wind, and rode on ahead, putting as much space between their horses as she could.

She passed Esmeralda, and caught up to Pete. "Let me ride first, will you?" she demanded in exasperation, pulling her cloak tightly about her shoulders. "*I'm* the one who has someplace to go; why should you be the navigator? You don't know the way through these mountains better than any of the rest of us, so why can't you let someone else take the lead occasionally?"

"I do; Colin led the group all morning," Pete responded, without looking at her.

"He doesn't count!" Bernadette hissed, immediately infuriated.

"Oh, right, I forgot, *he* isn't one of us; Esmeralda is," Pete replied, ironically. Bernadette had insisted that Pete and Esmeralda agree to a solemn pact to never reveal their true identity to anyone under any circumstances, *especially* not to Colin! For some inexplicable reason, this made Bernadette feel less dishonest about the whole matter.

"You're right, he isn't one of us!" Bernadette retorted angrily. "This is *my* adventure, as Father made quite clear to you before we even started, and you had no right to involve other people without my approval."

"On the contrary, I have a perfect right, which Uncle assigned to me, to ensure that your plans are carried out in a manner best consistent with your safety and interests," Pete returned quietly, refusing to let her anger arouse his. "I *could not* have guided you girls through this terrain by myself, which is why I had to ask Colin to accompany us. If you won't believe what I am or am not capable of accomplishing, there is nothing further I can say to convince you."

"I perfectly believe that you are not capable of protecting two defenseless maidens in a wilderness!" Bernadette shot back instantly. "But what *you* refuse to be convinced of, is that Esmeralda and I are not defenseless, and would be perfectly capable of making our way through here under any circumstances, with or without you and certainly without Sir Colin!"

"I already know what you both are capable of; you don't have to convince me of anything," Pete responded coolly.

"Oh!" Bernadette furiously turned her horse away, and rode back to Esmeralda. "It's useless to try to talk with either of them; we'll have to make do the best we can, and just depend on each other for company and understanding, Essie," she told her in a low aside. "I'm not even speaking to Pete just now. It's so infuriating, that we can't even be involved in our own travel plans or arrangements—why, what's the matter, Essie; are you crying?" she asked in surprise, gazing into her friend's downcast face.

Esmeralda straightened up and quickly drew the back of her hand across her eyes. "Yes, I am, a little," she acknowledged candidly. "It's very hard to return to your old home, and yet not be able to make yourself at home. I'm a mountain woodland girl, you know, Bernadette; this is the kind of life I know: climbing rocks, braving the cold, hearing the wind in the pine trees—everything that's wild and beautiful! And I was so happy to think that we would be going through here on our return journey, but it's just not the same. I can't enjoy this journey like I used to enjoy the ones with my caravan; it's no fun at all."

"It's no fun for me, either! I understand you perfectly, Essie," Bernadette replied, her heart aching with sympathy for her essentially homeless friend. "You should be the one leading this part of the journey. It's very unfair and wrong of Pete and that Sir Colin not to let you." She frowned blackly into the fog ahead.

"What makes it even more annoying," Esmeralda responded, still keeping her voice low so that the boys wouldn't overhear their complaints, "is that the further we get up into the mountains, the more obvious it is to me how little the two of them know about mountain navigation. I mean, it's not like we're going to get lost or fall down in a rockslide or starve to death or anything; but if they would only listen to me, instead of insisting on leading the entire trip their own way, we could journey much faster and more easily." She tossed her head and shrugged impatiently.

"Exactly," Bernadette agreed despairingly, and the two girls fell silent as they continued to ride along, further up into the High Ranges. They had been traveling for five days now, and were still far from the central summit.

After a while, Bernadette glanced anxiously up at the sky, which was growing increasingly dark and lowering. The dripping fog was all around them now, and the chill in the air was intense. "The weather doesn't look too good, Essie," she remarked presently.

"No, it doesn't, at that," agreed Colin, who had ridden closely up behind them unawares. "Hey, Pete," he called to their present leader. "Don't you think we ought to stop now and make some kind of shelter? Looks like a storm is coming up."

"So now *he'll* get all the credit for having noticed, when it was really me!" Bernadette grumbled to Esmeralda, who nodded and looked daggers at both Colin and Pete, who had ridden back to join them. The group huddled closely together, attempting to screen themselves from the bitter wind.

"I'd agree; it's getting almost too dark to see our way now, especially since the path leads down into a gorge, too dangerous to attempt in this fog. However, this isn't a very good place for making any kind of shelter," Pete remarked, glancing around at the rocky surroundings. "But maybe there's something else nearby. Suppose we make a lean-to and build a fire, and then you and I can go looking for something more stable, while the girls stay here by the path." Colin nodded his agreement.

"Why do *you* get to go searching, while we just sit around and do nothing?" Bernadette demanded, immediately up in arms against any plan that the two of them might propose. "I think we should all go; that way we can split into two parties and cover more ground faster."

"But someone ought to stay by the path," Pete explained patiently— as though he were talking to a child, Bernadette observed crossly to herself. "Besides, it's already starting to sleet, and so you girls should stay warm by the fire while we fellows continue braving the elements! And you could have dinner ready for us by the time we got back," he continued, dismounting and beginning to gather wood for the lean-to and fire.

"Is that all we're good for?" Bernadette inquired resentfully, ignoring Colin's outstretched hand and climbing ungracefully down from her own mount. "Just to make dinner in a sheltered environment, while you have all the fun and gain all the rewards and praise?" she added venomously, bending down to pick up a few sticks of her own.

"I don't think that there's any greater merit to finding a sturdier shelter than to making dinner for all of us," Colin returned, sounding a little surprised by her attitude. "They're *both* equally essential to our success in our journey. I should think you'd be proud of it."

"Well, I'm not!" Esmeralda grabbed a log that Pete had just placed on top of the lean-to and replaced it in another position. "Don't you know anything about building proper shelters, Pete? That's not the way at all; I tried to show you yesterday. Why don't you ever listen to me?"

"Because I know how to do it just as well as you do, or better," Pete retorted. "See, the wind's blowing through that gap where you placed it; I had it right before." He moved the log back.

"I hadn't finished!" Esmeralda raged. "Of course I was going to chink it. You never give me a chance to show what I can do, and . . ."

"Here now, we don't have time to quarrel," Colin interposed mildly. "Let me take your horse with the rest, Maiden Cecilia, and would you get the fire going?"

Gripping her horse's halter tighter, Bernadette demanded, crossly: "Why can't I put up the horses, and you tend to the fire?"

"Of course you *could*; but as matters stand now, it makes better sense if you *wouldn't*," Colin retorted with his usual cheerful lack of comprehension. "I've already got all of the other horses; why should we trade jobs? Just let me have the halter, will you?" He took it from her reluctant hand, and carelessly turned to lead the horses into the nearest thicket.

Bernadette stared regretfully after Midnight as Colin led her away, disappointment and indignation coursing through her veins. Colin somehow managed it so that she never had an opportunity to care for the horses; thus, her chances to pet Midnight were extraordinarily infrequent. She resented this more than anything else. But there was nothing to be done about it, so she knelt down to kindle the fire before the lean-to, which, in spite of their wranglings, Pete and Esmeralda had managed to raise into a decent structure by this time.

The four of them gathered under the shelter, with everyone except Colin trying to avoid sitting next to everybody else, while staying as close to the fire as possible. Bernadette silently passed around a snack of bread and cheese from one of her bags; and while they ate, the boys planned their search for a more permanent form of shelter, and the girls listened and burned inside with indignation and jealousy. The bread stuck in Bernadette's throat; she was too angry even to eat.

"I'm not hungry, and we need to save our rations; so unless anybody else wants it, I'll go over to the horses and pack mine away," she said, rising to go.

"I'd be glad to eat it if you don't, my little blind one," Colin answered, smiling up at her and reaching for the remainder of the sandwich. Bernadette let him have it and sat back down again, on the other side of the lean-to. No matter how hard she tried to avoid Colin, he was always there in her way! And his familiar way of calling her by the literal definition of her assumed name, Cecilia, was almost too much to be borne. When a girl makes it clear to a man that she does not like him and wants to stay out of his way, he should not behave so personally towards her!

Once they had finished eating, the boys prepared to go. "I'm sure the horses are rested by now. Keep the fire up high, girls; it's getting colder every minute. Whew, listen to that wind!" Pete buttoned his cloak closer and shook his head, as another limb was torn from the back of the lean-to. "We're in for a bad storm. We definitely need to find a more solid shelter, so come on, hurry, Colin!"

"If you'd just let *us* come and help . . ." Bernadette began, disagreeably.

"No, Bernie; we've already settled that you stay here. Just have something warm ready for us when we come back, which might not be for several hours, and that will be plenty good enough."

"*You* settled it, not us!" Bernadette retorted fiercely. "And I'm getting good and tired of you boys acting so all-knowing and superior to me and Es—Violetta all the time! We're just as good as you!"

"We never said you weren't," Colin returned, settling his black helmet more securely. "Come on, Pete." He headed for the thicket.

"And don't rebuild the lean-to while we're gone, either, Esmeralda! You've plenty to do without that," was Pete's parting thrust as he followed his comrade.

"Oh!" Esmeralda leaped to her feet, her face burning bright red. "I'm not your slave, Sir Peter! Who do you think you are, telling me what I can and cannot do? I'll jolly well do as I please; you have no control over me!"

"You are traveling under my protection; let's not forget that," Pete reminded her significantly, over his shoulder. He disappeared into the thicket, and the sound of hooves a moment later told the girls that the two young men had departed.

Bernadette and Esmeralda sat in silence for a while, staring dismally into the fire. As it began to burn lower, Bernadette sighed and shifted her weight. "Guess we might as well build up the fire," she said wearily, getting up to take a few more logs off the stack they had piled inside the lean-to.

"No, don't; let it burn all the way down," Esmeralda returned quickly, in a low tone, as she continued staring into the flames. Her eyes were intense, and she was evidently thinking very deeply about something.

"How can we make dinner, then?" Bernadette asked, staring at her curiously. She could tell that Esmeralda was up to something.

"We're not going to." Esmeralda got up, dusting off her skirt. "We're going to go look for a better shelter ourselves! I know I could find one before they do; they don't know where to look in these wilds. They can just make their own dinner!" She kicked clods of dirt over the glowing coals to smother them. "There; it won't burn up again now, but they can easily replenish it when they get back, having failed in their mission. And then we will come back, with a new warm, secure shelter all ready to lead them to! Then maybe they'll appreciate us a little more!"

"Let's do it!" Bernadette cried, fired with enthusiasm. "You're sure you know how to find a good place?"

"Nothing easier," Esmeralda replied, scornfully. "They went quite the wrong way; I can tell by the pattern of wear on these stones, and the sound of the river, that we'll find caves down there. As good as houses! But it'll be a tough journey, even now that the fog's lifted. However, *I* don't shirk from difficulty, if it's the quickest and surest means to success." She tossed her dark head up high.

"All right!" Bernadette was delighted at this opportunity to prove herself. "And you'll teach me all about the wilderness signs and how to use them, Essie, along the way?"

"What are friends for?" Esmeralda swung gaily astride her mount.

"Then let's go!" The two girls headed off together, not riding on the path, but taking a steeper, rockier way down into the gorge. It was faster, but also far more slippery. Bernadette felt nervous, but she gamely followed Esmeralda's lead. That young maiden was supremely comfortable and confident; she had traversed more precipitous passages than these before.

The sleet and rain were coming down in torrents; but Esmeralda seemed to know her way by instinct down the mountainside, turning her mount ever so slightly to navigate apparently impassable spots or regain the proper direction if the terrain forced them to stray momentarily. "We're heading for the river!" she shouted back over her shoulder.

Bernadette could not distinguish the sound of the river from the sound of the storm. Just as Esmeralda called to her, the second half of her sentence was all but drowned out by a mighty clap of thunder. Lightning flashed across the sky, illuminating their surroundings with an eerie blue light. Bernadette shivered and ducked down closer to her horse's neck. She almost wished they were back at the lean-to.

Esmeralda had no such reservations. She was in her element; getting struck by lightning was not a concern for her. No one had ever told her how dangerous it was to be out in a thunderstorm, so she didn't worry about it. She had gained the riverbank by now, and turning around in the saddle, sat and waited for Bernadette to come up alongside her.

As Bernadette drew up alongside her friend's mount, she stared in amazement, not unmingled with dismay, at the swollen, churning waters before her. "What are we going to do now? There are no caves on this side of the river," she said, glancing from one side to the other. The pebbly shore, lined with stunted brush, stretched both ways as far as the eye could see—and further.

"But look over there! Do you see those crags and trees?" Esmeralda waved her hand towards the opposite bank. "Those are sure signs of caves; the rocks are just the right shape. Come on; let's get across before the water gets higher! Or do you think you can make it?"

Nothing inspired Bernadette so much as a suggestion that she might actually be incapable of anything. She drew a deep breath and threw her head back, smiling bravely at Esmeralda. "Of course I can! I've crossed deeper rivers than this; they just weren't quite so swift."

"Follow me, then." Esmeralda gathered up her reins and headed into the river. Her horse started swimming, looking up and downstream with a panicked expression. Bernadette splashed into the ford after Esmeralda, urging her horse forward to catch up with her.

The current was strong, certainly. It pulled fiercely at Bernadette's legs and buffeted her horse back and forth. Bernadette glanced down into the ugly, swirling black depths, and shuddered. The river seemed like a living thing, intentionally battling against them. The rapids tossed the horses and their riders up and down like frail eggshells, and burst up into angry spouts of foam around the jagged rocks that jutted above the waters. The horses were being carried downstream about twice as fast as they were swimming across it, and Esmeralda's horse had been caught by an undertow that pulled her downriver even more quickly than Bernadette's horse; the two girls were widely separated now.

"We'll have to ride back up along the shore to the caves, once we reach the other side; we've already been carried down past the caves!" Esmeralda shouted over the raging torrent. The zigzag flashes of lightning illuminated her momentarily, cast in sharp profile against the darkness. She bent down low over her horse's neck, aiding his progress with her hand.

A tremendous burst of thunder prevented Bernadette from replying. Besides, it required all her energy to stay firmly atop her mount. The animal was tiring; he was swimming more slowly and falling behind. Suddenly fearing that he might not make it to the distant bank, Bernadette tried to urge him forward.

What went wrong, Bernadette never knew. Had something heavy carried down the stream struck her horse in the side? But her mount suddenly rolled over, spilling his rider into the water and helplessly succumbing to the raging waves that sent him tumbling downstream at a furious pace, dashing him against the cruel rocks.

Esmeralda saw it all. "Bernadette!" she cried, resisting the foolhardy impulse to immediately turn her horse around in an attempt to reach her friend. They would have been immediately swept downstream as well, had she done so. She slowed her horse's swimming, straining to discern a hand or skirt-edge floating above the tumultuous waters pouring fiercely down around her, splitting around one sharp boulder only to join again and rush on with redoubled intensity and deadly swiftness.

"Bernadette!" she called again, frantically.

But Bernadette was nowhere to be seen.

Chapter Twenty-two
Danger in the Water

Struggling in the water, her horse swept away from underneath her, Bernadette tried not to panic. As long as she did not oppose the raging current, it would carry her downstream and eventually cast her upon the shore. She surrendered herself to the pull of the waters, which almost immediately repaid her confidence by dashing several fully submerging waves over her head.

Gasping for breath, she surfaced once again and looked around for Esmeralda. Had she been knocked down as well? No, there she was, still on her horse, a little further downstream, looking about her anxiously. Bernadette called to her, trying to wave her hand above the foam, but her voice was drowned in the torrent, and then she was pushed under the water again. When she came back up, her lungs bursting, she suddenly realized the full extent of the danger she was in. Looming threateningly ahead, momentarily illuminated by the eerie flashes of lighting, and then instantly plunged again into darkness, were the same sharp boulders that had battered her horse downstream. The current ran right up against them; it required all of Bernadette's strength to fight it enough to avoid being crushed against their jagged edges.

Downstream, Esmeralda was using these same boulders to her advantage. She had seen Bernadette now, and thrown her reins over a projecting rock ahead, to keep herself and her horse in the same place, very close to the far bank, until Bernadette reached her. It would not be long; Bernadette was tumbling downstream at such a great rate of speed, sometimes above the water and sometimes under, that she would come alongside them in a few moments.

And then it all happened in a second. The undertow that had dragged Bernadette along, just barely carrying her past the treacherous rocks, suddenly changed its direction and flung her up against one of the most immense boulders in the river, brutally crushing her arm against it as she was swept past. She cried out in agonizing pain, and was thrust beneath the water once again. At the same moment, the taut reins that had anchored Esmeralda and her horse safely within reach of the shore, snapped off and left her and her horse at the mercy of the current.

Esmeralda was not the kind of girl who gave up. She could see that Bernadette was sinking and only half-conscious; she had to get to her. Somehow, as the river pulled her along as well, she slid off her horse and grasped an overhanging branch. It strained and cracked, but she caught hold of Bernadette's arm just in time and dragged her out of the current, into the calmer shallows by the bank. In another moment, dripping, shivering, and scarcely believing that they were still alive, the two girls were standing on the shore. The horse had also managed to struggle out of the rapids, and now climbed slowly out on the bank as well. With a dismal neigh, he took off running into the spruce trees that lined the river as fast as he could gallop.

"Hey, stop!" Esmeralda let go of Bernadette and chased after her former mount. Bernadette, reeling and exhausted, with the pain in her arm throbbing to her shoulder now, collapsed on the ground. Esmeralda immediately ran back to her.

"Are you much hurt, Bernadette?" she asked anxiously, bending over her in concern.

"It's my arm," Bernadette groaned, grimacing.

Esmeralda gently rolled her over and pressed her fingers capably around Bernadette' forearm. "It's broken, I'm afraid," she said simply. "But I know what to do. We've just got to make it back upstream to those caves . . ." A sudden boom of thunder interrupted them, and both girls looked up fearfully as streaks of lightning flashed up all around them. A nearby tree split and crackled at the impact. "We've got to get out of the open fast. Can you walk if I help you?"

"I *have* to." Bernadette struggled gamely to her feet. Esmeralda looped Bernadette's good arm over her shoulders, and cupped her hand beneath the broken one's elbow to steady it, as they made their way painfully up the riverbank, draggled and alone.

Bernadette groaned with every step, despite her best attempts to stoically endure the pain. She had never known pain like this before, and she was still somewhat in shock from the impact against the boulder and her long period of immersion. Both she and Esmeralda were shivering violently. The storm had died down a little, but it was still sleeting and very cold.

"Keep it up, Bernadette; we're almost to the rocks," Esmeralda encouraged, gasping a little as she half-carried her injured friend along. She stumbled once, and they both nearly went headlong, but Esmeralda managed to push Bernadette to a secure seat on a nearby stump before falling down herself. She picked herself up again, shaken but very glad that Bernadette had not been. She gave her arm once more to Bernadette, and they slowly continued on.

"Back here, Bernadette," Esmeralda guided her carefully in between the trees and overhanging rocks that lined the bank. "I can tell there's a cave here."

"How?" Bernadette just found the strength to whisper.

"Don't try to talk; I can hear running water, that isn't coming from the river. There must be an underground channel branching off from it, which doubtless runs through a cave—ah, here it is!" Excitedly, Esmeralda leaned down and held back the brush that all but concealed the opening in the stone face of the cliff. "Just crawl in there; I'm right behind you. Careful—oh, good, that little stream is off to the side where it won't bother us, but it's clean fresh water," she went on, tasting it.

"I can't see anything in here," Bernadette said wearily, flopping down on the musty-smelling dirt floor of the cave. "How can you?"

"I'm feeling more than seeing, and I've been in places like this before, so I know what they're like," Esmeralda replied, passing her hands investigatively over the stones. "But I'll build a fire in a minute."

"How can you? We've got nothing with us to start it, and the wood outside is all wet!" Bernadette protested, despairingly. Her throbbing arm would not allow her to take a bright view of the situation.

Esmeralda came to her side and patted her unhurt shoulder comfortingly. "I know what to do; don't worry. The wood on the underside of the brush always stays dry, I can find a quartz rock that will do for a flint, and I'll bring back a splint for your arm and some food, too! Aren't we lucky, though, that there's water here? It would have been difficult toting it from the river without buckets." She laughed and Bernadette shuddered; she didn't even want to think about that perilous river just now.

Esmeralda bound a strip of her skirt around Bernadette's arm, and put her shawl under her head. "Are you more comfortable now? You'll be all right while I'm gone? I won't be too long."

"I'll do fine." Bernadette gathered herself together and answered in a comparatively strong voice. "Thanks, Essie. I just hope you'll be all

221

right, out in that weather. Don't you need your shawl?" She raised her head and awkwardly put her good hand behind her, thinking of returning the wrap.

"Oh, no, you need it more than I do just now," Esmeralda assured her, making her way cautiously across the dim cavern towards its opening. "The rain's slowed down and the trees will shield me. I'll be back soon. Oh, and by the way . . ." she turned around in the entrance, and spoke so softly that Bernadette barely caught the whispered words. "I'm sorry that I got us into all this trouble."

Then she was gone, and Bernadette was left to reflect on what she had said. It hadn't all been Esmeralda's fault; Bernadette had been only too ready to fall in with her plan to try to show up the boys. They had both been extremely foolish, attempting dangerous feats they were entirely unprepared for, with no better reason for it than gratifying their own pride and stubbornness!

"The boys were right not to trust us to lead," Bernadette muttered to herself, tears of regret trickling down her cheeks. "We've just managed to prove ourselves quite as incapable of taking care of ourselves as they thought, nothing else! Oh, dear!" she sobbed quietly to herself in the darkness, longing miserably for Esmeralda's return.

Although it seemed an eternity to Bernadette, lonely and suffering as she was, Esmeralda actually dispatched her errand in extremely short order. When she returned, she was loaded down with wood, moss, a hastily-fashioned basket filled with mushrooms, and a bunch of herbs she had found. In less time than it takes to tell, she had a brisk fire roaring at the entrance of the cave, over which she hung a pot she had made out of a hollow log and filled with mushrooms and water to boil for stew. She piled the moss into a comfortable couch for Bernadette to rest on, once she had carefully bound up her arm with some narrow sticks she had found to use as splints. Esmeralda had also steeped some of the herbs she had gathered over the fire, and made them into a poultice for Bernadette's arm. Bernadette was very tired from her experiences that afternoon, and now that she was feeling slightly more comfortable, she fell asleep before the mushroom stew was finished cooking. Esmeralda ate some of it and—exercising a great moral effort, for she was hungry enough to have eaten it all and then more—saved the rest for Bernadette. She sat as close to the fire as she could, watching Bernadette sleeping beside her and trying to calculate how long they could survive in these circumstances, and what she would need to start doing first thing in the morning in order to successfully care for them both. But at last she fell asleep as well.

Chapter Twenty-three
The Girls on Their Own

Meanwhile, the boys had met with unexpected success in their own search for permanent shelter. A little further up the mountainside, off the path and in a sheltered glen, they had discovered a sturdy little thatched hut.

"Wonder who lives here?" Colin remarked, dismounting and going up to rap on the door. "Hello, the house!"

No one responded; and after waiting a moment, Colin and Pete decided to try the door. It was not locked, and so they went in, to find that the two-roomed house had evidently been unoccupied for some time. But it was still in good condition and contained some usable furniture and cooking utensils hanging on the wall. There were even some logs remaining in the fireplace and in the woodbox.

"It must have belonged to a hermit who came up here as a retreat from the world," Pete opined, as he and Colin came out and remounted their horses. "But we can still use it. Well, and so Bernie will get a chance to try out a hermit's life now! Wonder what she'll think of that?" Pete laughed out loud.

Colin smiled in his calmly amused way. "I can't imagine that it would be a particularly attractive lifestyle to her," he replied reflectively. "Although you should know her tastes better than I, Pete."

"I don't know that *anyone* knows her tastes, even herself!" Pete exclaimed, half impatiently and half laughing at his cousin's unpredictable ways.

"Well, never mind; it's shelter anyway, and that's what we went looking for. Now let's get back to the girls, so they—and us, too!—don't have to stay out in this miserable weather any longer," Colin suggested, and the two boys urged their horses back down the slope in the direction of the lean-to.

But when they came up to it, of course, the girls were gone. The fire was out, and the lean-to was leaning over precariously, battered down by the wind and rain. Pete and Colin stared at each other in consternation.

"What can have happened to them? Their horses are gone too," Pete cried.

"They've gone off to look for shelter themselves, obviously. We ought to have thought of that; they were none too happy about being left behind," Colin replied, surveying the ground in an attempt to discover any traces of the girls' tracks that might indicate which way they had gone.

"Oh, why do they always have to be so much *trouble!*" Pete stormed fiercely. "Come on, Colin; we'll have to go after them, I guess, though goodness only knows where they could be by now. Which way did they go; can you tell?"

"Down towards the river, I think," Colin replied, gathering up his reins again. "A sensible enough place for them to choose to look, I must say. We may end up fighting over whose discovered shelter to stay in," he added with a laugh, as they headed down the same slippery slope traversed by the girls only a few short hours before. Pete only frowned in response as he followed after his companion.

When they reached the river, it was raging higher than ever. "They can't possibly have crossed this," Colin observed, "so they must be somewhere downriver on this side."

"No, I don't suppose even they could be such fools as that," Pete rejoined ungraciously.

Colin cocked a reproving glance at him. "You shouldn't talk about them that way, Pete," he admonished. "I know you don't mean it, and it does you no credit to be rude concerning those you care about."

Pete did not answer. He knew Colin was right; but it was just the very fact that he *did* care very deeply about Bernadette and Esmeralda, and was by now profoundly worried about them, that caused him to give vent to his frustrations in this manner.

The boys felt their way cautiously down the slippery path beside the river, growing more anxious by the minute as they found no indications of the girls' presence in the vicinity. Where could they be? There were no caves or other coverings in which they might be concealed on this side of the river.

"I think we must have come the wrong way, Colin," Pete broke the silence eventually. "I don't see where they could be around here. Perhaps they headed back up the mountain another way and we missed them, or maybe those tracks we saw really weren't pointing this way at all. They were pretty hard to make out, you know."

"But I saw some more back up in the sand along the bank there," Colin replied, glancing uneasily into the depths of the fast-flowing current running alongside them. He was beginning to have some serious forebodings about what might have happened. "Let's just go down a little further; we can't see behind those rocks there, so maybe that's where they are," he proposed, as cheerfully as he was able, and they rode on again.

When they came up around the rock pile, they still saw no signs of the girls, but they did see something else. Jammed up against the sunken boulders in the river, half-submerged in the waters, was the broken body of Bernadette's horse.

For a moment, neither one of the two young knights could say anything. Then, having swallowed several times first before trusting his voice, Pete asked hoarsely: "Do you think there's any chance they may have made it out on the other side?"

"I don't know." Colin's dark eyes were shadowed and somber as he gazed into the river, following the swift, cruel motions of the current dashing against the rocks. There was very little chance, if any; and Pete knew that as well as he did, so there was no need to say so. However, neither of the girls nor the other horse were anywhere to be seen in the river at this point, and on this very slight circumstance the boys pinned all their hopes. Surely they all would have ended up at the same point if the current had overwhelmed them all, right?

"Let's get the bags; we may have need of what's in them," Pete said at last. Colin splashed through the shallows after him, and together they cut off the saddlebags with their swords and put them on their own horses. Then they carefully freed the body of the horse and carried it back to the shore.

"We'll bury him when we come back; right now, we need to go further down and keep on looking for the girls, before it gets too dark to see," Colin said determinedly.

"All right." The two young men rode on down the wet shore, anxiously calling the girls' names. But there were no answering calls in return.

Once total darkness fell, the boys were forced to admit temporary defeat. "We'll never find them in the dark," Pete stated bluntly. "If they made it all right, they'll still be all right in the morning, when we can cross to the other side and look for them there. It should have slowed down enough for us to be able to cross by then. I can't believe that they were foolhardy enough to . . ."

"Okay!" Colin cut him off, at the limit of his endurance. "You've said that enough already. I think they've probably been through enough by now without our coming down on them as well. That is, supposing we find them at all," he added in a lower tone, as he dismounted and began to prepare camp for the night. The boys were very hungry, but they still didn't manage to eat—or sleep—very well that night.

Back in the cave, the girls woke early, stiff and cramped from their damp, uncomfortable surroundings. Esmeralda got up and went to peer out of the entrance.

"It's still raining," she reported wearily. "And the fire's almost out, too. I guess I'll have to head out to find more wood to replenish it. But I think it's still hot enough for me to heat up the rest of the stew for your breakfast and prepare a fresh poultice for you. Are you still in pain?" She cast a solicitous glance at her friend as she bent down to blow on the flames.

"Some." Bernadette raised herself up cautiously, trying not to jiggle her arm too much. "What are you having for breakfast?"

"Nothing yet." Esmeralda didn't look up from her efforts with the coals. "I'll have to go out and try to find more food for today."

"We can share this," Bernadette offered, as Esmeralda handed her the warmed-up stew.

"No, there's only enough for you; I had mine last night," Esmeralda said, a note of finality in her voice. Bernadette didn't have the energy to argue; her arm had started to ache again, and so had her head, and she felt generally shaky and feverish. She devoured the soup and was still hungry, but she was glad to lie down again.

"I guess I'd better be going." Esmeralda wrapped herself in her shawl and headed slowly toward the mouth of the cave. She stood there for a moment, looking out and shivering slightly, then pulled herself together and stepped out into the cold morning wind. "I'll see you soon. I hope I can find something more nourishing for you than just mushrooms this time." With an encouraging nod of goodbye, she walked off with a brisk, purposeful step, and soon vanished from Bernadette's view.

Meanwhile, the boys had awakened early, hastily consumed a cold breakfast, and headed back down to the bank of the stream. It was still swollen and churning, but the violence of its rapids had diminished somewhat.

"Well, do you think we can make it across?" Pete glanced at Colin, one eyebrow raised quizzically.

"We've got to." Colin settled his black helmet more firmly, pulling the visor down over his eyes. "We should fasten our horses together; that way, we can offer more resistance to the current."

"But then if one falls, we both do," Pete objected. "No, Colin; just follow behind me." Gathering up the reins, he splashed into the waters at their narrowest point, urging his horse forward and keeping a sharp look-out to either side. Colin followed him, his horse cautiously picking its way along the sharp stones at the bottom of the river until it grew deep enough for him to swim. The current was still swift, but nothing like the night before, and the boys made it across without mishap.

"I saw no signs of them or their belongings in the river here; surely there would be some debris to be seen if—if anything had happened," Pete said hopefully, as they reached the opposite side. "So they've just *got* to be over here somewhere. Come on, let's start looking. Esmeralda! Bernie!" he called, urging his mount towards the woods.

"Here, wait a minute." Colin bent in his saddle and picked up something he had noticed on the ground. "Do you recognize this?" It was part of Bernadette's sash, which had loosened from the rest of her garment during her struggles in the water, and fallen off after she had reached the bank.

"Yes, yes, it's definitely hers," Pete responded excitedly. "And it's too far from the edge for it to have been washed up here; they must have made it! Come on!" With renewed hope and vigor, the two young men rode onward, repeating their anxious calls as they headed into the trees that lined the bank.

But there was no response; their voices could not penetrate the thick stone walls of the nearby cave where Bernadette lay, and Esmeralda was well off in the opposite direction along the riverbank, so she could not hear them either.

Esmeralda was hurrying as fast as the cold and her weariness would allow her to gather up a substantial amount of firewood. She had filled her pockets already with the herbs necessary for poultices, and was looking all around her for any signs of woodland edibles. But there was very little to be found; Esmeralda had greatly depleted the available stock the day before. After a period of fruitless search, she decided that it would be better to get back and build the fire up before it burned out entirely, and look for more food later. It would be better, she reasoned as she headed back towards the cave, bent under her heavy burden of firewood, for Bernadette to at least be warm while she waited for her next meal.

Somehow, the path back to the waterfront cavern seemed far longer and steeper now than it had the evening before. Esmeralda was panting and numb with exertion by the time she reached the cave-mouth, and let her load slip to the ground with a sigh of relief.

"So you're back, Essie?" Bernadette opened her eyes; she had been lying there and shivering for the longest while; the fire had gone out long ago.

"Yes; I didn't find any food yet, but I had to come back and build up the fire before you froze to death," Esmeralda returned quickly, kneeling down and piling up the fire. Once the embers caught, the two chilled-to-the-bone girls gathered as close to the welcome blaze as they could, gratefully warming themselves as Esmeralda put a fresh poultice around Bernadette's arm. For a while they just sat there, leaning against each other, and staring into the ruddy glow of the fire.

But at last Esmeralda roused herself. "I've got to go get food," she said dully, getting to her feet. She wavered and sat back down again rather hard, light-headed from hunger and exhaustion.

"Are you all right, Essie?" Bernadette looked up at her in alarm. Esmeralda's face was very pale, and she was breathing rather too heavily. But she answered gamely, rising more cautiously this time:

"Oh, sure I'm all right—I've got to be! As soon as I find some food and we can eat, we'll both be much better." Esmeralda once again headed out of the entrance to the cave, shivering as the outside wind struck her with its freezing blast. "And then we can discuss how we are to get out of here and rejoin the boys; I'm sure they're searching for us by now." She stepped away from the cave.

"Oh, yes; maybe you'll meet up with them!" Bernadette exclaimed eagerly. "Why don't you call to them occasionally while you're out?"

"I'm sure they're nowhere near here; they wouldn't have thought to cross the river. Our trail would have been all washed out by the rain, and they'd never suppose anyone would have crossed in that raging torrent last night," Esmeralda returned wearily. "But I'll keep an eye out for them, just in case." And indeed, by this time the boys had ridden quite a distance in the opposite direction from the cave, and so Esmeralda saw no traces of them as she searched for more food.

Back in the cave, Bernadette lay alone, tired and hungry and quite depressed by Esmeralda's crushing of her hopes for a speedy discovery by the boys. If they could not depend on Pete and Colin, they could depend on no one but themselves. If only it wasn't for her wretched arm! She looked down at it and shook her head in frustration, angry at her own weakness.

"When Essie comes back, I'm going to ask her if we can't figure out a way to bind it up a little tighter," she said aloud, gazing up at the cave ceiling. "And even if we can't, I'm not going to let a silly broken arm stop me from doing what's right. We need to get back; and there must be some safer shallower point across the river, maybe even some kind of natural bridge downstream. We'll plan it all out when Esmeralda comes back." Satisfied that she had now settled everything perfectly, Bernadette nestled down into her mossy couch and, despite the gnawing pangs of ever-increasing hunger, soon fell peacefully asleep.

Chapter Twenty-four
Rescued

Bernadette was roused hours later by the dragging sound of Esmeralda re-entering the cave, pulling her gatherings behind her. As Bernadette looked up into her face by the dim light of the dwindling fire, she was almost frightened by her friend's strained and utterly exhausted appearance. Esmeralda's deathly pale face was blotched with irregular fever-flushed patches, and her eyes were glazed over. She did not look towards Bernadette or speak to her at first; it seemed to take all her energy just to toss the light bundle of spindly fir branches on the fire, and then stumble thankfully past it into the depths of the cave, dropping a bundle of a few oddly-shaped roots into Bernadette's lap as she passed her, and collapsing on the damp cave floor.

"Essie!" Bernadette meant it to be a rousing cry of compassionate alarm, but it came out as a terrified whisper.

"Can you boil the roots yourself, Bernadette?" Esmeralda asked hoarsely, without lifting her head. "I am too tired to cook just now . . . I cannot even move. It was so cold, so far . . . I searched everywhere to finally find food . . . No signs of the others . . . I . . . ." her voice trailed off.

"Yes, of course, Essie; you just rest for a while. My arm is really much better, and I can easily get up a meal for both of us. Don't worry about it or try to talk any more right now," Bernadette replied compassionately, cautiously pulling herself up to a sitting position and drawing their pot towards her. She scooted over to dip it into the cave streamlet, and then hung it over the fire to boil. She dipped the roots into the stream as well to clean them, and then put them into the pot to cook. Picking up an overlooked stick with her good hand, Bernadette seated herself by the fire to stir the bubbling stew, stealing an anxious look over at Esmeralda from time to time. She was lying very still in the shadow of the rocks, her head resting on her arm.

"I guess she's asleep already," Bernadette murmured, slowly swirling her stirring-stick around in the broth and watching the rippling path it made. "I wish she had lain down closer to the fire, though." The heat felt very good on her arm, and she felt more like herself again. It would have done Esmeralda good too, surely, to be nice and warm now. But Bernadette couldn't make up her mind whether it would be better to disturb her so she could move over to the fire, or just let her sleep.

But once the vegetables had cooked down into a thick, flavorful mass, Bernadette easily decided she should wake her friend up now to enjoy the restorative meal with her. "Essie! Dinner's ready!" she called merrily, removing the heavy pot from over the fire with some difficulty, as she could only use one hand. "Oof!" She set it down rather heavily.

Esmeralda stirred and turned her head. The firelight faintly illuminated her still-weary expression and bleary eyes. "I'm too tired to eat, Bernadette," she whispered. "I just want to sleep. I haven't yet; I'm so cold."

"Well, come over here by the fire, then!" Bernadette leaned over and tugged at her friend's skirt to try and move her closer to the warming blaze. "And you would probably sleep better if you would eat; then you wouldn't be hungry and you'd be warm inside and out."

"No, I can't . . ." Esmeralda closed her eyes again.

"What's wrong with her?" Bernadette whispered to herself, greatly alarmed now, as she sat down by the fire again, rubbing her arm and eyeing her friend anxiously. Eventually she remembered the stew and ate some of it, leaving the pot close to the fire so it would keep warm for Esmeralda when she wanted to eat.

She seemed to be sleeping now; her eyes were closed and her mouth a little open as she drew in ragged, hoarse breaths at irregular intervals. Bernadette was extremely worried. The cold and exertion of having to care for both of them had evidently taken its toll on Esmeralda. She was certainly not going to be able to go out and find them more food for supper; and Bernadette had no idea how to find food in these mountain wildernesses.

"Oh, what am I to do?" Should she go out and try to find the boys, or at least look for some roots that looked similar to the ones Esmeralda had brought back, and some more wood? The fire was starting to burn down again.

As Bernadette gingerly attempted to rise to her feet, cradling her elbow like a baby, sharp stabs of pain rushed up her arm, making it tingle as though it were on fire, hurting so badly that she wavered and spots danced before her eyes. Bernadette cried out in misery and sank back down to the floor again.

"There's no way I could make it out there," Bernadette muttered to herself despairingly, rocking back and forth in an attempt to ease the renewed pain in her arm. Esmeralda hadn't brought back any more of the poultice herbs, either. Oh, if only the boys would come and find them!

"Isn't there *any* way I could reach them?" Bernadette crept along to the mouth of the cave, where she looked helplessly around for some means of signaling to the boys. And then she suddenly remembered how her father's herdsmen, back at the palace, used to tell her about their trips up into the mountains with their flocks. Sometimes they would become separated, but they never worried about it, because the rocks echoed so well that they could call to each other from miles away, using hollow wooden horns to help their voices carry.

Bernadette had no horn, but she was in a rock cave! Surely there was some way that she could utilize the rock formations at the cave entrance to amplify her calls to the boys, so that they could hear her and come to rescue them!

At first she couldn't figure out exactly what direction to call in, and the rocks didn't seem to be echoing at all. But after shifting around into various positions beside the cave entrance wall, Bernadette finally found the angle that made her voice echo until it sounded ten times louder than usual. The rocks rang above her; surely they could be heard anywhere on the mountain! She shouted again and again, calling until she was hoarse, and then calling some more.

Hours passed, and she was still calling, although far more weakly now. The air around her had turned dark at the edges, and Bernadette was afraid she was going to faint. But she couldn't! She just couldn't; she *had* to call until they came. Limp and half-conscious from exposure and pain, she strained to call again; the echoes of her own cries ringing in her ears.

But wait a minute—were those sounds wafting on the air around her the echoes of her calls, after all? They sounded somehow deeper, differently inflected, forming different patterns of syllables and words. "Where are you?"

Was she growing delirious, or could it be—? Bernadette drew a hasty breath, threw her head back, and screamed once again for all she was worth. Then she leaned against the rocks and listened eagerly for the returning echoes.

"Bernie! Where are you?" There could be no mistake now; Pete's voice cut loud and clear through the muddled resoundings of Bernadette's last call.

"Across the stream, in a cave! Downriver!" Bernadette had raised herself in her excitement, giving her arm a bad wrench. She slumped back against the rocks, unable to move or see; but she still kept calling, feebly, so Pete and Colin would know where to head for them.

In another moment, the sound of thudding hooves rang out close at hand. Bernadette gave one final shout of direction and fell silent, breathing heavily as she gave her tired lungs a rest at last.

The mist before her vision cleared slightly, but everything still looked black before her. Then she caught sight of Colin's face beneath his dusky visor. He bent over her, inquiring anxiously whether she were all right.

"My arm's broken—" motioning weakly toward the injured member—"but otherwise I'm just tired. I think Esmeralda's sick, though; she's inside . . ." Bernadette could not force her overstrained vocal cords to make one more sound. She dropped her head back on Colin's arm with a sigh.

"It's all right; Pete's gone in to get her. I'll take you on my horse." Colin lifted Bernadette in his arms, and even through the pain the movement caused, Bernadette managed to feel a twinge of delight at the thought of being carried away on Midnight. But even though Midnight had some of the smoothest paces of any horse around, the jolting proved to be too much for Bernadette to endure, and she soon fainted away entirely.

It was several hours later when she came to; Colin was still bending over her, and it was very dark and warm. Bernadette tried to sit up and take in a better view of her surroundings; but she found that she had several woolen blankets wrapped around her, so she couldn't move very well.

"Just lie still for now, Bernadette." Colin gently pushed her back onto what Bernadette now realized was a narrow bed. She sank willingly enough back down into the pillows. "Where am I?" she managed to whisper, gazing up into Colin's face, which was shadowed against the background of firelight flickering across dark-timbered walls and raftered ceiling.

"In an abandoned hermit's cottage we found, further up the mountain," Colin replied quietly. He laid his hand on her forehead for a moment, and then turned away to pick up a cup of some dark liquid sitting on a stand nearby. "Here, drink this."

He put the cup to her lips, and Bernadette swallowed the slightly bitter drink before she could ask: "What about Essie, and Pete?"

"They're here, on the other side of the room. Don't worry about anything; everything is all right now that we're together again. All you have to focus on is resting and getting well. Don't talk any more now; just go back to sleep." Colin pulled the blankets more snugly around her shoulders and sat back down beside the bed. "Is there anything else I could do to make you more comfortable?"

Bernadette shook her head. The medicine must have had some tranquilizing attributes; she was already beginning to feel very drowsy. "No, I'm all right, thank you," she whispered softly, gazing up into the strongly-marked face beside her. Colin had said that everything was all right now that *they* were all together again. And that was all that mattered. Bernadette closed her eyes and drifted willingly off to sleep.

Chapter Twenty-five
All Together Again

Colin sat quietly beside Bernadette, watching over her attentively until her deep breathing assured him that she was asleep. Only then did he get up and turn to the other side of the room, which he had hitherto carefully screened from Bernadette's view.

"How's Bernie?" Pete spoke low, and did not look up from where he was sitting beside the other bed.

"All right." Colin responded in the same hushed tones, as he noiselessly drew over his own stool and seated himself beside his friend. "There's no fever, and her arm already seems to be mending well, thanks to the skill with which it was bound up. She's just exhausted from her late experiences, and she's sleeping now, so I'm sure she'll be perfectly recovered by tomorrow morning or the next day. But what about Esmeralda?" The two boys gazed with genuine concern at the figure lying before them; Esmeralda's eyes were tightly closed, but she did not appear to be sleeping peacefully. Her face was flushed and her tangled hair clung damply to her clammy forehead. She was tossing and moaning continuously; the torpor of exhaustion had given way to the restlessness of fever. Pete's hand went out almost automatically in an attempt to soothe her agitated movements. "She doesn't recognize me, and she's completely delirious," he said, tonelessly. "I'm not sure what to do."

"Don't we have any medicine for fever?" Colin asked, concerned.

"We do; but it was in those saddle-bags on Bernie's horse, and was completely sodden," Pete replied, leaning over Esmeralda, who was making wildly futile attempts to raise herself, and gently maneuvering her to lie back down again. "I managed to get Esmeralda to take some, but I don't know what good it will do now."

"I'm sure the water didn't hurt it; don't we always steep such herbs into teas?" Colin suggested hopefully.

"Even so, we don't have much," Pete replied worriedly. He hadn't taken his eyes off of his patient once during the course of his and Colin's discussion.

Colin looked at him, a barely perceptible smile of knowing admiration just touching the corners of his lips. "Since Bernadette doesn't really require much attention anymore, perhaps we should take turns watching over Esmeralda while the other sleeps?" he proposed. "You're looking rather worn; let me take a turn." He gently laid his hand on Pete's shoulder, motioning for him to leave the stool and go lie down by the fire, where the boys had spread their bedrolls.

"No, you take the first rest, Colin; I don't want to leave Esmeralda. She's just gotten accustomed to having me here, and I think that I can keep her quiet now; a new hand and presence about her would probably only alarm her and stir her up again. Once she's sleeping better, and you're well rested and up to the vigil, I'll trade places with you." There was a note of utter finality in Pete's voice, even through its dreary anxiousness, and Colin somehow knew it would be useless to protest. Therefore, he wisely said nothing, but went and lay down comfortably before the fire, wrapping himself well up in his blankets, determined to be thoroughly refreshed by the time the care of their patients passed to him.

Bernadette was, indeed, much better—and *ravenously* hungry—when she awoke the next morning, and was so insistent upon knowing exactly how Esmeralda was, that Colin was forced to acquaint her with the full truth of the circumstances, in all their seriousness. Bernadette, naturally, wanted to help nurse Esmeralda—"after all, she's only sick because she wore herself out taking care of me! It's only fair that I do the same for her"—but Colin convinced her that it would only make Esmeralda worse if she found out that Bernadette was exerting herself to care for her before she had regained her full strength, especially when there were two other people in the hut perfectly capable of attending to her.

"Just rest for today, and we'll see how you both are tomorrow," he said reassuringly, smiling down at Bernadette with his usual imperturbable good-humor. Somehow, looking at that smile, Bernadette couldn't help but feel that even Esmeralda's illness was not so serious as it seemed, that it could not possibly prevail against them—or at least not against *him*!—and that everything would surely be all right very soon.

"She will get well though, won't she, Sir Colin?" she still inquired imploringly, wanting further assurance, as she rather unwillingly lay back down again. In spite of all that had happened, Bernadette still didn't feel close enough to Colin to address him without the "Sir," although she now felt rather awkward doing so, somehow.

He didn't appear to notice, though. He glanced over to where Pete was still sitting beside the other bed and then turned back to Bernadette, smiling affably. "Oh, don't worry; we'll all take such care of her that she can't *help* but get well!" he said, breezily confident—almost too confident, as usual, Bernadette thought to herself. But she could tell that he was mainly trying to be positive for her sake—and Pete's as well. "Here, Pete, now it's your turn to rest. Say good morning to your cousin, and then go and lie down and let me look after Violetta," he ordered, striding purposefully across the room.

241

As Pete rose, unwillingly, and turned towards Bernadette's side of the room, she was shocked to see how haggard he looked. He must have been extremely alarmed about them, and Bernadette felt a sudden pang of conscience. In her relief and joy over their successful rescue and return to safety, Bernadette had almost forgotten what had led to these circumstances in the first place.

"I'm awfully sorry we worried you so; we shouldn't have run off like that," she apologized awkwardly. "I guess you were right all along, that we aren't capable of taking care of ourselves." It still cost her an extreme effort to confess this.

But Pete shook his head, wearily, as he sat down next to his cousin and hugged her fiercely for a moment, indicating more clearly than words how much it meant to him to have her safely back again. He drew back and looked at Bernadette steadily. "We never said that about the two of you, Bernie, at least not in earnest."

"I never did at all!" Colin called pointedly from across the room, swiveling around on his stool to regard the others. Pete, knowing this was meant as a rebuke for his senseless teasing and criticisms, flushed consciously. "And you haven't shown yourselves incapable, Maiden Cecilia; yes, it was foolish to try and cross the river, but you had been provoked and it was understandable. We do owe you an apology for that, although it was certainly not our intention to disparage your abilities, at all."

"I realize that now," Bernadette responded, quietly.

"But anyone can make a mistake; the important thing is to learn from them and move on to undo them. The way in which you managed to survive the rapids and provide for yourselves in the wilderness, and your cleverness in figuring out how to contact us before it was too late, is worthy of nothing less than the highest admiration." Colin shrugged.

"I guess we've all learned something from this. But really, Pete, you ought to go to bed now. Your sister and I are *not* going to let you use this situation as an excuse to get sick as well!" he pretended to be very stern, and Bernadette laughed. She and Colin exchanged conspiratorially triumphant glances, as Pete finally submitted to their will and headed for his own cot.

But Esmeralda did not get well. If anything, her fever and delirium increased with the passing days, despite the constant care and attention given to her by the others. In spite of their best attempts to divide the nursing efforts equally, however, and much to their surprise, Colin and Bernadette were rarely able to convince Pete to leave her side. He slept only when it was absolutely necessary for the sake of his own health; and whenever Esmeralda seemed worse than usual, sometimes not even then. This attitude of his bewildered Bernadette somewhat, but she could do no less than admire her cousin for his display of compassion and constancy.

So as it turned out, Colin spent most of his time taking care of the hut and making meals. Bernadette helped with both this and the nursing as much as her arm would let her, but there were still many things she was unable to do. One morning, five or six days after their rescue, she was going aimlessly through the cabinets on the cottage wall, hoping to find something useful that she could do to help. Pete was bathing Esmeralda's hot forehead as she slept, and Colin was frying pancakes for breakfast and steeping a fresh supply of fever-tea. He reached into the pouch where the herbs were kept and felt the bottom of it.

"We're almost out of medicine," he said.

"Oh, we can't be!" Pete looked up despairingly. "Her fever still hasn't broken. We've got to find something!" He sounded almost desperate, but neither Bernadette nor Colin could think of anything to say to reassure him. Bernadette surreptitiously cast an anxious glance at her friend's pale, nearly unrecognizable face, and turned back to the cabinet to hide her tears. She fidgeted miserably with a small canister on one of the lower shelves, and, in her uneasiness, knocked the lid off. As she replaced it, she happened to notice some faded writing scrawled across the top. Without even really thinking about it, she bent down to try to decipher the wording.

"Maybe I should ride back down to the village we just came from, to see if anyone has a supply of the medicine that I could trade for," Colin suggested, going over to Pete's side. Bernadette put the canister back on the shelf and moved down to read the one next to it, bending her head attentively over the row. "What do you say about that, Pete?" Colin inquired.

"I don't know; it's several days' ride back down there, and the medicine will be long gone before you could get back, perhaps too late," Pete responded, hopelessly. Bernadette picked up another canister and inspected it closely. She looked up as if she were going to say something, her face tight with sudden excitement, but then changed her mind and looked back down again, carefully spelling out the writing on the top. "It's a good idea, but we should have gone before. As it is, either way she'll have to go without the medicine."

"No, she won't!" her face alight, Bernadette spun around, the small glass jar clasped tightly in her hand. "The hermit that owned this place must have been some kind of a doctor; he's got all kinds of herbal compounds and remedies in here! And there's three or four for fever, including one of the same formula we've been using! Look here!"

"Let me see that!" Pete almost snatched it from her in his haste to read the top. Not satisfied by the clear description of the contents, he unscrewed the lid and sniffed the herbs inside before he was convinced that it was, indeed, the very combination they required. "Oh, thank God! And thank *you*, Bernie, for finding them," he smiled up at her, for the first time in days. "Everything really *will* be all right now," Pete said in vast relief, turning back to Esmeralda with a sigh.

"My pancakes!" Colin yelled suddenly, catching up his spatula and rushing back over to the fireplace to hastily flip them before they burned.

Chapter Twenty-six
Friends

Esmeralda did get well. And as soon as she was recovered enough to sit up, she was anxious for them to be back on their way. "We've lost so many days already; if you are to get back in time, then we need to leave right now," she argued earnestly. "I am not going to be the reason that you fail in your mission."

"Well, it *might* have been helpful to have thought of all that earlier, Essie." Pete was quite his own man again by this time. "But it's no use starting on again before you are able to handle the journey. We still have a week or so of extra time; don't worry about it."

"And when Father said a year, he didn't mean to the exact day, anyway," Bernadette added reassuringly, coming over to them. "Just so long as I'm back before the wedding-date, which isn't for a full month after the year expires," she explained in a lower tone, casting a glance over her shoulder at Colin, who was apparently taking advantage of the opportunity for a nap, sprawled carelessly across both his and Pete's cots, in full armor except for his helmet. Bernadette shook her head at his disheveled appearance, smiling indulgently, and then turned back to the others. "Why don't you get some sleep yourself, now, Essie?" she suggested, carefully rearranging the covers more comfortably around her friend. "Then you'll be able to travel all the sooner."

"Oh, all right." Esmeralda lay back down, scowling blackly. "But we have to leave within this week, whether I'm better or not, do I make myself clear?" she challenged.

"We'll decide that," Pete was starting to say, when Bernadette's cast-covered elbow in his stomach abruptly checked his intended remark. And then by the time he had got his breath back, he had thought better about finishing it.

They actually departed the hermit's cottage four days later; leaving it in spotless condition and with two of their jewels prominently displayed alongside the canisters of medicine they had used. "If the hermit comes back, he'll find a full recompense for everything we used; and if he never comes back, well, maybe the jewels will be a fortunate find for another group of travelers that comes through here someday!" Bernadette stated cheerfully, accepting Colin's help into the saddle, since she still couldn't use her broken arm.

As Bernadette's horse was gone, the four of them had decided to pack all of their bundles and saddlebags onto Esmeralda's horse, and then ride double on the other two. Surprisingly, even now that Esmeralda was practically well again, Pete still insisted on having her ride with him, and left Bernadette to travel along with Colin. Not that she was complaining, though, Bernadette thought, stroking Midnight's smooth arched neck beneath the fine black mane, as Colin leapt on behind her and deftly gathered up the reins.

"Do you have a good hold, my little blind one?" Colin inquired solicitously, as they prepared to set off. He put his free arm firmly about her waist.

Bernadette squirmed into a more secure position, and grasped the front of the saddle tightly. "I'm all right; come on, let's go; the others are already way ahead of us." She twisted around to look up into Colin's face as they rode off after them. "Why do you always call me 'little blind one,' Sir Colin?" She really wanted to know, and she felt comfortable enough talking with Colin now to ask him.

"Well, that's what 'Cecilia' means; and that's your name, now, isn't it?" Colin smiled disarmingly down at her.

"Er—yes," Bernadette replied, feeling deceitful all over again. "But why not just call me Cecilia, and never mind the definition?"

"I do sometimes; I will more often, if you prefer it," Colin responded carelessly, guiding Midnight easily over a patch of uneven rocks underfoot with scarcely a jar. Bernadette tightened her grip anyway, and endeavored to shake her hair back out of her eyes.

"I can't wait until I have two hands to use again; it's amazing how much simpler it makes everything in life!" she exclaimed, half impatient and half laughing. "I really am blind now, but I'm not usually, and I won't be once I tie my hair back after we stop for lunch, so I don't see why you keep saying I am!"

"I don't mean that you're blind in general; you're not just anyone's 'little blind one,' but only with regard to me," Colin replied quietly, looking off into the distance as Bernadette turned around again in an attempt to catch his eye.

Bernadette did not forget what Colin had said; she thought about it often. Had she, in fact, been 'blind' regarding him? Had all her prejudices against him in fact been unfounded? Had she been wrong to dislike him without any real cause, and not even try to get to know him and like him? That was not fair; Bernadette usually approached everyone she met with the assumption that she was going to like them. Now that they were back together again, she was determined to rectify the past and give Colin the same opportunity to gain her friendship and esteem.

Of course, it was probably easier for Bernadette to make and keep this resolution now that she had practically the same share of ownership in Midnight as Colin himself! Not only were they both riding on her, but Colin had taken to letting her help him unharness and rub her down whenever they stopped for the night, and they vied to be the first to bring her treats every morning. And even after they stopped at another hermit's cottage to trade for a new horse for Bernadette, and the girls went back to riding by themselves, Colin still left the main care of all the horses to Bernadette, once her arm was strong enough for her to do so. Until then, they kept on doing it together.

Bernadette was surprised; maybe it had been her own attitude that had prevented her from being able to care for Midnight, and Colin had never really tried to get in her way at all! He certainly seemed to be fine with her helping out now.

"You really love horses, don't you, Maiden Cecilia?" he asked her one day, after they had stopped for the evening. Bernadette had gone over to fetch some more supplies for dinner out of the saddlebags, and paused to stroke Midnight's nose for a while—so long that Colin had to come after her.

"Yes, I do," Bernadette replied, leaning her cheek fondly against Midnight's dark muzzle. "But I love Midnight best of all."

"Oh, is that what you've named your new horse?" Colin inquired innocently, glancing over at the animal in question, who also happened to be black.

"That's what I call *my* horse, yes; but she's not new," Bernadette retorted meaningfully. She put her arm over Midnight's neck, and the mare turned to nuzzle her affectionately. "I wish you'd trade with me, Colin; I really don't think you care as much about having Midnight for your very own as I do." Bernadette had finally gotten around to just calling Colin by his name.

Colin only grinned at her, as he reached into the saddlebags to get out some more provisions, and took Bernadette's bundle from her to carry as they walked back to the fire. "If you hope to ever convince me that it would be better all around for you to own that mare rather than me, then you'd better at least call her by her right name! She's always been Sultana, and if you don't have enough respect for her royal status to refer to her by her proper title, how can I expect you to treat her accordingly?"

"Oh, Colin!" Bernadette rolled her eyes. "You know how well I take care of her, and all the horses!"

"Right; so why do you need to own her any more than you do, since you already have the same privileges with her as with your own horse and the others?" Colin effectively ended the discussion here; Bernadette just sighed at his lack of understanding and changed the subject. She was quite sure that she'd get Midnight from him eventually; and until then, as he said, it didn't really matter.

They took their time getting back to the fire, where Pete and Esmeralda were squabbling over the completely irrelevant question as to whether it was better to tell directions by the stars as knights did or moss on the trees as gypsies did. Considering that their route on this stage of the journey was entirely determined by keeping to the path, and that they weren't traveling by night and there was no moss growing on the trees on this particular mountainside, Bernadette could not imagine what had gotten them started on this topic. She traded exasperated looks with Colin; after all that had occurred, she had naturally expected that Pete and Esmeralda would continue getting along, but her hopes had been quickly dashed. If anything, matters were more contentious between them now than they had been before Esmeralda's illness and recovery—"making up for lost time, I guess"— Colin remarked in an ironical aside. In fact, it had gotten to the point that Esmeralda had insisted on the four of them going back to each riding their own horse even before she was quite ready—it certainly had not been Bernadette's idea; she would have been perfectly happy to continue riding Midnight, even with Colin, for a good while longer.

"Well, I don't care," Esmeralda said in exasperation. "Have it your way; we'll say that judging by the stars is more exact, then. But so what? As long as you're going in the general direction you want, you're bound to end up somewhere." She tossed her head impatiently, and moved off to the other side of the fire, where she busied herself ostentatiously with the stewpot.

"I suppose that doesn't matter to you gypsies: when you aren't heading for anywhere in particular, it wouldn't really matter if you ended up in the middle of the sea! But some of us care about getting to one specific place by the most direct route possible, because we have something to *do* there," Pete retorted.

"For your information"—Esmeralda looked up, her cheeks flushed from the heat of the fire and her own frustration—"we gypsies do plenty, wherever we are! We don't require some ideal location in order to be able to accomplish anything, unlike *some* people!"

"Hey, speaking of accomplishing things, how about we go berry-picking tomorrow?" Colin rushed into the midst of the circle of firelight with Bernadette right behind him, and spread out his hands to warm them over the blaze, talking energetically the while. "We're getting a bit low on food; of course we can always buy more from the hermits we pass by, but it might be wise to get what we can for ourselves as well, and I noticed some very tempting bushes down by the river when I went to get the water earlier. So what say if we don't leave until afternoon tomorrow, and spend the morning gathering the berries? Anybody game?" he looked around inquiringly at the other three grouped about the fire.

"Sure!" Esmeralda was immediately enthusiastic. "I'll run and get some rushes for us to weave into baskets right now; all right, Bernadette—Cecilia?" she jumped up from where she had been sitting. "It'll be just like old times, won't it?" she added merrily, throwing a saucy glance at her friend.

"I hope not *too* much like them," Pete muttered, poking at the fire. Esmeralda tossed him a contemptuous look and headed off down towards the river. "Don't fall in!" Pete called sardonically after her.

"Pete!" Bernadette protested vehemently. "Aren't you ever going to stop saying things like that to her? Anyway, it wasn't Essie who fell into the river; it was me!" She began slicing the chunks of dried vegetables that she and Colin had brought back into the bubbling stew. "Why don't you go and get some more wood for the fire and make yourself useful for a change?"

"Whew, why is everybody all down on me at once?" Pete demanded, only half serious, as he regretfully hoisted himself up from his comfortable warm spot and turned to go. "Why don't you ever order Colin off on these errands, Bernie, instead of me?"

Bernadette glanced over to the opposite side of the fire, where Colin had sprawled himself out, smiling up at her. She smiled back. "Perhaps because Colin doesn't need to be told to help out, Pete; he already got the water and helped me to bring back the food. Now it's your turn, so quit complaining and go on; the sooner you go, the sooner you'll get back to join us in having fun, now go on," she waved him off peremptorily with her wooden spoon. Pete shrugged, glanced from her to Colin, who didn't say anything, and headed off into the darkness of the nearby thicket. From down by the river, Esmeralda's voice, raised in song, came wafting back up to the campfire.

"So now that we're alone, what were we talking about?" Colin asked, immediately sitting bolt upright. Bernadette promptly settled down across from him, meeting his gaze across the fire, and the two friends plunged willingly back into their interrupted conversation.

Chapter Twenty-seven
Confidences in the Berry Patch

"Race you, Colin! First one to fill their basket gets to ride Midnight tomorrow!" Bernadette called across the line of bushes, where she was picking as fast as she could on one side and Colin on the other.

"You're on!" Colin hastily crammed a handful of berries into his mouth, and reached back into the bushes.

Bernadette looked over at him and laughed. "You should see how blue your lips are! It's not *that* cold out, now that we've reached the lower ranges of the mountains!"

"What about yours?" Colin retorted immediately. The four traveling companions had already been out picking for a couple hours; long enough for everyone to forget their heroic resolutions made at the beginning of the jaunt, to not eat any berries until after all the baskets had been filled.

The four of them had started out picking in the same area, but eventually Bernadette had grown tired of hearing Pete and Esmeralda's constant arguments, and had accordingly ordered them both off in opposite directions to finish their picking elsewhere. Esmeralda had gone back up to their camp to pick over the berries that had already been gathered. And so Colin and Bernadette were alone in the thickest part of the berry-patch, screened by a heavy tangle of thorny vines from where Pete had gone to pick further down the river.

Bernadette, quite pleased with her scheme for getting to ride on Midnight the next day, all by herself, picked so fast that her fingers could hardly be seen as they flew in and out among the vines. Up and down the rows of bushes she went, easily chatting with Colin. Eventually—exactly how he had maneuvered it I don't really know— Colin ended up on the same side of the bushes as Bernadette, picking next to her. Bernadette kept glancing first into his basket and then into her own to see how much further along she was than Colin, trying to avoid having him notice her covert glances, even though he was doing the exact same thing! Of course, after a while their eyes met; Bernadette laughed and brushed a wisp of hair out of her face to hide her confusion—leaving a noticeable purple streak behind—and picked faster than ever.

Bernadette dumped another handful of berries into her nearly full basket. As she reached back into the bushes, she glanced over again to check on Colin's progress. He had playfully put his basket on his other side where she couldn't see it. Bernadette leaned back to peer around him—and succeeded only in knocking over her own basket!

"Oh!" she cried in dismay, as the berries plopped squishily all around. "Oh, and I was just about finished, too!"

"Here, I'll help you pick them up; my basket's full," Colin offered, setting his berries aside and kneeling down next to her to help salvage as many of the fallen berries as possible.

"It'll be less work boiling these down into preserves, anyway," Bernadette remarked wryly, throwing a squashed clump into the basket. Colin reached over her to pick a few more good ones off the bushes, to replace those on the ground that could not be returned to the basket.

"I guess neither of us really won the race, then," he said casually, getting up and picking up the baskets. Bernadette sat back on her heels and wiped the back of her hand across her forehead again, gazing up into Colin's face as she did so. "Suppose we sit and rest for a minute before taking these back to camp? There's a nice seat on the roots of that tree there," Colin indicated the spot by swinging one of the baskets in its direction.

"Watch out; don't spill them all again!" Bernadette grabbed one of the baskets from him, and then followed him across to the tree, where she seated herself comfortably on the curved, moss-covered roots and set her basket down in a safe crevice beneath them. Colin established himself next to her, leaning back against the trunk with his long arms behind his head, relaxing.

"Well, so we're almost to the end of our journey," Colin began conversationally. "I suppose you're looking forward to getting back home, eh, Maiden Cecilia?" He raised an eyebrow inquiringly.

"I don't know," Bernadette replied slowly, plucking a daisy and beginning to absent-mindedly tear off its petals, one by one.

"You don't know?" Colin sat up a little straighter at this, now with both dark eyebrows significantly raised.

"I mean, I can't wait to see all my family and friends again, of course," Bernadette clarified quickly. "And I suppose it will be nice to have a rest from all this traveling, but . . ." she dropped her hands into her lap and gazed unseeingly into the distance, off beyond the final stretch of the High Ranges to where the castle stood.

"But . . . what?" Colin gently pressed her to complete her response.

"It's just . . ." Bernadette hesitated, feeling a sudden burning rush to confide in Colin about everything. He was always so calm and levelheaded, and so considerately good-humored; it would be wonderful to be able to share her concerns and longings with someone who would neither comfortably but unsatisfactorily agree with everything she said, as Esmeralda always did, nor simply tease her about her unrealistic ideas without providing a convincing alternative, like Pete. However, she was bound by a promise of her own instigation, to not tell Colin anything about who they were! What could she do? She cast an uneasy sideways glance at Colin; he was still watching her, smiling in his usual friendly fashion, but with a trace of concern deep down in his dark eyes. He reached out to put a hand over hers.

"What's wrong, my little blind one?" he asked compassionately. Bernadette made up her mind. Even if she couldn't tell Colin the full truth about herself, there was nothing stopping her from telling him about the situation anonymously, and getting his good advice and consolation that way.

"Didn't you ever wonder, Colin," she began decisively, sitting up straight and pulling her hand away to brush back her hair once again, "what a young maiden of my standing was doing going along with her brother on a trading-trip of such length and difficulty? Obviously I could not provide any necessary services to such a venture."

"Oh, I don't know about that . . ." Colin began deprecatingly, in an attempt at compliment, but Bernadette cut him off.

"Anyway, that's not why I came along. I've always led a sheltered upper-class life, where everything you are to do is already laid out for you to follow, and I got tired of it. I wanted some excitement and, well, a chance to decide for myself what I wanted out of life. Father gave me a year to travel with Pete and find out what I wanted to do."

"And have you found it?" Colin was not looking directly at her, having suddenly become absorbed in studying the pattern on the tree-trunk, but his head was turned to indicate that he was still listening attentively.

"I'm not sure. Sometimes I think that some of the things I've done on this journey are more enjoyable than my old life, and that I would rather keep on doing them than return to what I used to do, but then again I don't know. I've grown up somewhat from all these experiences; I don't think I'm quite so selfish now as I used to be, and I can't get rid of a nagging feeling that I *ought* to go home, that my duty in life is there, regardless of whether it's what I *want* or not. What we want can change from day to day. And every career has its ups and downs, its triumphs and pleasures and problems—so how do you choose one in particular?" Bernadette sighed and turned a little away, plucking at the wildflowers again.

"Well, if you feel a particular desire for one certain lifestyle over another, I would say to pursue it," Colin began again.

"But you see, I don't. I feel that there are many things that I would like and feel equally comfortable doing, including my old life, now. And I know Father and Mother want me to come home, and that there are—well, other people who are counting on me to fulfill my role there." Bernadette paused for a moment, confused. She sneaked a glance over at Colin to see if he looked at all suspicious, but he was still just smiling. Drawing a breath of relief, she rushed on. "So this puts me in a very difficult position. I could go in any number of directions."

"I don't see that. If you love and miss your family, and want to go back, which it seems that you do," Colin glanced at Bernadette for confirmation; she nodded, and he continued: "and if they want you to come back and you feel you have some obligations to fulfill there, it seems to me that the decision should be fairly easy, in regard to both what you ought to do and what you want to do."

"Oh, but I've left out the most tricky part of the situation!" Bernadette laughed in frustration over her own clumsy manner of explanation. "My biggest problem with my life back home is that girls like me have marriages arranged for them. I've been betrothed all my life, to a fellow that I've never seen. He's the son of my father's best friend. And if I go back, I have to marry him, and I don't want to!"

"Why not?" Colin posed the question as if it were a perfectly legitimate one.

"Colin!" Bernadette looked up at him in amazement, to see whether or not he were joking. His face was perfectly serious, however. "Would *you* want to marry someone you had never met?"

"Well, provided that I had been assured that she was tolerably pretty . . ." Colin started banteringly.

"Oh, Colin!" Bernadette brushed his nonsense aside impatiently. "Please try to understand. I—" she looked up at him again, and then in a sudden burst of confidence, admitted the whole truth to him, which she had never before so much as hinted to anyone else. "I'm scared."

"Scared of what? Of your betrothed?" Colin was giving her an opening to talk out her problem.

"Not *exactly* . . . but what if I don't like him?" she gazed agonizingly up into Colin's face, trying to gather courage from the calm strength she saw there.

"Well, you certainly won't like him with that attitude!" Colin returned immediately, with conviction. "Don't prejudice yourself against the fellow without any grounds whatsoever. I mean, after all, Bernadette, don't you more often like people when you meet them for the first time than dislike them?"

"Well—yes, usually," Bernadette acknowledged, guiltily conscious of the fact that it had been entirely her own preconceived notions about Colin that had led her to dislike *him* at first, and not any fault of his own. "But what if he doesn't like *me*; that's what really worries me, I guess."

"Did you ever meet a man that didn't?" Colin laughed, evidently quite assured on this point. Bernadette eyed him askance and did not answer. "Besides, I believe you told me that he's the son of your father's best friend?"

"What's that got to do with it?" Bernadette muttered, tracing out the pattern on her dress skirt with nervous fingers.

"Well, if you're anything like your father, and he's anything like his father, it would seem to follow logically that the two of you would be very compatible, too, and get along fairly well," Colin presented his case without a loophole remaining.

"But life isn't always logical, Colin!" Bernadette protested. "Yes, I think I am rather like my father, but I was brought up at home. My betrothed went to the Royal Military Academy here in Berklesgilands—you know, even princes from other kingdoms come here to train; we've got the best military school around—and since then, I don't know where he's been. Who knows what kind of influences he could have been exposed to as a young man; he could be simply awful! I tell you I'm scared," she reiterated.

"But Cecilia—" Colin paused for a moment and rolled his eyes in exasperation, and then continued more patiently. "Do you really think that your father cares so little for you that he would allow you to marry someone that he didn't know for certain was a good man who would try to make you happy?"

Surprisingly enough, this view of the case had never presented itself to Bernadette before. Its convincing appeal to her father's love for her almost took her breath away, and for a few seconds she was speechless. At last she replied, slowly, "Well, when you put it that way, Colin . . . but Father does not know my betrothed, either. He doesn't visit his friend very often, as he lives so far away; and the only time that Father ever saw his son, to my knowledge, was eighteen years ago, when he was just a baby."

"But surely he at least keeps up with your betrothed's progress and character through his friend?" Colin persisted, leaning forward earnestly.

Bernadette shrugged unconvincingly. "Oh, I'm sure they both talk about their children in their letters to each other; but what does that matter? Surely a father would be prejudiced on behalf of his son; my father isn't going to get any reliable information from that quarter."

"So your father's best friend isn't a man whose word is to be trusted?" Colin sounded slightly incensed. A little startled by the intensity in his voice, Bernadette glanced up at him in alarm. Colin's brows were knitted tightly together; and his eyes looked troubled, almost appealing, as though he sincerely wished she would not insinuate such things about anybody's character without full proof.

"Oh, no, I didn't mean that!" Bernadette rejoined earnestly, in haste to make amends. "I just—well, you know, Father only ever tells people about my good qualities, and so I'm sure his friend does the same. But shouldn't a husband and wife know about each other's negative qualities before they get married just as much as the good?"

"Well, that would be ideal, I suppose," Colin admitted. "But I do think parents can generally be trusted to understand who would best complement their children as a mate, as well as the children themselves can—perhaps even better sometimes, as love and such can get in the way." He pressed his hand unthinkingly over Bernadette's again, lacing his fingers through hers.

"Mm-hmm, I guess so," Bernadette agreed, thinking about how much trouble the Pete-Camille-Stephen triangle had always been back home. "But I still worry. I can't bear the thought of ending up with someone thoroughly disagreeable or, worse yet, morally questionable, and I have no guarantee otherwise."

"But what are the chances, really, that he is either?" Colin settled himself more comfortably and prepared to address the situation reasonably, whether Bernadette would or not. "And do you ever think of or hope for all the *good* kinds of people he might be?"

"No—I don't want to be disappointed if he isn't," Bernadette replied decisively.

Colin shrugged and looked away again. "But you could so easily be making yourself miserable over nothing! And besides, even supposing you don't like each other at first, why not treat it as an adventure, a challenging opportunity to win over somebody difficult either to like or to please. People can change, you know, provided they are willing to adapt to each other. And if you have that attitude towards it, I bet you could easily influence your husband." He glanced sideways at her, and smiled. "I think a fellow would have to be pretty bad to deliberately make himself disagreeable to *you*," he added significantly.

"It doesn't make much difference whether he does it deliberately or not; the effect is still the same," Bernadette pointed out dismally. "What if we simply can't get along, even if we both try to?"

"What is it you want out of a marriage, anyway, Cecilia?" the abrupt question took Bernadette rather off her guard.

"Well, I've never thought too much about it before," she replied, slowly. "But—you mean, if I could be married to whoever I wanted, what would I want him to be like? I have no idea!" she almost laughed at her own oversight in regard to this important matter, but then sighed dispiritedly instead. "Besides, I guess I've always felt that it shouldn't matter whether I am happy with someone or not, provided I did what was right."

"But you really can be happy and do the right thing at the same time," Colin insisted. "I do assure you, Bernadette. Don't you trust me?" he gently placed a hand under her chin and turned her face up to his.

"Certainly I do," Bernadette replied, feeling a little shy under his clear gaze. She quickly pulled back a little and turned away again, holding her head down. "But how does that help me with this?"

"Well—I mean, you'd take my advice if I offered it?" Surprisingly, Colin sounded momentarily flustered.

"Of course! Why do you think I've been telling you all this?" Bernadette looked back up at him again, unconsciously noting how uncommonly flushed his cheeks were.

"Well, I think that you ought to think about—and figure out who it is that you want to love," Colin went on, haltingly. "And once you've found him, even if he's not your betrothed, I think you should tell your father honestly about how you feel. I'm sure he would want you to marry only someone you really love, regardless of how much he might have initially wanted a match between his own and his best friend's family."

"Maybe that would have been the better way to begin with," Bernadette responded slowly. "But Colin—it's too late now for me to look for someone I can love. Once I get home, I have to make up my mind about my betrothed right away; and I have no one else to fairly compare him to."

"You don't?" Colin's voice was very quiet, but steady once again. "You don't know anyone, who, perhaps, loves you?"

"No; I've met a lot of fellows who might have found me more or less attractive; but as for anyone who seriously cared for me, I don't think . . ." Bernadette felt her words trailing off as the full impact of

Colin's words struck her, and she became suddenly aware that he was still holding her hand, very tightly now. She gasped and looked up at him, leaning towards her, his gaze fastened intently on her face. "You don't mean . . ." she began bewilderedly.

Colin finally let go of her hand, but he took hold of her shoulders instead and drew her towards him. His arms closed around her and he bent his head over her; his lips were nearly touching hers . . .

"Colin, wait!" Dizzy from this sudden revelation, Bernadette pushed him back with some difficulty, and reluctance on her own part. "I can't—not yet. Let me talk to Father first, after we get home. If he still wants me to marry my betrothed, it wouldn't be fair to him for me to let you kiss me first," she insisted, reluctantly.

"All right, I'll wait," Colin released her and stood up, leaning against the tree trunk and grinning down at her, entirely unperturbed by this development. Bernadette, still covered with confusion, kept her eyes on her lap and began picking nervously at her dress again. "But do you love me too, my little blind one? At least you could tell me that."

"Well, I—" Bernadette thought it over for a moment. She glanced up at Colin's amused and completely self-possessed countenance, and a little answering smile began to play around the corners of her mouth, as she considered how completely unprepared she had been for him to sweep her off her feet like this. "Can I have a little time to think it over?" she inquired, coquettishly, getting up and picking up her berry basket, and slipping her hand into his as they set off to walk back to their campsite together.

"No," Colin retorted unequivocally, casting a mischievous glance down at her. "You've had plenty of time to think it over already: with all the marked attentions I've given you, you should have realized my feelings for you long ago, my little blind one," he added teasingly.

"Well, I guess you don't call me that for nothing!" Bernadette responded gaily, and they laughed together as they continued on up the slope, hand in hand.

Chapter Twenty-eight
Pete and Esmeralda

They heard Pete and Esmeralda before they saw them. Their angry voices, raised in heated discussion, carried easily down to where Colin and Bernadette were still climbing up through the trees. Bernadette stopped momentarily, looked at Colin and sighed; then, swiftly disengaging her hand from his, she picked up her skirts and fairly flew the rest of the way up the slope to the camp, with Colin following right behind her.

"Can't you ever do anything right, Esmeralda?" Pete was storming, his face flushed with irritation. "Whatever possessed you to think it would be all right to destroy those things?"

"I didn't destroy them! I just used them for a different purpose," Esmeralda retorted indignantly. She was holding a bark container, doubtless full of some of the berry jam she was boiling over the fire, which she had carefully sealed by melting one of their few remaining gold coins over it. Several other similarly sealed containers were arranged neatly on the ground nearby. "There are plenty of jewels left to trade for provisions during the rest of our journey; you don't need the coins for that! They were all I had to use as seals, and so I did."

"It would be one thing if they were yours to use, but they're not. They belong to *us*, me and Bernie, and you had no right to take them," Pete insisted, picking one of them up to inspect it, and then setting it back down with a gesture of extreme impatience. "They're totally destroyed," he muttered, kicking at the dirt on the ground.

"They are not! Can't you ever see anything beyond the nose on your face? You never think anything is right unless it is used for the purpose *you* would have chosen! It's much more reasonable to use these coins to seal these jars of jam that we do need, rather than saving them for things we don't need, and I have as much right to them as you have! What, am I one of this group or not? At least keep me informed." Esmeralda brushed wisps of her beautiful hair back from her face, which was steamy and hot. She had obviously been slaving very hard over the fire to prepare the jams; Bernadette felt a pang of conscience over Pete's insensitive lack of appreciation.

"I don't know why we ever took you in as one of us; you've done nothing but cause us to lose precious time and possessions from the very beginning. But then, I suppose it was our own fault for allowing you to join with us in the first place; who can trust the right-hand helper of a common thief?" Pete scoffed, turning away from her.

Esmeralda flinched; his scorn jarred on a sensitive point with her. But she recovered herself instantly, and faced him gamely, her eyes flashing. "I got them all back for you, didn't I? And this is the thanks I get! Go ahead, deride and condemn me for what you know nothing about! What should I have done, starve?" she threw this unexpected challenge in his face. "And what would you have done, my upright and noble gentleman, alone and orphaned with no means of support? When the leader took notice of my skills and decided to appropriate them for his own purposes, what could I do against him? No one else in the band dared to oppose him or would have supported me had I done so; I was helpless in his hands, and I had to live someway, so why not that?" Esmeralda choked a little over her recital of her pitiful history; but then continued on, throwing her head back proudly in a final stand of defiance: "And I can tell you one thing, Sir Peter: if all the people who fell amongst my master's robber-band were like *you*, I wouldn't ever have felt the least bit bad about helping him discomfit them! And now, I've had enough of this; I'm through. You'll no longer be troubled with me; I'm leaving tomorrow. I'm going!" she reiterated, beginning to cry and burying her face in her hands.

Bernadette rushed to her friend's side and put her hand on her shoulder. "No . . . no, Esmeralda," she pleaded earnestly. "Look at me, Essie; please don't cry. Don't leave us; you are one of us, no matter what Pete says, and we want you with us. We need you with us; you've helped us in so many ways, including jarring up the jam today—how clever of you to figure that out! We couldn't do without you, dear friend, so please don't go. Pete didn't mean what he said, did you, Pete?" Bernadette cast an appealing look up at her cousin.

Pete met her gaze rather shamefacedly, but he merely shrugged and responded with his accustomed careless bravado: "You can't go, anyway, Essie. Wasn't the agreement that we would protect you from your old master on the condition that you joined forces with us?"

"And I did, and I've been with you long enough to complete my share of the contract!" Esmeralda fiercely wiped her tears away and turned on Pete again, avoiding Bernadette's restraining hand. "You can't keep me with you against my will; I'm not your prisoner!" she flared.

"You are if you try to return to that brigand," Pete responded significantly, in spite of Bernadette's and Colin's earnest attempts to silence him.

"Who said anything about going back? *I'm* no safer around him now than you are," Esmeralda retorted. "But I've a perfect right to go and join another band of my own people."

"Well, but how can we be sure we can trust you not to inform that former leader of yours of our whereabouts, even if you join a different band, once you are no longer under our supervision?" Pete demanded.

"Oh, Pete, that is really too much!" Colin exclaimed, capably taking charge of the situation, as usual. "Esmeralda has every right to go if she chooses; and you malign her unjustly if you so much as suspect her of being untrustworthy," he said evenly, a clear note of authority evident in his voice. "Did she not pledge you on her maiden honor to never betray you?"

"Well, yes," Pete responded somewhat reluctantly, tracing another pattern in the dirt with the toe of his boot.

"Very well then." Colin turned away from him dismissively, and directed his attention to the girls. "If you really feel that you cannot stay with us, Violetta, we will certainly respect that and not attempt to interfere with your leaving; however, I do hope that we can persuade you to overlook this unpleasant circumstance and remain with us. Surely there is some way we can make it up to you?" he queried, raising an eyebrow in sincere concern.

"Who put you in charge, Colin?" Pete muttered rebelliously, casting an indignant glance over at the little group.

"And who did *you*, Pete?" Bernadette flashed back at her cousin immediately, effectively silencing him for the time being. "Don't go, Essie; I want you to stay. Never mind what Pete says. But if you really can't bear it any more and would rather go, I understand," she said unwillingly, moving over to stand next to Colin. At least she could depend on *him* to stay with her, right?

"I'm sorry." Esmeralda blinked back tears again. "But I don't want to stay. Things just keep getting worse, and especially now that you and Sir Colin spend so much of your time together"—Bernadette gasped in surprise and glanced quickly up at Colin and then away, keeping her head down and blushing deeply. She hadn't realized that anyone else had noticed how matters stood between them.—"I'm thrown on Pete's company, and that is thoroughly disagreeable to both of us. It's better that I leave now," she reiterated more strongly.

"All right, then," Colin said, breaking a moment of silence. "But wait until tomorrow; it is already too late for you to make your way very far today. Continue on with us just for this last afternoon, and then we can take our separate ways tomorrow morning," he advised, moving to start packing up their camp. "So do you want to ride Sultana, my little blind one?" he inquired, assuming his accustomed cheerfulness as he bent to pick up another bedroll. "Neither one of us really won that race, but you can still ride her if you want."

"The race was for who got to ride her *tomorrow*, Colin, not today," Bernadette replied dispiritedly, miserably packing Esmeralda's jars into one of the bags. For once even the thought of riding on Midnight failed to cheer her. "It doesn't matter."

"Well, suppose we ride her together, then, and put all the bags on your horse?" Colin proposed, evidently not discouraged by her listless response.

"If you like." It would be comforting to have *someone* near her who could be counted on to not make life more difficult and perplexing than it already was!

The travels of the afternoon were uneventful, although they did not reach their campsite destination until rather late. Dusk had already begun to fall as the four alighted from their horses, and so they went about in silence to set up camp and start the fire as quickly as possible. An atmosphere of strain hung over all their proceedings; they scarcely spoke to one another, even once they were all settled around the fire

270

eating supper. Bernadette wanted desperately to talk to Esmeralda, knowing that it would doubtless be the last time they would ever see each other, but she could think of nothing to say. Colin did speak to her occasionally, but somehow the oppressive atmosphere of the situation forced them to talk in whispers, so at last they stopped trying and consumed the rest of their meal in silence.

"It's your turn to keep watch first tonight, Pete," Colin said shortly, unrolling his bedroll as soon as dinner was over. It was the first time he had spoken to Pete since that afternoon; clearly his feelings of disapproval had not lessened yet.

"Very well," Pete replied quite as shortly, taking up his weapons and settling himself to stand guard on the other side of the fire. Bernadette and Esmeralda brought over a few more logs to build up the blaze before retiring for the night as well, and an even deeper silence settled over the camp.

An owl hooted in the distance, and unfriendly rustlings sounded all around. From where he sat on guard, Pete shifted uncomfortably, a feeling of unaccountable loneliness and depression settling over him. Pete was usually never lonely, even on watch, because he generally found *himself* plenty good company. But tonight he did not; and the fact that he knew none of his traveling companions did either just now, doubtless contributed to his feelings of an outcast.

"Funny," he muttered to himself. "It's Esmeralda who's leaving, and yet I'm the one who feels deserted and alone." He looked over to the other side of the fire, where Esmeralda was sleeping. She was twisted up in an insecure sort of huddle, and her blanket had fallen down from off her shoulders. The night wind was chilly, and for some inexplicable reason, Pete got up and went and knelt beside her, reaching down to pull the warm covering back over her. She stirred and looked up at him;

apparently she had not been asleep after all. She immediately pushed his hand away.

"Go away; what do you want?" she whispered, her dark eyes snapping at him angrily. "I don't require your assistance in anything any more; I might as well start getting used to doing everything on my own," she hissed softly, not wishing to disturb the other sleepers, and turned her back on Pete, coldly.

"Oh, Esmeralda!" Pete sank down into a sitting position next to her. "Don't say that; I don't want you to go away," he whispered remorsefully.

"Of course not; then whom would you have to torment endlessly?" Esmeralda retorted, her tone laced with sarcasm.

"I didn't mean—Essie, please listen to me!" Pete caught her hand and held it, despite her best efforts to twist it away. "Just for a moment!"

"Haven't I heard enough from you? I should rather think so!" Esmeralda jerked away.

Pete regarded her rightfully indignant face somberly for a moment, and then dropped his head with a sigh. "I don't expect you would believe me, if I told you that none of my insults were directed at you personally."

"Oh, no, of course not; I suppose you were just talking to the wind!" Esmeralda rejoined scornfully.

"Directed at you *personally*, I said; of course I was talking to you," Pete responded, somewhat nettled. "But I didn't mean that I really thought that way about you."

"If you're hoping that I will ask you what you *did* think, I can tell you that I'm not in the least interested," Esmeralda replied shortly, curling back up again. "I'm going back to sleep."

"Well, I'm going to tell you anyway." Her resistance only bolstered Pete's resolution. "Please, Essie! You've got to listen. I was angry, Esmeralda, over being taken prisoner by that bandit who was your master, and I couldn't get over losing our freedom and property to him for so long, or endure the thought of him still having some of what rightly belongs to us. And I took it out on you because I couldn't get to him. But I was wrong," Pete went on, speaking probably more humbly than he ever had in his life before. "I realize now that you were not to blame, and I should have known that all along. But I never meant to hurt you; and then, when you were so ill, I realized—oh, what's the use of talking about it!" Pete broke off distressfully. "Please, Essie, give me another chance. Don't go away; I couldn't bear to let you out of my life now." He suddenly took her hands in his and bent down to kiss her earnestly, as the only means by which he could truly express how he felt.

Esmeralda pushed him back in astonishment and sat up, staring at him in the firelight with an expression of the blankest amazement. "You mean—you care for me like that?" she whispered, disbelievingly. "But how do you expect me to believe you really do, when you've never shown it before?"

"I tried to, especially when you were ill," Pete protested, a little hopelessly. "But I can show you now, if you'll let me." He had still kept her hands in his, and now leaned towards her again. Esmeralda offered no resistance this time.

"So you'll stay now?" Pete asked, in joyous confidence, as Esmeralda, suddenly remembering her maiden modesty, drew quickly away from him and turned to hide her blushing cheeks.

"Well, I'll think about it," she returned coyly. "We can talk it over in the morning; there'll be plenty of time then. Good night, Sir Peter." Esmeralda lay back down and pulled her blankets securely over her.

"Good night, Essie," Pete walked back to his place of watch with a light step and a lighter heart, the natural consequence of having done the right thing.

Now, whether the two slumbering figures on the other side of the fire had stirred more than once or twice during this interchange, and whether their eyes had remained perfectly shut the entire time, is a question that I would not venture to attempt to address satisfactorily. It certainly looked as though significant glances were exchanged, once Pete had returned to his post, and that the two of them then snuggled down into their respective bedrolls afterwards far more contentedly than before; but, you know, firelight *does* have a way of playing tricks on people's eyes.

Chapter Twenty-nine
On The Final Stretch of Their Journey

Neither Bernadette nor Colin evidenced any signs of surprise the next morning when they were informed, not only that Esmeralda would *not* be leaving them, but that she and Pete had established a perfect understanding between themselves. And as a result, when they arrived at the next hermit's cottage along their way, they stopped there long enough for a very important ceremony to take place.

"We're in luck; he's an ordained priest right enough," Pete came back in a hurry to where the other three were waiting with the horses. "Well, Essie, are you ready?"

"As ready as I'll ever be," she returned coquettishly, suddenly very busy with adjusting one of the bridles.

"And you're sure you're willing?" Pete pursued earnestly, though without seeming to be too concerned about the possibility of a negative answer.

Esmeralda finally looked up, her beautiful smile flashing in the sunlight. She looked lovelier than she ever had before; and Pete didn't wait for her to answer, but went up and kissed her in full view of Bernadette and Colin, who were pretending to not be at all interested.

"All right, all right, now, Pete, go on in," Bernadette ordered, pushing in between the two of them long before they were ready to separate. "Colin, you go with him; I suppose you're best man, as there's no one else around, and I'll get our bride ready. This ceremony is going to be conducted properly, even if the circumstances are somewhat irregular," she insisted, drawing Esmeralda away to the other side of the horses, where she had laid out her hairbrush and a garland and a few other accessories.

"Just don't take too long; we'll be inside waiting for you," Colin called over his shoulder, amusement ringing in his voice, as he took Pete's elbow and led him back inside the hermit's cottage, endeavoring to calm his friend, who was suddenly getting nervous.

Bernadette brushed out Esmeralda's hair until it shone like black gemstones in a river, and then twisted one thin portion into a braid around the top of her head, and pinned the flower garland to it. Both girls had their best dresses on, and Bernadette loaned Esmeralda her only pair of white lace gloves.

"You have to have something borrowed, you know," she said, as Esmeralda hesitated before putting them on. "And here, let me fasten your necklace. I've never seen this one of yours before; it's gorgeous!" holding it so that the stones would catch the sunlight and sparkle.

"It was my mother's; I wasn't supposed to wear it until my wedding-day; it's our family tradition," Esmeralda replied shyly, a soft blush mantling her cheeks as Bernadette put the chain about her neck.

"All right, you look simply lovely!" Bernadette said, standing back to admire her handiwork. "And here's your bouquet; it's rather small, but there aren't too many wildflowers growing up here, and I had to have one too!" she laughed as she looked down at the few insignificant blue forget-me-nots she held clasped in her hand. Esmeralda took the larger nosegay of daisies and early rosebuds, and turned towards the cottage.

"Don't you go in first, Bernadette?" she asked, her breath suddenly coming a little quicker and her cheeks burning brighter than ever.

Bernadette cast an admiring look at her friend. "If Pete weren't already crazy about you, you'd certainly win him over now!" she couldn't help exclaiming. "Yes, I'm supposed to lead you in. Stay right behind me." She walked purposefully up to the front door of the hermit's cottage and pushed it open, holding it for Esmeralda to pass through, and then preceding her slowly across the room to where the hermit-priest was waiting before his fireplace, a book open before him and Pete standing at his side, anxiously tugging at his mail gloves. Colin waited manfully next to Pete until the girls arrived alongside them; once Bernadette had put Esmeralda's arm through Pete's, she and Colin moved off to one side, as the other couple stood in front of the priest to recite their vows.

"You have the rings, Colin?" Bernadette whispered to him nervously, for about the twentieth time that day.

"Right here." Colin checked obligingly, yet again, in the breast pocket of his sable-colored mail shirt. "How clever it was of you to think of smelting both of them out of that last coin."

"And how clever of *you* to know how to do it," Bernadette turned the compliment back on him.

Colin laughed softly. "No good in learning how to do something if you never put it to use," he returned lightly, moving forward to give the rings to the priest.

"You may kiss the bride," that individual proclaimed, closing his book with the comfortable consciousness of a job well done.

And so Pete and Esmeralda were married, and afterward the wedding party enjoyed a fairly traditional reception, complete with Colin dancing with Bernadette and the newlyweds with each other while the hermit played several appropriately romantic tunes on his violin.

The four did not remain at the hermit's cottage for very long; the next morning, after thanking the priest for his services and hospitality, they were once again on their way, the same as ever. Well, not quite the same; now Esmeralda actually *insisted* on riding with Pete. Bernadette and Colin, of course, were nothing loath to follow their example, and accordingly rode Midnight together every day, with Bernadette's poor unappreciated horse following behind with all the saddlebags.

And so they headed on towards the crest of the final mountain in the High Ranges. Time was running out, and Bernadette was starting to worry that they would not get back in time to convince her father to stop her wedding.

"After all, if Prince Gerald-Reginald is already there, no one is going to allow me to turn him down in favor of somebody else, because it would be so rude," she explained to Colin one evening, after she had failed to convince the rest of the party to travel on for an extra hour before stopping for the night.

"Oh, you worry too much," Colin retorted, sprawling comfortably beside the fire next to her, with his hands behind his head.

"And sometimes I think you don't worry *enough*!" Bernadette immediately shot back, incensed that he failed to see the seriousness of the situation.

"Well, so you even each other out and make a fine pair, now, don't you?" Pete proposed teasingly from the other side of the fire, where he and Esmeralda were roasting apples on sticks for dinner.

"Come and get them while they're hot!" Esmeralda offered one stick, with two apples on it, to Bernadette. Bernadette slid one off, burning her fingers in the process, and dropped it quickly onto her plate, passing the stick to Colin, who simply ate his apple off of it. Esmeralda and Pete were doing the same, sharing their apples with each other in the age-old hopelessly romantic fashion. Pete held the stick for Esmeralda to take the best bite; she looked up at him and giggled, nestling affectionately within his encircling arm.

"It's incredible," Bernadette muttered to Colin. "Ever since they've gotten married, there hasn't been a speck of trouble between them. With most couples it's the other way around: they're all hearts and flowers during courtship; but then as soon as the knot is tied, they discover their differences and the arguments begin."

"Better idea to get it all out of your system beforehand, I would say, then; it seems to work," Colin replied in his carelessly debonair way, munching satisfactorily on his apple and watching the other two across the fire. "Maybe we ought to find something to fight over now, so we won't later," he grinned down at her.

"I still haven't said for sure that I'll marry you; I can't until I know whether Father will agree," Bernadette responded a little irritably. She didn't like Colin taking the entire arrangement of what she saw to be a majorly complicated affair so much for granted.

"Well, in my experience, people will generally agree with almost anything, provided that you can convince them it is the best option," Colin remarked with the utmost gravity, but with an unmistakably mischievous twinkle in his eye.

"Oh, now, that *is* an astonishing revelation," Bernadette rejoined sarcastically. "I never would have expected such to be the case." Colin laughed and attempted to put his arm around her shoulders, but Bernadette repulsed him and moved away out of his reach.

"My word, Bernie, what makes you so snippy lately?" Pete looked up away from his wife long enough to ask. "I should think you'd be extraordinarily happy with the way everything is turning out: we're almost home, you've experienced all kinds of exciting new adventures,

Colin loves you, and you know what you want to do now when we get back."

"But I don't know whether I'll actually be able to do it!" Bernadette exclaimed impatiently, getting up and walking a little ways off from the fire, to lean against a nearby tree. The firelight still lit up her features plainly as she faced the other three seated about the flames. "You all make it sound so easy, and I don't see it. Father doesn't change his mind very readily; no more than I do."

"Then, if I can change your mind, I can change his, too!" Colin pointed out cheerfully. "I tell you we've got nothing to worry about." He got up and came over to her, placing his hand persuasively on her arm. "Come on back to the fire, my little blind one; I didn't mean to upset you."

Bernadette couldn't help softening under his affectionate coaxing. "I'm not upset," she answered softly, following him back over and sitting willingly down next to him again.

Chapter Thirty
Parting Ways

But just three days later, Bernadette *was* seriously upset. They had reached the summit of the mountain, and were pitching camp for the night, even though it was barely four o'clock in the afternoon. Bernadette was still trying to argue everyone into continuing on a ways down the mountain; there was no reason to be stopping already.

"But we don't know whether we'll find another site as good as this by evenfall, Bernie," Pete explained patiently, yet again. "Can't you see how overgrown the next stretch is?" He indicated the scrubby slope below with a sweep of his hand.

"Aye, it is indeed a struggle to make one's way through!" a strange voice proclaimed from behind them. The four friends started and turned around, to find themselves facing three mounted knights who had just emerged into the clearing. "Well met, friends; may we join you?" requested their spokesman, a tall fellow in shining mail riding a little in advance of the other two. His eyes locked with Colin's; the latter had risen and reached for his helmet, just in case "friends" turned out to be a misnomer.

"Who are you, and whither do you come from?" Pete inquired, he and the girls rising as well. Esmeralda moved towards the horses to get more food out of the saddlebags, just in case these travelers really were friends and accordingly joined them for dinner.

"Knights of Berklesgilands," responded the other cautiously, pushing up his visor to mop his forehead with a fine linen handkerchief. He peered investigatively at the insignia on Pete's shield, to see whether it contained the motif common to all graduates of the Royal Military Academy. Colin's own shield, black of course, was entirely blank.

"How's the war effort going?" Bernadette demanded, pushing forward and, by her question, assuring the newcomers of their position before they had even figured out all the symbols. As Bernadette could now see, all three of their shields were stamped with the Berklesgilands emblem as well.

"That's why we're here," the leader of the small band explained, dismounting with his companions at Bernadette's silent invitation, and coming to join the others about the fire. Colin obligingly took their horses over to tie them up with their own in the thicket. "The King's troops are hard pressed on every side; the enemy appears to be alert to our every maneuver. It is beginning to be suspected that some traitors must have deserted to their side and are helping them. We have just left one of the strongest remaining forts, and are taking this unguarded shortcut through the mountains to reinforce the garrison at another. The tide of battle is not presently in our favor; but we are still strong and ready to defy the most powerful forces that can be arrayed against us, and the war is far from over! Long live King Friedrich and the Royal House!" he thundered inspiringly, raising his arm in a gesture of determination as his voice stirred the branches above.

"Long live King Friedrich!" echoed the others, including Colin, who had just returned.

"It's well we met with you," Pete said graciously. "We are deeply concerned about the outcome of the fray, though we have been out of the country for a while. We have been making all possible haste to return and offer our services to the war effort; perhaps we could join with you?"

"Well, that might be a proposal worthy of discussion," replied the leader ruminatively, accepting a biscuit from Esmeralda. "We shall consider it in the morning, shall we? If we may rest among you for the night, that is."

"Certainly you may stay with us tonight," Bernadette returned with gracious hospitality, getting up to refill everyone's drinks from the brook nearby. "But I'm afraid that we will not be able to join with you; we must get back to the palace by the most direct route possible. Pete, you know that we cannot do anything until we have seen Fa—the king," she remonstrated. "We have other matters to settle before you can go and join the battlefront."

"But isn't the state of the country a little more important than our own personal affairs?" Colin raised the question and his eyebrows at the same time, fixing Bernadette with an earnest look. "The King will hardly be able to help us if Berklesgilands falls to the enemy; I think our duty calls us to join with the war effort *now*, when it is needed."

"I must say that I agree," Esmeralda spoke up from her place next to Pete. "And what do you say, my husband?" she turned to him, her eyes soft with desire for his corroboration.

"Definitely," Pete confirmed, drawing her hand within his. "If the kingdom is in danger, we need to do whatever we can to stop the enemy, wherever we are at the moment." He looked across the fire to catch his cousin's eye.

"That is true enough," Bernadette replied distractedly. She did wish the others would not put her in this predicament of appearing selfish before these strangers! "But we cannot possibly know in what manner we may best serve the cause until after we have spoken to the King and found out what he wishes us to do," she explained somewhat lamely. "How do you know you are not needed elsewhere, Pete?"

"We can't know; and that's why I say we go directly to doing whatever we can to help," Colin responded. "Sometimes, in emergency situations, one just has to help wherever one is most needed at the moment, without waiting for prior instructions. That's life."

"It may be *your* life, Colin; but it's not mine!" Bernadette retorted immediately. It suddenly struck her, for the first time ever, as she looked at Colin's blank shield, that she really had no idea of where his allegiance lay or even where he originally came from. Perhaps this added some extra asperity to her voice as she continued, "*You* may not have any ties that bind you to one particular course, and so choose whichever path appeals most to you; but the rest of us have obligations that call us to go a certain way and not another right now. I am sure you understand, sir?" she turned to the other knights' leader with a pretty manner of appeal, which affected him enough to immediately nod his complete understanding of her position.

"Will you step aside and speak with me a moment, Maiden Cecilia?" There was a dangerously determined edge to Colin's voice, which Bernadette could plainly see was reflected in the glitter of his dark eyes when she glanced up at him. Colin was always so sweet and easygoing and generally good-natured, that it was easy to forget that he had been second-in-command during Sir Timothy's campaign, and knew very well how to enforce his will when he deemed it necessary. Unwillingly, but compelled by the magnetism of his gaze, Bernadette followed Colin over to a nearby cluster of trees.

"Sit down, my little blind one," Colin invited courteously, but with a more gentlemanly stiffness of tone then he usually used towards her. He leaned against the trunk of one of the trees, gesturing to Bernadette to take a seat among the roots. Bernadette, however, was beginning to feel her natural obstinacy rising in the face of his obvious resolve; and so she shook her head and remained standing, her arms crossed disagreeably over her chest.

"It's no use, Colin; I'm not going with them," she said doggedly. "I have to get home."

"And what good will it do for you to get home sooner, if I'm not with you?" Colin wanted to know. "Besides, what does your getting home have to do with going to see King Friedrich about the war effort, anyway?" He leaned forward until his dark curls were almost brushing her own, his eyes penetrating deeply into hers.

Bernadette looked away. How she yearned to tell Colin the whole truth, but she couldn't, and this knowledge made her angrier than ever. And so she replied to his first question, scornfully: "It does a lot of good if Father still wants me to marry my betrothed and not you; and either way, I want to go home. I'm not going to have my life controlled by what *you* think you ought to do, Colin. And if you'd rather leave me in order to join the war effort this minute—as though one man at one fort could really make any difference!—than wait until after we have everything important settled, I don't know that I care whether you go or not, in that case." She met his gaze fiercely, determined not to give in. He wouldn't go away with the other knights, not if it meant risking losing her, of that Bernadette was certain. She probably had not quite meant everything she had just said, but she wanted her threats to carry as much weight as possible, to be certain that she would convince him.

However, Colin's face had at first darkened during her address, and then assumed an expression of complete indifference. "I am sorry to hear you feel this way, Maiden Cecilia," he replied, even more stiffly than before. "I had hoped you would understand and join me in doing what I believe to be the only right course of action under the circumstances. I love you, but I would be wrong to allow any feelings, even the very highest known to man, to stand in the way of my duty."

"Spoken like a true knight," Bernadette rejoined, sarcastically. "You wouldn't go if you really loved me," she insisted, still keeping her arms tightly folded.

"Yes, I would." Colin's voice was perfectly steady, but there was a barely discernable look of pain in his eyes, balanced by one of steadfast resolution.

"Then you don't love me, and you can go wherever you want, and the sooner the better!" Bernadette exclaimed hotly. "And I'm certainly glad I found out you felt this way, before it was too late! I was right from the beginning not to trust you, but you deceived me and nearly brought me around. You *will* leave with them tomorrow, and I hope I never see you again!" With this annihilating conclusion, she turned on her heel and marched back to the fire; Colin followed silently after her and sat down next to the other leader, informing him of his intentions to accompany him and his companions the next day.

Bernadette ignored him, then and for the rest of the night as well. She had to argue with Pete for a long time about her own resolution to continue straight on home, but eventually her cousin was forced to give in; it was Bernadette's adventure, and he was duty bound to help her to carry it out in whatever manner she chose. And this situation was not one in which he could claim that his way of handling matters would be safer or more efficient than Bernadette's.

"Although it does mean that I'll be alone to take care of the two of you again," he pointed out at the end, after giving a half-hearted consent to her plan. "Since you said Colin is going with the other knights."

"But you don't have to worry now about us doing something rash, Pete; we've learned our lesson this time," Esmeralda assured him. "And are you sure Colin would leave us, anyway?" She glanced up anxiously at Bernadette in the darkness, the firelight glancing off her dark eyes and hair and multi-faceted bangles.

"Of course he will go," Pete replied wearily, before Bernadette had a chance to answer. "He's not selfish enough to shirk his responsibilities to the general population in preference for his own concerns, unlike some people I could mention." The implication was not lost on Bernadette, but for once she made no answer to her cousin's pointed thrust. "Come on, Essie; it's late, and we'll have a far road to travel in the morning, even if Bernadette does change her mind." The two of them moved slowly off together to retire for the night.

"Which I won't do!" Bernadette called indignantly after them, preparing to roll out her own bedding.

"Not even for me, my little blind one?" Colin's voice was sorrowful, as he materialized out of the darkness, and placed a hand on her shoulder, looking down at her in a last yearning plea for her consent.

"No!" Bernadette jerked away from him, and focused all of her attention on smoothing out her blankets, fully aware that Colin was still standing beside and gazing down at her. But presently he sighed, and went over to the other side of the fire to sleep as well. Bernadette, for her own part, did not sleep at all that night.

But she was up early the next morning with everyone else, working more energetically than anyone else to get the two parties off and on their separate ways as soon as possible. While the others were taking down the camp, Bernadette went over to saddle up the horses.

"Farewell, my beauty," she whispered to Midnight, stroking her nose one last time. Her pride would not allow her to ask Colin again if he would trade with her, not now.

"If you don't mind, Maiden Cecilia, I'll attend to my own horse," Colin spoke from behind her, as though he had read her thoughts.

"Not at all," Bernadette returned shortly. She left the thicket with her own horse and returned to the campsite. She did not see Colin again until everyone was mounted and ready to go.

"You are quite certain, Sir, that you do not wish to come with us?" inquired the other knights' leader one final time, addressing Pete. "There are accommodations for ladies at the fort whither we are bound; your wife and your sister would be quite comfortable there, I assure you. And we could certainly use the aid of every able-bodied man possible."

All eyes turned on Bernadette, who refused to acknowledge them, but sat fidgeting with the buckle on her mount's harness, until the silence became unbearable. As she looked up, she just caught Colin's eye, but he looked away indifferently, his face set toward his distant goal, on the other side of the mountain. Midnight arched her neck proudly and whinnied, seemingly expressing her approval of her master's chosen course of action. That decided Bernadette. Burning inside, she stubbornly set *her* face toward the downward path she had chosen for herself. Gathering up her reins, she only said, tersely:

"Come on, Pete, Esmeralda; what are we waiting for? We only have a few more days left to make it on time," and prepared to gallop off. Pete sighed, and having made an awkward apology to the leader of the other knights, and wrung Colin's hand heartily in bidding him goodbye, he and Esmeralda rode after Bernadette, calling earnest farewells and good wishes back to the others as they rode away.

Bernadette said nothing, and did not look back until just before the thickness of the underbrush completely obscured the view of the upper slopes of the mountain. Then, slowing her pace to allow Pete and Esmeralda to get ahead of her, she twisted around in her saddle and shaded her eyes, peering back up anxiously. The black horse and black rider, both proudly upright and silhouetted against the morning sun, were just slowly disappearing over the crest of the mountain. As they vanished from her sight, Bernadette felt a strangely tight, cracking sensation in her chest that she had never felt before. But she swallowed hard, past an inexplicable choke in her throat, and, tossing her head back proudly, turned and continued her downward ride, although her eyes were so dim that she could hardly see her way.

Book Three

And What Came of It

Chapter Thirty-one
Facing the Enemy

"Isn't it wonderful to be heading back down into the lowlands again? It's getting so much warmer; feel how balmy that breeze is!" Esmeralda exclaimed. Laughing, she caught at the edge of her scarf, which the wind had whisked away off her neck, and tucked the wrap into her pocket.

"Yes, indeed; it really feels like spring now," Pete agreed, turning to smile at her. Pete and Esmeralda were riding side by side as a matter of course, with Bernadette following behind. The other two would have been quite willing to let her take the lead if she had shown a preference for it; but truth to tell, Bernadette really did not care any more who went first.

"You know, I think I've been here before; I believe our caravan camped in these foothills a couple of years ago," Esmeralda continued conversationally. "I'm almost certain I recognize those crooked spruces, and that winding stream down that way," she indicated the direction with a sweep of her hand.

"Could be; considering that you've been traveling all your life, Essie, I should think you'd have seen just about every part of Berklesgilands by now," Pete rejoined, casually glancing in the direction his wife was pointing.

"Actually, no," Esmeralda responded. "For much of my early life, my band spent most of its time in the neighboring kingdoms, before we returned to Berklesgilands for good when I was about ten or twelve. But I hadn't left the country since then, until our escape last year."

"And now we're back again!" Pete said brightly, guiding his mount cautiously over a rocky place in the path.

Bernadette, bringing up the rear, had nothing to say. She was bitterly disappointed and angry with the present state of affairs, the prospective final outcome of her adventure, herself, and pretty much everything in general.

"Why are you so quiet, Bernie?" Pete turned around in the saddle to regard his cousin quizzically. "You've hardly spoken to either of us today. Did we do something to annoy you?"

"Of course not," Bernadette replied shortly. "I'm just feeling rather down, that's all." The moment the words were out of her mouth, she wished she hadn't said them.

"I don't see why; you got your own way, didn't you?" Pete retorted teasingly. Esmeralda touched him gently on the arm, to prevent him from saying anything further.

"You know, I think some of my people may be around here right now," she glanced around her uneasily. "I can see some traces of recent residence and use of the woodland resources. That tree over there with the bark stripped off, for example"—nodding towards it as she spoke—"it doesn't look like it was done by deer; the strips are too regular for antler marks. I just hope they're not my particular band." She glanced anxiously off to the side again. "I can't help feeling, though, judging from the signs . . ."

"Oh, how could you possibly tell, from the particular manner of bark-scratching, which gypsy band it was, Essie?" Pete rejoined impatiently. "Besides, your band was miles south of here when we left them. Come on, let's stop here for lunch," he proposed, dismounting and leading his horse to the brook to drink.

The girls followed his lead, although Esmeralda continued to keep a wary eye out as they rubbed down their horses and set out the midday meal. It was a rather silent luncheon: Bernadette still did not want to talk, Esmeralda continued silently uneasy, and Pete was busy eating. The stillness was pleasant, though; the springtime birds were singing and the breeze whistled gaily though the trees. Eventually a blue jay screamed, breaking into the low pattern of sounds, and Esmeralda gasped and looked quickly behind her.

"It's just a jay, Essie; my word, you're jumpy today!" Pete tried to laugh off her fears, and drew her to him affectionately. "There's no reason for you to ruin this beautiful day for yourself with unfounded anxieties. There's no one around here but us for miles."

"Ah, but that's where you're wrong, stranger," a heavy, coarse voice spoke from out of the underbrush, followed by a prodigious amount of rustling and crackling, as the owner of the voice issued forth into the clearing and stood facing the three travelers, his brawny bare arms crossed over his massive chest. He was a swarthy man of Herculean proportions, with a disagreeable countenance and ill-fitting clothes.

Esmeralda screamed once, and turned pale as ashes, as she drew further within the protection of Pete's arm, trembling. With his free hand, Pete gripped his sword with nervous intensity. There was no question who this man was: the gypsy chief's grandnephew, the tyrant who had been Esmeralda's harsh master and the cruel kidnapper of the other two.

Bernadette rose instinctively and stood in front of Pete and Esmeralda, hoping to block the latter from their enemy's view. But he had already recognized all of them. He laughed harshly, and took a step forward, directly addressing Esmeralda.

"Eh, so we meet again, now, don't we, my pretty bird? This is quite the windfall to a fellow who never expected to see the booty you double-crossed him out of, ever again! Well, that is what comes of taking on weak and undependable waifs, with their scheming, underhanded ways," he leered, drawing so close to the three of them that Bernadette was forced to step backward.

"So you thought you could run out on me, ay? And that I could not easily find you and bring you back, you contemptible little beggar? Did you consider the consequences of betraying me, girl?" he added menacingly. Esmeralda was shaking visibly.

"Do you consider the consequences of insulting my wife, brigand?" Pete abruptly broke in upon the fellow's threats, rising to his feet and confronting him with sword drawn. "She has nothing to do with you; so get you gone at once, you common thief and vagabond!" he ordered, gesturing back toward the trees with his weapon.

"And who is insulting now?" hissed the other, drawing an ugly-looking knife from one of his pockets, and at the same time loosening a curved, scimitar-like weapon from the other side of his belt. He stood on guard, awaiting Pete's onslaught.

"Pete, don't! You can't fight him; he'll kill you!" Esmeralda cried in terror, rushing to clutch her husband desperately by the arm.

"Never fear, my own one," Pete responded coolly, loosening his sleeve from her grasp. "I'd not stoop to combat with such a contemptible fellow as this, merely to suit my own preference; but only as it is necessary to defend my wife's safety and honor. As for killing me, that is the usual intent of one's opponent in a fight, and I have faced many such and am still around to talk about it. Never fear for me. Now for you, brigand," he turned resolutely back to the fiercely scowling outlaw, "I am prepared to give you better than your deserts and permit you to go on your way unmolested, provided that you first humbly beseech pardon for having so vilely spoken to a gentleman's wife, and promise to never attack any of the three of us or our possessions again. If you will not, I stand ready to punish you as you deserve!" his voice rang out forcefully.

The gypsy chief's grandnephew, laughing evilly, rushed on Pete, brandishing both of his weapons above his head. Pete only had his one sword, but he was fully adept at using that to parry the other's thrusts from both sides. "Keep back, girls!" he shouted, as the two of them closed on the patch of turf between the campsite and the woods.

They fought there fiercely for a long while; Pete's superior skill was balanced out by his opponent's greater strength and heavier weapons. The girls stood apart, watching the duel with strained faces and unblinking eyes, hoping for and yet fearing the end. At first they had held each other's hands tightly; but after a while, Esmeralda could no longer bear to watch her husband's struggles against his massive foe and cringed down on the ground, covering her face with her hands.

Bernadette remained standing. She had put on some of her old suit of armor and taken up her own sword; if the villain defeated Pete, he would have to make his way through her, too, before he would be able to harm Esmeralda!

It was well that she was prepared; for suddenly, the chief's grandnephew sprang to one side, taking Pete off guard. Quickly recovering himself, Pete prepared to swing around and face him again; but his opponent stuck out his foot and tripped him, sending him facedown on the ground and knocking his sword out of his hands. The scoundrel laughed cruelly and raised both of his knives above his head again. Esmeralda cried out in agony and fell back half-swooning.

"Foul play!" Bernadette rushed towards him at full speed, and thrust with all her strength into his upper right arm. The brigand howled, and dropped his scimitar, doubling over with the pain. Pete slowly rose to his feet, extending his hand. Bernadette put her sword into it.

"And here's yours again, Pete," Esmeralda had recovered herself and retrieved the weapon for him. "He's been fighting you two weapons to one all this time; I think it's about time you returned the service!" She darted a vindictive glance at their mutual enemy.

However, Pete was too much of a gentleman for that, and not only permitted his opponent to pick up his other sword, but also allowed him a breathing space before continuing the duel. However, Bernadette's saving thrust had done its work; the villain wearied quickly now, and laid himself open to Pete's lightning-quick attacks, one of which at length laid him stretched upon the ground.

"You are safe now, Essie; and your honor is avenged," Pete said quietly, wiping his forehead and gazing down upon his fallen foe.

"Is he dead?" Bernadette and Esmeralda had once again retreated to a safe distance from the battle, but now they returned to stand by Pete's side.

"No; just temporarily crippled from various wounds. We'll have to bind them up and take him along; hopefully we can drop him off at the next hermit's cottage we pass," Pete returned, sheathing his sword and gathering up the enemy's knife and scimitar. The victor in a duel is entitled to the other's weapons.

"I wonder what he's doing up here," Esmeralda whispered, looking down at her former master with scarcely repressed abhorrence. "Say"— she knelt down next to him, reluctantly—"are the rest of the tribe at hand?"

"Try and find out," growled the outlaw, striving to raise himself, but only succeeding in sinking back in a dead faint. Bernadette, moved with pity, hastily bent over him and began to bandage his wounds with her handkerchief.

"They can't be that close around here; he'd have summoned his minions to help," Esmeralda said musingly, sitting back on her heels. "He'd never go out on a raiding mission alone, and there are usually few travelers in these parts, anyway. What did he want here?"

"Perhaps this!" Bernadette plunged her hand into the enemy's pocket, and withdrew a bulky packet of papers, the corner of which she had seen protruding above the lining.

"He can't read; what good are those things to him?" Esmeralda sounded puzzled.

"Let me see them." Pete snatched the papers out of his cousin's hand and scanned them rapidly, his face darkening as he read. Bernadette finished binding up their vanquished foe's wounds and then rose to peer over Pete's shoulder at the papers.

"So *here's* our traitor who's been selling information to the enemy!" Pete exclaimed, looking down at the unconscious outlaw with unmixed scorn. "Of all the vile fellows! These papers are descriptions of every fort and battle plan of the entire armed forces of Berklesgilands; it's no wonder the enemy has been able to meet us at every turn."

"And what's this?" Bernadette caught at a letter, inscribed on a slightly thinner sheet of paper, and inspected it closely for a few moments, attempting to decipher the fancy martial handwriting. After a minute, she looked up, her face white.

"Pete, Essie, the enemy is planning to attack the Cergewillen Fort at the Fords of Bershwin *in three days*! The main force there is moving out that morning to go reinforce a more vulnerable location, and the enemy intends to fall upon them as soon as they are out of sight of the fort, take them by surprise and vanquish them, and then continue on and take the now undermanned fort. We've got to stop them!"

"How far away is this place? Can we make it in three days?" Esmeralda asked anxiously.

"No, we can't; but we've got to," Pete said tersely, turning away to start loading up immediately. "It's a good five days' regular journey from here; we'll have to travel nonstop if we are to make it."

"And God helping us, we will!" said Bernadette fervently, leaping into her saddle, still wearing partial armor.

"Don't you think we'd better head for the castle, first, though, Bernie, to ask Uncle whether or not he approves of this expedition?" Pete simply could not resist the temptation to inquire as the three of them galloped off.

"Don't tease, Pete; we have no time for that!" Bernadette exclaimed, her cheeks flushing distressfully. "This is an emergency; we've *got* to get there in time!"

Their travel speed was hampered for the rest of that day and night by the heavy burden draped across the back of Pete's saddle; but fortunately, they reached a hermit's cottage early the next morning. The inhabitant willingly agreed to take charge of the bandit and nurse him back to health, promising to immediately turn him over to the captain of the guard in the next village once he had recovered.

And then the race began. The three friends rode pell-mell through valley and dale, up hill and down, across rivers and gorges, without slackening their pace for an instant, even to eat or sleep. Through tangled woods and morasses they pushed onward, only Esmeralda's expert woodland skills preventing them from losing their way. After another day and night of hard riding, they finally came over the crest of a hill, to find themselves approaching a sizeable hamlet, and pressed on with renewed vigor.

"Say, Bernie, don't you recognize this place?" Pete inquired, glancing around him as they rode up the main street of the village with a thundering of hooves, attracting the attention of the stolid passersby, who did not appear to particularly appreciate this intrusion into their commonly quiet and undisturbed lifestyle.

"To be sure," Bernadette responded excitedly. "Isn't this the village on the other side of the Burlon Forest, where we joined Sir Timothy's regiment? Yes, it is; look, I can see Grandma Myrtle's sign down that road!" she gestured in its direction.

"Some of that gingerbread would sure taste good right now," Pete said wistfully.

"Well, we don't have time to get any," Bernadette rejoined decisively, a note of authority in her voice. "I've got my bearings now; we just came in from the opposite side. Come on, let's head for the inn and see whether or not we can find anyone there to help us! If we can raise a larger force to help us defend the fort, without delay, it might make all the difference! Come on!" and she led the way down the side road to the "Gander and Cheese."

There was something about this little town that made it the perfect gathering point for companies of traveling knights; there was a vast assembly of soldiers in the inn-yard, who were more than willing to join with them, especially once Bernadette had shown them her royal signet ring, stamped with the Royal Seal of the Kingdom of Berklesgilands, which she had carried with her as a safeguard throughout her entire journey. All the soldiers knew the Royal Seal by sight, and its authority was complete with them. They were all also aware of the Princess Royal's current adventure of absence, and immediately took it for granted that she had spent it in becoming acquainted with the arts of warcraft, just for the sake of such a situation as this.

Worthy Grand, the innkeeper, also was more than willing to help in any way possible; and in addition to heaping as many helpings of his cheeses on them as he possibly could, he offered the services of his daughter Bessie, who could ride on ahead of them and reach the force at the Cergewillen Fort before daybreak, to inform them that they were to remain on guard at the fort and await Bernadette's coming reinforcements. Bessie would be sure to get there on time; she was riding her father's horse Lightning, the fleetest of foot in the country.

The rest of the volunteer forces assembled and began the march to the Fords of Bershwin as quickly as possible, following Esmeralda's guidance through the tangled masses of the forest. The sun was already two hours high when they finally emerged from the woods the following morning. There were no signs of the enemy army, other than well-trampled footprints covering the meadow before them, clearly indicating that they had already passed that way and were well on their way to the fort. Dispirited looks were exchanged; Bernadette could feel the drop in morale, and made haste to encourage them once again.

"'Twas no more than I expected; they had a start on us. But if the innkeeper's daughter Bessie succeeded in her mission, the guard at the fort will have been warned and will keep the enemy off until we get there. But we have no more time to lose; come on!" and Bernadette set her men the example by spurring on her horse across the field. Raising a great hurrah, the knights stampeded after her.

Less than half an hour later, the battlements of the Cergewillen Fort loomed in the distance, and the sounds of combat carried clearly to the ears of the company. With redoubled vigor, the riders urged their horses across the swollen waters of the Fords of Bershwin, and thundered across the green and through the strand of trees before the fort.

Such a sight as met their eyes! The enemy army, under the command of their crown prince, was scattered all around the field, endeavoring to slingshot rocks up to the top of the fort walls, which were lined with archers shooting down into the confused mass below. Several wounded men were lying upon the ground, but they were all of the enemy's troops; none of the soldiers of the fort had yet been forced to come out in the effort to drive them away. The enemy army had clearly been taken aback upon finding the fort still fully occupied, but they had swiftly recovered their nerve and resource: a group of men was straining to roll a just-constructed battering ram against the strong front portal of the fort, and simultaneously endeavoring to shield themselves from a deluge of arrows from above.

"Now, men!" Bernadette, raising the Berklesgilands battle-cry and waving her sword above her head, led the shouting torrent of knights directly through the middle of the assembled enemy army, straight towards the battering ram. The enemy, taken completely by surprise, offered no resistance, until the battering ram had been smashed into a thousand pieces and trampled under the feet of the reinforcements' horses.

And then the fighting began in earnest. The archers on the walls kept the enemy away from the fort, while Bernadette's troops closed in on them from every side. Feeling themselves caught in a trap, the enemy knights fought like cornered wildcats, bringing down many a horse and rider. The outcome of the battle appeared by no means certain.

But Bernadette and her knights were determined; they were fighting on their own soil, for their own country, and that spurred them on. Bernadette galloped into the thickest of the battle, with her wealth of golden hair streaming out from beneath her helmet, and closed with one of the largest and most fearsome of the enemy soldiers, who had already taken down four of her ablest men. But he found Bernadette's skill and agility more than a match for his own brute force and power.

Pete, who had already unhorsed six of the enemy's knights, paused to wipe his sword and look about him, taking in the situation with a calculating eye. Matters were still up in the air; everywhere knights were fighting fiercely, some on horseback and some on foot. Esmeralda and Bessie (who had been prevented from leaving the fort by the arrival of the enemy) were running back and forth between the field and a small door leading into the fort, guiding their wounded safely inside.

The fort itself was still standing strong, without a single breach in its walls, or a gap in the line of archers lining the upper battlements. The enemy army was completely occupied with fighting against the Berklesgilandian knights who hemmed them in on every side, despite their efforts to break away and renew their assault upon the gates. Bernadette had unhorsed and severely wounded the enemy champion by now, which further demoralized their forces. They fell back as she galloped through their ranks once again; her identity as yet was only suspected by the opposing army, and few of them cared to grapple with this indefatigable female knight.

So far, well and good. Pete took a firm grip on his sword and looked about him for his next antagonist. Then out of the corner of his eye, he caught sight of some unusual movement in the portion of the enemy division surrounding the prince; they were headed away from the fort, but they did not appear to be fleeing. They were not fighting their way *through* the Berklesgilandian soldiers, but rather seemed to be surrounding them and driving them along. They were taking them prisoners! and would make their way back to their own country unmolested, unless they were stopped immediately.

Pete, shouting out to a number of the other knights to gather together and follow him, bore down upon the enemy prince; if he could take him down, the rest of the men around him would be discomfited and easily defeated. The Berklesgilandian prisoners raised a cheer as they discerned his efforts, and fought against their captors with renewed will.

However, few of the other knights had been able to follow Pete's lead; he was outnumbered, and before he could reach the prince, he felt a blow from behind, striking through his mail and wounding his shoulder, so that he dropped his sword and, reeling, fell from his horse. Triumphant, the enemy re-encircled their prisoners and marched off the field of battle without further pursuit from the Berklesgilandian soldiers.

But there was one, who was not a knight, who did pursue them. Esmeralda had seen her husband's capture; and without a moment of hesitation, she ran after the departing enemy division on foot, determined to aid her husband's escape or else share his fate, whatever that might be.

Bernadette had seen all of this, but was unable to assist in any way. She was surrounded on all sides by the best and bravest of the remaining enemy soldiers. It seemed that for every thrust she turned aside, three more were directed at her from the other side. She could not avoid them all, and between minor wounds and heavy blows landing upon her mail-protected shoulders and wrists, she was beginning to weary. Could this be where her adventure was to end?

"Bessie!" she shouted, seeing that maiden hastily skirting the danger area. "Summon a force from within the fort to my aid! We have more need now of men on the field than archers on the walls!" Bessie nodded and waved to indicate that she had heard, and returned within the fort. Bernadette fought on, breathing heavily; if she could but keep them at bay for a few more minutes, her other knights would arrive and drive them away.

And then, with a sudden rousing cry, several mounted Berklesgilandian knights bore down upon the struggling group. The enemy knights surrounding Bernadette, unprepared to meet this new attack, immediately fell back in the face of the knights from the Cergewillen Fort.

Perhaps Bernadette manifested her relief too soon; for the last of the retreating enemy knights turned around in his saddle and dealt a crushing blow to the top of her helmet, and before Bernadette could recover herself and turn to close with him again, he had thrust his sword through her side and upper arm, and knocked her from her horse. Then he turned and swiftly galloped away after his companions, pursued by the knights who had come to Bernadette's aid too late.

On the ground, Bernadette endeavored painfully to raise herself; through blurred vision, she could just see her horse rushing madly away. Bleeding and exhausted, she struggled to crawl out of the thick of the battle, which was still raging around her. Where was Bessie, to help her back to the fort? Suddenly renewed shouts, redolent of victory and defiance, rang out around her: what did they mean? Bernadette made one final effort to raise herself and take stock of the situation; finding the task beyond her strength, she sank down once again on the field of battle, unconscious.

Chapter Thirty-two
Peace Restored

When Bernadette finally opened her eyes again, groaning through the stiffness and pain in her side, it was dark and cold. She was lying on a hard and lumpy pallet, covered with an insufficient blanket, and, judging from the other groans audible around her, surrounded by other wounded sufferers like herself. As her eyes adjusted to the darkness, she could see the stone wall beside her; somehow she must have been brought into the fort. She had no idea how or when, nor of what else had happened out on the field of battle. Just now, all that mattered was that she was horribly thirsty. She was in a great deal of pain; but she really did not care, just so long as she could have one last drink of water.

Was there anyone around who could bring it to her? Bernadette attempted to raise her head. The stone floor of the room was covered with the wounded, lying in various positions of misery, and no one seemed to be attending to them. Where exactly was she, anyway?

Suddenly one of the figures next to her, who had been sitting propped against the wall, his head swathed in a stained bandage, leaned closer to her and gently pushed her back down. "Don't try to sit up," he said kindly. "There is no need."

"I just want some water," Bernadette replied, with great difficulty, falling limply back on her pallet.

"I'll get it for you." This knight was evidently not as badly wounded as some of the others; he made his way quite easily across the floor and brought back a dipperful of water, which he held to Bernadette's lips while she drank. Nectar and ambrosia were nothing compared to the taste of that water. It was not enough to quench her burning thirst, though, and she longed for more. But what she had drunk had cleared her head enough for her to consider the situation unselfishly; doubtless there were other people who needed water, and besides, she did not wish her fellow wounded soldier to exert himself beyond his strength for her.

This consideration did not appear to bother him, however. He reached over to adjust the bandages around her arm. Bernadette gritted her teeth against the pain; it did feel much better once he had rearranged them so that they did not stick so closely. "Thank you," she said softly, gazing longingly at the dipper he had set aside.

"How are you feeling now? Can I do anything else for you, my princess?" the voice somehow sounded almost cheerful and amused, even amidst the extremely disagreeable surroundings. Gracious, was she delirious or dreaming? It couldn't be, now could it? Bernadette peered up more closely into the face of her caretaker, trying to make out his features. A pair of familiar dark eyes sparkled knowingly down into hers.

"Colin?" Bernadette had just enough strength to whisper his name. He took her hands in his and bent down to press his lips warmly against her own. Bernadette couldn't move her one arm, but she got the other one loose and threw it around his neck, clinging to him as though nothing in the world could ever separate the two of them again. Colin held her closely in his arms for a long, long moment; his tenderness and devoted affection washing over her in waves of comfort.

But at length he drew away and seated himself beside her pallet again, smiling down at her in his usual companionable way. "Are you feeling all right now, darling?" he asked her gently, speaking the pet name he had never before used towards her so caressingly that Bernadette thought it was the most beautiful word in the world.

"I don't think I ever felt better," she breathed rapturously, trying to take hold of his hand once again. He closed his strong fingers over hers in a reassuringly supportive clasp. With his other hand, he reached down to brush her hair back from her damp forehead. For a moment, a silence far more eloquent than words remained between the two of them. But then Bernadette came back to the hard necessities of reality, accompanied by a very natural and pressing curiosity to fully understand the particulars of her current uncomfortable situation. "Where am I, Colin? And what are you doing here? What happened in the battle? How—oh, and I am *still* so thirsty," she ended plaintively, her dry throat preventing her rush of questions from finding full flow.

"I can get you more water; there is plenty of that in the fort, although there is a shortage of medicine," Colin replied, disengaging his hand from hers and going back over to the water bucket. "Are you in very much pain? Here," he put the water to her lips again and Bernadette drank gladly.

"I think I'm all right," Bernadette responded wearily. "I'm mostly just very stiff and tired."

"Well, the battle was over very shortly after you fell, so you were brought in and had your injuries bound up before there was a chance for infection to set in. You should do pretty well, but I wish I could get you something to ease your discomfort," Colin said, glancing about him a little impatiently. Men do not like to be put in the position of being unable to do absolutely everything possible for the girls they care for.

"But what about you, Colin? You were wounded too, weren't you?" Bernadette reached up to touch the bandage around his head, with womanly concern.

"Oh, it was nothing; I had my helmet knocked off and it banged my temple, and then I was slightly wounded in my ankle while trying to get away from the fellow before he could finish me off," Colin replied carelessly. "There are very few of your knights who were not injured to some extent; and so those who were only somewhat wounded have to care for those whose injuries are more serious."

"So what happened?" Bernadette still wanted to know. "Did we win the battle?"

"Technically, yes. The fort is still in the possession of the Kingdom of Berklesgilands, and the enemy force was driven off. The non-injured knights pursued them; hopefully they will be able to vanquish them entirely, but they will probably need reinforcements for that. Fortunately there's another outpost near here, so if they think to send a message there, the other force can join them and together they should be able to crush the enemy completely. Until we hear how that develops, it'll be safer for us to remain here in the fort, even supposing that the wounded could be removed without danger to their health, which most of them can't as yet," Colin replied calmly. He hadn't taken her hand again, although Bernadette had put it out so that he could if he wanted to, and was decidedly disappointed when he didn't.

"But what are you doing here?" Bernadette repeated, confusedly trying to piece the disconnected parts of the situation together, as well as her muddled brain would allow.

"I might ask the same of you," Colin came back at her immediately, and Bernadette flushed and her eyes fell. "The fort I was at fell last week, and those of us who escaped were making our way to another, when we ran across the enemy camp during a night march and heard that they were planning to make their way here. We followed them in order to lend our aid to the force at the fort, to find that you had gotten ahead of us. But our assistance did not seem to be superfluous, either."

"No, I dare say you turned the tide of the battle completely; it looked like we had an equal chance of falling as succeeding, the last I saw of it," Bernadette rejoined earnestly. "Oh, dear! And if I had gone with you to begin with, it would have worked out just the same. And it's what I should have done; I know that now. Forgive me, Colin," she pleaded, blinking back the tears that threatened to arise in spite of her best attempts to hold them back. Even wounded female knights do not cry while still in battle garb.

"I've nothing to forgive, my little blind one," Colin responded warmly. "It all worked out for the best; if you had been at the other fort with us, your force wouldn't have gotten here early enough to warn the battalion at this fort."

"But I was such a fool, to think that it could ever be right to leave one's country in the lurch for purely selfish considerations," Bernadette muttered self-reproachfully, twirling her tattered blanket between her fingers.

"Never mind," Colin said consolingly. "Everyone makes mistakes, and you certainly made up for yours, if it really even was one. Now you should really try to get some sleep." He reached down to soothe her nervous fingers still again.

"I'm too cold to sleep," Bernadette shivered, trying to close her ears to the moans of another injured knight across from her.

Colin did not respond to that, but went and got her some more water and then sat beside her and stroked her hair until she had relaxed enough to fall asleep in spite of the cold, much to Colin's relief. He had been worried that if she stayed awake any longer, she might ask him the one question that he really did not want to answer.

What had happened to Pete and Esmeralda? Colin did not know; he hadn't arrived until after they were already gone, but another one of the slightly wounded caretakers had informed him of the circumstances of their departure. There had not been enough healthy knights left to follow after them. The enemy prince was well known for being ruthless when it came to dealing with his prisoners; Colin was worried.

He was worried about Bernadette, too; despite her courageous words, he could tell that her wound was still serious, and that her chances of recovery were by no means certain. Colin had responsibilities to care for the other wounded as well, but he spent every spare moment at Bernadette's side. Under his tender and committed care, she began to gradually but consistently improve.

"I think I will get well," she said brightly, several days later. "And it can't happen any too soon, either; I want to get home as soon as possible. It's already past the date!" she exclaimed, plucking impatiently at her covers.

"Don't worry about it; you'll only make yourself worse and have to wait even longer," Colin offered his usual level-headed advice. He glanced over to where another knight was calling feebly for water. "I'll be back in a minute." He got up and moved over to the sufferer, bending over him and kindly offering to do whatever was possible to ease his pain.

Bernadette watched him, her heart in a warm glow. She loved Colin all the more when she saw his tender-hearted consideration for those who had no claim on him other than that of common humanity.

Occupied with these pleasant thoughts, she at first failed to notice the attempts made to gain her attention by another figure nearby. This individual did not even have a pallet, but was lying on the floor, and endeavoring to crawl closer to Bernadette.

"Bernadette! Oh, Bernadette, help me, please!" the cracked accents abruptly jolted Bernadette out of her reverie. She focused her gaze on the pathetic figure.

"Essie?" she gasped, scarcely recognizing her friend, as she dragged herself painfully to her side. "Are you hurt? What happened? Where is—" Bernadette did not finish her questioning. "Colin!" she called desperately, counting on his aid in this emergency as always.

Colin was at their side in a moment, stooping over Esmeralda and preparing to move her to a more comfortable resting place. But she feebly pushed his hands away.

"I'm not hurt, only exhausted from the journey and hunger. But Pete—" she choked momentarily and then continued, bravely: "I could not carry him up the stairs; he is unconscious down below. The lack of treatment for his wounds and the foul air of the enemy prison brought on a fever; we barely made it back here alive."

"I'll go and get him at once, Esmeralda," Colin assured her with alacrity. "But first let me put you to bed as well; you are obviously at the end of your strength and in need of proper care. Here, John!" he called to another one of the caretakers. "Pray go and prepare some nourishing gruel for this faint maiden, will you? Make haste!" he added, when the other did not move immediately.

"We're starting to run low on food, you know," Sir John said significantly. "Of course I'll get it for her; she needs it. But those of us who are stronger may need to start rationing our portions, if we are not to run out. I just thought I should warn you now," he spoke over his shoulder as he headed down to the fort cellars, where the food bags were stored.

"Right," Colin responded tersely, gathering the protesting Esmeralda up in his arms. She did not want to be taken care of until after her husband had been; he was in much more danger than she was!

"Lay her next to me, Colin; there's plenty of room," Bernadette offered, moving over on her narrow pallet. "Then you can go and get Pete and look after him, and move Esmeralda to her own bed at a more convenient time. I can keep her warm this way, anyhow, and I am sure she needs it," she took one of her friend's cold hands and began to rub it with her own good hand, trying to restore the circulation.

Colin thanked her with a look of approval for her consideration, and then was gone to bring up Pete. Esmeralda, meanwhile, once she had eaten the meal that Sir John shortly brought up for her, was able to tell Bernadette what had happened to them.

The enemy had carried Pete and several of the other knights off as prisoners to one of the forts they now held within the borders of Berklesgilands. Esmeralda had followed them at a distance, once it had become clear that any attempt on her part to free Pete single-handedly would only be folly. Arriving after Pete and the other prisoners had been thrown into the dungeon, without food or medical care, Esmeralda had snuck into the enemy's fort, daringly scaling the wall, and found her way down into the dungeons. In great danger of discovery, she had managed to pick the lock and free the knights of Berklesgilands and her husband. The rest of the knights had headed off to rejoin their respective regiments, and Esmeralda and Pete had turned back toward the Cergewillen Fort.

It had been a long and weary journey; Pete had soon become delirious and had been forced to lean heavily on Esmeralda in order to advance at all. Esmeralda had not dared to leave him even to forage for food, so they had been forced to make do with what few edibles

314

happened to be in their path. And even though they were both exhausted, Esmeralda had known that their only hope was to push on to the fort as quickly as possible, hoping that Pete would be able to hold out that far and that there would be aid available once they got there.

"We've been keeping some medicines back just in case of such emergencies; there will be enough for Pete, don't worry," Colin reassured the girls after hearing the story. "And I'll attend to him particularly; you're well enough now to look after Violetta while she recuperates, aren't you, Cecilia?" he spoke in a brisk, businesslike manner, obviously expecting that Bernadette would step up and take on the necessary responsibilities, in spite of her own only half-healed injuries, just as he and the others had.

"Of course," Bernadette said quietly, as Colin moved a pallet next to hers and lifted Esmeralda easily over onto it.

"I really don't need all that much care; I'm just very tired and need some rest," Esmeralda insisted hastily. "But first of all I need to be sure that Pete will be all right . . ."

"I can assure you that he will be fine; his wounds are neither deep nor serious, and the infection and fever are no worse than many cases I have seen treated to full recovery in very short order," Colin replied firmly. "Now you must rest and leave your husband's care to me; you have done all and more than could possibly be required of you. See to it that she doesn't exert herself before I give permission, Maiden Cecilia," he ordered playfully, moving off to go back to Pete.

"Aye, aye, sir," Bernadette returned with a mock salute, leaning back on her good elbow and turning her attention to her own patient. Esmeralda's eyes were already closed; she was in desperate need of sleep.

After a few days of needed rest and care, Esmeralda was quite herself again, and Pete was recovered enough to recognize his wife, cousin, and friend, although he was still too weak to talk much. Bernadette's own wound was still mending, steadily though slowly, and Colin appeared so well that everyone had forgotten that he had even been scratched in the late battle. Besides, there were more important considerations at hand.

"There really is not enough food left to last out the week; what are we to do?" Sir John had just come up from the cellars with the day's rations, which were decidedly small.

"It is simple," Colin rejoined assertively. "I will leave the fort today to find and bring back provisions."

"You oughtn't to go alone, Colin; what if you run across more enemy soldiers along the way? Let me go with you," Bernadette pleaded earnestly, half-rising from her pallet.

"You're not well enough; and besides, one person is half as much likely to be noticed as two," Colin replied curtly, getting to his feet and heading for the fort stairwell.

"And can also carry only half as much food," Bernadette pointed out.

Chapter Thirty-three
Home Again

Nonetheless, Colin went alone, and returned three days later with a wagonful of provisions, and some extremely good news.

"The war is over!" he proclaimed, running up the stairs into the sick ward and throwing his black helmet triumphantly in the air. The recuperating knights broke into rousing cheers. Esmeralda got up and danced a fandango the length of the floor, and Pete and Bernadette hugged each other in delight. "We've won!"

"How did it come about, Colin, and where did you find out?" Bernadette asked eagerly, getting up and coming over to help him and Sir John distribute the much-anticipated delicacies he had brought back.

"At the village where I bought the food, of course; it was all over town," Colin responded, straining at the knots on one of the bundles. "Apparently our success in holding the fort here utterly demoralized the enemy's forces. The enemy king and the largest division of his army had just been preparing to meet King Friedrich and his forces in battle at the Fields of Kergewellin, which is not far from the Royal Palace, when they heard of this. The enemy king was alarmed, and attempted to slip away the night before the battle was to take place, to gather and reorganize the rest of his scattered army; but King Friedrich pursued and defeated them, and so they were forced to sue for peace. It's all over now, and we can go home!" Colin reiterated, to further thunderous cheers. There are perhaps few people in the world to whom the word "home" means more than a war-weary soldier.

And so a gradual exodus from Cergewillen Fort began, almost immediately. Only a skeleton garrison was required to remain at the fort in times of peace, so the rest of the recovered soldiers left to rejoin their hometown divisions or go to new assignments. Those who were still recuperating were only waiting to be well enough to travel in order to follow them.

Colin had left with one of the very first companies to depart. He was no longer needed to care for any of the other three, and none of them had invited him to remain and travel back with them. Bernadette had longed to, but did not dare. She had noticed a change in Colin's manner towards her, shortly after Pete and Esmeralda had arrived. He seemed to have gone back to considering her simply as a friend. Had she been mistaken in assuming what passion it was that had driven him to plant that one burning kiss on her lips, when they had first met again? Perhaps he had thought, then, that she might die, and only wanted to assure her of his friendship and forgiveness. Certainly he had shown no signs of especial tenderness towards her once she had begun to recover. Did he no longer care for her, or was it that he thought she no longer cared for him, and therefore did not wish to trouble her with unwanted attentions? Bernadette did not know, and before she could scrape up the courage to ask Colin straight out, he was gone.

And it was time for the rest of them to be gone as well; no doubt everyone at the palace was worrying about why they had not arrived back on time. Oddly enough, now it was Pete who was the most anxious to be getting home; as soon as his injuries were healed enough to ensure against recurring infection, he was ready to go. Bernadette's own wound was still stiff and sore, but she could travel if she tried, and she wasn't going to be a weakling and ask for a few more days of rest, as much as she would have liked them. Nothing really mattered now.

Besides, it was neither a very long nor a very hard journey; three days of easy going brought them within sight of the castle towers. Upon first seeing them, Bernadette roused from her apathy enough to feel a lump rising in her throat; she had been gone for so long, away from those she loved and had missed so much, and now they were right there in front of her. Soon she would see them all again.

"Come on, let's go!" Pete urged, gathering up his reins and preparing to descend the final hill that lay on their way to the castle. Esmeralda was right behind him, but Bernadette gazed thoughtfully at her beckoning home for a couple of moments longer before following, torn inside with various conflicting emotions.

Shortly thereafter, they rode into the palace yard, three weary, mud-splashed, and bedraggled figures on three equally travel-worn horses. There were no grooms present to take their mounts, so they had to take them to the stable and rub them down themselves, before finally trudging up to the castle door.

Obviously, as they were past the return date, no one was expecting them on this specific day. But all the same, they had barely gotten up the front steps before Stephen pounced on them, welcoming his princess home as warmly as one would a returning hero long given up for lost.

"Come in, come in! Oh, it is so good to see you again, Princess Bernadette; you cannot imagine how much you have been missed here! So much has occurred that I have to tell you, and I am certain you have as much to share with me, yes indeed!" Stephen could scarcely check his enthusiastic flow of conversation long enough to hear Bernadette's own greeting, while he nearly wrung her hand off in his excitement. Turning to Pete, he clapped him heartily on the shoulder, exclaiming: "And how are you, Sir Peter, my friend? So good to see you back again!" just as though they had always been the very best of chums! "I'll go and let everyone know you're back; oh, they will all be *so* happy to see you!" and he rushed off distractedly, leaving the other three standing in the Great Hall. Fortunately, Cecil had just been on his way down to relieve Stephen as door-porter, and therefore was able to take their cloaks and find a suitably durable mat for them to scrape their muddy boots on, meanwhile offering his own expressions of welcome, which, if not quite as exuberant as Stephen's, were equally heartfelt and sincere.

And then everyone was there: King Friedrich, Queen Anna Marie, Camille, Princess Roxanne, the cook, the butler, the ladies-in-waiting, and all the rest of the palace staff. There was such a hubbub of hugging and kissing and merry greeting, with everyone talking at once, that it was a long time before any one particular voice could be clearly distinguished.

The one that finally was, however, was of course King Friedrich's hearty, booming accents. "Well, well, so we have the return of the wanderers now, eh? At last! So, are you glad to be at home again, daughter?" he looked down at her with a fondly quizzical expression, to where he was still holding her tightly clasped in one large encircling arm.

"Oh, yes, Father," Bernadette replied fervently, nestling closely against his vest, feeling like a little girl again. She reached over his shoulder to get hold of her mother's hand, basking in the warmth of her tender, fond smile. It was good to be home.

"And how about you, my nephew? Survived the mission, I see," King Friedrich went on jovially, turning to Pete, who was standing nearby, looking surprisingly uncomfortable.

"Barely!" he responded immediately, rousing himself to roll his eyes significantly at his cousin and then moving away awkwardly, to address one of the last people in the palace he still had to greet, who in times past had always been one of the very *first* he had greeted.

"How are you, Maiden Camille?" he asked, in an unnaturally stiff tone, clearly very ill at ease. Bernadette freed herself from her father's arm and watched with interest to see how this interchange would turn out. Camille seemed embarrassed as well; perhaps Pete's distant manner troubled her, for she responded at random, with flushed cheeks and without looking up, seemingly seeking an excuse to get away.

"And who is this lovely young lady you have brought back with you?" King Friedrich reclaimed Bernadette's attention, placing his hand on her shoulder and directing an affably inquiring glance towards Esmeralda, who had remained shyly in the background throughout the reunion bustle, looking about her uncertainly. But now, emboldened by King Friedrich's welcoming smile, and Queen Anna Marie's gracious one, she came forward without another moment's hesitation.

"I am Esmeralda, the gypsy maiden," she introduced herself with a respectful curtsy, but with head held high. No one could have thought for one minute that she considered herself below the level of any of the upper-class ladies of title who frequented the palace and courted the attention of the King and Queen.

"And my very closest friend!" Bernadette added warmly, putting her arm around Esmeralda's waist and eagerly seeking to further the favorable impression she saw that her friend had already made upon her parents. "Without her, I don't know what Pete and I would have done at times."

"Oh, really, I . . ." Esmeralda began to deprecate the tribute's application, but King Friedrich interrupted her.

"Well, any friend of my daughter's is sure of a hearty welcome here, always! You must consider our house as your own, my dear," he offered the whole of the palace with one inviting sweep of his hand.

"I should hope so, uncle, as it really is her only home now," Pete said, almost desperately, turning away from Camille and back to them, as if resolved to get the truth out once and for all. "Esmeralda is my wife, so of course my home here is hers as well." He did not look back at Camille as he said this; Pete hated to disappoint or hurt anyone, even by accident (except of course for an enemy soldier on the field of battle).

"You're married, too!" Camille did not appear to be at all hurt, only extremely surprised, and strangely enough, almost relieved.

"Yes," Pete laughed, very glad to have the confession over with, and immediately feeling like himself again. With the conscious pride of a newlywed, he reached for Esmeralda's hand and began to explain: "You see, we were married on the way, because . . . what do you mean, 'married too,' Camille?" he turned back to her as the significance of her words struck him.

"Yes, we are!" Stephen bounded over to take Camille's arm, beaming into her downcast, blushing face. "And it's all due to you, Princess," he added warmly, turning to Bernadette with inexpressible gratitude written all over his face. "Since you told me to take care of Camille while you were away, she couldn't very well forbid me to approach her, for that would be going against your wishes."

"And of course, Camille would never do that!" Bernadette rejoined merrily, throwing a laughing glance at her maid. "I know; that was why I told you to do it."

"Yes; and so I was finally able to court her as I wished, and she finally said yes, and so now I am the happiest man in the world!"

322

Stephen concluded triumphantly, drawing Camille closer to him, with the air of a man who knows he possesses the world's greatest treasure and values it accordingly, which was very pleasant to see.

"Quite the way to get the woman you want, to take advantage of the fact that she can't properly reject your addresses," Pete observed moralistically, apparently not too impressed.

"We'll be generous, and not ask how *you* got *your* wife to agree to the marriage," Stephen retorted immediately, evidently enjoying the chance to keep on wrangling with Pete in a friendly fashion, even now that their old competition had been so neatly resolved all around.

"But anyway, I'm so happy for you both!" Bernadette exclaimed, rushing over to kiss Camille on the cheek and shake Stephen heartily by the hand.

"So, daughter, are you going to set up in business as a matchmaker now, seeing how well your first efforts have been rewarded; or do you have something else in mind?" King Friedrich asked playfully, bringing Bernadette back to the business of reality. She had almost forgotten the bargain conditions now to be fulfilled, in the joy of being at home again. But now she had to announce her decision, and everyone in the Hall was looking at her expectantly. Bernadette drew a deep breath and threw her head back, looking her father directly in the eye as she replied, and carefully choosing the right words to express her decision, which had cost her so much to make.

"I daresay you knew from the very beginning, Father, that what I would learn from my adventure would not be how to find out what I wanted in life, but to realize that I had had it all along," she said in measured tones. "I have learned a great deal about life and about our kingdom and the people who will be my future subjects, and I take greater pride than ever in the thought of leading them someday. I would not have gone without the experiences of this past year; I know I am now much better equipped than I was to take on my rightful duties, and I know that I could not truly desire to do anything else. I am Princess Bernadette, and not anybody else; and nothing can change that, and I do not wish that it could be changed," Bernadette continued slowly. "I've enjoyed some of the other things I have done on this journey; but that isn't what matters, whether you enjoy something or not. Everything in this world can be enjoyable if handled right! What matters is whether your life is truly *yours*, and I know that the place where I can make my life mine is here, in the castle, with you and the rest of the family," she concluded with strong emotion, running to hug her father, mother, and Roxanne all over again. She drew back and smiled through a mist of earnest tears. "Does this make you happy, Father? Do you think I have made the right decision?"

"I always knew you would; my only concern was whether you would be happy with it," the King responded, looking down at his daughter with pride.

"But there is one more thing I've learned on this trip, Father," Bernadette prepared to broach the dangerous subject cautiously. "Sometimes you can do what you are supposed to do, without necessarily including all the aspects of it that don't suit you. I should have told you this long ago," she went on resolutely, "but what I really wanted was not to get out of being a princess and taking on my corresponding duties, but simply to avoid my planned marriage. I don't want to marry Prince Gerald Reginald of Saxe-Habsburg, and I never have. Can't Roxanne still take my betrothed, even if she doesn't take the kingdom?" she ended hopefully, but a look up into her father's serious face immediately dashed her positive expectations. She waited in dread for what he might say.

"But your marriage to the son of King Vincentius *is* part of your royal duties, my dear; I thought that we had been quite clear on that," her father told her gently, but quite firmly. "It would not be fair of you to ask Roxanne to take on some of the responsibilities of your station, while you kept all of its privileges."

"But why is it part of my duties, Father?" Bernadette challenged, unwilling to give in without a determined effort first. "What has marriage to do with running a kingdom?"

"You can't do it alone, my dear, believe me," the King smiled at the Queen. "I'd never manage anything half so well without your mother. You need a husband, and as a matter of diplomatic policy and alliance, Prince Gerald Reginald is your best choice available."

"But why cannot we split the two duties? They need not be connected," Bernadette proposed, as diplomatically as she could, although her heart was pounding away at a mile a minute within her chest, making it difficult for her to speak as calmly as she wished.

"What do you mean?" her father looked confused.

"Why can't the diplomatic part be covered by having the prince marry Roxanne, thus creating the needed alliance; and then I can marry someone else, and fulfill my part of the duty that way," Bernadette explained. She thought it sounded pretty reasonable, and she sincerely hoped her parents would agree.

Maybe they did, but unfortunately, that didn't matter at this point. "I'm afraid that's impossible, dear," King Friedrich replied, with a barely perceptible twinkle in his eye, "because, you see"—turning to his younger daughter with a look of fond pride—"Roxanne is already married."

"Wha-at!" Bernadette gasped in shock, staring at her sister with a completely dumbfounded expression, at which the rest of her family could not help laughing.

"Yes, Bernadette, I'm married," Princess Roxanne replied, in her prettily innocent manner, "to an Officer of the Guards, Sir Timothy," she turned to look up at a tall, handsome knight standing close beside her, glowing with gentle happiness as she placed her small hand confidingly in his.

"Sir Timothy!" Bernadette repeated blankly, gazing wide-eyed on the spectacle for another stunned minute. Then, abruptly recovering herself, she snapped to attention and saluted smartly. "And how are you, Commander?"

"Well; and you, Sir George?" Sir Timothy replied gravely, but with smiling eyes twinkling at his erstwhile aide.

"Did you know who I was all the time?" Bernadette demanded immediately, moving a step closer, and ignoring the confused looks all around her over this exceptionally unexpected method of greeting between her and her new brother-in-law.

"I did not. But I thought that I recognized Sir William—" Sir Timothy nodded in Pete's direction—"as an officer I had met in another regiment under another name. But I couldn't remember for certain, so I inquired about him from that regiment's commanding officer when I next returned to those barracks. And once I found out that he was your cousin Sir Peter, I naturally put two and two together."

"Well, I can't say I'm surprised at this turn of events; I remember how strongly you supported my praises of Roxanne at the dinner-table that night," Bernadette remarked, glancing from him to her sister and back again. "But how did it come about?"

"My division was with your father's troops during the final battle of the war, and we were invited here on furlough afterwards," Sir Timothy explained, glancing over at Sir Tousle-head, who was standing over by the wall; and who, judging from the complacent looks he was trading with a finely-dressed young lady by his side, whom Bernadette recognized as her lady-in-waiting Letitia, had also found matrimonial happiness upon his arrival there. "And your sister was so kind to me that I could not help but offer myself as her suitor, and was graciously accepted," he bent to kiss Princess Roxanne lightly on the forehead, pressing her hand fondly within his own.

All these happy couples surrounding her! It simply wasn't fair. "Well, I wish you joy, of course," Bernadette said slowly. "And I can't think of anyone I would rather have for a brother-in-law than you, Timothy; but don't you think you should have waited until I got back? What if I hadn't decided to take up my inheritance; what would you have done about my betrothed then, with Roxanne already taken?" she directed the last question to her father, turning back to him half-indignantly, half-appealingly.

"I knew that I could depend upon you not to be so selfish as to reject your duties, especially if doing so would wreck your sister's and another's happiness," King Friedrich rejoined quietly, but with pointed emphasis. Bernadette flushed consciously, but she was not done yet.

"Yes, but what about *my* happiness?" she exclaimed, a little hotly. "Why should my life's happiness be dependent upon the whims of that Gerald-Reginald prince fellow, whom we know nothing about, and who could be extremely distasteful to me, for all I know? I've met men from several walks of life during this journey, and I know full well that I'd prefer to marry almost anyone—knight, landlord, tinker, peasant, even *bandit*—rather than a high-ranking, spoiled, indolent, arrogant—"

Bernadette was choking on her running list of applicable terms for the mindless patrician coxcombs she so detested.

"Gracious me, Bernadette, hush!" admonished her mother anxiously, with a glance behind her at the door leading into the castle parlour. "Would you have him hear you?"

"Hear me? Is he here?" Bernadette gasped in horror, also looking at the door, with a terrible sinking feeling concerning the frightful mysterious personage waiting behind it.

"Of course; your wedding-date was several weeks ago, and you were expected to be back by then, so your betrothed and his family and all the rest of the wedding-guests were assembled here for the occasion," the Queen reminded her daughter patiently. "When you were not able to make it in time, most of the guests departed, but your betrothed remained to wait for you."

"Well, he can keep on waiting, then!" Bernadette exclaimed, not caring if he *did* hear her. "I think this is extremely unfair, to rig everything so that I don't have time to figure out how to handle this matter before I am forced to take action on it."

"Sorry, daughter, but it's too late to do anything about it now," her father replied, trying to be sympathetic. "If you want to get out of this, I'm afraid you'll have to provide a much more concrete objection than 'it's not fair.' Have you one?" he inquired, looking quite ready to consider it if she had.

Oh, how Bernadette longed to say "yes." But her only concrete objection was miles away; and besides, she could no longer be sure that she could have depended on his support, anyway. So she reluctantly shook her head. "No, I'm afraid I don't, Father."

"Then perhaps before we concern ourselves about the situation any further, you should really meet the others involved," King Friedrich suggested pleasantly. "Why don't you go up and get changed, all three of you—" glancing from one tattered and muddy figure to another as he spoke—"and then come down and get a more comprehensive view of the matter? You can't make up your mind against the prince without having met him, you know, daughter," he added.

"Yes, I know," Bernadette replied, drearily. The temporary burst of animation that had buoyed up her spirits upon her enthusiastic welcome home had died away entirely, leaving her feeling dull and lifeless, and really not caring how anything might turn out anymore. She followed Camille passively towards the stairs leading up to her room.

Back in her pretty childhood room, Bernadette looked around her with the vacant gaze of a shipwrecked sailor lost for years, who had returned to his old hometown to find everything strangely different, and yet poignantly the same. She let Camille choose a dress for her and fuss over her to her heart's content while she got into it; Bernadette was so much more wiry and athletically shaped now, that none of her dresses fit quite right anymore, and Camille had to take them in and tie them up to make them hang nicely enough to please her critical eye.

"You will want to look your best to meet your betrothed, Your Highness," she told her, gently encouraging. "I think you will like him, truly; he seems very kind and the perfect gentleman, and notices everyone in the palace in the most considerate way. He and Stephen"— blushing here again—"have become quite good friends."

"Yes, of course," Bernadette responded wearily. She did not want to talk about it any more. "Thank you, Camille; that will do. Go on back to your husband now," she added, with an attempt at her usual cheery flippancy, as she slipped out the door and headed slowly back down the stairs.

"There you are! What took you so long? Essie and I have been down here for ages." Pete was standing at the base of the stairs. "All the rest are already in the parlor; I came out to tell you when you came down. What's wrong, Bernie?" Pete broke off to ask his cousin seriously, coming up the first few steps to take her arm.

"You know perfectly well what!" Bernadette jerked away and stood facing him, her arms crossed tightly over her chest. "I don't want to marry him!"

"Really, Bernie, marriage is hardly fatal and actually very healthy; I ought to know," Pete responded jestingly, trying to lighten the situation (and very poorly timed his attempt was, Bernadette thought).

"Pete! Stop it! You of all people must understand how I feel; I love *Colin*, and you know it!" Bernadette cried desperately. No one but Pete could help her out now.

"Do I?" he responded indifferently, folding his own arms together and leaning back against the banisters. "Are you sure *he* knows it, Bernie? You haven't always made it profoundly obvious, you know."

"I know," Bernadette replied miserably, looking down and twisting her skirt nervously between her fingers. "But I do love him, and so I don't know what to do about all this now."

"Well, what do you think Colin would want you to do?" It was a very good question on Pete's part; he met his cousin's eyes with an intent, even gaze. Bernadette took a deep breath: yes, Pete was right; if she truly loved Colin, she would let his counsel be her guide.

"He would want me to not be afraid to do my duty for fear it would wreck my happiness; not to worry, but to do the right thing, knowing that it would all work out for the best in the end," she replied slowly but with conviction. She could almost hear Colin's voice corroborating her decision; he had said the same sort of thing to her so many times before.

"Very well, then; let's go in." Pete took her arm and led her into the parlor. "He's over there," Pete nodded towards a crowded back corner of the room, and then left to go back over to Esmeralda, who was standing by the fireplace, talking with Princess Roxanne and Sir Timothy.

Bernadette remained uncertainly by the door, not sure what she was expected to do. Her parents were talking with a couple further back in the room; Bernadette did not recognize the lady at all, but she thought that the dark, strongly-built, clean-cut gentleman looked vaguely familiar.

Several young men and women were grouped around a couch in the corner of the room where Pete had said her betrothed was; she would have to go over there to find him. Bernadette slowly threaded her way through the clusters of people that thronged the room, feeling as though she were trying to swim through jelly. Her arms and legs felt almost too heavy to lift.

"Ah, there you are, daughter!" her father's voice abruptly rose above the buzz of idle chatter. "Come and meet your prospective in-laws: my old friend King Vincentius and his wife Queen Beatrice!"

So she couldn't have recognized the gentleman after all; Bernadette had never met King Vincentius. He must just look like someone else she had met before. Not that it mattered. Bernadette went over and curtsied to the royal couple, hoping that they wouldn't detain her for too long. Now that it was almost here, she just wanted to get the dreaded first interview with her betrothed over with.

"Ah, so this is your spirited, independent-minded daughter, now isn't it!" King Vincentius exclaimed, regarding Bernadette with obvious approval. His wife smiled at her pleasantly, as well. "A pleasure to meet you at long last, my dear. I hope you had a pleasant and instructive journey?"

"Yes, I did, thank you," Bernadette responded tonelessly, dutifully returning the hearty kiss he planted on her cheek. "Very pleased to meet you," she remembered her manners, turning to greet Queen Beatrice in like manner.

"So, have you seen that rascal son of mine yet? Where is he hiding?" King Vincentius demanded jovially, sending keen, inquiring glances all around the room. Bernadette could see why he was her own father's best friend; they were really very much alike.

"Oh, he's over with the rest of the young folks in the corner; come now, daughter, allow me to introduce you," King Friedrich took Bernadette's arm and guided her towards the opposite corner of the room; the many young men and women chatting around the couch all paused in their conversations and looked up at her. Bernadette's head was swimming, and she could not distinguish any of their faces clearly, as her father stopped at a conspicuous point in the room, so that everyone could clearly hear and see what was going on.

"Prince Gerald Reginald, may I present my daughter, Princess Bernadette? Bernadette, this is your betrothed, Prince Gerald Reginald of Saxe-Habsburg," her father performed the introduction formally but heartily, and then released his daughter's arm and moved back, as did the crowd in the corner from around her betrothed.

The young man, who had been sitting on the couch, turned a little away from Bernadette's view, now rose and turned to face her directly. "My pleasure, Princess Bernadette." Those even tones, the keen gaze, the strongly-modeled features—there was no mistaking who this arresting figure really was. Bernadette felt the room spinning around her and fought to keep her balance; it couldn't be, it simply couldn't be, but . . .

"Colin?" Bernadette gasped.

Chapter Thirty-four
The Bargain Settled

"Colin!" Bernadette repeated disbelievingly, as she flung herself across the room and into his arms; he caught her up and kissed her, his lips pressed ardently to hers. After a moment he set her down and gazed deeply into her eyes.

"You're not crying, are you, my little blind one?" he asked, his keen eyes searching her face. "Come now: you've been wounded in battle, captured by bandits, nearly drowned in a river, and traversed the most treacherous of mountain passes and woodlands—you're not going to cry now, just over unexpectedly running into an old acquaintance, are you?" He was laughing, and Bernadette, shyly meeting his gaze, had to laugh, too.

"Well, if my eyes can't see, and don't cry, what on earth are they good for, then? Answer me that, Colin," she replied archly, brushing away the tears that had risen up out of sheer relief and incredulous joy.

"Well, they're very beautiful; have I ever told you that before?" Colin came back banteringly, smiling down at her, and drawing her down to sit next to him on the couch.

"Oh, I expect so," Bernadette returned carelessly. She leaned up against Colin's shoulder, pulling at him eagerly. "But how did you get here, Colin?"

"Well, your parents happened to invite me to the wedding, so I came as soon as I knew I would be wanted to participate in the happy occasion," Colin began, with a perfectly serious expression. "It had nothing to do with my own personal preference, of course, as I believe

334

has been previously mentioned in the course of our acquaintance, so we don't need to go into that again, now do we?" he glanced down at her, one eyebrow pointedly upraised, his ever-ready smile tugging at the corners of his mouth. Bernadette smiled back, and kissed him again.

"Would you two mind letting us in on the jest?" King Friedrich's voice easily carried over to their cozy corner. "Some other people in this room might be interested to know what on earth is going on."

"Yes, you might as well explain the whole thing now, son," boomed King Vincentius, in corroboration. Bernadette sat back and looked inquiringly up into Colin's face. He leaned back comfortably against the sofa cushions, and prepared to enlighten the entire assembled company.

"Well, I don't know whether it ever occurred to you, Cecilia," he glanced slyly over at Bernadette, "that your betrothed might have wondered as much about what you were like, as you did about him! When we first heard the news of your proposed journey—your father wrote mine all about it, of course—I was very eager to meet you, since you were so clearly different and so much more full of life and decision than most of the young ladies I'd ever met. And so I decided to go after you. That way I could see what you were really like."

"So you knew who I was the entire time!" Bernadette exclaimed, drawing back to look him in the face more directly. Out of the corner of her eye, she suddenly caught sight of Pete's broadly grinning face, and memories of certain formerly inexplicable occurrences flashed up in her mind, now laced with suspicion. She turned on her cousin. "Don't tell me you knew all about it, too, Pete!"

"Of course he did; we were at the Royal Military Academy together," Colin said quietly. "Pete recognized me the first night at the inn, and guessed my plan even before I got a chance to tell him. He fell in with it immediately, and as you know, helped me out considerably when it came to joining with you later."

"Oh, and how you both must have laughed in your sleeves over how utterly ignorant and unobservant I was about the whole thing!" Bernadette shook her head ruefully.

"On the contrary, darling, we had to be very careful not to slip up and give ourselves away, because you were so sharp that we knew you would catch on at the least sign that we had known each other before," Colin insisted warmly, pressing his hand over hers. "And of course," his eyes lit up with suppressed humor, as he turned to address his next remarks more particularly to the rest of the room, "the very first thing I did once we were all together was to commit the most serious blunder I possibly could have: buying that horse you love so much!" he darted another highly amused glance at Bernadette. "After that, I realized that I had just succeeded in making the task I had set for myself just about one hundred times harder," he shook his head in mock consternation and self-pity.

"If you had sold her to me when I first told you I wanted her, that would have solved everything," Bernadette pointed out.

"No; I didn't want you to get the idea that you could just walk all over me from the very beginning," Colin retorted coolly. "I had to win you over some other way, or I never could have had any confidence in my diplomatic abilities again."

"Well, you seem to have redeemed yourself well enough, Reggie, my boy," King Vincentius drawled approvingly, coming over behind the couch, to lay a hand on each of their shoulders.

Bernadette looked up at him alertly. "Well, now I know why you seemed so familiar to me when I first came in, Your Majesty," she remarked, brightly. "Colin looks so much like you," glancing from the father to the son. "Oh, and by the way, what do you want me to call you now? Prince Gerald-Reginald, or . . ." she broke off, laughing.

"Goodness me, no!" Colin shook his head decidedly, chuckling embarrassedly at the bare idea. "That's just my formal title; no one has ever called me Gerald, and I don't think I could stand it if anyone did."

"It certainly doesn't suit you at all," Bernadette agreed, surveying his splendid physique and handsome dark features, which certainly deserved a more manly appellation than the poetic "Gerald."

"I was always Reggie to the family and my early tutors," Colin went on explaining, "but once I went away to study, I couldn't go by that nickname any more; it sounded too childish. And 'Reginald' is worse than Gerald; so stiff! The only reason Father and Mother even *gave* me those two names in the first place was to honor two old uncles, who had to inconveniently choose the very time of my birth to pass away. So I've always gone by my third name—like all royalty, I've got a string of a couple dozen to do what I like with, as I dare say you do too."

"So your name really *is* Colin, then," Bernadette said musingly. "And I can keep on calling you that; I'd rather, for I could never think of you as 'Reggie.' But Cecilia *isn't* one of my names—I wish it were, I wouldn't have felt so profoundly deceitful in telling you it was—so I'd rather you start calling me Bernadette, if you don't mind."

"I certainly don't; I always think of you as Bernadette, because I knew who you were the whole time," Colin responded, twining his fingers more closely around hers. "But I don't intend to drop my own nickname for you, my little blind one," he smiled down into her eyes.

"I wouldn't want you to!" Bernadette tossed her head back coquettishly, and nestled comfortably closer to his side. "Now I understand why you left the fort early; you wanted to be here to surprise me. And was that why you were in such a rush to get back,

Pete; tired of having to keep it all secret?" she directed a laughing glance over at her cousin.

"I told him a year was long enough to wait, and that if he didn't bring you back here the first moment he possibly could, I would know the reason why," Colin said, crossing his arms over his chest and fixing Pete with a knowing look.

"And I didn't want to know the reason why," Pete returned wryly. "I've been severely beset from all three sides at various times during this journey; sometimes, Uncle, I've frankly wished that you had never suggested I go along." He shook his head with the air of a martyr.

"Oh, honestly, Pete! You don't really mean that, do you?" Bernadette tore herself away from Colin's side long enough to run over and nearly knock her cousin over with a terrific bear hug. She stepped back and regarded him levelly, eye to eye. "I never could have made it through this journey without you; and I really did appreciate having you there by my side, every second of the way, even though I didn't always show it, and certainly never said so!"

"Then don't now," Pete retorted, grinning down at her. "We get along well enough, Bernie, without having to bother with needless demonstrations of affectionate gratitude. That's not our style; save that for your husband," he shot a mischievous smile over her head in Colin's direction.

"Well, at least you two still seem to be talking to each other, so I would say that the experiment was quite a satisfactory success all around," King Friedrich remarked complacently, beaming upon them with a benignant expression.

"Father, did you know about this all along, too?" Bernadette demanded, whirling around and running over to confront him.

"Well, I knew that His Highness Prince Gerald-Reginald-Colin had decided to follow after you in hopes of meeting up with you; King Vincentius wrote me about his plan," her father responded. "But neither of us knew whether or not he had succeeded, my dear, and certainly we were not involved in conniving at any of the circumstances of your acquaintance, if that's what you want to know."

"And even after Reggie got back here, we still couldn't find out what had actually happened between the two of you," King Vincentius entered the conversation. "It's always impossibly difficult to get any information out of Reggie, if he chooses to withhold it," he shook his head at his son, with mock severity.

"Don't I know it!" Bernadette went back and primly seated herself next to Colin again, clasping her hands in her lap. "Do you know, Colin, that you never told me the least thing about who you were or where you had come from, and never even considered that I might be curious? It's a wonder that I ever came to trust you," she added teasingly. Colin merely smiled at her in return. "Well, and now to business," Bernadette turned briskly to her mother. "When are we having the ceremony?"

"Well, dear, it will take at least several weeks to re-invite all the guests and prepare for such an important event . . ." the Queen began, indulgently, trading looks of thoughtful consideration with Queen Beatrice.

"Goodness, Mother!" Bernadette sat bolt upright in shocked horror. "You don't mean that we have to wait still longer, do you? We're already late, and I want to get married tonight!"

"Tonight! Why, don't be ridiculous, dear; you know that's impossible," her mother smiled.

"But why?" Bernadette argued. "I don't care how many guests we have; and who comes to see the ceremony, anyway? We could have a grand reception later to honor the occasion and invite all the 'anybodies who are anybody' to that instead, which would give us time to have a dress made and decorate and all the rest of it; but why couldn't Colin and I be married already? We'll wait until after the reception for the honeymoon; that's really all that matters for the proper timeline, and I'm in no hurry to rush off again, believe me." She went over to hug her mother again. "Please, please, please," she coaxed earnestly. "Father, convince her, do!"

"You too, Father," Colin joined in the urging. "If the two of us don't feel any need to wait for the grand celebration, why should anyone else mind? I'm sure there's enough food and guests in the palace already for a decent banquet and dance tonight, and we don't want anything else, do we, Bernadette?" he raised his eyebrows questioningly, desiring her approbation.

"No!" Bernadette shook her head emphatically. "*Please*, Mother and Father," she begged her very hardest.

The four parents exchanged glances, and the two kings shrugged and laughed. "We may as well resign ourselves to the inevitable, my dear; they will give us no peace until we agree," King Friedrich said, and Queen Anna Marie sighed and nodded her consent.

"Hooray!" Bernadette jumped up and down, clapping her hands (forgetting again how very unladylike it was to do so), and ran gleefully back over to Colin. He swung her around, laughing. "Put me down, please; I want to at least go up and change into a white dress!" Bernadette endeavored to free herself.

"Just a minute; I have a wedding present that I want to give you first." Colin kept a fast hold on her and started to pull her unyieldingly across the room.

"Can't it wait until after the ceremony?" Bernadette wanted to know. She was in a hurry, and right now she was only interested in Colin himself, not in presents.

"You won't want to once you see what it is," Colin replied. "Come over to the window."

"The window?" Bernadette followed him over, curiously, and peered out at the ground below. She took one look at what was standing placidly in the nearby pasture, looking around with intelligent eyes, and then turned and threw her arms around Colin's neck with a gasp of incredulous delight. "Oh, Colin, darling, do you really mean that I am to have Midnight for *my very own*? Oh, I love you more than ever now!" Bernadette let go of him and twirled about the room in ecstasy.

"Sometimes I almost think that you care more about that black animal than you do about me," Colin rejoined, calmly readjusting his collar.

"I'm not even going to dignify that with an answer," Bernadette flung back at him over her shoulder as she raced out of the room. "I'll be ready in five minutes, Mother; you and Roxanne can have everything set up by then, right?"

Chapter Thirty-five
The Next Morning in the Palace

"Time to get up now, Bernadette; it's already past nine o'clock."

Bernadette yawned and stretched luxuriously before opening her eyes, puzzled. It had been months since she had slept in such a comfortable bed with smooth, soft satin sheets. She looked up into Colin's smiling face above her; sunlight was pouring in through the nearest window, illuminating the corners of her bedroom. "Oh!" she laughed, remembering. "We were married last night, weren't we, Colin?"

"According to the castle chaplain and all those witnesses, we were; and there were certainly enough of them," Colin responded lightly, as he got up and slipped on his black-broadcloth dressing-gown, belting the garment snugly around his waist. Bernadette watched her handsome husband admiringly, her mind busy with the events of the past evening.

"It wasn't just a beautiful dream, then," she said with a happy little sigh. "I'm glad."

"So am I," Colin smiled over his shoulder at her. He threw open the curtains and then turned back to the bed. "Come on, get up."

"I don't think I want to yet," Bernadette returned saucily, snuggling down into the comfortable warm nest she was by no means ready to relinquish.

"Oh, really?" Colin did not appear to be impressed, and simply pulled all the covers off the bed, dumping Bernadette unceremoniously on the floor.

"Colin!" Bernadette jumped up, protesting. He dropped the bedclothes and prudently retreated, laughing. Bernadette looked around for something to throw at him; she caught up a pillow lying nearby, and flung it across the room with remarkably good aim. Colin caught it by the corner and threw it back at her, and then, laughing, came back over and started to help her gather up the scattered bedclothes. It was a good thing they did, too, for when Camille came in a few minutes later to assist her mistress in dressing, she looked around at the shambles they had made of the room with an astonished and slightly disapproving eye.

"Well, I'll leave you ladies to your morning preparations, and meet you in the hall to go down to breakfast, Bernadette," Colin said easily, throwing the last of the comforters back onto the bed, and exiting into his own dressing-room, nodding a polite good-morning to Camille as he passed.

Bernadette scrambled hastily into her own dressing-gown, and permitted Camille to herd her into the next room to fix her hair. The procedure felt familiar, even though Roxanne was not sharing Bernadette's dressing-room any more; she and Sir Timothy had their own brand-new suite of apartments on the other side of the palace.

Bernadette was dressed and ready to go in record time, escaping to the hall well in advance of any of her bustling ladies-in-waiting, even Camille. She had no mandatory bouquet to burden her this morning; Colin gave her a pretty nosegay (and a kiss) as she came up to him in the hall, but it was daintily and tastefully arranged, and Bernadette could easily have pinned it to her shoulder, if she found it got in her way.

Pete and Esmeralda met them at the foot of the stairs, just in from a romantic early-morning ramble in the garden. Esmeralda was dressed in her old gypsy finery, with a freshly plucked rose tucked behind her ear and glowing strikingly against her lustrous dark hair; she looked wonderfully at home.

"So, there you are, sleepyheads," Pete greeted them, with the lofty condescension of an old married man who feels that he has earned the right to look upon all newlyweds with detached indulgence and a pardonable sense of superiority. His wife gave him a half-amused, half-reproving look, and then ran over to bid Bernadette good-morning herself.

"It's wonderful to be able to dress how I please once again, without having to worry about fitting in with other people's mandatory disguises!" she laughed, putting her arm confidentially through Bernadette's. "Your father said I could have whatever I wanted to wear, and so I took him quite at his word, you see."

"He's *your* uncle, now, you know, Essie, so why don't you call him that, instead of 'your father,' " Pete said pointedly, stepping up beside them and drawing his wife away, planting a kiss on her blooming cheeks. "Come on; I don't know whether anyone else is hungry for breakfast, but I am!"

Camille, who had gone over to the door to talk to Stephen, now came back with him to join the procession into the breakfast hall. Cecil had come downstairs in the meantime, and he patted Bernadette's shoulder in a grandfatherly way, on his way to his post.

Upon entering the breakfast-room, Bernadette rushed immediately over to the King's Table to take her old place by her father, sinking delightedly down into her own chair. "Oh, I have missed this!" she exclaimed, catching up her napkin to place in her lap, and leaning over to kiss her father and mother good-morning.

"Wouldn't you rather sit next to your husband, though, dear?" King Friedrich inquired teasingly, trading knowing glances with his wife.

"And since when didn't I have two sides, Father?" Bernadette demanded, highly amused. Colin, meanwhile, had coolly come over and appropriated the seat at her left hand. "Besides, Camille sits with Stephen at one of the other tables now," she nodded towards her maid, who was walking demurely across to the other side of the room, attended by her dedicated husband.

"Well, but I thought you might like a table of your own to preside over now, what with your newly elevated status as a married couple," the King retorted, grinning down the length of the table at King Vincentius, who was established prominently at the foot with Queen Beatrice, nodding proudly at his son and new daughter-in-law.

Bernadette laughed. "No, thank you; there's plenty of time for that, isn't there, Colin?" She glanced fondly up at her husband and then back over at her father. "Today I want to be with *all* the people I love," she smiled around the table at Pete and Esmeralda and Sir Timothy and Princess Roxanne, who were all gathered there as well.

"All right, then!" King Friedrich said grace, and then picked up his spoon before anyone else. "Eat up and enjoy, everyone!"

"What's the plan for the day, father-in-law?" Colin inquired pleasantly, helping first Bernadette and then himself to scrambled eggs and bread pudding. Bernadette savored each bite delightedly, remembering the many breakfasts on her journey that had consisted of stale bread and water. It certainly made one appreciate their blessings a little more, once they had them again.

"Well, I have some things to attend to with your father this morning, my boy; so you and Bernadette can do as you please until after lunch, when I will want to discuss with you what notable developments have occurred since you have been away, daughter, and lay out some plans for our future political procedures," the King replied, looking from Bernadette to Colin for their approval of his proposal.

"Certainly, Father; it still is my very favorite thing to do," Bernadette responded, smiling and thinking back to the last time she had spent with her father in his study.

King Friedrich winked at her. "That's settled, then. Are you ready to go over those negotiations with me now, Vincentius?" he rose from the table and addressed his friend confidingly.

"Yes, indeed! See you later, son—and daughter," King Vincentius also winked at them on his way out.

Bernadette and Colin finished their breakfast and went back out into the Great Hall. "How about we go for a ride this morning, Bernadette?" Colin proposed. "We could go and see the nice peasant lady who started this whole adventure for you, whom I am very interested to meet, and be back in plenty of time for lunch and the meeting with our fathers afterward."

"A wonderful idea; I'd love to take you to meet Old Saphronia," Bernadette heartily approved. "I'll just run back up to our room and change my dress real quick." She let go of his arm and ran lightly up the staircase, holding up her elegant skirt in one hand and resting the other gracefully on the banister.

Colin, his arms folded on the top of the column at the bottom of the balustrade, regarded his bride's progress with fond admiration. At the curve in the stairwell, Bernadette turned to smile down at him, and then quickened her pace, in a hurry to get back to him. "I'll go out and get both of our mounts saddled and ready, and be waiting for you at the door, with your precious Sultana," Colin called up to her, rousing himself and heading for the front door.

"*Midnight*!" Bernadette shouted in exasperation, whirling around and clamping both her hands down hard on the banister, glaring fiercely down at her husband. But Colin, laughing heartily, had already slammed the door behind him, effectively cutting off any further protestations she could make. Bernadette stood staring after him for a moment, chewing impatiently on her lower lip; and then an involuntary smile lit up her entire face and heart, as she continued merrily on her way up to her chambers, looking forward to her ride together with Colin—and their happily ever after together, too.

The End